Christine Merrill lives o̶̶̶̶̶̶̶̶̶̶̶̶̶̶̶̶̶̶
her husband, two sons, and̶̶̶̶̶̶̶̶̶̶̶̶̶̶̶̶̶̶
like her to get off the com̶̶̶̶̶̶̶̶̶̶̶̶̶̶̶̶̶̶

She has worked by turns in theatre costuming, where sh̶̶̶̶̶̶
paid to play with period ballgowns, and as a librarian, where
she spent the day surrounded by books. Writing historical
romance combines her love of good stories and fancy dress
with her ability to stare out of the window and make stuff up.

Don't miss these other Regency delights from Mills & Boon® Historical romance's bestselling authors!

REGENCY
Redemption

Christine Merrill

Mills & Boon, an imprint of Harlequin (UK) Limited, Eton House, 18-24 Paradise Road, Richmond, Surrey TW9 1SR

REGENCY REDEMPTION © Harlequin Books S.A. 2011

The publisher acknowledges the copyright holder of the individual works as follows:

The Inconvenient Duchess © Christine Merrill 2006
An Unladylike Offer © Christine Merrill 2007

ISBN: 978 0 263 88734 1

052-0511

Printed in the UK
by CPI Mackays, Chatham, ME5 8TD

The Inconvenient Duchess

To Jim, who knows I'm crazy,
but loves me anyway. And to James and Sean.
Making your own breakfasts and mating your own socks
builds character. You'll thank me later, but I thank you now.

Chapter One

'Of course, you know I am dying.' His mother extended slim fingers from beneath the bedclothes and patted the hand that he offered to her.

Marcus Radwell, fourth Duke of Haughleigh, kept his face impassive, searching his mind for the appropriate response. 'No.' His tone was neutral. 'We will, no doubt, have this conversation again at Christmas when you have recovered from your current malady.'

'Only you would use obstinacy as a way to cheer me on my deathbed.'

And only you would stage death with such Drury Lane melodrama. He left the words unspoken, struggling for decorum, but glared at the carefully arranged scene. She'd chosen burgundy velvet hangings and dim lighting to accent her already pale skin. The cloying scent of the lilies on the dresser gave the air a funereal heaviness.

'No, my son, we will not be having this conversation again. The things I have to tell you will be said today. I do not have the strength to tell them twice, and certainly will not be here at Christmas to force another promise from you.' She gestured to the water glass at the bedside. He filled it and offered it to her, supporting her as she drank.

No strength? And yet her voice seemed steady enough. This latest fatal illness was probably no more real than the last one. Or the one before. He stared hard into her face, searching for some indication of the truth. Her hair was still the same delicate blonde cloud on the pillow, but her face was grey beneath the porcelain complexion that had always given her a false air of fragility. 'If you are too weak…perhaps later…'

'Perhaps later I will be too weak to say them, and you will not have to hear. A good attempt, but I expected better.'

'And I expected better of you, Mother. I thought I had made it clear, on my last visit to your *deathbed*—' the word was heavy with irony he could no longer disguise '—that I was tired of playing the fool in these little dramas you insist on arranging. If you want something of me, you could at least do me the courtesy of stating it plainly in a letter.'

'So that you could refuse me by post, and save yourself the journey home?'

'Home? And where might that be? This is your home. Not mine.'

Her laugh was mirthless and ended in a rasping cough. Old instincts made him reach out to her before he caught himself and let the hand fall to his side. The coughing ended abruptly, as though his lack of sympathy made her rethink her strategy.

'This is your home, *your Grace*, whether you choose to live in it or not.'

So if fears for her health would not move him, perhaps guilt over his neglected estate? He shrugged.

Her hand trembled as she gestured towards the nightstand, and he reached for the carafe to refill her glass. 'No. The box on the table.'

He passed the inlaid box to her. She fumbled with the catch, opened it and removed a stack of letters, patting them. 'As time grows short, I've worked to mend the mistakes in my past. To right what wrongs I could. To make peace.'

To get right with the Lord before His inevitable judgement, he added to himself and clenched his jaw.

'And recently, I received a letter from a friend of my youth. An old school companion who was treated badly.'

He could guess by whom. If his mother was planning to right her wrongs chronologically, she had better be quick. Even if she lived another twenty years, as he suspected she might, there were wrongs enough in her past to fill the remaining time.

'There were money problems, as there so often are. Her father died penniless. She was forced home and had to find her own way in the world. She has been, for the last twelve years, a companion to a young girl.'

'No.' His voice echoed in the still sickroom.

'You say no, and, as yet, I have asked no questions.'

'But you most certainly will. The young girl will turn out to be of marriageable age and good family. The conversation will be about the succession. The question is inevitable and the answer will be no.'

'I had thought to see you settled before I died.'

'Perhaps you shall. I am sure we have plenty of time.'

She continued as if there had been no interruption. 'I let you wait, assuming you would make a choice in your own good time. But I have no time. No time to let you handle things. Certainly no time to let you wallow in grief for losses and mistakes that are ten years past.'

He bit off the retort that was forming on his tongue. She was right in this at least. He needn't reopen his half of an old argument.

'You are right. The girl is of marriageable age, but her prospects are poor. She is all but an orphan. The family lands are mortgaged and gone. She has little hope of making a match, and Lady Cecily despairs of her chances. She fears that her charge is destined for a life of service and does not wish to see her own fate visited on another. She has approached me, hoping that I might help…'

'And you offered me up as a sacrifice to expiate the wrong you did forty years ago.'

'I offered her hope. Why should I not? I have a son who is thirty-five and without issue. A son who shows no sign of remedying this condition, though his wife and heir are ten years in the grave. A son who wastes himself on whores when he should be seeing to the estate and providing for the succession. I know how quickly life passes. If you die, the title falls to your brother. Have you considered this, or do you think yourself immortal?'

He forced a smile. 'Why does it matter to you now? If St John inherited the title, it would please you above all things. You've made no effort to hide that he is your favourite.'

She smiled back, with equal coldness. 'I am a fond old woman, but not as foolish as all that. I will not lie and call you favourite. But neither will I claim that St John has the talent or temperament to run this estate. I can trust that once you are settled here, you will not lose your father's coronet at cards. Your neglect of your duties is benign, and easily remedied. But can you imagine the land after a year in your brother's care?'

He closed his eyes and felt the chill seeping through his blood. He did not want to imagine his brother as a duke any more than he wanted to imagine himself chained to a wife and family and trapped in this tomb of a house. There were enough ghosts here, and now his mother was threatening to add herself to the list of grim spirits he was avoiding.

She gave a shuddering breath and coughed.

He offered her another sip of water and she cleared her throat before speaking again. 'I did not offer you as a sacrifice, however much pleasure you take in playing the martyr. I suggested that she and the girl visit. That is all. From you, I expect a promise. A small boon, not total surrender. I would ask that you not turn her away before meeting her. It will not be a love match, but I trust you to realise, now, that love in courtship does not guarantee a long or a happy union. If she is not deformed, or ill favoured, or so hopelessly stupid as to render her company unbearable, I expect you to give serious thought to your offer. Wit and beauty may fade, but if she has common sense and good health, she has qualities sufficient to make a good wife. You have not, as yet, married some doxy on the continent?'

He glared at her and shook his head.

'Or developed some tragic *tendre* for the wife of a friend?'

'Good God, Mother.'

'And you are not courting some English rose in secret? That would be too much to hope. So this leaves you with no logical excuse to avoid a meeting. Nothing but a broken heart and a bitter nature, which you can go back to nurturing once an heir is born and the succession secured.'

'You seriously suggest that I marry some girl you've sent for, on the basis of your casual correspondence with an old acquaintance?'

She struggled to sit upright, her eyes glowing like coals in her ashen face. 'If I had more time, and if you weren't so damned stubborn, I'd have trotted you around London and forced you to take your pick of the Season long ago. But time is short, and I am forced to make do with what can be found quickly and arranged without effort. If she has wide hips and an amiable nature, overcome your reservations, wed, and get her with child.'

And she coughed again. But this time it was not the delicate sound he was used to, but the rack of lungs too full to hold breath. And it went on and on until her body shook with it. A maid rushed into the room, drawn by the sound, and leaned over the bed, supporting his mother's back and holding a basin before her. After more coughing she spat and sagged back into the pillows, spent. The maid hurried away with the basin, but a tiny fleck of blood remained on his mother's lip.

'Mother.' His voice was unsteady and his hand trembled as he touched his handkerchief to her mouth.

Her hand tightened on his, but with little strength. He could feel the bones through the translucent skin.

When she spoke, her voice was a hoarse whisper. The glow in her eyes had faded to a pleading, frightened look that he had not seen there before. 'Please. Before it is too late. Meet the girl. Let me die in peace.' She smiled in a way that was more a grimace, and he wondered if it was from pain. She'd always tried to keep such rigid control. Of herself. Of him. Of everything. It must embarrass her to have to yield now. And for the first time he noticed how small she was as she lay there and smelled the hint of decay masked by the scent of the lilies.

It was true, then. This time she really was dying.

He sighed. What harm could it do to make a promise now, when she would be gone long before he needed to keep it? He answered stiffly, giving her more cause to hope than he had in years. 'I will consider it.'

Chapter Two

The front door was oak, and when she dropped the heavy brass knocker against it, Miranda Grey was surprised that the sound was barely louder than the hammering of the rain on the flags around her. It would be a wonder if anyone heard her knock above the sound of the late summer storm.

When the door finally opened, the butler hesitated, as though a moment's delay in the rain might wash the step clean and save him the trouble of seeing to her.

She was afraid to imagine what he must see. Her hair was half down and streaming water. Her shawl clung to her body, soaked through with the rain. Her travelling dress moulded to her body, and the mud-splattered skirts bunched between her legs when she tried to move. She offered a silent prayer of thanks that she'd decided against wearing slippers or her new pair of shoes. The heavy boots she'd chosen were wildly inappropriate for a lady, but anything else would have disintegrated on the walk to the house. Her wrists, which protruded from the sleeves of the gown before disappearing into her faded gloves, were blue with cold.

After an eternity, the butler opened his mouth, probably to send her away. Or at least to direct her to the rear entrance.

She squared her shoulders and heard Cici repeating words in her mind.

'It is not who you appear to be that matters. It is who you are. Despite circumstances, you are a lady. You were born to be a lady. If you remember this, people will treat you accordingly.'

Appreciating her height for once, she stared down into the face of the butler and said in a tone as frigid as the icy rainwater in her boots, 'Lady Miranda Grey. I believe I am expected.'

The butler stepped aside and muttered something about a library. Then, without waiting for an answer, he shambled off down the hall, leaving her and her portmanteau on the step.

She heaved the luggage over the threshold, stepped in after it, and pulled the door shut behind her. She glanced down at her bag, which sat in its own puddle on the marble floor. It could stay here and rot. She was reasonably sure that it was not her job to carry the blasted thing. The blisters forming beneath the calluses on her palms convinced her that she had already carried it quite enough for one night. She abandoned it and hurried after the butler.

He led her into a large room lined with books and muttered something. She leaned closer, but was unable to make out the words. He was no easier to understand in the dead quiet of the house than he had been when he'd greeted her at the door. Then he wandered away again, off into the hall. In search of the dowager, she hoped. In his wake, she detected a faint whiff of gin.

When he was gone, she examined her surroundings in detail, trying to ignore the water dripping from her clothes and on to the fine rug. The house was grand. There was no argument to that. The ceilings were high. The park in front was enormous, as she had learned in frustration while stumbling across its wide expanse in the pouring rain. The hall to this room had been long, wide and marble, and lined with doors that hinted at a variety of equally large rooms.

But…

She sighed. There had to be a but. A house with a peer, but without some accompanying problem, some unspoken deficit, would not have opened its doors to her. She stepped closer to the bookshelves and struggled to read a few of the titles. They did not appear to be well used or current—not that she had any idea of the fashion in literature. Their spines were not worn; they were coated with dust and trailed the occasional cobweb from corner to corner. Not a great man for learning, the duke.

She brightened. Learning was not a requirement, certainly. A learned man might be too clever by half and she'd find herself back out in the rain. Perhaps he had more money than wit.

She stepped closer to the fire and examined the bricks of the hearth. Now here was an area she well understood. It left a message much more readable than the bookshelves. There was soot on the bricks that should have been scrubbed away long ago. She could see the faint smudges on the walls, signs that the room was long overdue for a good cleaning. She rustled the heavy velvet of the draperies over the window, then sneezed at the dust and slapped at the flutter of moths she'd disturbed.

So, the duke was not a man of learning, and the dowager had a weak hand on the servants. The butler was drunk and the maids did not waste time cleaning the room set aside to receive guests. Her hands itched to straighten cushions, to beat dust out of velvet and to find a brush to scrub the bricks. Didn't these people understand what they had? How lucky they were? And how careless with their good fortune?

If she were mistress of this house…

She stopped to correct herself. When she was mistress of this house. That was how Cici would want her to think. When, not if. Her father was fond of myths and had often told her stories of the Spartan soldiers. When they went off to war, their mothers told them to come back with their shields or on them. And her family would have the same of her. Failure was not an option. She could not disappoint them.

Very well, she decided. When she was mistress of this house, things would be different. She could not offer his Grace riches. But despite the dirt, the house and furnishings proved he did not need money. She was not a great beauty, but who would see her here, so far from London? She lacked the refinements and charms of a lady accustomed to society, but she'd seen no evidence that his Grace enjoyed entertaining. She had little learning, but the dust on his library showed this was not his first concern.

What she could offer were the qualities he clearly needed. Household management. A strong back. A willingness to work hard. She could make his life more comfortable.

And she could provide him an heir.

She pushed the thought quickly from her mind. That would be part of her duties, of course. And, despite Cici's all-too-detailed explanations of what this duty entailed, she was not afraid. Well, not very afraid. Cici had told her enough about his Grace, the Duke of Haughleigh, to encourage her on this point. He was ten years a widower, so perhaps he would not be too demanding. If his needs were great, he must surely have found a means to satisfy them that did not involve a wife. If his needs were not great, then she had no reason to fear him.

She'd imagined him waiting for her arrival, as she made the long coach ride from London. He was older than she, and thinner. Not frail, but with a slight stoop. Greying hair. She'd added spectacles, since they always seemed to make the wearer less intimidating. And a kind smile. A little sad, perhaps, since he'd waited so long after the death of his wife to seek a new one.

But he did not seek, she reminded herself. Cici had done all the seeking, and this introduction had been arranged with his mother. She added shy, to his list of attributes. He was a retiring country gentleman and not the terrifying rake or high-flyer that Cici had been most qualified to warn her about. She would be polite. He would be receptive. They would deal well together.

And when, eventually, the details of her circumstances needed to be explained, he would have grown so fond of her that he would accept them without qualms.

Without warning, the door opened behind her and she spun to face it. Her heart thumped in her chest and she threw away the image she'd been creating. The man in front of her was no quiet country scholar. Nor some darkly handsome, brooding rake. He entered the room like sunlight streaming through a window.

Not so old, she thought. He must have married young. And his face bore no marks of the grief, no lines of long-born sorrow. It was open and friendly. She relaxed a little and returned his smile. It was impossible not to. His eyes sparkled. And they were as blue as…

She faltered. Not the sky. The sky in the city had been grey. The sea? She'd never seen it, so she was not sure.

Flowers, perhaps. But not the sensible flowers found in a kitchen garden. Something planted in full sun that had no use but to bring pleasure to the viewer.

His hair was much easier to describe. It shone gold in the light from the low fire.

'Well, well, well. And who do we have here?' His voice was low and pleasant and the warmth of it made her long to draw near to him. And when she did, she was sure he would smell of expensive soap. And his breath would be sweet. She almost shivered at the thought that she might soon know for sure. She dropped a curtsy.

He continued to stare at her in puzzlement. 'I'm sorry, my dear. You have the better of me. As far as I know, we weren't expecting any guests.'

She frowned. 'My guardian wrote to your mother. It was supposed to be all arranged. Of course, I was rather surprised when there was no one to meet the coach, but…'

He was frowning now, but there was a look of dawning comprehension. 'I see. If my mother arranged it, that would explain why you expected…' He paused again and began cautiously. 'Did you know my mother well?'

'Me? No, not at all. My guardian and she were school friends. They corresponded.' She fumbled in her reticule and removed the damp and much-handled letter of introduction, offering it to him.

'Then you didn't know of my mother's illness.' He took the letter and scanned it, eyebrows raised as he glanced over at her. Then he slipped off his fashionable dark jacket and revealed the black armband tied about the sleeve of his shirt.

'I'm afraid you're six weeks too late to have an appointment with my mother, unless you have powers not possessed by the other members of this household. The wreath's just off the door. I suppose it's disrespectful of me to say so, but you didn't miss much. At the best of times, my mother was no pleasure. Here, now…'

He reached for her as she collapsed into the chair, no longer heeding the water soaking into the upholstery from her sodden gown.

'I thought, since you didn't know her… I didn't expect this to affect you so. Can I get you something…brandy…? Decanter empty again…Wilkins! Damn that man.' He threw open the door and shouted down the hall, trying to locate the muttering butler. 'Wilkins! Where's the brandy?'

So she'd arrived dripping wet, unescorted and unexpected, into a house of mourning, with a dubious letter of introduction, expecting to work her way into the affections of a peer and secure an offer before he asked too many questions and sent her home. She buried her head in her hands, wishing that she could soak into the carpet and disappear like the rain trickling from her gown.

'What the hell is going on?' His Grace had found someone, but the answering voice in the hall was clearly not the butler. 'St John, what is the meaning of shouting up and down the halls for brandy? Have you no shame at all? Drink the house dry if you must, but have the common decency to do it in quiet.' The voice grew louder as it approached the open doorway.

'And who is this? I swear to God, St John, if this drowned rat is your doing, be damned to our mother's memory, I'll throw you out in the rain, brandy and girl and all.'

Miranda looked up to find a stranger framed in the

doorway. He was everything that the other man was not. Dark hair, with a streak of grey at each temple, and a face creased by bitterness and hard living. An unsmiling mouth. And his eyes were the grey of a sky before a storm. Strength and power radiated from him like heat from the fire.

The other man ducked under his arm and strode back into the room, proffering a brandy snifter. Then he reconsidered and kept it for himself, taking a long drink before speaking.

'For a change, dear brother, you can't blame this muddle on me. The girl is your problem, not mine, and comes courtesy of our departed mother.' He waved the letter of introduction in salute before passing it to his brother. 'May I present Lady Miranda Grey, come to see his Grace the Duke of Haughleigh.' The blond man grinned.

'You're the duke?' She looked to the imposing man in the doorway and wondered how she could have been so wrong. When this man had entered the room, his brother had faded to insignificance. She tried to stand up to curtsy again, but her knees gave out and she plopped back on to the sofa. The water in her boots made a squelching sound as she moved.

He stared back. 'Of course I'm the duke. This is my home you've come to. Who were you expecting to find? The Prince Regent?'

The other man grinned. 'I think she was under the mistaken impression that I was the duke. I'd just come into the library, looking for the brandy decanter, and found her waiting here…'

'For how long?' snapped his brother.

'Moments. Scant moments, although I would have enjoyed more time alone with Lady Miranda. She's a charming conversationalist.'

'And, during this charming conversation, you neglected to mention your name, and allowed her to go on in her mistake.' He turned from his brother to her.

His gaze caught hers and held it a moment too long as though he could read her heart in her eyes. She looked away in embarrassment and gestured helplessly to the letter of introduction. 'I was expected. I had no idea...about your mother.

'I'm so sorry,' she added as an afterthought.

'Not as sorry as I am.' He scanned the letter. 'Damn that woman. She made me promise. But it was a deathbed promise, and I said the words hoping her demise would absolve me of action.'

'You promised to marry me, hoping your mother would die?' She stared back in horror.

'I promised to meet you. Nothing more. If my mother had died that night, as it appeared she might, who was to know what I promised her? But she lingered.' He waved the paper. 'Obviously long enough to post an invitation. And now here you are. With a maid, I trust?'

'Ahhh...no.' She struggled with the answer. It was as she'd feared. He must think she was beyond all sense, travelling unchaperoned to visit strangers. 'She was taken ill and was unable to accompany me.' As the lie fell from her lips, she forced herself to meet the duke's unwavering gaze.

'Surely, your guardian...'

'Unfortunately, no. She is also in ill health, no longer fit to travel.' Miranda sighed convincingly. Cici was strong as an ox, and had sworn that it would take a team of them to drag her back into the presence of the duke's mother.

'And you travelled alone? From London?'

'On the mail coach,' she finished. 'I rode on top with the driver. It was unorthodox, but not improper.' And inexpensive.

'And when you arrived in Devon?'

'I was surprised that there was no one to meet me. I inquired the direction, and I walked.'

'Four miles? Cross-country? In the pouring rain?'

'After London, I enjoyed the fresh air.' She need not mention the savings of not hiring a gig.

'And you had no surfeit of air, riding for hours on the roof of the mail coach?' He was looking at her as though she was crack-brained.

'I like storms.' It was an outright lie, but the best she could do. Any love for storms that she might have had had disappeared when the rain permeated her petticoat and ran in icy rivers down her legs.

'And do you also like dishonour, to court it so?'

She bowed her head again, no longer able to look him in the eye. It had been a mistake to come here. Her behaviour had been outlandish, but she had not been trying to compromise herself. In walking to the house, she had risked all, and now, if the duke turned her out and she had to find her own way home, there would be no way to repair the damage to her reputation.

He gestured around the room. 'You're miles from the protection of society in the company of a pair of notorious rakes.'

'Notorious?' She compared them. The duke looked dangerous enough, but it was hard to believe his brother was a threat to her honour.

'In these parts, certainly. Does anyone know you're here?'

'I asked direction of a respectable gentleman and his wife.'

'The man, so tall?' The duke sketched a measurement

with his hand. 'And plump. With grey hair. The wife: tall, lean as a rail. A mouth that makes her look—' he pulled a face '—a little too respectable.'

She shrugged. 'I suppose that could be them. If he had spectacles and she had a slight squint.'

'And when you spoke to them, you gave them your right name?'

She stared back in challenge. 'Why would I not?'

The duke sank into a chair with a groan.

His brother let out a whoop of laughter.

The duke glared. 'This is no laughing matter, you nincompoop. If you care at all for honour, then one of us is up a creek.'

St John laughed again. 'By now you know the answer to the first part of the statement. It would lead you to the answer to the second. I suppose that I could generously offer—'

'I have a notion of what you would consider a generous offer. Complete the sentence and I'll hand you your head.' He ran fingers through his dark hair. Then he turned slowly back to look at her. 'Miss…whatever-your-name-is…' He fumbled with the letter, reread it and began again. 'Lady Miranda Grey. Your arrival here was somewhat…unusual. In London, it might have gone unnoticed. But Marshmore is small, and the arrival of a young lady on a coach, alone, is reason enough to gossip. In the village you spoke with the Reverend Winslow and his wife, who have a rather unchristian love of rumour and no great fondness for this family. When you asked direction to this house, where there was no chaperon in attendance, you cemented their view of you.'

'I don't understand.'

St John smirked. 'It is no doubt now well known around

the town that the duke and his brother have reconciled sufficiently after the death of their mother to share a demi-mondaine.'

'There is a chance that the story will not get back to London, I suppose,' the duke said with a touch of hope.

Which would be no help. Because of her father, London was still too hot to hold her. If she had to cross out Devon, too… She sighed. There was a limit to the number of counties she could be disgraced in, and still have hope of a match.

St John was still amused. 'Mrs Winslow has a cousin in London. We might as well take out an ad in *The Times*.'

The duke looked out of the window and into the rain, which had changed from the soft and bone-chilling drizzle to a driving storm, complete with lightning and high winds. 'There is no telling the condition of the road between here and the inn. I dare not risk a carriage.'

The look in his eyes made her wonder whether he expected her to set off on foot. She bit back the response forming in her mind, trying to focus on the goal of this trip. A goal that no longer seemed as unlikely as it had when Cici first suggested it.

'She'll have to stay the night, Marcus. There's nothing else for it. And the only question in the mind of the town will be which one of us had her first.'

She gasped in shock at the insult, and then covered her mouth with her hand. There was no advantage in calling attention to herself, just now. Judging by the duke's expression, he would more likely throw her out into the storm than apologise for his brother's crudeness.

St John slapped his brother on the back. 'But, good news, old man. The solution is at hand. And it was our mother's dying wish, was it not?'

'Damn the woman. Damn her to hell. Damn the vicar. And his pinched-up shrew of a wife. Damn. Damn!'

St John patted his apoplectic brother. 'Perhaps the vicar needs to explain free will to you, Marcus. They are not the ones forcing your hand.'

The duke shook off the offending hand. 'And damn you as well.'

'You do have a choice, Marcus. But Haughleigh?' The title escaped St John's lips in a contemptuous puff of breath. 'It is Haughleigh who does not. For he would never choose common sense over chivalry, would he, Marcus?'

The duke's face darkened. 'I do not need your help in this, St John.'

'Of course you don't, your Grace. You never do. So say the words and get them over with. Protect your precious honour. Waiting will not help the matter.'

The duke stiffened, then turned towards Miranda, his jaw clenched and expression hooded, as if making a great effort to marshal his emotions. There was a long pause, and she imagined she could feel the ground shake as the statement rose out of him like lava from an erupting volcano. 'Lady Miranda, would you do me the honour of accepting my hand in marriage?'

Chapter Three

'**B**ut that's ridiculous.' It had slipped out. That was not supposed to be the answer, she reminded herself. It was the goal, was it not, to get her away from scandal and well and properly married? And to a duke. How could she object to that?

She'd imagined an elderly earl. A homely squire. A baron lost in drink or in books. Someone with expectations as low as her own. Not a duke, despite what Cici had planned. She'd mentioned that the Duke of Haughleigh had a younger brother. He had seemed the more likely of the two unlikely possibilities.

And now, she was faced with the elder brother. Unhappy. Impatient. More than she bargained for.

'You find my proposal ridiculous?' The duke was staring at her in amazement.

She shook her head. 'I'm sorry. It isn't ridiculous. Of course not. Just sudden. You surprised me.'

She was starting to babble. She stopped herself before she was tempted to turn him down and request that his brother offer instead.

'Well? You've got over the shock by now, I trust.'

Of course, she thought, swallowing the bitterness. It had been seconds. She should be fully recovered by now. She looked to St John for help. He grinned back at her, open, honest and unhelpful.

The duke was tapping his foot. Did she want to be yoked for life to a man who tapped his foot whenever she was trying to make a major decision?

Cici's voice came clearly to her again. *'Want has nothing to do with it. What you want does not signify. You make the best choice possible given the options available. And if there is only one choice…'*

'I am truly ruined?'

'If you cannot leave this house until morning, which you can't. And if the vicar's wife spreads the tale, which she will.

'I'm sorry,' he added as an afterthought.

He was sorry. That, she supposed, was something. But was he sorry for her, or for himself? And would she have to spend the rest of her life in atonement for this night?

'All right.' Her voice was barely above a whisper. 'If that is what you want.'

His business-like demeanour evaporated under the strain. 'That is not what I want,' he snapped. 'But it is what must be done. You are here now, no thanks to my late mother for making the muddle and letting me sort it out. And don't pretend that this wasn't your goal in coming here. You were dangling after a proposal, and you received one within moments of our meeting. This is a success for you. A coup. Can you not at least pretend to be content? I can but hope that we are a suitable match. And now, if you will excuse me, I must write a letter to the vicar to be delivered as soon as the road is passable, explaining the situation and requesting his presence tomorrow morning. I only hope gold and good intentions will smooth out the details and convince him to waive the banns. We can hold a ceremony in the family chapel, away from prying eyes and with his wife as a witness.' He turned and stalked towards the door.

'Excuse me,' she called after him. 'What should I do in the meantime?'

'Go to the devil,' he barked. 'Or go to your room. I care not either way.' The door slammed behind him.

'But I don't have a room,' she said to the closed door.

St John chuckled behind her.

She turned, startled. She'd forgotten his presence in the face of his brother's personality, which seemed to take up all the available space in the room.

He was still smiling, and she relaxed a little. At least she would have one ally in the house.

'Don't mind my brother overmuch. He's a little out of sorts right now, as any man would be.'

'And his bark is worse than his bite?' she added hopefully.

'Yes. I'm sure it is.' But there was a hesitance as he said it. And, for a moment, his face went blank as if he'd remembered something. Then he buried the thought and his face returned to its previous sunny expression. 'Your host may have forgotten, but I think I can find you a room and some supper. Let's go find the butler, shall we? And see what he's done with your bags.'

She'd done it again. Marcus had been sure that six feet of earth separated him from any motherly interventions in his life. He'd thought that a half-promise of co-operation would be sufficient to set her mind at rest and leave him free.

Obviously not. He emptied a drawer of his late mother's writing desk. Unused stationery, envelopes, stamps. He overturned an inkbottle and swore, mopping at the spreading stain with the linen table runner.

But she'd cast the line, and, at the first opportunity, he'd risen to the bait like a hungry trout. He should have walked out of the room and left the girl to St John. Turned her out into the storm with whatever was left of her honour to fend for herself. Or let her stay in a dry bed and be damned to her reputation.

But how could he? He sank down on to the chair next to the desk and felt it creak under his weight. He was lost as soon as he'd looked into her eyes. When she realised what she had done in coming to his house, there was no triumph there, only resignation. And as he'd railed at her, she'd stood her ground, back straight and chin up, though her eyes couldn't hide the panic and desperation that she was feeling.

He'd seen that look often enough in the old days. In the mirror, every morning when he shaved. Ten years away had erased it from his own face, only to mark this poor young woman. She certainly had the look of someone who'd run afoul of his accursed family. And if there was anything he could do to ease her misery…

He turned back to the desk. It was not like his mother to burn old letters. If she'd had a plan, there would be some record of it. And he'd seen another letter, the day she suggested this meeting. He snapped his fingers in recognition.

In the inlaid box at her bedside. Thank God for the ineptitude of his mother's servants. They'd not cleaned the room, other than to change the linens after removing the body. The box still stood beside the bed. He reached in and removed several packs of letters, neatly bound with ribbon.

Correspondence from St John, the egg-sucking rat. Each letter beginning, 'Dearest Mother...'

Marcus marvelled at his brother's ability to lie with a straight face and no tremor in the script from the laughter as he'd written those words. But St John had no doubt been asking for money, and that was never a laughing matter to him.

No bundle of letters from himself, he noticed. Not that the curt missives he was prone to send would have been cherished by the dowager.

Letters from the lawyers, arranging estate matters. She'd been well prepared to go when the time had come.

And, on the bottom, a small stack of letters on heavy, cream vellum.

Dearest Andrea,

It has been many years, nearly forty, since last we saw each other at Miss Farthing's school, and I have thought of you often. I read of your marriage to the late duke, and of the births of your sons. At the time, I'd thought to send congratulations, but you can understand why this would have been unwise. Still, I thought of you, and kept you in my prayers, hoping you received the life you so richly deserved.

I write you now, hoping that you can help an old friend in a time of need. It is not for me that I write, but for the daughter of our mutual friend, Anthony. Miranda's life has not been an easy one since the death of her mother, and her father's subsequent troubles. She has no hope of making an appropriate match in the ordinary way.

> *I am led to believe that both your sons are, at this time,*
> *unmarried. Your eldest has not found another wife since*
> *the death in childbirth of the duchess some ten years*
> *past. I know how important the succession must be to*
> *you. And we both know how accidents can occur, espe-*
> *cially to active young men, as I'm sure your sons are.*
>
> *So, perhaps the matchmaking of a pair of old school*
> *friends might solve both the problems and see young*
> *Miranda and one of your sons settled.*
> *I await your answer in hope,*
> *Cecily Dawson*

An odd letter, he thought. Not impossible to call on an old
school friend for help, but rather unusual if there had been
no word in forty years. He turned to the second in the stack.

> *Andrea,*
> *I still await your answer concerning the matter of*
> *Lady Miranda Grey. I do not wish to come down to*
> *Devon and settle this face to face, but will if I must.*
> *Please respond.*
> *Awaiting your answer,*
> *Cecily Dawson*

He arched an eyebrow. Stranger still. He turned to the
third letter.

> *Andrea,*
> *Thank you for your brief answer of the fourteenth,*
> *but I am afraid it will not suffice. If you fear that the girl*
> *is unchaste, please understand that she is more inno-*
> *cent in the ways of the bedroom than either of us was*

at her age. And I wish her to remain so until she can make a match suitable to her station. Whatever happened to her father, young Miranda is not to blame for it. But she is poor as a church mouse and beset with offers of things other than marriage. I want to see her safely away from here before disaster strikes. If not your sons, then perhaps another eligible gentleman in your vicinity. Could you arrange an introduction for her? Shepherd her through your social circle? Any assistance would be greatly appreciated.

Yours in gratitude,
Cecily

He turned to the last letter in the stack.

Andrea,
I am sorry to hear of your failing health, but will not accept it as excuse for your denial of aid. If you are to go to meet our Maker any time soon, ask him if he heard my forty years of pleadings for justice to be done between us. I can forgive the ills you've caused me, but you also deserve a portion of blame for the sorry life this child has led. Rescue her now. Set her back up to the station she deserves and I'll pray for your soul. Turn your back again and I'll bring the girl to Devon myself to explain the circumstances to your family at the funeral.

Cecily Dawson

He sat back on the bed, staring at the letters in confusion. Blackmail. And, knowing his mother, it was a case of chickens come home to roost. If she had been without guilt, she'd have destroyed the letters and he'd have known nothing about it. What could his mother have done to set her immortal soul in jeopardy? To make her so hated that an old friend would pray for her damnation?

Any number of things, he thought grimly, if this Cecily woman stood between her and a goal. A man, perhaps? His father, he hoped. It would make the comments about the succession fall into place. His mother had been more than conscious of the family honour and its place in history. The need for a legitimate heir.

And the need to keep secret things secret.

He had been, too, at one time, before bitter experience had lifted the scales from his eyes. Some families were so corrupt it was better to let them die without issue. Some honour did not deserve to be protected. Some secrets were better exposed to the light. It relieved them of their power to taint their surroundings and destroy the lives of those around them.

And what fresh shame did this girl have, that his family was responsible for? St John, most likely. Carrying another by-blow, to be shuffled quietly into the family deck.

He frowned. But that couldn't be right. The letters spoke of old crimes. And when he'd come on the girl and St John together, there had been no sense of conspiracy. She'd seemed a complete stranger to him and to this house. Lost in her surroundings.

She was not a pretty girl, certainly. But he'd not seen her at her best. Her long dark hair was falling from its pins, bedraggled and wet. The gown she'd worn had never been fashionable and being soaked in the storm had made it even more shapeless. It clung to her tall, bony frame the way that the hair stuck to the sharp contours of her face. Everything about her was hard: the lines of her face and body, the set of her mouth, the look in her eyes.

He smiled. A woman after his own heart. Maybe they would do well together, after all.

She looked around in despair. So this was to be her new home. Not this room, she hoped. It was grand enough for a duchess.

Precisely why she did not belong in it.

She forced that thought out of her mind.

'This is the life you belong to, not the life you've lived so far. The past is an aberration. The future is merely a return to the correct path.'

All right. She had better take Cici's words to heart. Repeat them as often as necessary until they became the truth.

Of course, if this was the life she was meant to have, then dust and cobwebs were an inherent part of her destiny. She'd hoped, when she finally got to enjoy the comforts of a great house, she would not be expected to clean it first. This room had not been aired in years. It would take a stout ladder to get up to the sconces to scrub off the tarnish and the grime, and to the top of the undusted mantelpiece. Hell and damnation upon the head of the man who thought that high ceilings lent majesty to a room.

She pulled back the dusty curtains on the window to peer into the rain-streaked night. This might be the front of the house, and those lumps below could be the view of a formal garden. No doubt gone to seed like everything else.

Was her new husband poor, that his estate had faded so?

Cici had thought not. '*Rich enough to waste money on whores,*' she'd said. But then, she'd described the dowager as a spider at the centre of a great web. Miranda hadn't expected to come and find the web empty.

Cici would have been overjoyed, she was sure. The weak part of the plan had always been the co-operation of the son. The dowager could be forced, but how would she gain the co-operation of the son without revealing all? Cici had hoped that one or the other of the two men was so hopelessly under the thumb of his mother as to agree without question when a suitable woman was put before him. But she'd had her doubts. If the sons were in their mother's control, they'd have been married already.

To stumble into complete ruin was more good fortune than she could hope for.

She smothered her rising guilt. The duke had been right. She'd achieved her purpose and should derive some pleasure from it. She was about to become the lady to a very great, and very dirty, estate. She was about to marry a duke, the prize of every young girl of the *ton*. And have his heir.

She sat down on the edge of the bed. That was the crux of the problem. To have the heirs, she would have to become much more familiar with the Duke of Haughleigh than she would like. She was going to have to climb in the bed of that intimidating man and…

Lie very still and think of something else, she supposed. Cici had assured her that there were many types of men. And that the side they showed in the drawing room was not what she might see in the bedroom. She hoped not, or he'd spend the night interrogating her and tapping his foot when things did not go as fast as he'd hoped. She imagined him, standing over her on breakfast of their second wedded day, demanding to know why she wasn't increasing.

'Unfair. Unfair,' Cici remonstrated in her head. *'How can you claim to know a man you just met? Give him a chance.'*

All right. A chance. And he had offered for her, when he'd realised her circumstances. He could have left her to ruin. If he could get over his initial anger at being trapped into a union, he might make a fine husband. She would try to make a decent wife.

And in a house as large as this, they might make do quite well without seeing each other. There was certainly enough space.

A soft knock sounded at the door. 'Lady Miranda? His Lordship sent me up to do for you.' A mob-capped head poked around the corner of the slightly opened door. 'May I come in, ma'am?'

'Yes, please.'

'I'm Polly, ma'am. Not much of a lady's maid, I'm afraid. There's not been any call for it. The dowager's woman went back to her people after the funeral.'

'Well, it's been a long time since I've had a lady's maid, Polly, so we'll just have to muddle through this together.'

The girl smiled and entered, carrying a tray with a teapot and a light supper. She set it down on a small table by the window. 'Lord St John thought you'd be happier eating up here, ma'am. Supper in these parts is somewhat irregular.'

'Irregular?' As in, eaten seldom? Eaten at irregular times? Was the food strange in some way?

She glanced down at the meal, which consisted of a runny stew and a crust of dry bread. Certainly not what she'd expected. Too close to the poor meals she was used to. She tasted.

But not as well prepared.

'The house is still finding its way after her Grace's death.' The maid bowed her head in a second's reverent silence.

'And what was the pattern before?'

'Her Grace would mostly take a tray in her room, of the evenings.'

'And her sons?'

'Weren't here, ma'am. Lord St John was mostly up in London. And his Grace was on the continent. Paris and such. He din't come back 'til just before his mother died, to make peace. And Lord St John almost missed the funeral.'

It was just as well that she was disgraced, she thought. It didn't sound like either of the men would have had her because of the gentle pleadings of their mother.

'When will we be expecting the rest of your things, ma'am?' Polly was shaking the wrinkles out of a rather forlorn evening gown, surprised at having reached the bottom of the valise so soon. There was no good way to explain that the maid had seen the sum total of her trousseau: two day dresses, a gown and the travelling dress drying on a rack in the corner, supplemented by a pair of limp fichus, worn gloves and darned stockings.

'I'm afraid there aren't any more things, Polly. There was a problem on the coach,' she lied. 'There was a trunk, but it didn't make the trip with me. The men accidentally left it behind, and I fear it is stolen by now.'

'Perhaps not, ma'am,' Polly replied. 'Next time his Grace goes into the village, he can enquire after it. They'll send it on once they have the direction.'

Miranda could guess the response she'd receive if she asked him to inquire after her mythical wardrobe. He would no doubt give her some kind of a household allowance. She'd counted on the fact. Perhaps his powers of observation weren't sharp and she could begin making small purchases from it to supplement her clothing. She turned back to the topic at hand.

'And was her Grace ill for long before her death?'

'Yes, ma'am. She spent the last two months in her room. We all saw it coming.'

And shirked their duties because no one was there to scold them into action. By the look of the house, his Grace had not taken up the running of the house after the funeral. 'And now that his Grace is in charge of things,' she asked carefully, 'what kind of a master is he?'

'Don't rightly know, ma'am. He tends to the lands and leaves the running of the house to itself. Some nights he eats with the tenants. Some nights he eats in the village. Some nights he don't eat at all. There's not been much done with the tenants' houses and the upkeep since he's been away, and I think he's feelin' a bit guilty. And there's no telling what Lord St John is up to.' She grinned, as though it was a point of pride in the household. 'Young Lord St John is quite the man for a pretty face.'

'Well, yes. Hmm.' The last thing she needed. But he'd been pleasant to her and very helpful.

'He was the one that suggested we put you up here, even though the room hasn't been used much. Thought the duke'd want you up here eventually.'

'And why would that be?'

Polly stuck a thumb in the direction of the door on the south wall. 'It's more handy, like. This was his late duchess's room, although that goes back to well before my time.'

'H-how long ago would that be, Polly?' She glanced towards the bed, uncomfortable with the idea of sleeping on someone's deathbed, no matter how grand it might appear.

'Over ten years, ma'am.' Polly saw the look in her eyes and grinned. 'We've changed the linen since, I'm sure.'

'Of course,' she said, shaking herself for being a goose. 'And her Grace died…?'

'In childbed, ma'am. His Grace was quite broken up about it, and swore he'd leave the house to rot on its foundation before marrying again. He's been on the continent most of the last ten years. Stops back once or twice a year to check on the estate, but that is all.'

Miranda leaned back in her chair and gripped the arms. The picture Cici had painted for her was of a man who had grieved, but was ready to marry again. And he hadn't expected her. Hadn't wanted her. Had only agreed to a meeting to humour his dying mother.

No wonder he had flown into a rage.

She should set him free of any obligation towards her. Perhaps he could lend her her coach fare back to London. Prospects were black, but certainly not as bad as attaching herself to an unwilling husband.

Don't let an attack of missish nerves turn you from your destiny. There is nothing here to return to, should you turn aside an opportunity in Devon.

Nothing but Cici, who had been like a mother to her for so many years, and her poor, dear father. They'd sacrificed what little they had left to give her this one chance at a match. She couldn't disappoint them. And if she became a duchess, she could find a way to see them again.

If her husband allowed.

'What's to become of me?' she whispered more to herself than to Polly.

The night passed slowly, and the storm continued to pound against the windows. The room was damp and the pitiful fire laid in the grate did nothing to relieve it. Polly gave up trying, after several attempts, to find a chambermaid to air and change the bedding or to do something to improve the draw of the chimney. She returned with instructions from his Grace that, for the sake of propriety, Miranda was to remain in her room with the door locked until morning, when someone would come to fetch her to the chapel for her wedding. She carefully locked the door behind Polly, trying to imagine what dangers lay without that she must guard against. Surely, now that the damage was done, her honour was no longer at risk. Did wild dogs roam the corridor at night, that she needed to bar the door?

The only danger she feared was not likely to enter through the main door of her room. She glared across at the connecting door that led to the rooms of her future husband. If he wished to enter, he had easy access to her.

And the way to rescue or escape, should she need it, was blocked. The hairs on the back of her neck rose. She tiptoed across the room and laid her hand against the wood panel of the connecting door, leaning her head close to listen for noises from the other side. There was a muffled oath, a rustling, and nothing more. Yet.

She shook her head. She was being ridiculous. If he wanted her, there was no rush. She would legally belong to him in twenty-four hours. It was highly unlikely that he was planning to storm into her room tonight and take her.

She laid her hand on the doorknob. It would be locked, of course. She was being foolish. Her future husband had revealed nothing that indicated a desire for her now, or at any time in the future. He'd seemed more put out than lecherous at the thought of imminent matrimony and the accompanying sexual relations.

The doorknob turned in her hand and she opened it a crack before shutting it swiftly and turning to lean against it.

All right. The idea was not so outlandish after all. The door to the hall was locked against intruders and the way was clear for a visit from the man who would be her lord and master. She was helpless to prevent it.

And she was acting like she'd wasted her life on Minerva novels, or living some bad play with a lothario duke and a fainting virgin. If he'd been planning seduction, he'd had ample opportunity. If there were any real danger, she could call upon St John for help.

But, just in case, she edged the delicate gold-legged chair from the vanity under the doorknob of the connecting room. Remembering the duke, the width of his shoulders, and the boundless depths of his temper, she slid the vanity table to join the chair in blocking the doorway. Then she climbed back in the bed, pulled the covers up to her chin and stared sleeplessly up towards the canopy.

Marcus woke with a start, feeling the cold sweat rolling from his body and listening to the pounding of his heart, which slowed only slightly now that he was awake and recognised his surroundings.

Almost ten years without nightmares, since he'd stayed so far away from the place that had been their source. He'd been convinced that they would return as soon as he passed over the threshold. He'd lain awake, waiting for them on the first night and the second. And there had been nothing.

He'd thought, after his mother's funeral, they would return. Night after night of feeling the dirt hitting his face and struggling for breath. Or beating against the closed coffin lid, while the earth echoed against the other side of it. Certainly, watching as they lowered his mother into the ground would bring back the dreams of smothering, the nightmares of premature burial that this house always held for him.

But there had been nothing but peaceful sleep in the last two months. And he'd lulled himself with the idea that he was free. At least as free as was possible, given the responsibilities of the title and land. Nothing to fear any more, and time to get about the business that he'd been avoiding for so long, of being a duke and steward of the land.

And now the dreams were back as strong as ever. It had been water this time. Probably echoes of the storm outside. Waves and waves of it, crashing into his room, dragging him under. Pressing against his lungs until he was forced to take the last liquid breath that would end his life.

He'd woken with a start. Some small sound had broken through the dream and now he lay in bed as his heart slowed, listening for a repetition.

The communicating door opened a crack, and a beam of light shot into his room, before the door was hastily closed with a small click that echoed in the silence.

He smothered a laugh. His betrothed, awake and creeping around the room, had brought him out of the dream that she was the probable cause of. He considered calling out to her that he was having a nightmare, and asking for comfort like a little boy. How mad would she think him then?

Not mad, perhaps. It wasn't fear of his madness that made her check the door. Foolish of him not to lock it himself and set her mind at rest. But it had been a long time since he'd been over that threshold, and he'd ignored it for so long that he'd almost forgotten it was there.

He smiled towards his future bride through the darkness.

I know you are there. Just the other side of the door. If I listen, I can hear the sound of your breathing. Come into my room, darling. Come closer. Closer. Closer still. You're afraid, aren't you? Afraid of the future? Well, hell, so am I. But I know a way we can pass the hours until dawn. Honour and virtue and obligation be damned for just a night, just one night.

Too late, he decided, as he heard the sound of something heavy being dragged across the carpet to lean in front of the unlocked door. He stared up at the canopy of his bed. She was, no doubt, a most honourable and virtuous young lady who would make a fine wife. The thought was immeasurably depressing.

Chapter Four

The vicar was shaking his head dourly and Marcus slipped the explanatory letter off the blotter and towards him. 'As you can see, I was just writing to you to invite you to the house so we could resolve this situation.' His lips thinned as he fought to contain the rest of the thought.

Of course I needn't have bothered. You hitched up the carriage and were on your way here as soon as the sun rose. Come to see the storm damage, have you, vicar? Meddling old fool. You've come to see the girl and you're hoping for the worst.

The vicar looked sympathetic, but couldn't disguise the sanctimonious smile as he spoke. 'Most unfortunate. A most unfortunate turn of events. Of course, you realise what your duty is in this situation, to prevent talk in the village and to protect the young lady's reputation.'

A duty that could have been prevented yesterday, if you actually cared a jot for the girl or for silencing talk.

'Yes,' he responded mildly. 'I discussed it with Miranda yesterday and we are in agreement. It only remains to arrange the ceremony.'

The vicar nodded. 'Your mother would have been most pleased.'

'Would she, now?' His eyes narrowed.

'Hmm, yes. She mentioned as much on my last visit to her.'

'Mentioned Miranda, did she?'

He nodded again. 'Yes. She said that a match between you was in the offing. It was her fondest hope—'

'Damn.'

'Your Grace. There's no need—'

'This was all neatly arranged, wasn't it? My mother's hand from beyond the grave, shoving that poor girl down the road to ruin, and you and your wife looking the other way while it happened.' He leaned forward and the vicar leaned back.

'Your Grace, I hardly think—'

'You hardly do, that's for certain. Suppose I am as bad as my mother made me out to be? Then you would have thrown the girl's honour away in the hope that I would agree to this madness. Suppose I had been from home when she arrived? Suppose it had been just St John here to greet her? Do you honestly think he would be so agreeable?' He was on the verge of shouting again. He paused to gain control and his next words were a cold and contemptuous whisper. 'Or would you have brushed that circumstance under the rug and rushed her back out of town, instead of trumpeting the girl's location around the village so that everyone would know and my obligation would be clear?'

'That does not signify. Fortunately, we have only the situation at hand to deal with.'

'Which leaves me married to a stranger chosen by my mother.'

He was nodding again, but without certainty. 'Hmm, well…under the circumstances it would be best to act expediently. The banns—'

'Are far from expedient, as I remember. We dispensed with them the last time. A special licence.'

'If you send to London today, then perhaps by next week…'

'And I suppose you will spirit the girl away to your house for a week, until the paperwork catches up with the plotting. Really, Reverend, you and my mother should have planned this better. Perhaps you should have forged my name on the application a month ago and we could have settled this today. You needn't have involved me in the decision at all.' He thought for a moment and stared coldly at the priest. 'This is how we will proceed. You will perform the ceremony today, and I will go off to London tomorrow for the licence.'

'But that would be highly improper.'

'But it would ensure I need never see your face in my house again, and that suits me well. If you cared for impropriety, you should have seen to it yesterday, when you met Miranda on her way here. When I come back with the licence I will have a servant bring it to you and you can fill in whatever dates you choose and sign the bloody thing. But this morning you will see the young lady and myself married before the eyes of God in the family chapel.'

His head was shaking now in obvious disapproval. 'Hmm. Well, that would hardly be legitimate.'

'Not legal, perhaps, but certainly moral. And morality is what you are supposed to concern yourself with. If you don't question the fact that you coerced me into taking her, then do not waste breath telling me my behaviour is improper. Open the prayer book and say the words, take yourself and your bullying harpy of a wife away from this house and leave me in peace. Now go to the chapel and prepare for the ceremony. Miranda and I will be there shortly.'

The vicar hemmed and harrumphed his way out of the study, not happy, but apparently willing to follow Marcus's plan without further objections. A generous gratuity after the ceremony would go a long way towards smoothing any remaining ruffled feathers and soon the scandal of his new marriage would fade away as though there had been nothing unusual about it.

His mind was at rest on one point, at least. The interview with the vicar exonerated Miranda of any blame for the unusual and scandalous way she had appeared on his doorstep. She had hoped to make a match, but there was no evidence that she had tried to trap him by ruining herself. There was no reason to believe that she was anything other than what she appeared to be.

Unless she was dishonoured before she arrived at his home.

The letters from the mysterious Cecily said otherwise. They said she was innocent. But, of course, they would. No sane person would send a letter, claiming that the girl was a trollop but had a good heart. He struggled with the thought, trying to force it from his mind. He was well and truly bound to her by oath and honour, whatever the condition of her reputation.

But not by law. Until his name was on the licence he was not tying a knot that could not be untied, should the truth come to light soon. He would watch the girl and find what he could of the truth before it was too late. And he would protect her while she was in his home; make sure he was not worsening an already bad situation. He rang the bell for Wilkins and demanded that he summon St John to the study.

After a short time, his brother lounged into the room with the same contempt and insolence that he always displayed when they were alone together. 'As always your servant, your Grace.'

'Spare me the false subservience for once, St John.'

St John smirked at him. 'You don't appreciate me when I do my utmost to show respect for you, Haughleigh. It is, alas, so hard to please the peer.'

'As you make a point of telling me, whenever we speak. You can call a truce for just one day. Today you will grant me the honour due a duke, and the master of this house.' He was close to shouting again. His plan to appeal to him as a brother was scuttled before he had a chance to act on it. To hell with his quick temper and St John's ability to reduce him to a towering rage without expending any energy.

'Very well, Marcus.' The name sounded as false and contemptible as his title always did when it came from his brother's lips. 'A truce, but only for a day. Consider it my wedding gift to you.'

'It is about the wedding that I meant to talk to you, St John.'

'Oh, really?' There was the insolent quirk of the eyebrows that he had grown to loathe. 'Is there anything you need advice on? I'd assumed that the vicar would give you the speech on the duties of the husband. Or that perhaps you recalled some of them, after Bethany. But, remembering your last marriage, I could see where you might come to me for advice.'

Marcus's fist slammed down on the desk as though he had no control. 'How dare you, St John? Damn you for speaking of Bethany, today of all days.'

'Why not, Marcus? She is never far from my mind. Just because you wish to forget her does not mean that I will.'

He flexed his hands and pushed away the image of them closing on St John's windpipe, and then placed them carefully on the blotter. 'You promised a truce and I see how quickly you forget it. Let us pretend for a moment, St John, that you have any honour left as it pertains to this house.'

'Very well, brother. One last game of "Let's Pretend", as we played when we were little. And what are we pretending, pray tell?'

'That you are planning to go willingly from this house, today, and that it will not be necessary for me to have the servants evict you.'

'Go? From this house? Why ever would I do that, Marcus?'

'Because you hate it here as much as I do. And you hate me. There. There are two good reasons. I must remain here to face what memories there are. As you are quick to point out to me, whenever we are alone, I am the Duke of Haughleigh. And now I am to be married, and chances are good that I will soon have a son to inherit. There is no reason for you to wait in the house for me to break my neck on the stairs and leave you the title and the entail. I am certain that, should the happy accident you are waiting for occur before a son arrives, my wife will notify you and you can return.'

'You are right, Marcus. I do hate you, and this house. But I have grown quite fond of Miranda.'

'In the twelve hours you have known her.'

'I have spent more time with her during those hours than you have, Marcus. While you were busy playing lord of the manor and issuing commands, I was stealing a march. And now, I should find it quite hard to part myself from my dear little sister, for that is how I view her.' The smile on his face was deceptively innocent. Marcus knew it well.

'You will view her, if at all, from a distance.' Marcus reached into the desk drawer and removed a leather purse that clanked with gold when he threw it out on to the desktop. 'You will go today, and take my purse with you. You need not even stop in your room to pack, for Wilkins is already taking care of that. Your things will be on the way to the inn within the hour.'

'You think of everything, don't you, Marcus? Except, of course, what you will do if I refuse to accede to your command.'

'Oh, St John, I've thought of that as well.'

'Really?'

'Yes. You can leave for the inn immediately, and from there to points distant. Or you can leave feet foremost for a position slightly to the left of Mother. The view from the spot I plan for you is exceptional, although you will no longer be able to enjoy it.'

'Fratricide? You have become quite the man of action in the ten years we've been parted, Marcus.'

'Or a duel, if you have the nerve. The results will be the same, I assure you. I can only guess how you've spent the intervening years, but I've studied with the best fencing masters in Italy, and am a crack shot. I've allowed you a period of mourning and have made what efforts I could to mend the breach between us and put the past to rest. It has been an abject failure. After today, you are no longer welcome in my home, St John. If you do not leave willingly, I will remove you myself.'

'Afraid, Marcus?'

'Of you? Certainly not.' He shifted in his chair, trying to disguise the tension building within him.

'Of the past coming back to haunt you, I think.'

'Not afraid, St John. But not the naïve young man I once was. There is no place for you here. What is your decision?'

St John leaned an indolent hand forward and pulled the purse to himself. 'How could I refuse your generosity, Marcus? I will say hello to all the old gang in London, and buy them a drink in honour of you and your lovely new wife.'

Marcus felt his muscles relax and tried not to let his breath expel in a relieved puff. 'You have chosen wisely, St John.'

Miranda waited politely as Mrs Winslow and Polly examined the gown. 'But it's grey.' Mrs Winslow's disappointment was obvious.

'It seemed a serviceable choice at the time.' Miranda's excuse was as limp as the lace that trimmed the gown.

'My dear, common sense is all well and good, but this is your wedding day. Have you nothing more appropriate? This gown appears more suitable—'

'For mourning?' Miranda supplied. 'Well, yes. My own dear mother…'

Had been dead for thirteen years. But what Mrs Winslow did not know would not hurt her. And if the death seemed more recent, it explained the dress. The gown in question had, in fact, been Cici's mourning dress, purchased fifteen years' distant, after the death of a Spanish count. While full mourning black might have been more appropriate, Cici had chosen dove grey silk, not wanting to appear unavailable for long. It had taken some doing to shorten the bodice and lengthen the skirt to fit Miranda, but they'd done a creditable job by adding a ruffle at the hem.

'Your mother? You poor dear. But you're well out of mourning now?'

'Of course. But I've had little time to buy new things.' *Or money,* she added to herself.

'Well, now that the duke will be looking after you, I'm sure that things will be looking up. And for now, this must do.' Mrs Winslow looked at her curiously. 'Before your mother died…did she…?' She took a deep breath. 'There are things that every young woman must know. Before she marries. Certain facts that will make the first night less of a…a shock.'

Miranda bit her lip. It was better not to reveal how much she knew on the subject of marital relations. Cici's lectures had been informative, if unorthodox, and had given her an unladylike command of the details. 'Thank you for your concern, Mrs Winslow.'

'Are you aware…there are differences in the male and the female…?'

'Yes,' she answered a little too quickly. 'I helped…nursing…charity work.' Much could be explained by charity work, she hoped.

'Then you have seen…' Mrs Winslow took a nervous sip of tea.

'Yes.'

'Good. Well, not good, precisely. But at least you will not be surprised.' She rushed on, 'And the two genders fit together where there are differences, and the man plants a seed and that is where babies come from. Do you understand?'

Cici had made it clear enough, but she doubted that Mrs Winslow's description was of much use to the uninitiated. 'I…'

'Never mind,' the woman continued. 'I dare say the duke knows well enough how to proceed. You must trust him in all things. However, the duke…is a very—' words failed her again '—*vigorous* man.'

'Vigorous?'

'In his prime. Robust. And the men in his family are reported to have healthy appetites. Too healthy, some might say.' She sniffed in disapproval.

Miranda looked at the vicar's wife with what she hoped was an appropriately confused expression, and did not have to feign the blush colouring her cheeks.

'And the baby that his first wife was delivering when she died was said to be exceptionally large. A difficult birth. He will, of course, insist on an heir. But if his demands seem excessive after the birth of the first child…many women find…a megrim, perhaps. A small lie is not a major sin when it gains a tired woman an occasional night of peace.'

Miranda stood at the back of the chapel, waiting for the man who was to seal her destiny. When the knock had sounded at her door, she'd expected the duke, but had been surprised to see St John, holding a small bouquet out to her and offering to accompany her to the chapel. The gown she'd finally chosen for the wedding was not the silk, but her best day dress, and, if he thought to make a comment on the state of it, it didn't show. It had looked much better in the firelight as she'd altered it. Here in Devon, in the light of day, the sorriness of it was plainly apparent to anyone that cared to look. The hem of Cici's green cotton gown had been let down several inches to accommodate her long legs, and the crease of the old hem was clearly visible behind the unusually placed strip of lace meant to conceal it. The ruffles, cut from the excess fabric of the bodice when she'd taken it in, and added to the ends of the sleeves, did not quite match, and the scrap of wilted lace at their ends made the whole affair look not so much cheerful as pathetic.

'There now, mouse. Don't look so glum, although I could see where a long talk with the vicar's wife might not put you in the mood to smile. Did she explain to you your wifely duties?'

She blushed at St John's boldness. 'After a fashion. And then she quizzed me about my parents, and about the last twenty-four hours. And she assured me that whatever you might have done to me, if I felt the need to flee, they would take me in, and ask no questions.'

His laugh rang against the vaulted ceiling and the vicar and his wife looked back in disapproval. 'And God does not strike them down for their lies when they say they wouldn't question you. At least my brother and I make no bones about our wicked ways. They cloak their desire to hear the salacious story of your seduction in an offer of shelter.'

'My what?'

'They hope for the worst, my dear. If you were to burst into tears at the altar and plead for rescue, you will fulfil all of their wildest dreams and surmises.'

'St John.' She frowned her disapproval.

'Or better yet, you could fall weeping to my arms and let me carry you away from this place, as my brother rages. I would be delighted to oblige.'

'As if that would not make my reputation.'

'Ah, but what a reputation. To be seduced away from your wedding by the duke's roguishly handsome younger brother and carried off somewhere. Oh, but I see I'm upsetting you.' He pointed up to the window above the altar, where the bleeding head of St John the Baptist rested in stained glass. 'I don't know what my mother was thinking of, naming me for a saint. If it was to imbue me with piousness and virtue, it didn't work.'

'Was the window commissioned in your honour, then?'

'Can you not see the resemblance?' He tilted his head to the side, tongue lolling out of his mouth and eyes rolled to show the whites. And, despite herself, she laughed.

'No, it's an old family name, and the window was commissioned after some particularly reprehensible St John before me. Probably lost his head over a woman, the poor soul.' He touched his blond hair and admitted, 'There is a slight resemblance, though. Most of the art in this room was made to look like family. It is my brother who looks more like my mother's indiscretion than my father's first child.'

'I don't think so,' she remarked, pointing at a marble statue. 'That scowling martyr in the corner could well be him. See the profile?'

St John laughed. 'No, my brother was never named from the bible. He was named for a Roman dictator. Quite fitting, really.'

'What are you doing still here?' St John was right. It was an imperious voice, and its owner did nothing to hide the contempt in it as he spoke to his brother.

'You needed witnesses for this little party, Marcus. And how could I miss my brother's wedding?'

'You could miss it because I ordered you to,' growled Marcus. 'I believe I told you to vacate your rooms and be off this morning.'

'But you meant after the ceremony, certainly. I doubted

you'd allow me as best man, but surely someone must give the bride away.'

She frowned. She'd already been given away, certain enough. She didn't need any presence of her father to remind her of that.

'And I suppose that is why, when I went to Miranda's chamber to fetch her, I found it empty.'

'Dashed bad luck for the groom to see the bride before the wedding.'

'For you as well as me.' There was a murderous tone in her future husband's voice.

'Please, your Grace,' she interceded. 'Would it be so wrong of St John to stay for just one more hour, if I wish it so?'

'If you wish.' The short phrase seemed as though it was being wrenched from the heart of him. The duke pointed down the aisle and towards the altar and muttered to his brother, 'If you insist on being party to this against my specific instructions, then try my patience no further. Walk her to the altar and we can commence.'

St John linked his arm with hers and set off on the short walk to the front of the chapel at a leisurely pace, with Marcus a step behind. She could feel him behind her in a cloud of irritation as thick as incense. St John twitched next to her as his brother's hand prodded him to speed up.

'In a rush, Marcus? I could see why, of course, with such a lovely bride awaiting you. But we must try to respect the solemnity to the occasion. No need to race up the aisle, is there?'

'Just walk.' He almost spat the words. She was afraid to turn and face him, but could already guess his expression. It was the one he got right before he began to swear.

They reached the front of the chapel and the vicar looked down at them with a beneficent smile. 'Dearly beloved, we are gathered here today in the sight of God, and the face of this congregation…' He faltered as he looked out over the empty pews and a snort escaped from St John.

His voice rose and fell monotonously. '…nor taken in hand, unadvisedly, lightly or wantonly…'

She bit her lip. Taken into unadvisedly, indeed. What could be considered unadvisable about this?

'…let him speak now, or else hereafter for ever hold his peace.'

There was a loud and disapproving sniff from the vicar's wife in the front pew, to fill the dramatic pause.

He turned back to them. 'I require and charge you both, as ye will answer at the dreadful day of judgement when the secrets of all hearts shall be disclosed, that if either of you know of any impediment…'

Dear God, forgive me for what I am doing today. I swear that I will be a good and faithful servant to this man, she prayed fervently. *And do not punish me for the secrets in my heart, for I swore to keep them. It was wrong, I know, but I swore to Cici and to my father…*

She felt her husband's hand tighten on hers even as she was praying. Without realising it, he had pulled her closer to him and she leaned against his arm, which was as solid as a marble pillar. Perhaps this was some sort of sign, his strength guarding and upholding her as she faced her fears.

The vicar led them through the vows, the duke answering with a firm, 'I will', and maintaining the grip on her arm that inspired her to manage the same.

He plighted his troth with equal confidence, although his

eyes barely flickered in her direction as he said the words, and she promised 'to love, cherish, and obey'.

Then the vicar called for the ring, and the duke looked down at her with a dazed expression, clearly having forgotten. He glanced once at an amused St John, then slipped the signet from his own finger and handed it to the vicar to bless. When he muttered, 'With this ring I thee wed, with my body I thee worship and with all my worldly goods I thee endow', his voice was a self-conscious apology for everything that had happened in the last twenty-four hours. And he kissed the ring once before slipping it on to her finger.

He folded her fingers into a loose fist to keep the ring from slipping off and for a moment she felt as though she had trapped the kiss in her palm and could feel the warmth of it seeping through her.

The vicar droned the ceremony to its conclusion and she clung to the kiss in her hand. Cici had been correct all along. It was going to be all right. He might be gruff, but there was a tenderness in the way he'd said the vows and made her believe the words, and supported her when she was afraid, and given her his ring.

Then it was over, and her hand was firmly trapped in the crook of her husband's arm as they turned to accept the congratulations of the congregation. All two of them.

The vicar's wife sniffed politely and allowed that it had been a lovely ceremony, such as it was, and wished them happiness in a tone that stated she thought the chances of it were remote.

St John's smile was as bright as ever, if a trifle sad. He clasped his brother's hand, and Marcus accepted stiffly.

'Good luck, Marcus. Once again you have more good fortune than you deserve.' He turned to her. 'Miranda, dear sister.' He reached out to grip her hands as well and said, 'I must be going this afternoon, as my brother wishes. But if there is ever anything I can do for you, the innkeeper in the village will know where to reach me. And now—' his eyes sparkled '—let me be the first to kiss the bride.'

And before his brother could object, although she saw the storm gathering in his eyes, St John's lips had come down quickly to buss her own. It was sweet and harmless, and she couldn't help but smile at his impertinence.

'St John, I believe it is time for you to be going. Long past time, as a matter of fact. And you...' He looked down at her and she realised again how massive a man he was and shrank away from him, but he pulled her close. 'You must learn to take care whom you kiss, madam.'

He stared into her eyes and his own grew dark. She was lost in them, paralysed with nerves and anticipation. Then his mouth covered hers and his hand went to the back of her neck, stroking her hair and sending shivers down her spine. Despite herself, she relaxed and leaned against him, running her hands under his lapels to feel the solidity of his body, letting it support her as his other hand slipped to her waist.

This was wrong. It must be. The ideas rising within her had no place in a chapel. She opened her mouth to protest and his tongue dipped into it, stroking her tongue and thrusting again, simulating... And she felt the feeling rushing through her in a great shudder.

She fought for control of her emotions. Dear God, no. She mustn't respond so. What must he think? She pulled herself out of his arms and stood back, staring up at him in shock. He smiled down at her, one eyebrow raised in surprise. And then he turned away, staring past her at St John's retreating back.

Chapter Five

She was still shaking with mingled passion and panic. How dare he? In a church! In front of the vicar! And she had responded like a common whore. If the kiss had been some sort of test of her experience, she'd probably confirmed his worst fears. Her empty stomach roiled and she covered her mouth, afraid to look at the vicar's wife lest she be sick on the marble floor. It would only have made the situation worse.

And her husband would not have noticed. He was already striding out of the chapel and down the hall, following St John at a safe distance, probably to make sure that he was headed towards the stables and away.

She straightened her back and turned to the vicar and his wife, forcing a smile to her face. 'Well.' The word was artificially cheery. 'I must thank you, Reverend Winslow, and Mrs Winslow, for your concern in the matter of my safety and honour.'

'Hmm. Well, of course, the concern continues, your Grace.'

For a moment she looked around, expecting to see her

husband behind her, and then realised that he was addressing her, the new duchess.

'Thank you, yet again. But I am certain, now that we are
married, I will do well here.'

They continued to stare at her. She had hoped that 'good
day' was implied in her thanks, but they showed no sign of
leaving. They must be expecting something. 'Well,' she said
again but the cheer in her voice was running thin.

'Perhaps, over the wedding breakfast, we might speak to
his Grace once more. To make sure there is nothing further
required of us.' Mrs Winslow's pointed remark led the way
to yet another problem.

'Ah, yes. The wedding breakfast.' Miranda wondered if
anyone on the staff had considered guests. She doubted, after
watching his mood in the church, that her husband cared to celebrate. Still, if she could not come up with a bit of cake and
some champagne, she might as well find a maid to ready a room
for the Winslows. They showed no sign of leaving. 'Let us go
back to the house and see what the servants are preparing.'

She walked them back and abandoned them in the drawing
room with promises of a speedy return, then ran into the hall
and shouted for Wilkins.

He appeared looking as stooped and addled as he had the
day before, giving her a long, fishy look that made her suspect
he had forgotten who she was.

'Wilkins.' Her tone was sharp, hoping to cut through the
fog of gin in his mind. 'I need you to find his Grace and ask
him to return to the house to say goodbye to the Winslows.
And I need to speak to the housekeeper about preparing a
small wedding breakfast.'

'Breakfast.' The word had registered, judging by the panic

that crossed his face. 'That won't be likely, miss. House-keeper's off today.'

In a flash, the mess she had landed in spread itself before her. The house was unmanageable, the servants intractable, the duke antisocial and oblivious to the chaos around him.

And, after twenty minutes of rote prayer, she was in charge.

'First, Wilkins—' her voice was silky smooth '—you will no longer refer to me as "Miss". After the ceremony in the chapel this morning, my title is her Grace, the Duchess of Haughleigh. Since I doubt you remember my old name, you need waste little time in forgetting it. If the housekeeper is off, than she needs to make other arrangements for the management of the house while she is gone. Who, exactly, is in charge in her absence?'

Wilkins's blank eyes and furrowed brow were answer enough.

'Very well. I will assume no one is in charge, since this is certainly the appearance the house creates. Is the cook available? Sober? Alive? Do we even have a cook, Wilkins?'

'Yes, miss—ma'am—your Grace.' With each new title, his back got straighter as he addressed her.

'Then you will inform the cook that, if she values her position here, there will be a wedding breakfast laid in the dining room in forty-five minutes. I do not expect a miracle. Just the most she can manage on such short notice. And a bottle or two of the best champagne in the cellars to take our mind off the food. Please find the duke and ask him to join us in the drawing room.'

The speech must have hit home, for Wilkins toddled off in the direction of the kitchen at a speed as yet unseen by her.

Then she turned with as much majesty and command as she could muster and headed back into the drawing room, trying to radiate her half of marital bliss.

The Winslows were perched on the edges of their respective chairs, awaiting her arrival. She informed them of the brief delay and set to holding up her end of the conversation, which was rather like supporting a dead ox. Topics such as family, past, friends, and thoughts for her future had been exhausted or avoided in the morning's interviews with Mrs Winslow.

Efforts to draw the Winslows out on their own lives proved them to be neither well travelled, nor intelligent.

The clock was ticking by with no evidence of the arrival of the duke. It would serve him right to enter and find himself the topic of conversation. She tried hesitantly, 'Have you known the Radwell family long, Reverend? For other than connections with the dowager through a guardian of mine, they are strangers to me.'

'Hmm. Well, yes. I've been in the area, man and boy, most of my life. Things were different under the old duke,' he hinted.

'How so?' She doubted such a direct request for information was going to be met with an answer, but it was worth a try.

The vicar shot a nervous glance at the doorway, as though expecting the appearance of the current duke at the mention of his name. But Mrs Winslow was no longer able to contain the dark secrets she knew. 'The old duke would not have held with the nonsense his sons have got up to. He knew his duty and the land was a showplace while he controlled it. The fourth duke tried for a few years to hold up to his father's standards, but gave up the ghost after his first wife died, leaving the poor dowager alone to manage as best she could. And Lord St John…' she shook her head and sniffed for emphasis '…has never made any effort to make his family's life any easier. From the moment he was old enough to distinguish the difference between the sexes and read the numbers on a deck of cards or count the spots on the dice, there has always been a debt that he has been running from. It is my opinion that the dowager died more of a broken heart than anything else.'

'The current duke…'

And, as if summoned, the door opened and framed Marcus.

The vicar's wife shut her mouth with a snap.

'If I might see you for a moment in the hall, Miranda.'

The word 'now' was unspoken, but plain enough. And the sound of her name on his lips was strange, indeed. There was something about the way he said the 'r' that seemed to vibrate into a growl.

'If you will excuse me, for a moment, Reverend, Mrs Winslow?' And she rose quickly to join her husband in the hall.

'Your Grace?'

'You demanded my attendance, Miranda?' He sketched a mocking bow to her.

'Not demanded. I requested that Wilkins find you and bring you back for our wedding breakfast.'

'I ordered no breakfast.'

'I did.' She glared at him in frustration. 'Perhaps you see no need to celebrate the day, and I could do without a continuation of this… this…melodrama, but the Winslows expect it of us and will not leave until the niceties are performed.'

'Damn the Winslows!'

'Damn them indeed, sir,' she whispered, 'but do it quietly. They are probably listening at the door.'

'I do not care what they hear. If they lack the sense to clear off—'

'Very well, then there will be no breakfast. And since I am to have no authority in this house I will leave it to you to step into the drawing room and request that they leave. Order them from the house. You seem to be good at that.'

'Ahh, we come to the crux, finally. This is about St John, is it? I told him this morning that he is no longer welcome here and my decision stands.'

'St John? Don't be ridiculous. This is about your unwillingness to live by the proprieties for more than a few minutes at a time.'

'I followed them when I offered for you. And I married you, didn't I?'

She forced a smile and muttered through her gritted teeth, 'And now you must pretend to celebrate the fact, as I am doing. Choke down a piece of cake and a glass of wine. We both must eat something, and it will not kill us to eat it together. Then thank the vicar for performing the ceremony. Pay him. Make him go away.'

The door to the drawing room swung open and the vicar's head appeared in the opening. 'And how are you two managing together?'

Her husband smiled with such ferociousness that the vicar retreated behind the protection of the door. 'As well as can be expected, Reverend. I understand my wife has arranged a feast for us. Let us retire to the dining room and see what the servants have prepared.'

He led the way, Miranda noted in relief, since the dining room was not a place she had had need to visit since coming to the house. It was about as she had expected: dirty and dusty, but with lurid painted silk on the walls, depicting poorly drawn shepherds and shepherdesses bullying sheep up and down the hills.

The breakfast was also as she expected. Weak tea, runny eggs, a passable ham accompanied by another serving from the endless supply of dry bread. She wondered how the cook managed it. Had she found a way to dry it before baking? The wedding cake itself was the most frightening part of the meal. There had been no time to prepare a true cake, and cook had made do with something that had been leftover from another meal. Whose, she was not sure—she certainly had not seen it during her brief stay. The cut edge had been trimmed away and the whole thing heavily iced and scattered with candied violets that were unable to conceal the lopsided nature of the whole.

And Marcus ruled over the table without saying a word, maintaining the same horrible smile he'd shone in the hallway. The vicar offered a brief prayer of thanks, to which Marcus blinked in response, and they all ate.

To her relief, Wilkins had followed her instructions and provided the best champagne that the cellars had to offer. She had never tasted it before and was surprised at how light and easily drinkable it was. And equally surprised, twenty minutes later, that she had downed three glasses of it, and barely touched the food on her plate. She opened her mouth to speak and hiccupped, making the Winslows jump in their seats and bringing a critical glare from her husband. She offered a quiet apology and shielded her glass from any further attempt of the eager footman to fill it.

Shortly thereafter the duke removed his napkin from his lap and threw it on his plate with a note of finality. He stood and advanced slowly on the vicar with an evil grin and such a deliberate pace that all at the table were convinced that they were about to see the poor man murdered and perhaps eaten. The duke reached into the front pocket of his jacket and the vicar cringed against the oncoming blow.

The duke merely produced an envelope thick with bank notes and dropped it on the plate in front of the vicar. 'Thank you for your assistance in this matter, Reverend, Mrs Winslow. Good day.'

And then he stood there, stock still, above the vicar. And waited. All in all, Miranda decided she much preferred it when he was yelling. But the effect was impressive and it took less than a minute before the vicar's composure cracked and he was making his apologies and wishing them well before hustling his wife to the door.

She saw them off with an artificial courtesy that she hoped was not too obvious and turned to find that her husband had followed them to the door as well.

'I trust that was sufficient, madam?' He stared at her with only the barest trace of the annoyance he'd shown for the last hour.

'Yes. Thank you.' She looked up at him and wondered what was actually going through his mind. He was capable of so many emotions, and able to exchange them so quickly.

'Very well.' He continued to look at her, as if seeing her for the first time.

She gazed down and clasped her hands together and remembered the ring he had given her and the kiss, and blushed, running her finger over the surface of the gold and feeling safe and warm.

He glanced down. 'Ah, yes. I had forgotten that. May I have my ring back, please?'

She looked up at him in shock.

'I have need of it. And it would not do for you to lose it.'

'Lose it? It's just that…I thought…' She stared down at it, unsure what to say. She thought that the gift had meant something. Perhaps not.

And her eyes met his, and she was lost in them. Her fingers relaxed and the heavy ring slipped off and bounced on the marble floor.

He stooped and caught it, before it had rolled too far, nodding as if this confirmed what he had suspected about her negligent care of it. 'Thank you. And now, if you will excuse me, I'm sure I will see you in our rooms, later.'

Chapter Six

She stared up into the canopy of the bed, watching a spider spinning in the gloom of a corner. Her husband would come soon, and do what he would do, and it would be over. She tried not to review in her mind the detailed explanation that Cici had given her of marital relations. It would hurt the first time, but she was not to be afraid.

She mentally cursed Cici for explaining it so. It must not hurt so very much or women would never allow a second time. She was not unfamiliar with pain. It could not hurt her body as much as leaving home had wounded her heart. She would survive.

Cici had said that with some men it was not painful, but actually quite pleasant. When the man was loving and gentle, there was nowhere else you'd rather be than joined with them. Cici had known many men and had a chance for comparison.

Since she was to know only one, whether it might be pleasant somewhere else need not concern her. As a matter of fact, it was annoying to think that things could be better in a different bed. Hadn't she always known that there were better places to be than the circumstances she'd been given? And wasn't the foolish quest for better circumstances the thing that had led her here?

She remembered her last job, helping in the kitchen of one of the great houses near her home. She'd been carrying strawberries from the garden for the cook, when an unnamed lord had spotted her in a secluded hallway. He'd blocked her way, and smiled, wishing her a good morning.

And she'd smiled back, and made to go around him.

And he'd asked her name.

She'd responded politely and continued her progress towards the kitchen.

He was upon her before she realised and her back was against the wall. He'd reached into the bowl of berries she was still holding in front of her and brought one to his lips, biting and letting the juice trickle on to his chin. And he'd taken another, and brought it very deliberately to her lips and bade her bite. She'd been hungry and unable to resist the temptation to have just one. And she'd eaten from his hand like a tamed animal. Then he'd thrust a hand down the front of her dress and seized her breast.

She stood there, frozen in shock as he felt the slight weight of it, then rolled the nipple between his fingers.

Her mind had screamed that she must run. But her traitorous legs would not move. And he'd leaned closer, nipping her earlobe and whispering that, Miranda, there were many easier ways to earn a shilling than fetching and carrying for the cook. And, Miranda, there could be pretty dresses and baubles for a pretty girl, a quiet girl, if she were to bring her bowl of berries and come with him now.

And, to her shame, she'd been tempted. The part of her that

was weak and tired and frightened told her that he was right. It would be easier just to lie back and give up. But he'd begun to describe what he wanted in whispering gasps, and anger had broken through the fear in her mind. She'd dropped the bowl and run from the house. She'd saved her honour, but lost her position. And considered herself lucky that he hadn't taken what he wanted without benefit of discussion.

Cici had warned her, if a man turned out to be a brute, it was better not to resist, but to lie still and let him finish.

Which brought her mind back to her new husband. The kiss in the church had been strange enough. It had been pleasant at first, but overwhelming and inescapable. She imagined being trapped beneath him tonight as he grunted and rutted like some stallion in a stable yard. She'd be still, let him take what he wanted and perhaps he'd lose interest and return to his own rooms. She must look on the bright side, such as it was. He kept himself cleaner than the servants kept his house. His face had been shaven smooth and his body smelled of cologne and not sweat. His breath was fresh enough. His teeth were good. The advantages of wealth, she thought. The improved circumstances that Cici said her father had wanted for her. It was inevitable that she would marry and have some man in her bed. At least a rich man would be clean and the bed would be large.

And the result would be the same, whether she'd married a beggar or a peer. A swollen belly, the pain of childbed and a baby. At least her new husband could afford to keep his children. She never need worry about food or a roof over her head or the clothing on her back. That was the gift that her father had wanted for her and she should be grateful that he had been sensible enough to look to her future.

She listened for sounds from the other room, and her nerves ratcheted still tighter. How long was he planning to wait? It was past midnight and still there was no sign.

Her stomach growled, and the hollow ache in it drove the acid up and into her throat. She should have choked down a meal. She should have partaken of that miserable wedding breakfast. Now she was starving as well as scared and could feel a faint pounding beginning behind her temple.

Perhaps she should ring for Polly to bring her some tea. As if she'd want to come at this hour— Miranda had too much sympathy there to draw the servants out of their warm beds to fulfil needs that should have been dealt with earlier in the evening.

Of course, there was no law to say that she couldn't take care of things herself. Great houses were all alike. Bedrooms were up, and kitchens were down and there were servants' stairs between. It was possible, at this advanced hour, that the duke had no plans to visit her. And if he did, she should hurry and be back before he arrived and no one would be the wiser. She left her door open a crack and tiptoed down the hall to the place where she was sure the servants' stairs must lie.

The duke stared down in to his brandy glass. He should be upstairs by now, waiting on his new wife, not in the library, gathering Dutch courage.

He poured another glass and drank. This was not how the day was supposed to run. He'd had no desire to take a wife and certainly not to yoke himself to the odd duck that had washed up on the doorstep yesterday. Eventually, he would have had to make a decision, but he had been enjoying the relative quiet in the house without the presence of his mother.

He would get the estate back in order first. And something would have to be done about St John. An uneasy truce at least. They'd need to work through enough of the old problem so they would not be at each other's throats. He had no real desire to throw his only living relative from the house for good, but it might be necessary if no solution could be found.

He'd never intended to bring a wife into the mess that existed now. But one had forced her way into it and now he had another problem to deal with. And he'd done a ham-handed job of it so far, railing at her in the hall for problems that weren't of her doing, and goaded by St John's sneers to that kiss after the wedding. He could tell by the thin set of her lips at breakfast that she was convinced she'd married a lout.

And now, instead of apologising and getting on with the business at hand, he was hiding in the library with a brandy bottle. As if an excess of spirits would do anything but inhibit his ability to perform the new duty added to an already long list.

At the least, it would leave him careless and he imagined the deflowering of a virgin required a certain amount of finesse.

If that truly was her state. He suspected not. To be rushed unescorted out of London raised doubts. He knew nothing of her family other than it had been wronged by his, which did not narrow the field much in choice of a wife. It was how he'd gained his last wife as well. He suspected, between his mother, his brother and himself, that there was quite a list of eligible females whose families had been wronged. But he could not take a harem to assuage the family honour.

It might be best, he thought, swirling the liquor in the

snifter, if the consummation were postponed, at least until he could ascertain the reason that his mother had been so eager to have him wed to this particular woman. It would be the rational course of action to proceed with caution.

And what would be the fun of that?

Marcus smiled at the thought that had crept unbidden in to his head. Throw caution to the winds? He was a brother to St John after all. While it might be sensible to save the wedding night until he was sure he had any intention of staying married to the woman in question, it was in no way satisfying. If the woman came to his home hoping to be wed, surely she must be expecting his visit.

He set down his glass and walked slowly towards his room.

If she was honourable, and this was all some horrible mistake, she deserved the protection of his name, and should be willing to submit graciously to her new husband. She'd had ample opportunity to stop this farce of a marriage at the beginning, yet she'd said nothing. She now had no reason to cry nay at the inevitable climax of the day.

But if she was some trollop foisted on him by a combination of bad fortune and his mother's need for redemption? Then he could enjoy his wife's favours, knowing that he was not taking any liberties that she had not given elsewhere. And when he found the truth he would throw her out into the street, bag and baggage, reputation be damned. She could scream and cry all she liked, but where there was no wedding licence, there was no wedding. He was bound by no legal contract and no amount of crying women and hand-wringing preachers would persuade him to keep her.

Besides, the quickest way to discover her honour or lack

of it might be to do the deed. Seeing the wench naked, he could look for a telltale bulging belly or lack of modesty.

But if she was innocent? Then planning was required.

He arrived in his room and paused with his hand on the knob. How best to set the scene? His room or hers? Hers, he suspected. Then, when it was through, she could have the comfort of familiarity, if such could be gained by twenty-four hours' occupancy.

Dressed or undressed? Undressed would be easier. There was certainly a pleasure in slow discovery, but, perhaps in this case, expediency might be better.

Undressed, then. But how far? Not totally. To arrive naked in her room? Certainly not. If she was a virgin, there was no telling how much information she'd received on the activities of the marriage bed. Unclothed and fully aroused was no condition in which to give anatomy lessons. Perhaps even now, she was sitting primly in her bed in her best nightrail and cap, waiting for her husband.

And the thought made him smile.

Very well. Her room. He'd arrive in his dressing gown, and sit on the corner of her bed so as not to alarm her. They'd chat. And soon he would be sitting beside her. He would take her hand to reassure her. Then he'd take her lips.

And soon he'd take the rest of her and the business would be done.

He stripped without the help of his valet, and put on a brocade dressing gown. He pulled the knot of the robe tight and nodded in approval of himself. There. A plan was in place and things would continue to their successful conclusion.

And he opened the connecting door to her room.

They could continue, except for the absence of one important component. His wife was nowhere to be found.

She glared in to the pantry. How did the house run on such a meagre store of food? A bit of cheese and bread was all she wanted, but she'd expected to find more. The snack she was taking seemed hardly fit for the mice she'd startled when she came into the room.

Such stale bread. And such dry cheese. It was as unpalatable as the lunch and the supper. She imagined writing a plea to her family.

Dear Cici and Father,
I have come to Devon and married a duke. And I'm more tired and hungry than I have ever been in my life. Please let me come home.

'What the devil are you doing in the kitchen?'

And why must everything you say to me be shouted? she wondered, rubbing her temples.

The duke was standing in the doorway, his arms folded in front of him. His words rolled over her in a torrent. 'I came to your room, expecting to find you waiting, and had to chase through the whole of the house before I found you. And here, of all places. Did you expect to sleep next to the fire, like the kitchen cat? Was I to call the servants to locate you? Wouldn't that be rich? To have the household know that his Grace has had a wife for less than a day and already misplaced her.'

'Because it is all about you, isn't it?' she snapped. 'And about what people think. That is why you had to marry me. That is the only reason I'm still here and I expect you'll have cause to mention it whenever I make a mistake for the rest of my life.'

'If you wish to stay in this house, then, yes, it is all about my wishes. And if I say that what people think is important, then you'd better believe it and act accordingly.'

'But that's just it,' she retorted. 'I don't wish to stay in this house. What reason would I have to stay here?'

'Many would think that a great house and a duke is reason enough,' he growled.

And the rage and confusion broke in her and poured out. 'Then many people have not met you. If they had, they might change their opinion. For I swear that I have never been so miserable in my life. Sir, you are foul tempered and foul mouthed.' She sniffed the air. 'And drunk. You do nothing but storm at me, but expect me to wait meekly in my bed for your arrival. You were eager enough to kiss me at the altar and yet show no hurry to come to my bed on our wedding night. I sat there for hours, and finally was too starved to wait longer and came to the kitchen for some food.' She gestured around her. 'And, lo, you keep none here. What a surprise that things should be managed more like the poorest hovel than the greatest of houses. Are you a miser as well as a bully, that the meals in this house should be so poor and the rooms so cold and filthy?'

He looked, she thought, like a dog that had been slapped across the muzzle in the moment of stunned realisation before he must choose attack or retreat. And she felt the world shift under her as she understood what she had done. The Duke of Haughleigh was unlikely to turn tail and run.

'If you feel that way, madam—' and his voice was ice and not fire '—then perhaps I should pack you off back to London.'

And she realised that she'd gone too far. She'd failed her father. She'd failed Cici. She'd enraged the duke. And she had nowhere to go. The room spun around her.

'Damn.' He saw her begin to crumple and lunged to catch her before her body hit the floor. Who would have thought, after such an admirable rage, that she would turn out to be a fainter? Then he pulled her body close and knew the answer. The poor thing was skin and bones. She hadn't been exaggerating when she'd claimed that she was cold and tired and hungry. She was merely stating the truth of the abysmal hospitality he'd shown her.

He scooped a hand behind her knees and lifted her in his arms, surprised that, despite her height, she was so light a burden.

She roused and struck feebly at his chest, murmuring, 'Put me down.'

'And let you fall to the ground in a heap? Certainly not.' He negotiated the stairs and made his way towards their rooms.

When she realised the direction, she struggled against him, but he held her tighter.

'No. Please.' And he felt the tremor rush through her body as they crossed the threshold to her room.

He looked in amazement at the top of her head, trying to see down into the rat's nest that this woman must call brains, and suspected he understood. 'Madam, fear not. Necrophilia is not among my many vices. I do not mean to drag you unconscious to bed and force myself on your lifeless body.' He dropped her down on to the bed, and she curled up in to a ball, hands screwed in to fists and pressed to her face.

He looked down at her in the firelight, surprised at what

he saw. She was amazingly thin, and the flames cast shadows in the deep hollows under her eyes and cheekbones. The nightrail was not the delicate trousseau he expected to find, but rough cotton, darned many times and a little too short for her.

He pulled her hands away from her face and looked down at them, rubbing his thumbs gently along the palms. They were rough with calluses and showed fresh blisters and the healing cuts and scars of someone who knew what it meant to work for a living. He let go and she hid them, looking at him in horror, and waiting for his response.

'I will send Polly to your room with some nourishment. In the future, do not be afraid to ask for what you want, whether it be an extra log for the fire or an extra meal. I go to my room now, and expect nothing of you but that you rest and gain strength before making any decisions. Goodnight, Miranda.'

He closed the door softly behind him. What a strange bird she was. And willing to fly full into the teeth of a storm and beat her wings against it. He had a foul temper and a foul mouth, did he?

He smiled, then sat at his desk. She had his measure after only a day. And the sight of her in a towering rage against him had been quite—he stirred in his chair—arousing. Not the delicate flower he'd been afraid to touch. Or the calculating seductress meaning to trap him. This one had fire in the blood and didn't give a damn for him or his title. And if anger and passion were intertwined? Then perhaps it was time and more for this marriage.

Of course, he'd need to undo some of the damage he'd done in the last day, if he hoped for her to come to him willingly. He needed to be cautious. It was thinking such as that that had led him into the disaster of his first marriage. With Bethany, it had been the sweet temper and dazzling looks that allowed her to wrap him so thoroughly in her web before sucking the hope out of him. This one could do it through sheer force of will, seducing him with passion, rendering him weak with a desire to please her.

He needed to know where she came from, before dropping upon him unsuspecting. Why she was roughened from work. What wrong his mother had done to her.

He thought for a moment and drew up a course of action, taking paper and pen from his writing desk.

Dearest Miranda.

He crumpled the paper and threw it into the fire. How should he start a letter to a wife who was a complete stranger to him?

Miranda,

Somewhat cool, perhaps, but accurate.

I think it best, after last night, that we proceed with cau-tion on this journey set before us. Your perceptions are accurate. I would not have chosen you, had the situa-tion not been forced upon me by honour, just as you would not have sought me out, based on my behaviour of the last two days.

But that does not mean that our union is impossible. Sometimes it strengthens a marriage to see the worst and find the sweetness of happiness later. Thus I've de-cided to visit London for a few weeks and leave you alone to become accustomed to your surroundings. The house is yours; do with it as you please. The staff, also, is yours to command. I think you will find that there are advantages to a title and an estate that might make up for the sad deficiencies in the character of its owner.

Take two weeks alone, and use it to rest from your journey and adjust to your new home before we begin anew. I will do my best to leave my temper in the city and return to you a contrite and respectful husband.

And, if still you decide that you wish to return home, we will arrange it when I get back. There should be no trouble procuring an annulment, as I have absented myself from the marriage bed and left you your honour.

Until my return, your husband,

Marcus Radwell, Duke of Haughleigh

He sealed the letter and left it for a maid to place at the breakfast table in the morning. Then he rang for his valet and made quiet and succinct instructions for the carriage to be readied and the grooms to be woken.

And, last, he took the letters his mother had received from the mysterious Lady Cecily. Two weeks away should be time enough to find her direction and gather information on his new bride.

Chapter Seven

The day dawned uncomfortably bright and early, and Miranda pulled the hangings shut against it. After her visit from the duke the previous evening, she was at a loss as to what she could possibly say in the morning. No doubt her bags were packed and waiting for her in the entrance hall. But would he think to arrange transportation, or assume that she could purchase a ticket from her own funds?

She laughed bitterly. As if there were such a thing. Her purse had been emptied by the trip to Devon, and showed no signs of magically filling itself for the return trip. And if she should return, where would she go? Her father had made it quite clear that there was to be no turning back from this course, and while the parting had been sweet, she knew he was sincere in his desire to get rid of her, for her own safety and his peace of mind.

Unless she abandoned all pride and made a living on her back, as more than one nobleman had suggested. And what fool thought it better to be the whore of a rich man then to be a wife?

There was nothing for it. This morning, she would seek out her husband and throw herself on his mercy, such as it was. If she ate nothing else today, it would be her words of the previous evening.

'Your Grace, are you up?' Polly poked her head between the curtains and offered her the tea tray. 'I was wondering if you'd like to eat downstairs this morning. Cook says there'll be something in the breakfast room. Not what you're used to, I'm sure, but a bit better than you've been having.' The tea was at least warm today, and she hoped that this was a sign of things to come. She took a small sip and felt a wee bit better.

'His Grace told me that you'd no doubt be tired this morning, and that I was to make sure you had plenty of sleep and a decent breakfast, if I had to stand over you and force it in,' she said, proudly.

'He did, did he?' She considered refusing to eat, but reminded herself of her promise of a few minutes ago. 'And what else did he have to say?'

'That you'd know what you wanted to do, and that you was the mistress of the house now, and I was to help you in any way, but to make sure that you ate and rested. And then he was in the carriage and gone.'

'Gone?'

'Last night, after midnight. He was off to London and then Lord St John was back from wherever he goes. It was busy as the courtyard of the inn here.'

'St John, back?' She tried not to let the relief show in her voice. Perhaps he could help her understand the actions of her husband.

Polly helped her to dress and she crept down the stairs

towards breakfast, then stopped herself halfway. Why was she hesitating? This was her house. Her stairs. Her servants.

Well, not really hers. Her husband's, perhaps, until he came back from where ever it was he went. Probably with the necessary paperwork for an annulment if such was necessary, since she'd assumed she would have to sign some sort of licence and it hadn't happened yesterday. She was sure of that fact. Well, reasonably sure. The day had gone by so fast, and she'd been so tired…

She raised her hands to her temple and pushed against them, trying to silence the thoughts that were running through her head. It did no good to try to analyse the events of the last two days. Even if she had been clear headed, they'd have made no sense and they just seemed to get stranger and stranger.

She was going to focus on the task before her. Not one step behind. Not one mile ahead. Just one step at a time until she could walk herself out of the maze she was lost in.

And the first step was breakfast. She entered the breakfast room to see St John, lounging at the head of the table in the place she'd expected to find the duke. He was reading the mail as though he owned the place. She wondered what her husband's reaction would be if he were there to take in the picture, and then checked herself.

She knew perfectly well what it would be. Similar to all the other reactions she had seen him make when he saw something that displeased him. Yelling. Threats. And St John banished from the house without a hearing. If she could do nothing else in the house, perhaps she could find a way to end the foolish bickering that these two seemed to revel in.

'Miranda.' He stood and beamed at her and she felt unaccountably less lonely than she had. 'You are already having a positive effect here. There is breakfast for a change. And, although I would not trust the kippers, the eggs today seem fresh enough. Come, sit down.'

'Aren't you a trifle free with your brother's hospitality, for one I saw banished from the house yesterday?'

He smiled again. 'Perhaps. Perhaps. But they informed me at the inn that my brother was riding out for London. And although he cannot abide my company, the servants here are still quite fond of the black sheep and I count on them to hold their tongues when he comes home to pasture. And…' he looked probingly at her '…I wondered if the new duchess might need assistance after being abandoned by her husband on her wedding night. Are you well?' The question was gently put, but he was no longer smiling and he tensed, waiting for a response.

'Of course,' she lied. She had not been dismissed, if Polly's attitude was any indication of the duke's mood. And to be left alone by her new husband, but allowed to stay in the house was quite the best of all possible results, if a trifle annoying. 'I am beginning to feel at home here already. Is that the mail?' She reached towards the letter in front of him and he gathered it to himself.

'Expecting a *billet-doux*, little sister? No, not the mail. Just something I brought with me to dispose of. Damn bill collectors tracked me to the inn. Let us show them what I think of them.' And he resealed the letter, than twisted it into a roll and walked towards the fireplace. 'The less time spent with this odious missive the better for all concerned.' He struck a lucifer on the mantelpiece and held it to the paper, watching it blaze before tossing the smouldering end into the fire.

'Really, St John, you should not be so casual with your responsibilities.'

'Miranda, my dear, I am quite serious at times, when a goal is before me. You have not yet seen me at my best. And I am sure, if you have talked to my brother, you have heard nothing but the worst of my character.'

'Oh, no, I assure you. There was very little time to discuss anything with the duke last night.' She paused, embarrassed. It sounded rather like they were occupied in other ways. She looked down at her plate and nibbled on a slice of toast.

'Did he take the time to tell you, then, why he was leaving you so quickly?'

'I am sure he has a good reason for his actions,' she answered.

St John nodded over his coffee. 'I'm sure he does. There might be certain people in London that need to be informed of his nuptials. So as to avoid embarrassment later.'

'Certain people?' She waited for him to continue.

He cleared his throat. 'Well. Yes. It doesn't do to let the rumours come back to town before him. It needn't change the current situation, if he has married again, but it is wise to put her mind to rest. To let her know that her position is still secure. Jealousy, thy name is woman, and all that.' He looked at her and a faint blush was visible on his cheek. 'I know I shouldn't even hint at such things, especially not to a lady, and on your first day here. But I felt you deserved to know the lay of the land. I meant no insult.'

So her husband had left the marriage bed still cold and gone to London to be with his… She very deliberately buttered another slice of toast and bit into the corner, chewing as it turned to sawdust in her mouth. And there was no reason that it need bother her in the least. She had expected something of the sort. And this was neither a love match, nor she some giddy girl. 'It is all right, St John. Thank you. You are right. It is better to know how things stand.'

He sighed in obvious relief. 'Good. I am glad you are taking this so well. And remember, as I offered before, if you need a strong arm to support you, and my brother is nowhere to be found, you can always call on me.'

'Thank you.' She smiled wanly back at him.

'And now, my dear, I must be off. To see about the responsibilities you would have me attend to.' He sighed. 'To appear as idle as I do requires a surprising amount of effort. May I have the honour of joining you at supper this evening?'

'Of course.' As she watched him go, it occurred to her, if he was to join her for dinner, it meant that there must be a meal. Which required menus, shopping, and co-ordination of the staff. Perhaps the duke had managed to subsist on weak tea and stew, but surely there must be something else in the kitchen.

She was in charge here. At least until the duke came and relieved her. And if she was in charge, there were going to have to be some changes.

She stiffened her spine as she walked down the last of the steps to the servants' hall and the kitchen where she had been the night before. The remains of breakfast were congealing in plates on the table. That they had not been cleared bespoke a slovenliness she wouldn't have believed possible.

When she examined the contents of the plates, the situation grew worse still. The crusts of bread were soft and light. Jam. Porridge in bowls. A single rasher of bacon still sat on the edge of one plate.

She remembered her runny eggs and the inedible kipper and fought down an urge to scoop up the remains on the table before her and sneak them back to her room for later. As she stood there, a door at the far end of the room opened and a woman entered. She was short, stout and sour faced, and fixed Miranda with a glare. 'Who might you be and what are you doing below stairs?'

Miranda drew herself up to her full height and smiled. 'I am the lady of the house. And who, exactly, are you?'

'There ain't a lady of the house. Least not since the dowager, her Grace, died.'

'There is since yesterday, when his Grace and I were married. Mrs...?'

'His Grace didn't say nothing to me about it.'

'As I understand it, you were out, and the servants had no idea how to contact you. Mrs...?'

'His Grace didn't say nothing about getting married,' she argued.

A kitchen maid crept in to stand quietly in the corner, drawn by the housekeeper's raised voice.

'It was a bit of a shock to him as well. Perhaps he neglected to inform you. But surely Wilkins...'

'That old drunk ain't allowed to get within ten feet of me or I'll—'

Clearly the woman was used to having her way with the running of the house. Miranda took a firmer tone and a half-step forward. 'His Grace didn't have to say anything to you, Mrs...?'

She paused again and the woman reluctantly supplied, 'Clopton.'

'Mrs Clopton. You knew I was here, since you must have sent breakfast up to me earlier.' She decided against mentioning the quality of the food. It could wait until she'd mollified the housekeeper.

'I don't pay no attention to what ladies they keeps upstairs. It's no never mind to me.'

'But it should be, Mrs Clopton. You are, after all, the housekeeper, are you not?'

'I am in charge here,' the lady informed her.

Miranda waved a hand in the direction of the house, and glanced around the room, noting the growing cluster of servants gathering to witness the dispute. Whatever was to come of this, it would be known all over the house by the end of the morning and she could not afford to lose. 'If you are responsible for what I have seen in this house, you had best not brag of it. It is no point of pride.' She pointed down at the staff dining table. 'I see evidence that someone in the house is sustaining themselves in comfort, but that is not the case above stairs.'

'An' I suppose you'll be expecting the staff to work like dogs without a full stomach.'

Miranda countered, 'But I see no evidence that the household staff works like dogs. Perhaps in the stables, where the duke has had time to observe.'

'The household staff does the work they're paid to do, and they're paid damn little.'

She raised her eyebrows in shock at the curse. 'I'll be the judge of that, Mrs Clopton. If you'll gather the household expense books, we will see what can be done.'

At the mention of books, the housekeeper took a step back. 'His Grace never thought it was necessary to check the bookwork.'

'His Grace is not here.' The words snapped out from

between her clenched teeth as she gave the housekeeper a share of the morning's marital frustrations. 'But I am. And, whether you choose to recognise it or not, I am the duchess and from now on you will be dealing with me. Mrs Clopton, bring me the books.'

A murmur ran through the staff, and Mrs Clopton pulled herself up to her full height, glaring. 'I don't think that will be necessary.'

Miranda kept her voice flat, but firm. 'I do. Unless there is some reason you don't want to show them to me.' She waited.

'When the old duchess was alive…'

'She never checked the books either, I suppose. How many years, Mrs Clopton, have you been skimming from the household accounts? Skimping on the food and the staff and lining your own pockets.' It was a blind shot.

'Who do you think you are, callin' me a thief?' Mrs Clopton shot back. 'And you, stealin' into this house, no better than you should be. Tryin' to pass yourself off as a duchess.'

Mrs Clopton was shooting blindly as well, and Miranda struggled not to show how close the bolts were to hitting their target.

'I don't know what you are, but you ain't quality.'

'Because I won't let you steal from the duke?'

The housekeeper spat back. 'Helpin' yourself from them that don't need it is no great crime. But stealin' a title…'

'Sacked!' The word came out of her in a roar that would have been worthy of the absent duke. 'I hope you took enough, Mrs Clopton, to last you for a long time. I want you packed and out of this house before noon.'

She ignored the gasps and tears from the staff in the background. 'Wilkins?'

The butler had joined the audience at some point and stepped forward in answer.

'See to it that *this woman* finds her way out of the house. And then assemble the staff in the entrance hall. I wish to speak with them.'

'Yes, your Grace.' He looked doubtful, but the words were what mattered, not appearances. And he'd obeyed an order. It would have to do.

Messieurs Binley and Binley had been family friends and solicitors since the first duke, when the two names on the sign had belonged to the ancestors of the man currently in the office. Binley the elder was retired now, but his son Claude, a man slightly older than Marcus himself, kept the name on the sign out of respect and simplicity. After several years at Oxford, there would be a new Binley in the office, and it hardly seemed necessary to repaint.

Claude ushered him in to the oak-panelled office and seated him in a heavy leather wing chair before taking his own seat behind the enormous desk. 'And to what do I owe this honour, your Grace?'

'I have a problem, Claude.'

'We have a problem, then. As I must always remind you, do not feel that you need face these things alone.'

'This one, I might. The utmost discretion is required.'

'Discretion is my watchword.'

Marcus smiled. There were times at Oxford when discretion was the last thing he'd sought when in Claude's company.

'There is a lady involved.'

'And St John?' Claude Binley reached for the chequebook on the corner of the desk.

'I don't believe so.'

Claude relaxed into his chair.

'This time, I am the one most intimately involved.'

Claude's body snapped back into alertness. 'You, Marcus? This is most surprising. I have been relieved to find you most circumspect in these matters.'

'Unlike the previous Dukes of Haughleigh?' Marcus grinned.

'Your family has found its way into some damned awkward situations in the last few generations.'

'And your family has got us out of them.'

'But you? I'd thought after—' Claude stopped in mid-sentence, before stepping beyond the acceptable boundaries of both friendship and employ. 'Well, you haven't been much of a problem for the last ten years.'

'And I had hoped to go another ten before finding myself in this position. This particular situation washed up on the doorstep almost a week ago. It seems I have got myself leg-shackled.'

'Married?'

'But not legally.'

Claude choked on his tea.

'To a complete stranger.' Marcus stepped around the desk and pounded his lawyer smartly on the back, refilling his teacup.

'No tea,' he gasped. 'There is whisky in the decanter behind the bookshelf.'

'So early in the day?'

'When the situation calls for it. Pour one for yourself and explain.'

Marcus went to the decanter and poured a healthy inch into the bottom of each empty teacup. Behind him Claude muttered, 'I knew you were too good to be true. My father warned me about the Haughleighs. And I thought, perhaps, that we might skip a generation. Or that the mess would limit itself to your scapegrace brother.'

Marcus smiled and offered him the cup. 'We can never be truly free of our heredity, Claude.' And he began at the beginning, telling of his mother's request and of finding Miranda in the drawing room.

Claude sat, fingers steepled and a look of intense concentration on his face. When the story was finished he reached again for the chequebook. 'The solution to this problem is simple. A substantial settlement. Enough to set the girl up in a respectable trade, preferably somewhere far away.'

'But if she is a gentlewoman as the letters claim?'

'Then enough to get her home to her family where she can seclude herself.'

'The marriage?'

'Is not legal. Or consummated. Breach of promise, perhaps. But I doubt it would hold in court since you were trapped into your offer. Another thousand pounds should still any complaints.'

'And the blackmail?'

'Would have surfaced before now if the charge were serious. The claim, whatever it is, is forty years old and made against a dead woman.'

'But I want to know what the scandal was. And if this girl was hurt by it…'

'Then you were not at fault. If you truly want my advice, Marcus, you'll buy her off. If you'd come to me earlier, I'd have told you to send her packing. A family who cared for her reputation would never have sent her to you, and when she arrived…'

'She met St John. If I had not taken her in, there is no telling what might have happened to her with him there, ready to offer assistance. And in my own home. Was I to stand by and watch?'

'If you'd taken my advice about St John, you'd have cut him off long ago. He continues to be a problem because you continue to pay his bills. And now your soft heart and your soft head combine to land you here.'

Marcus drew himself up in his chair, but, before he could speak, the lawyer cut him off.

'I apologise, your Grace, for speaking so freely.' His tone was anything but apologetic. 'But if you do not wish to follow my counsel, then give me instruction. Just what is it you want from me in this situation? Congratulations on your nuptials?' His gaze was cold and intent and his fingers drummed on the edge of the desk as he waited for Marcus to make a decision.

'I want…' What did he want? He wanted to make a wise decision that would benefit everyone involved, not just save his own skin. He wanted to be a better man than his brother. Or his father. Or the other Haughleighs down through the generations. Men who had, invariably, chosen folly and self-interest over the needs of others.

'I want to know the truth of the matter. I want to know where the girl came from. And what part my mother played in her life. If there is truly some fault, if she needs my help in any way, I want to assist her.' He inhaled and went on. 'And I want you to procure a special licence.'

Claude exploded. 'You don't seriously mean to make this

marriage legal. Your Grace, I cannot condone such a course of action. It is madness.'

'Did I do any better when I married for love? For better or worse, I am home to stay and there is much work to be done. I was going to have to settle the matter of marriage and succession sooner, not later. St John is sniffing around the house, drinking my brandy and hoping that I choke on my soup. The household is in shambles and I have no idea how to bring it round. This Miranda Grey may be a fortune hunter, but, by God, she'll earn her fortune if she means to stay. When I return in two weeks, if she hasn't already fled in despair or locked herself in her room, or if I have not found evidence that she is disgraced beyond all acceptance, I might do worse than to make the situation permanent and keep her on.'

'Marcus, you talk as if you are hiring a housekeeper.'

'At least I am not so crack-brained as to be pining for eternal love and divine happiness. I am not the green fool that I used to be, Claude, whinging for my broken heart and shattered dreams. One woman is much like another, once the lights are out. I never thought I'd say it, but my mother was right. If this girl is chaste and willing, I could do worse. At least she gave no indication, in our brief time together, that she was some empty-headed, society chit. Nor prone to illogical tears or fits of giggles.'

But, occasionally, to shouting. He smiled as the picture formed in his head of his new wife, storming up at him, and could almost feel the weight of her in his arms as he'd carried her to her room. The next time he carried her there, it would be different.

'No, Claude. If I can find no major fault, I mean to keep her.' He laid the blackmail letters on the table in front of him. 'And I wish you to direct me in my search for her family.'

Chapter Eight

Marcus entered his third stationer's shop of the day, with a growing feeling of despair. Perhaps Claude had been right when he'd offered to make the inquiries himself. But, since there was no telling what he might find at the end of the journey, he had wanted to do the leg work himself.

And he'd discovered that there was indeed a Lady Miranda Grey, aged three and twenty, daughter of Sir Anthony, but that neither had been seen in years. Sir Anthony had run through the family fortune after the death of his wife, and was rumoured to have decamped to the continent like a filthy coward, or quietly put a bullet through his brain. What remained of the family goods had been sold at auction years ago, but the daughter had not been present. There was no known family, although one would have expected to hear of an aunt or female relative of some kind to step forward and claim the girl. The name Lady Dawson did not appear in any of the accompanying records, nor was it familiar to those questioned.

He looked imperiously at the stationer in front of him and tried to hide any hopes that he might feel for the outcome of the visit. His title was enough to send the clerk scurrying to get the storeowner, who fell over himself in an effort to win what he'd hoped would be a lucrative order.

'How can we help you, your Grace?'

'I am recently married and will need a wide variety of things. Announcements. Engraved cards for my wife. Some writing paper for her, I think. With a monogram. And a watermark. The family crest. Can you manage that?'

'Of course, your Grace.' The man was fairly drooling at the prospect.

'I've seen some fine work recently, letters posted to my late mother, and am looking for the purveyors of the papers in question. Would you be able to identify things you've supplied to others, so that I might know I have found the correct store? I've tried several, but have been unsuccessful.'

'Would it not have been easier simply to ask the senders of the letters to give you direction?'

Marcus responded with a look so cold that the man was immediately sorry he had asked.

'But of course, if it is my work, I would recognise it. Perhaps… if I could see the letters?'

Marcus fanned the pack of blackmail notes on the counter before him.

His eyebrows arched. 'All the same signature and ink, and all different papers.'

Marcus said, 'The contents of the notes need not interest you. It is the paper I am wondering about.'

The man cleared his throat. 'The words, of course, do not concern me. But I find the ink interesting. Not a particularly good brand for the paper. And the writer could have done with a new quill. May I?' He reached for the letters.

Marcus nodded.

The man held them up to the light. 'Three different watermarks. I know these two. They are clients of mine. The third is from a shop in Bond Street, but I recognise the coat of arms of the client. The fourth?' He shrugged. 'It does not match the others. It is a good grade, but a common paper, available in most of the shops in London. As it happens, I recognise the pressed monogram, which has been rubbed flat here at the top of the page. The writer seems to have been trying to disguise the origin of the paper. This was sold by our shop to a cit. A factory owner, I believe.' He laid the papers back on the desk. 'Is this sufficient information, your Grace? I would do nothing to jeopardise the privacy of my customers.'

Marcus smiled in a slow, expansive way that hinted of gold to come. 'Of course. I would not want anyone jeopardising my own. Should I choose to shop here, I would want to know that my business remained secret.' He fanned the letters, then stacked them and folded them, making them disappear into the pocket of his greatcoat. 'But I am curious on one point. Do these customers live in the vicinity of your shop?'

The man shook his head. 'As a matter of fact, they don't. Not frequent customers. If you give me a moment, I could perhaps find addresses for them. If you care for references?'

Marcus smiled more warmly. The man had hit on a more convincing lie than he had been able to create. 'References. That would be most helpful. And while you are gone, if I might see a sample book, I will begin making my selections.'

He left the shop, having placed an order for more paper than he and his new duchess could use in several years of industrious writing.

And a map of east London and outlying villages, where the homes of three minor lords and a cit lay within a three-mile radius of each other. It was not much. There was no guarantee. But it gave him a place to look for the mysterious Cecily Dawson.

Chapter Nine

The staff stood before her, terrified. Clearly, they had heard the contretemps below stairs, and were all hoping that the next sacking would be someone other than themselves.

She tried to return a gaze that was cool and indifferent. 'By now, you all know the fate of Mrs Clopton. This will, of course, cause a certain amount of disarray below stairs, but…' she paused to run a hand along the woodwork and wipe the smudge into her handkerchief '… I care more for the state of things above stairs, and doubt that anything I've done could create greater disorder than was here already.' She smiled. 'My difficulties with the previous housekeeper were based solely on the errors in the accounts and the state of the house. I assume that these problems are now solved. If I am mistaken, I wish that you will come to me and that we can reach a solution. I will be replacing Mrs Clopton shortly, and we will manage as best we can until that point. In the mean time…' she presented a list of tasks '…I would have you begin in the entryway and continue through the house, with a thorough cleaning. I've written the procedure I would have you follow and a few of the cleaning formulas I wish you to use.' The looks of wariness on the faces of the maids were replaced by a grudging respect.

'And since it has been so very long since things have been done properly, I believe more help will be needed. Jenny?' She gestured to the chief parlour maid. 'Do you know anyone in the village in need of work? Older sisters? Aunts?'

Jenny allowed as how she might know a few girls and was sent to the village to fetch them. The rest of the women were divided into teams and began conquering the tasks on the list in each of the reception rooms. Once things were underway, Miranda felt it safe to retire to the study and hope that she could find some means to pay the expenses she was about to incur.

She sat down at the desk. Her husband's desk, she thought nervously, then willed herself to relax. The chair was imposing but comfortable. Fit for a duke. She let an imagined sense of power envelope her, and pressed her hands flat against the mahogany surface in front of her, surveying the room. It was cleaner than the rest of the house. Perhaps Mrs Clopton was unable to defy the duke in such an obvious way. The desk was clear of paper, the ink well filled, the pens clean and of good quality. It was an orderly and comfortable workspace. Her husband must spend much time here, when he was on the estate.

On an impulse, she reached for a drawer pull, expecting to find it locked. It slid open easily, and she peered inside. Resting at the top of a stack of papers, as though hurriedly discarded, was a sheet of paper covered with notes.

The hand was clear and firm, not rushed. Miranda had heard that it was possible to tell the soul of the writer by the way he formed his letters. If so, her new husband was—she studied the paper—strong. Decisive. There was no trace in the writing of the anger she'd seen in him.

She read the words. There was a short list of supplies—for the estate or the tenants, she knew not. Neat rows of figures, totalled accurately and without hesitation. And nearer the bottom of the page a reminder to call on the vicar first thing in the morning. She smiled and traced the line. He'd written it the night she'd arrived. And below it was a single word: MIRANDA?

She could almost hear it, as though he were there, speaking to her. And how strange, because the tone she imagined was not one she'd heard from him in life. The voice she imagined was soft and inviting, and full of promise.

A soft cough from the direction of the doorway indicated the presence of Wilkins. 'Your Grace?'

She slid the drawer closed and looked the butler in the eye. 'Yes, Wilkins?'

'I have something I…' He dropped his hands to his sides in defeat. 'I'm afraid I must give notice, ma'am.'

Oh, dear. She had been afraid this might happen, but could she stand the loss of both main retainers? 'I'm sure his Grace would be most disappointed to lose you, Wilkins. What is the reason for this sudden decision?'

'I rather thought, your Grace, that once you got the lay of the land, you would be asking me to leave. I'm just saving you the trouble.'

'I appreciate your honesty. And your coming to me, like this. Despite what I told the staff just now, the problem with Mrs Clopton…' she sighed in exasperation '…was not so much the crime—which was bad enough, certainly—but her unrepentant attitude. How can I run a house when the housekeeper thinks me such a fool as to be bullied into accepting her flimsy excuses out of hand?' She looked steadily at the butler. 'Is there something you would like to discuss, Wilkins?'

'Ma'am, when you get around to inventorying the cellars, you will find that there is much I have to account for.'

'And is there no way to make up the difference?'

'None that I can think of, ma'am. May I speak frankly?'

'Please.'

'The wages in this house have long been the talk of the district. You'll find it hard to replace the housekeeper, once they hear what is offered, and what is expected. And my own wages, even supplemented by the occasional stolen brandy bottle, are insufficient to meet my needs and repay his Grace.'

She held up a hand to him. 'Let us say no more about your leaving at this time, Wilkins. It is certainly not a problem that needs to be dealt with before my husband's return.'

There was a polite knock and a chambermaid poked her head around the doorframe. 'Your Grace? Something awful's happened in the dining room. Come quick.'

Had the first day of her new regime been marred by an accident? Had someone fallen off a ladder? She'd forgotten to check on their stability before sending the footman to bring down the chandeliers.

When she entered the dining room, she saw that the problem was far worse, at least in the eyes of the maids.

'We tried the formula you suggested for the walls, but look what happened.' They were lined obediently up at the end of the room, waiting to be sacked.

She glanced up at the silk covering the walls and stood mesmerised in shock. The sheep that had been grazing on the green of the hillside were either totally obliterated or oozing towards the wainscoting. The shepherd who had been looking in adoration at his shepherdess was still largely extant, but his smile had been replaced by a runny leer before the maids had given it up as a bad job and run for help. 'Hand painted,' she muttered under her breath. 'It would have done well for regular paper. Even for patterned silk.'

'We only did what you requested, your Grace.' There was no trace of sarcasm in the comment, only fear. The poor girl was waiting for her to explode.

'Yes, of course you did. It was my fault for not thinking of the surface to be cleaned before making that suggestion. There is nothing to be done for it now. We will have to replace the wall coverings. Please continue cleaning the windows, the floors and the fireplace. But do not worry about the walls until I can think of what is to be done.'

She trudged down the hall to her room. What was to be done was to have a megrim, alone in her room. Surely that was allowed. She would have to order new silk from the shops in the village. She doubted they would have anything appropriate. Something could be brought from London. And she had not a penny in her pocket, or any idea how to get one.

She smiled to herself. If she was a duchess, then perhaps she no longer needed money. She could not remember, on outings with her mother, ever seeing a coin change hands. Even after the money was gone, the shopkeepers extended them credit because of her father's title, lowly though it was. All she need do was ride into town surrounded by the Haughleigh livery, find an appropriate sample and point. It would be delivered in all due haste, and might be hung on the walls before her husband returned to find her mistake.

He would, of course, be angry. But in the two days she had

known him, he had been angry about so many things that she doubted one more would make a difference.

Supper that evening was a very different affair than breakfast had been. After a short nap, she had composed herself and returned to the kitchen to confront the cook. The woman had been wary at first, but when she was told that she might choose her own ingredients and order what was needed to undo the artificial famine created by Mrs Clopton, she seemed most happy with the change.

Miranda, at Polly's insistence, allowed her hair to be dressed and changed into her only decent gown for supper. The gown was a burgundy satin that had been much more fresh fifteen years ago, when it had been one of Cici's ball dresses. They'd cut down the puffed sleeves, removed large amounts of skirt to hide the worn spots and managed, by cannibalising the train and adding some lace from another gown, to create something almost presentable.

St John met her at the dinner table and kissed her hand. 'Enchanted as always, my dear. You look lovely this evening.' He looked over his shoulder at the destruction on the walls. 'Dear God, what happened in here?'

She sat and took a large sip of wine before speaking. 'My first act today, as duchess, was to fire the housekeeper. My second was to destroy the dining room, attempting to clean it.'

'The wall coverings,' he said, 'were imported from France by the second duke.'

'Expensive?' she asked.

'Irreplaceable.'

'Oh. And what is the current duke likely to say, when he realises they are gone?' She held her breath.

'I suspect that you will have done me a great service. The apoplexy will leave you a widow and me as the fifth duke. I will then absolve you of any guilt. They were uncommonly ugly, for all their value.' He reached forward and snuffed several candles on the table, darkening the corners of the room. 'And hardly visible now. Isn't this much more intimate?'

She laughed, despite herself. He seemed pleased, and continued to amuse her during dinner.

After the meal he stood up and offered her his arm. 'Would you like to retire to the drawing room, your Grace? Or would you prefer a more interesting pastime? I could give you a tour of the house, if you wish.'

'It would be dark in the unused rooms,' she protested.

'Then the servants can go ahead and light our way. It is their job, after all, Miranda, to follow your instructions. But suppose we limit ourselves to a single room. It will further your education and not trouble the servants overly much if we spend the evening in the portrait gallery.'

'That is an excellent idea, St John.'

He rang for the butler, explained their needs and then escorted her to a long room on the second floor. Once there, he entertained her with stories of his ancestors. The first duke, awarded the title after a battle. His son, the mad second duke. Their father, who had been killed in a riding accident when both boys were young. He stopped before a portrait of his mother, and seemed to pause in respectful silence.

She looked up at the face in the painting. Definitely mother to St John, with the same startlingly blue eyes, but with hair so blonde as to be almost white. She was as pretty as Cici had said, and Miranda looked for any indication that the woman was a threat, but could find none. There was nothing in her face to show that she was other than sweetness and light.

She compared the mother to the picture of her new husband. Even for the portrait, he had not managed a smile. The painting in front of her must be several years old. There was no grey in his hair and the face had fewer lines. But the look in the eyes was the same intense stare that she had seen. Eyes that did not miss much, she thought. They were judging her as she stood in front of them, holding her fast and looking deep into her soul.

She shuddered. If only he would smile at her, perhaps the effect would not be so disturbing. There had been kindness on his face during the wedding. And when he put her to bed the night before. He had not seemed at all frightening to her then, when she had felt a protective warmth radiating from him, that had drawn her to him. Perhaps, when he returned from London, things would be different.

If he returned.

She tore her gaze away from her husband and walked a few steps further down the gallery to where St John stood before the portrait of another beautiful woman. When he turned from the painting and looked to her, there was a tear in his eye.

'I'm sorry,' she whispered. 'I did not mean to interrupt.'

'Quite all right, Miranda, dear. It was I who brought you here, and then I was rude enough to forget that fact.'

She looked up at the painting he had been admiring. It was of a beautiful blonde woman in a rose-coloured gown. But beautiful was too mild a word. The woman was radiant. Her hair was gold and her cheeks a delicate pink overlaying the cream of her skin. Her breasts were high and round, and outlined against the curve of her bodice. Her height must have been almost a head below Miranda's own. And yet the painting was more than life size, and she felt dwarfed by it.

'This is Bethany. She was quite the loveliest woman ever to grace this house.'

'Is she an ancestor of yours?' Even as she said it, she revised her estimate. The gown was only slightly out of fashion. This woman must be her contemporary.

'No ancestor of mine. But you have much in common with her. You share a husband. Bethany was my brother's first wife.'

She stared in stunned silence. No wonder he was angry to find himself attached to a dowdy hen after losing this angel. 'And she died in childbirth?' She could see how it was possible. The narrow-hipped girl in the picture scarcely seemed large enough to bear a child.

'That is what they say.' His voice was strangely flat.

She stared at him in curiosity. 'Do you have any reason to doubt the story?'

'Oh, she died in childbed, sure enough, but I always thought...' he sighed '...had she married happily, the end might have been different for her.'

'She was not happy?' It seemed so odd that a woman such as this would not have been happy.

St John's smile was tight-lipped. 'You have met my brother, Miranda. And seen his moods. It was like throwing a butterfly into a storm to wed the two together. They were married less than a year when she died, but her spirit had fled long before her body failed her.'

'But, why—?'

'Why did she marry him?' St John sighed. 'Why would

any woman choose my brother? Be honest, my dear. For the same reason that you came to him.'

Desperation, she thought, bitterly.

St John continued as though an answer wasn't required. 'The title. Say what I might about him, my brother is a powerful and a rich man. There is much temptation in that. And she had much to offer.' He paused, looking back at the picture. 'This does not do her justice. Her eyes were bluer than that. Her hair more gold, and soft as silk to the touch. She sang like an angel, and her laugh itself was music. And she was delicate. To look at her made you think of a crystal goblet.' His eyes grew hard. 'My brother saw her once and knew he must have her. She was dazzled by his wealth and went willingly into his arms.' His body tensed. 'And when I saw her, just a few months after the marriage, she was desperate to get away. He terrified her. When I think of her, soft as a rose petal, in the hands of that—' He choked on the last word, unwilling or unable to say what he was thinking. 'But there was nothing I could do. I was only eighteen, had no power, no money to offer her.' He gripped her by the shoulders and spun her to look at him. 'I will not make the mistake again. Miranda. My means are limited, but, should you need them, all I have is yours to command.'

She struggled for a response. Foremost in her mind were the words, *too late*. 'If you had a warning to share, yesterday would have been a better time than today.'

'Yesterday my brother was still in the house and the servants obey him, not me. He's gone, now, and I can speak freely. Say the word and I will help you flee and you can be long gone before he returns.'

Flee to where? There was no home to return to, no friend

to take her in. 'I am not afraid of the duke,' she lied. At least, with Cici's training, and St John's warning, she would not go into the marriage as empty headed as the late Bethany. Foul words left no mark and bruises healed. And if the duke threatened her with worse, she would cross that bridge when she came to it.

'I thank you for your kind offer, and will remember it if I need you, but am sure it need not come to that.'

Chapter Ten

Marcus looked up at the fading paint on the inn's sign: The Duke's Right Arm.

It sounded promising. Lucky, if he believed in luck. But the picture, which was of a dismembered arm lying on a grassy background, spoiled the image he wanted of a place that offered aid and succour. It would have been his last choice if he needed a bed for the night, or a drink, for that matter. The windows were dirty, and the door forbidding. It was his last choice now, as he'd visited all the other inns in the area.

Gentle questioning of the innkeepers had revealed a thorough knowledge of the area's great houses and their inhabitants. Everyone knew the local lords, and their families. If he combined the information gained from the various places, he had a good idea of the comings and goings of the guests in the area. Small amounts of gold, spread amongst the ostlers and stable boys, told him all there was to know about who had visited whom and what they drove to get there.

And no one, anywhere, knew anything of Miranda Grey

or Cecily Dawson. Or recognised the vague description he could give of a woman in her fifties and her tall ward.

They were not members of any of the families. They had not stayed in any of the inns at times corresponding to the dates on the letters. They had not been seen travelling. They were not known to be residing in any of the places he had visited.

Short of barging up to the front doors in question and demanding to know how Cecily had come by her writing materials, there was little hope in that direction.

This was his last chance. A disreputable inn in a miserable village that was little more than a cluster of cottages for workers at the nearby textile mill, owned by the cit whose stationery he kept folded in his pocket. It was not the place he wanted to find information about his new wife, but it made an irritating sort of sense. The factory owner's stationery had been used to write the last of the letters to his mother. If the writer had worked hardest to create a good impression for the first letter, perhaps she'd grabbed what was closest to hand when writing the last.

He opened the grimy door and stepped into the taproom of the inn, and all faces turned towards him. The wave of disdain from the other customers was palpable.

He stepped forward and took a seat, staring back and daring them to find his presence strange. The thought crossed his mind that no one knew his location, and his purse was dangerously heavy. If he did not watch his back on the way out, he was likely to finish this search by receiving a knock on the head and a push into the nearest ditch.

The serving girl fixed him with a sullen glare, not bothering to flirt or flounce. Apparently, she felt the chances of gaining a few coppers by courtesy were not worth the effort. Without asking for his order she put a pint of ale in front of him. 'If you want else, go elsewhere. You get what we have.'

He caught her wrist as she turned away from him. 'Maybe you can help me. I'm looking for two women.'

She pulled her arm out of his grasp. 'I said, this is all we serve. You will get nothing more from me.'

'I apologise for the familiarity.' He tried to look as harmless as possible. 'I need nothing more than information.'

'You'll find little of that here.' Her gaze never wavered. 'But I can offer you advice. We serve ale. It sits in front of you. Drink it and go back where you came.'

He laid a gold coin from his purse on the table in front of him and she glanced at it hungrily. 'Cecily Dawson. Or Miranda Grey. Have you ever heard the names?'

For a moment her eyes sparkled with something more than lust for the gold in front of her. Then she walked back to the bar and muttered something to the man behind it. He cast a look in Marcus's direction, and they conversed between themselves. The girl was trying to persuade him of something and he was shaking his head. She persevered. At last, he shrugged and ambled towards the table.

He sat across from Marcus without asking permission and scooped the coin off the table, tossing it to the girl. 'You're a brave man, your lordship, coming here alone to ask questions you've no business asking.'

He let the title slip by without responding. 'How do you know I have no business with them?'

'The likes of you rarely has business with the likes of us. And when you do, it's never good news.'

Us? So he knew them. Marcus kept his face impassive. 'I mean them no harm. I have already met Miranda. I just wanted to satisfy my curiosity about certain events in her past before…' Before what? What could he say that would not reveal too much? 'Finalising her position.'

'If it's references you want—' the man shrugged '—I can give them as well as anybody. She's a hard worker and honest.'

A barmaid?

'Ask at any of the houses in the area and the housekeepers will assure you. She's a good girl.' The man glared at him. 'And you'd better not be offering any position that's less honourable than scullery work. Because if you are, the lads will take you out back and cure you of that notion.'

'Nothing dishonourable, I assure you, sir. And Lady Dawson? Where can I find her?'

'I thought your business was with Miranda.'

'But I want to thank Lady Dawson for sending her to me,' he lied. 'She was once a friend of my mother's.'

The man stared at him, long and hard, as if searching for a crack in his composure.

'And if I mean her any harm, she can always send for the lads,' Marcus added. 'I am, as you pointed out, alone here, trusting in your good reputation to see me safely to my goal.'

The man sighed. 'If you're lying, it's a damn fool errand you're on after all this time. There is no money there. You'll come away empty handed. But if you've come about little Miranda, they'll be glad of news.' He pointed down the street and gave direction to a place on the west side of the village.

'Thank you.' Marcus slipped another coin on to the table and the man looked at it a long time before sliding it off the table and into his own pocket.

Chapter Eleven

Miranda looked up at the workman on the ladder and resisted an urge to supervise him. The removal of the old hangings was not her job. Or the cleaning of the chandeliers, for that matter. But it had been so long since some of the household chores had been attended to that the process had been difficult and after the ruination of the dining-room silk she'd felt the need to take an active part in most of the major jobs. It was only eleven o'clock and she was already exhausted. And itchy, as though a thin layer of grime covered her body. The staff had been cleaning for a week and she noted with satisfaction, the improvement was beginning to show. When and if her errant husband chose to return home, he would be well pleased.

'Not still working in here, are you?' St John had come up from behind her, spinning her around to face him.

'It needs to be done,' she said and stepped out of his grasp. 'The house was sorely neglected.'

'It needs doing, certainly, but not by you. I seriously doubt that my high-and-mighty brother would be pleased to see his new wife acting like a scullery maid.'

She let this pass in silence, since there was no indication that her husband would be pleased to see her in any capacity. What if she had done this, only to anger him further? She pushed the thought from her mind. She was doing the best she could for him. He would be pleased. He must be.

'And,' St John added, touching her face, tipping her chin up until she was looking into his eyes, 'you have a smudge on your nose. Charming, but most unusual for a duchess.' He offered her his linen handkerchief and she wiped at the offending soot.

'Miranda, darling, you should not be spending so much time indoors, working. It can't be good for you. I have a remedy.'

'And what would that be?'

'A ride with your new brother. I can show you the lands. I'll wager you have no idea of the size of the property.'

She had a pretty good idea, she thought wanly, after walking through so much of it to get to the house that first day. But a ride? Perhaps he meant carriage.

'What you need is a few hours on one of my brother's fine mares, galloping across the countryside. That will put colour back into your cheeks.'

The colour in her cheeks would be grey. A horse? And galloping, no less? It had been at least twelve years since she'd last ridden, and that had been a tethered pony.

But St John warmed to the idea. 'I've been meaning to try out my brother's new hunter, and this is just the excuse. You can have your pick of the horseflesh, there's sure to be something to suit you.'

'St John,' she began, 'I don't know that a ride would be possible. I did not bring a habit with me when I came from town.'

He frowned, but only for a moment. 'Certainly your maid can find something of my mother's that will do until your own clothes arrive. Call her immediately and we will see.'

'But, St John, I…' and inspiration struck her '…I am afraid of horses.' It was close enough to the truth.

'Afraid?' He stared at her, dumbfounded. 'And you married my brother. Oh, dear. This will not do, Miranda. You must overcome this unfortunate problem before my brother reappears if the two of you are to manage at all. Marcus is quite the man for the sporting life. The thrill of the hunt is in his blood. He is never truly happy unless he's haring around after one poor animal while on the back of another.' St John frowned. 'When he finds that he has married someone who does not share his interests…' He shook his head. 'He will be most put out.' He smiled down at her. 'But, fear not, little sister. I am here. And I can teach you. A few quiet rides through the country on the back of a gentle beast will be just the thing. When it is time to jump fences—' He saw the alarm on her face. 'Well, that may never be needed, so there is no point in worrying about it.'

Polly was able to cobble together bits of the late dowager's riding apparel to leave her suitably, although not fashionably covered. Miranda limped down the stairs in too-tight boots, cursing the need to force her unnaturally tall frame into the clothing of yet another petite woman. The dowager had been several inches shorter than she, with delicate feet and a trim figure. Once again, she was showing too much wrist and ankle, immobilised in a jacket that lacked room for her shoulders, but had plenty of space for the bosom that she did not possess.

She met St John in the entry hall; if he found anything unusual in her appearance, he was too polite to say so. He led her to the stables, where he chose a docile mare and helped her up, before mounting the magnificent black stallion beside it.

Horses were taller than she remembered. Certainly taller than they looked from the ground, where she wished she still was. She felt the horse twitch under her and forced the thought from her mind. If it realised that she wanted to be back on solid earth, it might decide to throw her and grant the wish without warning. She did not wish for the ground, she reminded herself. She wished to remain in the saddle.

St John set off at a walk and her own horse followed his with a minimum of direction on her part. She relaxed a little. He was right; this was not so bad. She called on what little she could remember of her childhood rides and manoeuvred her horse to walk beside St John's so they could converse.

'See?' he encouraged. 'It is not so bad as all that, is it?'

'No. Not so bad,' she lied.

'We will ride down the main road and into the farm land, towards that little copse of trees yonder—' he pointed towards the horizon '—then back to the house. And you will find the fresh air and exercise will do you good.'

He led her on and kept a running commentary on the local landscape. That farm held the oldest tenant. There lay the berry bushes that he and Marcus had raided as boys. That tree was the rumoured hanging spot of a notorious highwayman.

As he did so he encouraged his horse to a trot, and she did likewise. Her seat was not good and she jolted on the horse, wishing that they could return to the walking pace.

'You are managing quite well. I was sure it would only

take a short while to bring you back up to snuff.' His voice was full of encouragement.

'St John, I am not sure—'

'It is only a little further. We will stop to rest in the woods and then walk the horses home.'

She gritted her teeth. If it was only a little further, she could manage. And, perhaps it was her imagination, but his pace seemed faster still, and her horse speeded up without encouragement to follow St John's stallion. She glanced to the side, then quickly ahead to fight down the churning in her stomach. It was better to focus on the approaching woods. When they arrived there, she could stop and rest.

She looked with worry at the path before her. It appeared to be narrowing. And her horse was still abreast with St John's and too close to the edge of the road. She tugged at the reins, but her mount ignored her, refusing to give way. She tugged more firmly, but the horse showed no sign of interest.

They were almost to the trees and there was no path left. St John realised her dilemma and spurred his horse forward and then pulled up short at the side of the path.

She pulled too hard on the reins and her own horse at last realised what she expected of it and stopped without warning, lowering its head to graze.

And, in the way of all objects in motion, she continued forward, and over the horse's head. One minute she had an excellent, if alarming, view of the rapidly approaching trees. And then everything spun around and she had landed in a heap and was looking into the face of her own horse as it tried to nudge her out of the way to get to the tender grass that had broken the worst of her fall.

St John's face appeared in her field of vision, horrified. 'Oh, dear. Oh, Miranda. I never thought…'

'Perhaps,' she managed, 'a ride was not the best idea, St John.'

'Perhaps not,' he agreed, his light tone at odds with the worry in his eyes. 'Are you injured?'

'I do not believe so.' She tried to stand, then sat down again as her ankle collapsed beneath her. 'Maybe,' she conceded.

'Stay right where you are,' he commanded. 'Do not move. If there is a break in the bone, moving will make things worse.'

She lay back on the grass and stared up at the trees above her. What a fool her husband would think her if he returned to find her bedridden, unable to manage even a simple horseback ride. 'It is not broken,' she insisted. It simply could not be. She would not permit it.

She felt St John lift her skirts and realised with shock that he was removing her boots. She sat up, and then collapsed again as the blood rushed to her head. 'What are you doing?'

'What must be done if we are to establish the extent of your injuries. Now lie still and I will try not to hurt you.'

There was a firm tug and she bit back a cry as the boot came free. He reached for the other foot and she pulled it away. 'I am sure that that one is not injured.'

'But it is better to be safe than sorry in these things.' He tugged the other boot free.

She felt his touch against her stocking as he probed first one ankle and then the other. Now that the offending boots were gone, the pain was not so severe. Perhaps it was only loss of circulation that had caused her to stumble. The pins and needles were subsiding and she could feel his hands on her feet.

It was good there was no groom along to see this, for it would seem highly improper. He was taking his time, touching each bone to make sure it was in place. Through the roughness of her stocking, the sensation tingled and she involuntarily twitched her toes.

His hand tightened on her foot. 'You have feeling there?'

She nodded and bit her lip.

'Then the fall could not have been too severe.'

'I am glad to know that. Now, if you don't mind, I'll put my shoes back myself.'

'It is better to leave them off, lest there be swelling.'

She reached for them. 'I cannot ride back to the house stocking footed.'

'And you cannot ride if your boots are so tight that you cannot feel your feet in the stirrups.' He tossed the offending boots into the bushes.

'St John! Those belonged to your mother.'

'She has no plans to use them again. Nor should you, if they do not fit. When we go riding in the future, we will find another solution.'

When hell freezes and your mother needs her boots back, she thought, but kept her face placid and co-operative. 'Very well. Now, if you will help me back to my horse, we can return home.' His hand was still resting on her ankle, and she gave a shudder of pleasure and tried to pull away.

His grin was wicked as he pulled her foot into his lap. 'Not so fast. I think I've discovered your weakness.' He stroked the foot again, massaging the sole. 'A moment ago, I very nearly saw you smile. I refuse to release you until you do me the honour of laughing, for I swear I cannot live in this house a moment longer without hearing you laugh.'

'St John, please. This is most improper.' She sat up and frowned at him and twitched the too-short skirts of the dowager's habit down to cover her feet, but they covered his hands as well and it made the situation worse because she could not see what he was doing.

'You are right. And that is why we must finish quickly before someone finds us. Laugh for me and I'll let you go.'

'St John, stop this instant.' She tried to sound stern, but the effect was spoiled by the breathiness of her voice.

He trailed his fingers along the sole of her foot, 'When you know me better, Miranda, you will find it impossible to oppose me. Save yourself the trouble and give me what I want. Then I'll help you back on to your horse and we can return to the house.' He was massaging now, alternating firm touches with light, and the sensitivity was increasing with each stroke.

'St John…' She wanted to lecture him, but the feeling of his hands on her was delightful. And he was so devilishly unrepentant. And the situation so absurd. Air escaped her lips in a puff, and then she gasped, as the feeling became too frustrating to ignore and a last featherlight touch of her toes reduced her to a fit of giggling. She lay back in the grass and shook with laughter as he took his hands away and smoothed her skirt over her feet.

'There, you see. It was not so awful, was it, giving in and taking a little pleasure?'

She shook her head, dropping her eyes from his, and feeling the blush creeping up her cheeks as she smiled again.

'Good. For I would have you be happy here, Miranda. There is much to be happy about here. My brother…' She looked up at him as he frowned, trying to find a way to complete the sentence. 'My brother was not always as he is now. When we were young he was not so cold. So distant. If you cannot find the man that he once was, then know that you will always have a friend in me and need never be lonely or afraid.' He stood. 'Now, take my hand and I will help you mount. If you are strong enough, that is. You could always ride in front of me on the saddle and I could lead your horse.'

It was such an innocent offer. Too innocent, she suspected. His eyes were the clearest blue and there was not a hint of guile on his face as he said it.

And yet, she felt the heat of his hand as he helped her from the ground, and her mind drifted to the thought of them, together on the saddle, the gentle rocking of the horse between their legs, and him, close behind her, rocking against her… 'No. I am quite all right. I'm sure I can ride alone.' She stumbled in the direction of her horse.

'Are you sure? You look unsteady. Let me help you.' And his hand burned through her clothing as he lifted her easily up into the saddle. She kept her face averted from his, so he couldn't see the crimson in her cheeks.

There was something wrong with her. There must be. Some wickedness brought on by too much knowledge. She wished that she was as naïve and innocent as she pretended to be. But Cici had told her everything and had been so matter of fact about the pleasures of the flesh. Perhaps that was why she responded so quickly to a man's touch. And the touch of a man who was not her husband. The fact that the man in question was her husband's brother made it even worse, for she would have to be in close proximity to him, probably for the rest of their lives. She must master the feeling. Gain control of herself so that no one would ever know. Not the duke. And certainly not St John.

Chapter Twelve

Marcus looked at the house in surprise. Not what he had expected. Not at all. He'd imagined a quiet cottage where two ladies might spend their years in modesty, waiting for an improvement in position. Genteel poverty.

There was nothing genteel about his new wife's old home. It was poverty, pure and simple. Smaller than the homes of his tenants and packed cheek by jowl between other similar houses. He strode to the door and knocked.

The woman who answered dropped a curtsy, but looked at him with undisguised suspicion. 'Lost your way, milord?'

'Lady Cecily Dawson?'

She glared back at him. 'The "Lady" is long retired from her profession, and you'd best seek your amusements elsewhere.'

'If I could see her, please.'

'Come to get a look at her after all these years? What are you, then? The son of one of her clients, come to be initiated? A bit old for that, aren't you?'

'I beg your pardon.'

'You take my meaning plain enough. Get yourself off, in every sense of the word. The lady will be no help to you.'

He got his foot in the door in time to halt the slam, and pushed roughly past her, into the tiny room. 'Close the door. The questions I have to ask are better handled away from prying eyes.' He tossed his purse on the table and watched her eyes light as it made a satisfying clink. 'I require information. The money's yours if you can provide it.'

She dropped another curtsy, this one not tinged with irony. 'At your service, milord.'

'I want the whereabouts of Lady Cecily Dawson, and any information you can provide about her ward, Lady Miranda Grey.'

The colour drained out of the woman before him. And she clutched the table edge. 'Why would you be wanting that?'

'To satisfy my mind in certain details of Miss Grey's life before her recent marriage.'

'She's done it, then?' The avarice in the old woman's eyes changed to a glint of hope. 'She's safely married.'

'Yes.'

The woman pushed on. 'And her husband. What is he like?'

'He is a very powerful man, and impatient for information. Provide it, and keep the gold on the table—delay any longer and things will go bad for you.'

A man's voice rose from the curtained corner of the room behind him. 'That's enough, Cici. I'll talk to the gentleman.' The last word was said with a touch of scorn. The man that appeared from behind the curtain was in his mid-fifties, but hard work had left him much older. He walked with a cane, and the hands that held it were gnarled and knotted, the knuckles misshapen. He glared at the duke as though this were the reception room of a great house, and not a hovel, and said in a firm tone, 'And whom do I have the honour of addressing, sir?'

'Someone who wishes to remain anonymous.'

'As do we. But you are the one who forced his way into my home, and you can take your gold and go, or introduce yourself properly. You have my word that your identity will go no further than these walls.'

'Your word? And what is that worth to me?'

'It is all I have to offer, so it will have to do.'

'Very well, I am Marcus Radwell, Duke of Haughleigh.' He heard a sharp gasp escape the lady behind him. 'And you, sir?'

'I, your Grace, am Sir Anthony Grey, father of the young lady you are enquiring after.'

Marcus resisted the temptation to grab the corner of the table for support. Just what had he wandered into this time? 'Her father? I was led to believe—'

'That she was an orphan? It could well have been the case. Indeed, it would have been better had it been true.' He looked at the duke in curiosity. 'Tell me, Your Grace, before we go further—are you my daughter's husband?'

'Yes.' The word came out as a croak, and he cleared his throat to master his voice before speaking again.

'And you have come to London, seeking the truth.'

'I left on our wedding night.' He coughed again. Facing the girl's father, even under these circumstances, it was a damned difficult subject. 'Before an annulment became impossible.'

'And where is my daughter, now?'

'Safely in Devon. At my home.'

'And your decision about her depends on the results of your search here?'

'And on her wishes. I have no desire to force marriage on her, if she is unwilling.'

Her father set his face in resolve. 'Do not trouble yourself as regards her wishes, your Grace. Delicate sensibilities can be saved for those women that can afford them. My health is failing and I can no longer pretend to support the three of us. Her choices here are a place in service in a great house, or walking the street. If you still wish to have her, after today, she will choose you and be grateful.'

'Proceed then, Sir Anthony.'

The man barked a laugh at the title. 'How curious to be addressed so, after all this time. Very well, then. My story.

'Once, some thirteen years past, I was a happy man, with a beautiful wife, a daughter who was a joy to me and expectations of a son to carry on my name. Unfortunately, my wife died, giving birth to our second child, and the child died as well. The grief quite unhinged me. Your Grace, are you, as Cici remembered, a widower for similar reasons?'

Marcus gave a faint nod.

'Then you can understand the grief and disappointment, and perhaps sympathise with the depths to which I sunk. I turned from the daughter I loved, and, in the space of a few years, I destroyed her inheritance and my own, gambling away the land, drinking until late in the evening. When I ran out of money, I borrowed from friends. I depleted all resources available to me, and hoped to blow my brains out and avoid the consequences of my actions. When I was loading the gun to end my life, my daughter came into the room, still so innocent, and pleaded with me to spend just a few moments with her as I used to. One look into those eyes changed my course and hardened my resolve to find a way out of my difficulties.

'Alas, there was no honourable course available. The creditors were at my door. So I decamped—' he gestured around him '—to a place so low that my friends and creditors would never think to look for me. It must be better, I thought, to find honest work and keep what little I earned than to face debtors' prison in London. And if I went to prison, what would happen to my Miranda?

'There was a factory here with an opening for a clerk. It was less than we were used to, but if we lived simply we could manage. I spent my days in the office, totting up figures and copying, and things were well for a time.' Sir Anthony waved a clawed hand before his face. 'But it was not too long before my eyes would no longer focus on the small print, and then even the big print became hard to decipher. And my hand cramped on the pen. The owner had an opening in the factory proper, running a loom. It was not so much money, of course. But it was not a difficult job to learn and when the last of our savings ran out and there was nothing left worth selling, I was not too proud to take my place with the other workers. If people in these parts had any suspicions about the strangers in their midst, time set their minds at rest. Cici and Miranda did what was necessary to help keep us afloat, taking in washing and mending, and hiring themselves out to the great houses in the area when they needed extra help. And thus, slowly, my daughter forgot the world she was born to.'

'And now that she is neither fish nor fowl, you think she should marry a *duke*?' Marcus stared in disbelief at the man before him.

Sir Anthony's mouth tightened. 'Yes, I do. I can no longer work.' He held out his twisted hands in evidence. 'I am useless, too clumsy to run even the simplest machine. Unless we can find another means of support, it's the poorhouse for us all. Do you understand what it means to watch your daughter forced to wait upon people who would be her inferiors, had I but kept a cool and sober head some years back? To sit idle and watch my only child forced into service to expiate my sins?'

And it grew still worse. Marcus listened in horror as Sir Anthony explained. 'Recently, Miranda had grown popular at a certain house—her occasional position serving there was to be made permanent. Humiliating, perhaps, if I'd had any pride left. But then it became clear to me that the lord wished to offer her a position above stairs that had nothing to do with service. Miranda is a bright girl, and she loves us too well. It was only a matter of time, your Grace, before she realised that she was the solution to all our problems and agreed. I needed to get her away and safely married before a local lord took what he wanted and I completed my daughter's ruin by sacrificing her honour to put bread on the table. It was Cici's idea to try to find her a husband that suited her station in life. Someone who seldom visited London, and was unaware of the scandal attached to our name.'

'But why me?' There must be something, a sign on his face perhaps, that labelled him easily gulled.

The woman spoke. 'Your mother owed me for a wrong, done long before you were born. I called in the debt.'

'I read your letters. You threatened her with exposure. Exposure of what?'

'There was little threat, really, other than the weight of her own guilt. And perhaps the embarrassment of having known me. But she responded to the letters I sent and I took advantage of the fact.'

'She was dying.'

Lady Cecily looked coldly into his eyes. 'I know. And I can't say that I cared, other than that it left me little time to form my plan. I am sorry to be so blunt. But your mother, as I knew her, was a hard woman, and jealous. If she wished to repent before death, she had much to repent for.'

He nodded. 'Please explain.'

'We knew each other first as children. We went to school together and shared a room. We were best friends as girls and both as sweet and beautiful as one could hope. When I was fourteen, my father died. He left sufficient funds to see me through school, and provide a modest Season when I came of age, and left my guardianship to an aged aunt who knew little of what happened while I was away.'

Her mouth twisted in a bitter line. 'There was a trustee there who took, shall we say, a personal interest in my case. He took every opportunity to remind me that my funds were limited, and my position at the school in jeopardy. Finally, he persuaded me to meet him one night in an office. To go over the details of my father's will. How was I to know what he intended? I was only a girl.' There was anguish in her voice and Marcus felt the man next to him tighten protectively.

'I returned to my room afterward crying and shaking and your mother helped me clean away the blood and swore she would tell no one what had happened. And she kept the secret for me because I begged her to, even though the man continued to use me on and off for the rest of the term. I escaped to my aunt's home after that, and saw nothing of your mother until the year we had our Season.

'She was a great beauty, as was I.' Cecily smiled as she remembered. 'I'd put the difficulties at school far behind me and hoped to make a match with an understanding man who would not question the lack of blood on the sheet. I had several fine prospects, including my dear Anthony, and…' she looked appraisingly at Marcus '…your own father. Many of the same men who hovered about your mother, in fact. We had been friends at school, but we were rivals now. When it looked like your father might be ready to offer for me, when it looked like she might lose, your mother let my secret slip out, and then spread it enthusiastically about the *ton*. Suddenly I was not a poor, abused girl, but a young seductress. And the offers I received?' She laughed. 'Well, they were not offers of marriage. Eventually, I accepted one. And when he tired of me, I found another. And that is when I was known as "Lady Cecily". And why I responded as I did when you came to the door. Anthony was the last of the men that kept me, and I loved him from the time before my fall from honour. When he became too poor to keep me?' She shrugged. 'I kept him. And he ran through all I had saved before I could persuade him to take his daughter, abandon his honour and run.'

'And you sought to ruin me, as my mother ruined you?'

'No, your Grace. I swear we meant you no harm. I only sought to find the best possible home for Miranda. And I do you no disservice in sending you a wife. She is not so great as the ladies you might choose, but she has had no opportunity to be a lady since she was ten, and no mother to guide her. Had the past been different, she would be every bit as fine as the woman you would select for yourself.'

The words were distant in his ears, drowned out by the memories in his head.

'The poor girl…'

'Your family honour...'

'Look at her and think of what will happen to her if you beg off now...'

'The child needs a name...'

'Your Grace?' Cecily Dawson was looking at him in puzzlement and he snapped back to the present.

'I beg your pardon, madam. Pray continue.'

'We never meant to trap you into a marriage with Miranda. It was our hope, rather naïve perhaps, but our hope all the same, that if she could only meet a few gentlemen of her own class, she might by her modesty and good sense attract the attention of one of them. I thought, if your mother was unable to persuade one of her sons to take a wife, we might, by continued threat, convince her to take the girl as a ward and introduce her to other gentlemen in the area. At the very least, a position as companion to your mother...'

'Delivering the girl into the hands of your enemies?' He quirked a brow and smiled ironically back to them.

Sir Anthony responded, 'At this point, it was the frying pan or the fire for her. I apologise for my candour, your Grace. Your mother may have had a tongue like a viper, but words are not capable of hurting my daughter. Her acceptance of my daughter was an admission of guilt and fear of exposure.'

'But my mother is dead,' Marcus said silkily. 'And I am under no such compulsion.'

The looks on the faces of the other two went from resolve to alarm.

'I beg pardon for what I have said. I'm sorry for your loss, your Grace,' Sir Anthony said.

'No, you are not and neither am I. What you've said about my mother is the truth. She cared for herself, and her status, and very little else. The fact that you managed to blackmail her into any action that was not solely for her benefit speaks to the heaviness of her soul at the end of her life. I married your daughter because I felt bound by honour to protect her good name after she came unannounced to my house and spent the night there unchaperoned. By her untimely death, my mother has trapped me yet again into choosing honour over good sense and secured the success of your scheme.' He looked around him, 'Of course, now that I have learned the origins of my wife…'

Tears began to trickle from under the closed eyelids of the woman before him and he looked away. Better not to look and be fooled by a whore's tears.

Lord Anthony's voice shook as he began. 'Yes, your Grace, your new wife was raised by a drunkard and a gambler, and mothered by a whore. She has worked as a servant, cleaning privy pots and scrubbing hearthstones and doing whatever jobs were considered beneath the dignity of the regular staff. And now, if you turn her off, she has nowhere to go and will sink lower still to keep from starving to death. I am sick unto death myself of watching her pay for my sins. I wish to God when I held the pistol that day I had shot us both, rather than doom her to a life of servitude, for she has done nothing to deserve it but follow where I have led her. And when I sent her to you, she resisted, saying she'd rather stay with us and do what was necessary than leave us when we needed her. I made her swear, your Grace, on her mother's Bible, that she'd do as I commanded and keep her tongue about it. I made her swear that, should she manage marriage to an honourable man, she would serve him with all her heart, and never, ever turn back to the place she had come from. She is a pearl, and a pearl buried in a dung heap is no less valuable for its surroundings.'

Marcus kept his face impassive. 'A pearl, you say? In what way? What can she bring to our marriage? There is no dowry, certainly. And as yet, she has not won me with her sweet nature and soft looks.'

'She can bring her strength, your Grace. And her honour.'

'Which she has proved to me by lying to gain access to my house and concealing the circumstances of her life.'

'A thing that she would never have done had I not required it of her. She begged, your Grace, not to be forced to do this. And I'm sure that keeping the secret from you pains her almost as much as the separation from us. If you can relieve her of it, you will see her true nature and she will be eternally grateful to you. Look into your heart, your Grace, and ask yourself what you would do in the circumstances. Have you never lied to protect another? For that is all she is guilty of.'

Marcus closed his eyes against the question, struck to the heart with a random blow. Maybe he and his new wife had more common ground than first he realised.

He thought back to her, the way exhaustion had broken her the night he'd left, when the cool courtesy had cracked and the way a glimmer of the truth had come spilling out. The horror on her face, when she realised what she'd said and done.

He stared at the people before him. 'And what are you willing to do for your daughter's honour, Sir Anthony?'

'Anything you require of me, your Grace. If you wish us to work as servants in your house, say the word. As long as Miranda is safe, I am yours to command.'

'And, Lady Cecily? Can you speak for yourself in this matter?'

'I've raised the girl as my own daughter for twelve years, your Grace. It is as Sir Anthony says. I will do what you ask.'

'Then I ask that you gather your belongings and prepare to remove yourselves to my home in Northumberland. Not the most comfortable of abodes, certainly. I use it for hunting. But there is a small staff and it is very private. You can wait there until decisions are made. And, Lord Anthony, I assume your debts still stand on someone's books?'

'Such things are never forgotten, your Grace.'

'Then they will need to be settled.'

'I have not the means…'

'Of course you don't, but I do.'

'I never intended—'

'That's as it may be,' he snapped, and heard four generations of Haughleigh in his voice. It was a voice people couldn't help but obey.

Lord Anthony fell silent.

He continued. 'You may not have intended to saddle me with the debts, but I mean to see them paid. I will accept no argument. Write down what you can remember of them and think no further on the subject. You will retire to my hunting lodge, while I clear your name and discuss with Miranda her wishes for the future.

'When some agreement is reached between us, you will be contacted by her or me, and reunited. Whether she comes back to you with her honour and her freedom, or you come to us at Haughleigh is yet to be decided, but I will not return her to you if you must only sell her to some other man of privilege. Whatever her future may be, her duty to her past will stop with me.'

Chapter Thirteen

Miranda was screaming. It was odd, he thought, that he should know her voice. They'd been together so briefly. But it was her, he was sure. Screaming in terror. He tried to run to her, but the ground turned to mud beneath his feet, sucking at his boots and dragging him downward.

'Marcus! Help me! Marcus! Please.' Her voice trailed off as though she was losing the strength to call him.

He fought. Fought the sensation of sinking and the fear that at any moment the treacherous ground would close up and swallow him. There was a branch beneath his hand and he closed on it and hauled himself forward out of the mud and towards the place where he knew she must wait for him.

He jerked awake, panting and stared around the room. He was in bed in his townhouse in London. There was no mud, of course. He was not even wearing boots. And he could not hear his new wife because she was miles away in Devon.

It was folly to place too much credence in dreams. They were not omens of the future, after all. They were only the fancies created by an overheated mind as it sought rest.

And that was why he'd stayed away from home all these years. Because dreams meant nothing. He sneered at his own folly. He might have stood his mother's presence and taken up his position at Haughleigh if it hadn't been for the damned dreams of suffocation. He'd set his life's course by dreams.

But what of the future? In his dreams, Miranda wanted him to come to her. If the real Miranda knew it, she would be appalled. What reason had he given her to trust him? She probably felt she needed protection from him.

The faint morning light was seeping between the bed curtains and he rang for his valet. A shave and a wash would shake the last of the clouds from his mind. It had been ridiculous. A rescue fantasy. But, at least, not as frightening as a premature burial. He had been able to move, this time. And he had needed to get to Miranda.

She was in need, whether she realised it or not. Her father was a pleasant enough sort, if more than a bit of a fool. He had ruined his daughter, never thinking of the future. Marcus remembered her standing in the kitchen. Trembling skin and bones. Hands with long tapering fingers, covering her face in shame and horror. Hands, which could have been bedecked with rings and toying with an ivory fan, were rough from years of hard labour marred with burns and scars.

His mouth thinned to a tight line. Her eyes had been guarded, afraid to let out a glimmer of passion or pain, afraid that any weakness would be used against her. And her father had done it all, dragging her down in the name of love and family togetherness. And who knew what ideas she had after twelve years of listening to her surrogate mother?

He winced as he remembered the story and the valet paused in his shaving to avoid cutting his throat.

There was a tangled mess, and the end of the string led back to his own doorstep. The Dawson woman need not have been a whore if it hadn't been for the machinations of his hellhound of a mother. She could have hid her shame and married well. Anthony Grey, perhaps. Or his own father. Which would make Cecily Dawson... He shrugged. His mother. Or Miranda's. And either choice could have been a happier fate for all concerned.

He could not turn back the clock for Cecily, but it was not too late for Miranda. His dream told him that much.

The late summer sun was bright on the shop windows as he walked into the shopping district, warm on the fine wool of his jacket. But it had been too nice a day for the carriage, quite the nicest day he'd seen in some time, and he felt he must walk.

Tum te tum... How did it go again? He tried to remember the ditty that had been running through his head. Something about milkmaids. Brown eyes. Wooing. Something. Folksongs were all alike. There was always a shepherd or a tinker and a milkmaid. And the results were certainly the same.

He whistled.

What was coming over him? He was wandering down Bond Street like he hadn't a care in the world.

He was acting like St John.

And stopped in his tracks so suddenly that the package-laden man behind him collided with an oath. He apologised with a smile, helped the man collect his purchases and helped him on his way with more good grace than he'd felt in years.

It was dashed strange, considering the mood he'd been in when he'd come to London, to find himself so carefree now.

Especially considering the burden of responsibilities loaded on to his back. A wife had been shock enough. But a wife that could clean privy pots and draw ale? And in-laws. And their debts. And a surrogate mother-in-law who would turn the vicar's hair snow white, should he realise her former profession.

It could probably be kept hushed, he decided. But he must find a way to persuade Anthony to legitimise the union before he could accept them into the house. The vision of Cecily Dawson at Christmas dinner floated into his mind. Perhaps he would have the servants put her in his mother's room. The thought gave him a moment's wicked pleasure.

It was mad.

He ducked through a nearby door and into the salon of a noted dressmaker. It had been years since he'd crossed the threshold, trailing after Bethany on one of her many shopping trips, but Madame Souette recognised him immediately.

'How may I help you, your Grace?' She signalled to a shop girl to bring tea, and offered him a seat on a divan.

'I need…I need everything. That a woman might require.' He pulled out the worn gown and slippers that Cecily had provided. 'In this size, or slightly larger.'

She glanced down at the worn clothing in front of her and almost managed to hide the moue of displeasure at their poor condition. 'And the woman in question? What is her taste?' Madame was probing gently, afraid of giving offence. 'Will you be spending your time with her at the opera? The theatre? Or will you be remaining at home?'

She was looking at him closely, probably trying to guess the identity of his new mistress.

He grinned. 'Oh, all of the above, I should think. When I

bring my new bride to London, she will attend many such functions. But for now, clothing suitable for a quiet life in the country.'

'A wardrobe worthy of a duchess?'

He nodded.

'And she needs everything.' The woman's eyes sparkled as she totalled the bill in her mind.

'Everything. There was an accident involving her trunks when she travelled to Devon.' He waved his hand in dismissal. 'All lost.'

'How unfortunate.' Madame tried and failed to look grieved.

'I trust that you will be both discreet and quick, for I need the clothing in three days.'

Her eyebrows arched, but she did not refuse him.

'It will require a miracle, but you will be generously compensated for it. Her colouring is pale, but her hair and eyes are dark. Do what you can to flatter her. I trust your judgment in these matters more than my own.'

Giving her his card and direction, he left the shop.

It was strange seeing the small rooms where his wife had spent so many years, poor beyond his ability to imagine, but more warm and welcoming than his own home had been. And then to come into the great mausoleum that was Haughleigh Grange.

She deserved better.

His next stop was a jeweller's shop, where he pulled a flat, velvet-lined case from his pocket. The jeweller was as ingratiating as the dressmaker had been; ready to bend over backwards to please his Grace.

He spilled the hated necklace on to the table in front of him. 'I have recently remarried and wish to present the family emeralds to my wife.'

The jeweller remarked that they were most fine which, of course, Marcus knew.

'A new setting, I think. A new wife should not have to wear the cast-offs of the old. I would like to start fresh.' Not that that was ever possible, with the weight of tradition heavy on his shoulders. Perhaps a change in the necklace would remind him of something other than his mother, or Bethany, whenever he had to look at them.

The jeweller made hurried notes, wincing only a little at the proposed timeline. 'Will there be anything else, your Grace?'

'No. I think… Wait.' The image of his new wife standing in the hall as his signet rolled across the floor popped into his mind. 'Yes, there is something. I need a ring. A wedding ring. We married hurriedly and she deserves better than my temporary solution.'

The jeweller brought forth a prodigious tray of diamonds, rubies, emeralds and plain gold bands. He stared over the selection, but none of them reminded him of the strange white-faced girl he had left behind in his home. Then he smiled up at the man in front of him. 'Do you have any sealing wax?'

The man disappeared into the back room of the shop and returned with a lump of casting wax and a candle.

Marcus melted the stuff on to the counter in front of him and plunged his signet into it, leaving the clearly defined mark of the crest imbedded in it. 'That is what I would like for her. On a plain gold ring, but to fit a woman's finger.'

'Unorthodox, Your Grace.'

'But it will suit her better than these baubles.'

* * *

His last stop was the family solicitor. Claude Binley looked at him over the stack of papers on the desk and pushed his spectacles further down his nose.

Marcus grinned at him in response. 'How are things progressing?'

'That would depend, your Grace, on the point of view. From my position, they are progressing much too quickly.'

'Too quickly? But successfully, I trust.'

The solicitor nodded. 'I have made arrangements for the licence. I have altered your will to reflect the marriage. I have settled accounts at Boodle's and White's for Sir Anthony Grey.'

'And you can expect to see some additional bills from a dressmaker and a jeweller,' Marcus added.

Claude sniffed his disapproval.

'Is there some problem with funds?'

'No, your Grace.'

'It would hardly do to let my duchess sit in rags, Claude. Money will have to be spent.'

'May I speak frankly, your Grace?'

'Not if you insist on calling me "your Grace". We have known each other since childhood, Claude.'

'Very well, Marcus, since we have known each other so long. I remember your first wife, and the speed with which you courted and wed her. And I remember the details of the union and the result. I would hate to see a repeat of that mistake.'

Marcus felt his spine stiffen. 'I don't think it would be possible to repeat a mistake quite that substantial.'

'I see similarities.'

'And what might you think they are?'

'A woman you barely know. Recommended to you by

your mother. A sudden marriage. And distinct signs that you have a head full of clouds. Lavish gifts. The refusal to heed the counsel of those around you. Heroic measures on your part to rush to the aid of a damsel in distress.'

'But Miranda is nothing like Bethany. And my mother, should she have lived to see her, would have been appalled.'

'To marry her in spite of your mother is no different from marrying with her consent. You are still leg-shackled.'

'And you have been in that state for nearly fifteen years, Claude. Is it not time that I joined the fraternity of the married and settled?'

'Certainly. But not in this way, Marcus. Perhaps to this girl, if you are so set upon her, but not until matters in her own family and yours are properly resolved. You know nothing of her except what you have been told and yet you are willing to believe what is a most extraordinary story. And you do not doubt her honour. Time alone will prove that. Even a few weeks might confirm—'

'That the next duke will not be some other man's bastard?' His voice was ice now. 'Thank you for the warning, Claude. But take care. You are speaking of my wife.'

'Who was raised by a wastrel and a slut.'

Marcus rose out of his chair, ready to challenge, to fight.

Claude stood against the threat, unmoved. 'I speak the truth, though you don't want to hear it, your Grace.'

Marcus sighed. 'And I, Claude, am the son of a drunkard and a shrew. Perhaps we are well suited after all. For, if parentage matters so much, then I am not such a great bargain, but for the title. My last wife was raised by exemplary parents. Her family history was without blemish. And in the end, it made no difference.'

Claude sighed. 'Yes, your Grace. And it has hardened you to good advice. Now you will do as you will do, no matter what I might say to the contrary, for you have a head harder than a paving stone. I pray that you are right and wish you well.'

Chapter Fourteen

'Your Grace, did you purchase anything new in the village shops?'

'No, Polly. My things will do nicely.' With each trip to the village to arrange for help or supplies or to check on the progress of the silk Miranda had ordered for the dining room, Polly had become more insistent that she buy something for herself. Miranda sighed. There would be hell to pay when the bills came due, if she could not find a husband to write the cheques. Why add additional purchases for herself to the growing stack of necessities?

Polly picked up the hem of the evening gown. She'd found the section where the trim simply ended, only to reappear from a seam a foot away. 'The cloth was fine enough once, your Grace—'

When it was new, Miranda added to herself.

'—But I don't know how much longer these sleeves will hold. Perhaps if you bought lace to freshen them up?'

'No need, Polly.'

'A new bonnet, perhaps?' There was a note of desperation in the maid's voice.

With her husband gone and no real understanding of the accounts, she dared not risk such a frivolous expense. She'd better wait until he returned and set some kind of allowance. 'I think not,' she said.

'Oh, well, ma'am. I could see that you might find the stuff you can purchase hereabouts a mite simple for a fine London lady. And when his Grace returns, he'll have brought back presents for you.'

Perhaps when his Grace returns, he'll have forgotten he's married. She held no great hopes of him purchasing hat trims.

'Now, about your hair.'

'My hair?' Miranda touched the plait, worried for a moment that Polly was going to suggest they purchase a wig.

'It's not quite the style that ladies are wearing nowadays. Rather unusual.'

And easy to keep up, thought Miranda. No need for curling irons or a maid to dress the back.

Polly pulled a much-handled sketch from behind her back. 'I thought, perhaps, you might let me try something more like this.' It was a page from *Le Beau Monde* or some other fashion magazine, and had probably been through the hands of most of the ladies' maids in the area.

Polly pointed a stubby finger at a style in the background. 'Maybe a bit longer in the back, but not much. Parted on the side, here. The curls would call attention to your eyes, your Grace, and you do have lovely eyes.'

It could be a disaster, she thought. A scissors and curling iron in untrained hands. 'Do you know much about hair, Polly?'

'Oh, yes, your Grace. I do for my whole family. My sisters look right smart.'

'Do any of them work here?' She crossed her fingers that it would not turn out to be the parlourmaid with the horrible squint that looked like she'd trimmed her hair with hedge clippers.

'No, your Grace. But I've got three of them, all younger. I know all about hair.'

'All right.' She must throw a bone to the poor woman, to make up for the sorry wardrobe and the lack of excitement she must present as the new lady of the house.

'Oh, thank you, your Grace. You stay right here and I'll get the scissors.'

Now? Dear Lord. She'd imagined sitting down for this in some distant future, and agreed, hoping that it would satisfy the maid. She sank on to the chair by the dressing table. No time to prepare herself.

Polly was back and holding a pair of scissors. She gave an experimental snip, the gleaming blades slicing the air. The maid nibbled her lip.

Do your worst, Miranda thought, eyes closed, listening to the sound of the snipping going on behind her back. She felt the first lock fall away and felt strangely lighter, like the headache that had plagued her for days was the result of the hair dragging upon her mind.

The snipping continued and she relaxed under Polly's ministrations. It really was rather nice to be done for, rather than doing for others. And Polly was good humoured, one of the few such people in this house. She kept a steady stream of information coming about her sisters, their hair, their beaus, and then she stopped. 'You can open your eyes now, your Grace. See, it wasn't so bad as all that, now was it? I'll get you a cup of tea and heat up the curling irons. You'll see it will be most fine when we've finished.'

She stared at her reflection in shock. Polly had been right. It changed her face, when the hair was trimmed away and the bone structure allowed to show. And she had good eyes. Not dull and hard as she had thought. Surrounded by curls, she looked almost playful. She was not so grand as Bethany had been, but then, no one was. Perhaps a touch of rouge… She wondered what Marcus would think, when he saw her.

And realised that the rouge was not necessary for the colour appeared on its own in her cheeks. Dear God. She scrubbed at them, as though the thought that had put the roses there might be easy to interpret.

Polly returned with her tea and she sipped it gladly, ignoring the slight rattle as she placed it on the saucer.

She walked down to dinner that night with her head held high to accent the graceful neck she had never known she possessed. And when she entered the dining room, St John was there and sprang to his feet at the sight of her.

'Miranda.' He said her name in a kind of sigh, unlike the usual playful tone he used when addressing her. 'I swear I had no idea.' He crossed the room, and she cast her gaze to the floor as he walked slowly around her. 'Whose plan was this, then? Have you been to London and back in an afternoon that you appear so fine?'

'No,' she said. 'This was Polly's doing. She insisted.'

'Then you must take her advice in all things, for she is wise for one so young. Is that a new gown as well?'

'You spoil your compliments with base flattery, St John. This is the same dress I have worn to dinner these two weeks.'

'I did not mean to flatter you. It is just that…your transformation is so startling… Frankly, Miranda, I can hardly look at the dress, the woman wearing it is so radiant.'

She tried not to take pleasure in the comment, reminding herself that it was not St John that she needed to please.

She asked hesitantly, 'Do you think the duke will approve?'

St John looked elsewhere, then busied himself with his soup. Finally he muttered, 'I am, perhaps, not the best person to ask on my brother's taste when it comes to women. After all, it has been several years since we spent any time together. Tastes change.' He paused, taking another spoonful of soup. 'But how could he not like it? It really is most becoming.'

Wonderful. He must have a fancy for long, undressed hair. Had she changed what in his eyes was her only good quality? She took a deep drink of wine and allowed the footman to refill the glass. She would not let worry about the duke ruin her evening. She tossed her head and felt the curls bob against her neck. It made her smile. 'If he does not like it, then I care not what he thinks, for it looks fine.'

St John laughed at this little rebellion. 'That's my girl. Keep your chin up and show me more of that beautiful neck. Your brief stay here has done you good.'

She could feel the colour in her cheeks again. There was no point in hiding it. He could no doubt see what effect his compliments had on her, but was too polite to comment. Soon he would artfully turn the conversation to topics more general that she could respond to without a blush or a giggle.

She took another sip of wine. She would enjoy them while

she could, for her husband must come back soon and he would send St John away. Already, he was describing some fine-blooded mare he'd seen at the inn today and laying plans, as he did occasionally, to start a stud farm in the area. She nodded in feigned interest as the entrée passed away and the dessert course arrived. St John's plans were always expansive and he told them well, but she suspected that they were a source of the conflict between himself and his brother. The family's younger son had not received much of an inheritance, and what he had seemed to have disappeared in the two months since his mother's death. St John's debts were bigger than his dreams, and he relied on the duke to keep his creditors at bay.

He gazed at her over the dessert and they fell into a silence that was at first comfortable, then pregnant with expectation. Too much wine tonight, she thought. It would be best to retire early and put an end to this foolishness.

'And what of this evening?' St John asked as if reading her thoughts and tempting her from them. 'Port in the library? I could read to you. The music room, perhaps? There is a pianoforte there. I don't suppose you play? I can manage a few simple tunes that won't offend a lady, although my voice is nothing to speak of.'

He was so eager. So willing to please. And it would be enjoyable, as evenings spent in his company often were. Too comfortable. She felt the danger of growing too used to them. The parting would be bitter enough. 'Not tonight, St John. I am rather tired. I think I will retire to my room and read.'

'Come...' he took her arm '...I'll escort you.'

'That won't be necessary.'

'Ah, but I insist.' He stood and came to stand beside her,

giving her arm an innocent squeeze, and she felt an unaccustomed tightening in her body. 'You shouldn't have to wander this great house alone.'

'But, really, I prefer…'

'To be alone? Bah. It is not healthy to be too much by one's self. You will find that there are many enjoyable activities that are better in the company of others.'

He led her out of the room and they proceeded down the hall and up the first flight of stairs towards her room. She made to break away from him then, thanking him again for unnecessary courtesy.

'But we are barely halfway there, Miranda.'

'I know the way. Honestly, St John, it is not as though I am likely to get lost in my own house.'

His expression flickered in the candlelight. 'It was my house too, once. Everyone forgets that I am a member of the family.'

'Of course you are family, St John. To me at least. Just like a brother.' The words sounded false in her ears and she hurried on. 'I never had a brother.'

'You certainly never had mine. But I will rectify this lack of family and make you welcome.' And before she could pull away, he kissed her on the cheek.

It was only a peck, but it burned against her skin and she stood dazed beside him, feeling the weight of his hand pressing on her shoulder.

He touched her on the cheek and his finger traced the line of her nose, and to her shock she sighed.

'My word. You truly haven't had my brother. He's gone, but left you untouched.'

She blushed. 'It is not proper to talk of such things.'

'Not proper. But it's true, isn't it?' He did not wait for her answer, but read it in her eyes.

'My brother is a bigger fool than I thought to abandon a gem to chase after the dross he'll find in London.'

'He did not abandon me.' But her voice did not sound as sure as she wanted to make it.

'Perhaps not. He will no doubt come back when he tires of the sport where he is hunting, and expect to find his innocent waiting at home. It would serve him right if someone came and stole you away.'

'I have more honour than that, sir.'

'Of course you do, my darling Miranda. But you'll find there are men who have no scruples against tempting a lonely wife away from her virtue.'

'And I suppose you mean to protect me from them,' she said tartly.

'Perhaps it is not protection you need.'

'St John, you go too far.' She turned away from him and he took her shoulders and gently turned her back to face him.

'Miranda.' His voice was injured innocence itself. 'I was only teasing. Your secret is safe with me.'

'Thank you,' she murmured.

'There. Much better. Am I forgiven? I could not bear to see you angry with me. Who would I have then to talk to and to walk with?'

'I was being foolish.' He was right, she thought. It was better to be alone together than for the two of them to be alone separately.

He pulled her to him and gave her a salute on the other cheek, another brief peck, and she felt the blood rushing to her face.

He did not let go. 'I would miss you, you know, if you

were to withdraw your affection.' His voice was ever so slightly hoarse.

She looked up into his eyes, and saw the sadness in his smile.

'Without you, I would be quite desperately unhappy. This is such a cold house, without the warmth of another human being, is it not? You must feel it yourself, at night when you are alone in that great bed in the duke's apartments.'

She did not want to think of the loneliness. Not just now, when she was standing too close to another.

'And you, Miranda dear, should not be abandoned to the darkness that is our family home. You deserve better.'

She closed her eyes against the words. Everyone kept insisting that she deserved more than she wanted. She could be happy but for the desire of those around her to improve her condition when she was content.

'A flower like you must not be kept in the cold and dark, but must be given light and warmth so it may flourish.' His hands brushed slowly up her arms as if to dispel the chill, but she shivered at his touch, realised their proximity and made to pull away.

But his arms were strong and held her fast, and they seemed to leech the strength from her body as his eyes gazed down into hers. And then, instead of holding her, they were drawing her closer and his head was dipping down and his lips met hers.

The kiss was sweet, and all the more seductive because she knew it was wrong. Cici had said that the good church-going people who worried so about temptation didn't know the real danger: they didn't understand the joy in falling.

There was a strange liquid sensation running through her

body, as though her blood had been replaced with honey. And she could feel by the way he was rubbing his tongue against her closed mouth, that he meant for her to open her lips and the good Miranda cautioned that this would be disaster, but the wicked girl told her that the damage was done and the only danger now was discovery. And she opened her mouth to him and let him take it, and it was good.

And the honeyed feeling had reached her stomach, and her body cried that it wanted to be closer still.

He felt the change. And suddenly his hands were roaming freely over her body, and his mouth was hard and demanding on hers, not sweet and coaxing, and she struggled against him.

And she pulled her arm back as far as she could and brought it forward fast and struck him in the head.

Years of hauling water and scrubbing floors had put muscle in her arm that embroidery and harpsichord playing never could. She noted with satisfaction that the blow had been hard enough to leave him dazed when he let go of her and leaned against the wall.

When his eyes rose to meet hers, they were dark and calculating, not full of love.

And she ran. She raced like a mad woman down the corridor into her room where she slammed the door behind her and turned the key in the lock.

And then she heard footsteps in the hall pausing outside her door. The knob turned, one way and then the other.

Let me go, she pleaded silently.

'Miranda. Let me in,' he was whispering at the keyhole and his quiet voice echoed through her room like a shout. 'Sweeting, open the door to me.'

She mouthed the word, *No*. And wrapped her arms around her as she sat upon the bed.

'You know you want to.'

She didn't know what she wanted. Not any more. She wanted to be home. She wanted somewhere to be home.

'Miranda.' He sang the name. 'Does my brother know how sweet your lips are?'

She wiped her mouth with the back of her hand.

'I'll wager not, for that was a mouth that had never known kisses. Do you think I should tell him?'

'No,' she said the word aloud this time and cursed herself for responding.

'Then it is a good thing that he abandoned you to me, for what he doesn't know will not trouble him. Open the door, Miranda, and let us finish what we started.'

'Go away.'

'You are too late to send me away. It is unfair of you to tempt me so and then deny me what you were freely offering before.'

'I did not tempt you, you snake.'

'But I'm not a serpent, darling, and this is certainly no Eden. Can it be so wrong for two people to huddle together for warmth when freezing in a tomb such as this?'

'Yes. And if you do not know why, then you should leave this house immediately.'

'I'll come and go here in my own good time, your Grace, just as I always have. Unless you want to explain to my brother why you feel I must go. He will not take it well.'

'Then you must stay away from me, and I plan to keep as far away from you as possible.'

His voice was soft, and the hairs on the back of her neck rose. 'At first, perhaps. But soon you will see, my darling, that he does not want you the way that I do. And when you lie in bed at night unfulfilled, longing for the touch of a warm hand, you will find that my door will always be unlocked for you.' And he laughed. And she heard his light footsteps retreating down the hall.

She ran to her own door and checked it again, to find it still locked fast. She sank to the ground in front of it.

It was true, then. Just as she'd always feared. There was something wrong with her, that she could succumb so easily when temptation presented itself. She loved her father and she loved Cici. But living with them had not taught her the skills she needed to survive as a lady. They had not taught her circumspection or restraint. They certainly had not taught her chastity. Instead, Cici had taught her the truth of what happened between a man and a woman, and she'd listened to the stories eagerly. And remembered. And wanted to hear more. To know more.

Tonight she had been ready, and some of her was still ready, to open the door to a man who should be her brother. To let him take her and use her as he would. She'd opened her lips to him when she should never have allowed so much as a kiss on the hand.

And when the lord had kissed her... She remembered how she'd licked the berries from his fingers and felt the low flutter inside her that she felt whenever she thought of such things. She never should have let him stop her. When he spoke, she should not have answered. She should have run sooner. Perhaps she'd wanted to feel that hand on her breast. That and more.

She wanted to feel a man inside her, even if the man was not her husband. She knew it was wrong, but she wanted it all the same. And St John must have felt the weakness in her or he'd never have tried what he did.

She knelt by the door and offered a silent prayer for forgiveness and for strength. And that her husband would never find the wickedness in her amongst all the other lies in her faithless heart.

Chapter Fifteen

There was a hubbub in the courtyard. Miranda could hear it through the open window. She rose from where she'd slept, leaning against the door, and straightened the cramps out of her back. Through the wood she could hear more sounds, fainter, of servants rushing about trying to look busy.

Fire, perhaps?

No, someone would have come for her, even if they disliked her management.

There was a sharp rapping on the panel near her ear and she started back in surprise.

'Your Grace, are you awake? I'd come in, but the door is locked. It's time to dress. Quickly. His Grace, the duke, is back.'

Oh, God. He'd returned. Just as if he'd seen what had happened the night before and come to call her to account. She unbolted the door and Polly hurried into the room.

They threw together her morning dress and combed her hair, and she surveyed the results in the mirror. If possible, she looked even worse than when he had left her. The dress, which had been sorry when she'd arrived at the house, was looking even more tired. There were places where the thread-bare trim had given way, and Polly had made the best of it by removing the ruffles all together, but the blank lines looked almost worse. The fit was not loose, as it had been, but uncomfortably tight across the breasts.

Her hair. She ran a quick hand through the curls, remembering what St John had said about his brother's love of long flowing hair, remembering the portrait in the hall upstairs of the winsome blonde surrounded with the cloud of waves.

And her face was worst of all. She was tired, she knew, but not paler for it. She had the guilty flush of a woman just kissed, and there was nothing she could do to force the colour from her cheeks.

Miranda left the room and descended the stairs, trying to keep her head high.

Her husband, if that was still what he was, was in the entry way, shouting orders to servants and directing various bags, boxes and crates to their chosen destination. He shrugged out of his many-caped coat and passed it to the waiting valet. His boots were still dusty from the road, but the black suit he wore was immaculate, his shirt points were crisp and his cravat fell in a complicated knot and was held in place by a jet stick pin. He was every bit the smart town gentleman, rich and well bred. She felt a flash of pride and admiration, knowing that she was his.

He glanced up the stairs when she reached a point about halfway down, and stopped his instructions to the butler, following her with his eyes as she descended. She was again conscious of her sorry appearance. She looked like what she was: hardly good enough to claim a job as maid in the house that she was mistress of.

She reached the floor and stopped a few feet in front of him, dropping into her best curtsy. 'Welcome home, your Grace.' *And where have you been?* Her mind forced the words to remain unspoken, but they bubbled just below the surface.

'And a pleasant homecoming it is, to find you here to greet me.' His expression was appraising, but there was a slight smile on his lips, as if he approved of something. He gestured to the boxes surrounding him. 'I seem to have arrived at the same time as some purchases of yours. They were waiting at the inn and I had them brought along. Have you used the last two weeks to spend my money?'

She blushed. It was not the first impression she'd wished to give her new husband, one of profligate spending while his back was turned. She'd hoped that the new draperies would be up, the paper hung and the debts hidden in the accounts. Men seldom noticed improvements, once they were in place, and the changes would not have been drastic. An enormous pile of boxes, however, made it all look worse than it was.

'I can explain,' she assured him.

'Then let us retire to the study, and you may explain.' He strode ahead of her, leaving the boxes behind them. Once in the room, he sat at the desk and began going through the stack of mail that had accumulated in his absence.

She stood in silence, in front of him, waiting for an opportunity to begin.

'Well?' He addressed her without looking up.

'The boxes in the hall…'

'Are no doubt filled with some frippery which you do not need to explain to me.'

'Are filled with curtains and paper for the dining room,' she corrected, with a glare. 'When we attempted to clean the room, the velvet shredded as we touched it. And I understand the value of the silk on the walls, but it was so stained under the grime that it was beyond redemption. I've made no great change in the colour or style of the room, but once the new purchases are installed, I'm sure you will appreciate the difference.'

'You attempted to clean the dining room,' he repeated.

'Of course. It needed doing. I have not touched any of your private rooms—' *as yet*, she thought, glancing at a particularly noxious spider's web in the corner '—but felt the common areas of the house could stand a thorough scrubbing.'

'Come here,' he commanded, and she stepped closer. He reached out and took her hands, turning them palm up and running a finger along the softening calluses. 'I trust you were not carrying out this work all by yourself.'

'You have servants, your Grace, although I found it necessary to find some extra help from the village. I'm sure that it is only a temporary expense.'

'And what did the housekeeper think of your plans?'

And here is where he'll speak his mind, she thought grimly. 'She had very little to say after I sacked her. The new housekeeper was most agreeable to change.'

'Sacked her?' he repeated.

'Um, yes. She did not prove willing, and I felt that there was no going on if I was to remain here.'

She thought she saw the barest flicker of a smile before he went on. 'So you've spent several hundred pounds on new hangings and sacked the housekeeper. Is there anything else?'

There was a delicate cough, which announced the presence of Wilkins the butler.

'Not now, Wilkins, I'm speaking with my wife.'

'No, I suppose this would be as good a time as any to speak with Wilkins.' She was emboldened, having survived so far without incident. 'For I'm sure he'd like to speak with you. I've not sacked him, yet,' she added, 'since he is an old family retainer, and I thought that it might be better if you handled things.'

His eyebrow arched. He was unaccustomed at being told by anyone that it was his job to 'handle' anything.

'Wilkins has been unhappy of late, and this unhappiness has led to an unfortunate dependence on your wine cellar and the brandy decanter. I have not calculated how much you are losing, but the amount is considerable and it's affecting his ability to complete his duties.'

'Is this true, Wilkins?'

Wilkins must have hoped to come and plead his case before the duke had had a chance to talk to his mad new wife, and was at a loss as to how to continue.

'Things have been somewhat better this last week, and I think I've found a solution,' she hurried on.

'Oh, really?'

'I've been looking at the household expense books, which is why I got the idea for the new curtains. Your mother did not—your mother was—' She hunted for words that would express the truth without speaking ill of the dead. 'Although the servants are devoted to your mother's memory, your mother had not adjusted their salaries in several years.

'The rate of pay here, from the butler to the scullery maids, is much lower than what I'm accustomed to seeing.' She should know, she thought, since she was intimately familiar with the pay of a servant.

'Are you seriously recommending that we reward drunkenness and theft with a rise in salary?'

Wilkins looked as though he'd rather die on the spot than suggest such a thing.

'Yes, I am,' she continued. 'When people are forced to do menial tasks for an ungrateful master, they find ways to take back some of their own. They steal; they shirk their duties; they skim from the budget, short-change the grocer and water the wine. I know that your estate must be profitable and can afford a significant increase in the household budget. At the moment, your servants are robbing you blind and the house is a shambles.'

He stared up at her. 'Plain speaking, madam.'

'I speak the truth. The housekeeper is gone because she bought inferior cuts of meat, doctored the books and kept the difference. The staff is in turmoil, but at least dinner will be edible. A rise in pay will smooth the ruffled feathers below stairs, prove that I have the ear of my husband in these matters, and allow me to get the house in order.'

'And what of Wilkins?'

Wilkins's lower lip twitched, which was the closest she'd seen to a butler cringing in terror.

'If he can shake himself of the need to pilfer the cellars, he is welcome to return to his post.'

'Wilkins, does this meet with your satisfaction?'

'Yes, your Grace.'

'Very well, then. And, before you go, see to the money that her Grace suggested. Five per cent.'

She gave a covert, palm-raised gesture.

He glanced at her. 'Ten per cent, all around. And let it be known that her Grace is to thank for the change in situation.'

'Yes, sir.' He evaporated, leaving them alone.

'Well, if that will be all, your Grace…' She made to follow the butler out of the door.

'No, it will not.'

She turned back, feeling the dread creeping down her back.

His expression was impassive. 'You seem to have been busy, these last two weeks.'

'Well, yes. But I saw that there was much that needed doing.'

'And your situation here, does it meet with your satisfaction?'

His eyes were cold and grey and staring into her.

'My situation?'

'When we spoke before I left for London, you seemed somewhat less than happy with our marriage. You expressed a desire to return home. I take it this is no longer the case.'

She curtsied before him and dropped her eyes to the ground. 'It was a childish and hysterical fit of nerves, your Grace. It will not be repeated. You honour me by marrying me and I am grateful and intend to return that honour as a faithful and submissive wife.'

She thought for a moment that she heard a derisive snort at the last words, but when she looked up his face was as stern as ever.

'Very well. And I notice, while I was gone, that you felt free to spend my money with abandon.'

Was he as clutch-pursed as his mother? She dropped her eyes to the ground again. 'You left no specific instructions of how I was to go on. I thought it best to take control of the household as quickly as possible. I am sorry if the expenditures were more than you intended.'

'In the future, please let me see any receipts over a hundred pounds, but, if you continue the way you have begun, I see no reason not to accede to your judgment in household matters.'

'Thank you, your Grace. And now, if you'll excuse me?'

'Of course.'

She turned and fled, but as she reached the door he said softly, 'Miranda.'

'Yes?'

'Your hair.'

Her hand flew to the forgotten curls at her ears.

'It is most becoming.'

Despite herself, she smiled. 'Thank you, your Grace.' And she fled to the safety of her room.

Most curious, she thought. Most curious indeed. Not a word of explanation as to where he'd been or what he'd been doing. He had said London, but that was all. And she'd lacked the nerve to ask. When she'd arrived, he'd claimed to be a rake. Perhaps there was a demi-rep waiting in a rented house somewhere, wearing silk and jewels and smiling in satisfaction at two weeks spent with Miranda's solemn husband.

While she'd been working her back to near breaking, he'd no doubt been enjoying the pleasures of the city and thinking himself well away from this hated house and its new encumbrance. She pushed against the door to her room and it resisted.

'Oh, your Grace, just a moment, let me clear your things out from in front of the door.'

Her things? She peeked her head around the crack in the door, and started in surprise.

'Isn't it wonderful? His Grace found your trunks. They

were not lost after all. And so many beautiful things you have, ma'am. You'll no doubt want to be changing out of that dress you're wearing, into something more appropriate for luncheon.'

'No.' She wrapped her arms around her body, as though afraid that Polly would snatch the hated dress off her body.

Polly was looking at her as though she were mad.

'I mean, I don't want to change until we have a chance to unpack.' *And until I can figure out to whom these clothes belong*, she thought miserably. The tags on the trunks were clearly marked for her. The directions were plain enough. Of course, they were marked with her title and her married name. Perhaps Marcus had found some woman's unlabelled luggage and assumed that it must belong to her.

Unlikely, she thought, examining the contents. The clothing was new; some of the dresses still had the basting stitches in the hems. It was a rushed job that the seamstresses could barely finish.

She picked up a gold silk slipper with diamanté clips and tried it on her foot. It was very comfortable. She held the gown that matched it against her body and felt the hem brushing correctly at her feet.

'Do you like them?' Her husband was lounging against the doorframe between their rooms, and she noticed, for the first time, the resemblance between the brothers. His eyes followed her, hungry, and his smile was pure devilment. As though he'd entered the room without crossing the threshold and laid a hand against her skin.

She stared at him without answering and Polly piped up, 'Oh really, your Grace, they are the most splendid things. You'll have every eye in the county on you when you walk out in this.' She was swishing an apple-green day dress in front of her and listening to the crisp ruffles scrape against each other.

'Glad they meet your approval, Polly. Run along now, and let me have a word with my wife.'

The maid dropped a curtsy and disappeared with a giggle.

Her husband crossed the threshold and moved towards her, sitting on her bed, looking even more masculine when surrounded by frills. 'I trust you'll be more comfortable,' he said cryptically, 'now that your things have arrived.'

She spun to face him. 'They're not my things, and you know it full well.'

He replied, 'Of course they are yours. The trunks are labelled, and, if you notice, the tags in the gowns bear your name. Madame Souette in Bond Street. A very fine dressmaker and milliner.' He touched the silk of a bodice. 'You have exquisite taste.'

'Is this what you've been doing for the last two weeks?' she snapped. 'Playing dolls at a dressmaker?'

'Of course not. I left general instructions and she filled the order. It is hardly necessary for me to oversee every aspect of your wardrobe.'

'I did not ask you to oversee any part of it.'

'But clearly someone must. I notice, although you ran up considerable expenditures for household items and furnishings, and have insisted that I compensate even the lowliest scullery maid, you are wearing the same tired frock that you wore on the day we married.' He walked around her in close scrutiny. 'Although your hair is a vast improvement, and you no longer look as pinched and haggard. I could almost say that there are roses in your cheeks this morning. Country air must be agreeing with you.'

She could feel the guilty flush on her face grow even more pronounced. 'So you took your purse to London and brought me back a wardrobe. And now what do you expect of me?'

He leaned close and, as she pulled away her hand, brushed a collection of dainty lingerie. And she knew what he expected, what he would demand, what it would be his right to take when he chose.

He leaned closer and he whispered into her ear, 'I expect you to say, "Thank you for the lovely clothing".'

'Thank you, your Grace,' she parroted back.

He sighed. 'Your gratitude overwhelms me. Try again. And this time, and in future, when you address me, I expect to hear my Christian name. I will have no more curtsying, no scraping and bowing like a servant before me. It pleases me to be able to look into your eyes when you speak to me.' He twisted a curl between his fingers and she pulled away from him and glared into his eyes.

'Thank you, Marcus, for the lovely dresses. And now, if you'll excuse me?' She gestured towards the door.

'I'm dismissed, am I? Madam, I'm accustomed to my gifts being greeted with more enthusiasm. To win such mean thanks and a dismissal for a room full of presents? I've had women collapse, shrieking in joy for mere baubles…'

'Your mistresses, perhaps, are easily swayed by any attention you give them. And if you are foolish enough to expect such immodest and mercenary displays, then perhaps you should return to them. But I am your wife and should not have to fall prostrate in ecstasy whenever you deign to bless me with your company.'

He exploded in an oath and threw the shoe he'd been holding to the floor. 'No, of course not. Why would I expect that my wife might be the least bit glad to see me? Why would I expect a sincere welcome in my own house? Toadying to my title—well, of course I'll be allowed that. But no offer of warmth or friendship is to be unpunished. Very well, then, let us get on as you would choose. As your husband and a duke, I order you to burn every stitch of clothing you brought with you to this house and wear the things I've purchased for you or, so help me, I'll lock you in your room. Good day, madam.' He strode past her through the adjoining door and slammed it so hard that the pictures on the walls swayed. A few seconds later, she heard him slam the door to his room as well, and stride down the hall, no doubt looking for other doors to slam.

She sat on the bed, surrounded by silks and ribbons and numb with shock. The interview in the study had gone so well, and she'd been lulled into a vision of what she'd thought their relationship might be. Passionless, perhaps, but they would deal well with each other. And if he felt the need to jaunt off to London on their wedding night, without a word of explanation, leaving her alone to fight off the lecherous advances of his brother, and then to reappear without warning, it was no concern of hers. Hers would be the running of the household, his the running of the lands. They'd hardly see each other. Except at night, when…

She got up off the bed and sat in a chair.

And if none of it mattered to her, why had she just banished him from the bedroom and for bringing her gifts?

Because he'd ordered her to do things. First he'd ordered her not to be subservient; then he'd continued to order her to burn her clothes.

Which were ill-fitting rags. That she hated.

'Your Grace?' Polly's head poked around the door of the bedroom. She'd no doubt heard the end of the exchange, as had people in the neighbouring villages. The last door slam was probably strong enough to frighten wildlife in adjoining counties.

'Yes, Polly?' She succeeded in keeping the tremor out of her voice when she spoke.

'May I get on with the unpacking now?'

She smiled with more confidence than she felt. 'Yes, Polly. That would be most helpful.'

'And can I lay out a dress for your Grace, for luncheon? The green one, perhaps?'

Polly liked the green one. She could tell. But after the storm she'd just witnessed, it would serve him right if she showed up at the luncheon table wearing the same dress she had on. And let him rage on and storm out of luncheon, too. He could go without eating for all she cared and see if it improved his temper any. She raised a hand to her curls, wishing they'd grow long again, just out of spite.

Rip.

The sleeve of her dress, already weakened from turning and years of hard labour, finally gave up the ghost, and she felt the draft as her elbow poked through the unmendable hole.

'All right, Polly. The green one. And burn this.'

He stared towards her room through the ceiling of his study, overcome with frustration. How was he to manage with such a woman when she provoked him at every turn? He'd thought she would have at least something in common with Bethany and all the other women of his acquaintance, that the clothing would send her into fits of feminine joy. He could then lay the prize of her father's safety at her feet, and have a purring kitten of contentment for the rest of his life.

He had not expected to see the first part of the offering viewed with such suspicion, and the gift of his house, his lands, and his title, 'and all his worldly goods endow' treated as a great sacrifice that she must endure.

He shuddered to think what it would be like when they got to the part of the vow that required him with his body her to worship. If she held her current attitude, it would be an uncomfortable experience.

And telling her now that he knew all and her father would visit at Christmas might be the most effective way to bring her quickly to heel, but not the most satisfying. She was a proud woman, the proudest he had ever met, despite the fact that she had nothing but a shred of honour. She would not be grateful that she no longer kept a secret; she would be shamed. And when she found out that he had helped her, she would go to his bed quietly as a hostage to her father's continued safety.

And why must it be that way? Had he grown so repellent in his years away that no one could want him? Did debauchery show in his face? Were sins of pride and weakness so obvious in his character that no honest woman, no matter how desperate, could stand to be bedded by him?

And he had found an honest woman, hadn't he? Willing to sacrifice blindly to fulfil her father's dream. How well he could appreciate the burden of family obligation. They were not unalike and, once she realised it, they would do well together.

But, as usual, he'd been a ham-handed husband, thinking

that with a show of wealth, things could be done quickly. She was accustomed to simplicity and hard work, and he had offered her splendour. Of course she was uncomfortable. She seemed at her best when she was active. No china-doll duchess for him. Not this time. He must find work suited to her station and ability.

He smiled. And, once she was happy, certain other, more pleasurable tasks could be slipped into her schedule at the end of the day and accomplished with a minimum of fuss. If he could get her to come to his bed with a light heart, then he could share the information about her father, and cement the relationship without making her an obliged slave to his desires.

Chapter Sixteen

She sat alone at the luncheon table with cold salmon and trepidation. She was being punished, she suspected, for the outburst in the bedroom.

And then she heard the distant sound of doors opening, and commotion in the hall. She was beginning to suspect that, wherever he went, a cloud of noise and action swirled around the duke.

He strode into the dining room and took his place at the head of the table, barely noticing her, as footmen rushed forward to fill his plate and glasses. He fell to eating, without saying a word, but stopped after a few bites, to look up at her. His expression held no cloud of memory of his earlier outburst.

'This salmon is uncommonly good. Did you sack the cook as well?'

'No. I merely oversaw the purchasing of the foodstuffs. You'll find, now that the food that is ordered actually makes it to the table, the quality of the meals has improved.'

'And will continue to improve, after the cook hears of the increase in pay?'

'I believe she has already heard, your Grace. Marcus,' she corrected. 'Today's luncheon is noticeably better than yesterday's supper.'

He shrugged and took another bite. 'If the trend continues, I'll have to consider eating supper at home.'

'If there are dishes that might tempt you to dine here, please inform me, so that I can provide them.'

The fork stopped, midway to his mouth, and he examined her before answering. Then he took a slow sip of wine. 'Of course. If there is anything that might tempt me to remain home, you'll be the first to know.'

He continued to stare over his fork at her until she blushed from the attention.

Then he went on. 'That dress is most becoming on you. It brings out the colour in your cheeks.'

'Thank you. Marcus,' she added with difficulty.

The conversation died.

She chewed in silence. It was going to get awfully monotonous if the course of every meal involved a remark on the food, a remark on her dress, and silence. What did she talk about, when in the bosom of the family? What they'd done. What they were planning to do.

And if she asked Marcus where he'd been for two weeks? He could tell her, and she might not like the answer, or the silence could grow even deeper.

'Do you have plans this afternoon, Marcus?'

He looked over the fork again. 'Why? Do you have a suggestion?'

It was an innuendo, she suspected. She chose to ignore it. 'No, Marcus. Only table talk. You needn't answer, if you don't wish to.'

They ate in silence for another bite.

'I was thinking,' he said at last, 'of visiting some of the outlying farms.'

She nodded and took another bite.

'You may accompany me. If you wish, that is. I mean, the tenants might think it quite an honour to receive a visit from the duchess. It's something they've come not to expect, in the years my mother held the title.' He contemplated his wine. 'Of course, if you do not wish…'

'Oh, no. I mean, of course I'd like to ride with you.' If only the land were small enough to walk. Of course, the house was barely small enough to navigate with walking. 'I'm sure it will be very interesting.'

When I fall off my horse again and you have to carry me home.

He nodded in approval. 'Very good, then. I will meet you by the stables in half an hour.' He tossed his napkin on to his plate and rose, looking down at her with the very slightest of smiles. 'Dress appropriately.'

She stood before the stables thirty-five minutes later, cursing all men who thought it was easy to run up the stairs and slip into a riding habit, as though it were a pair of gloves, and then rush outside and down to the stables in less than an hour. And all so she could get up on some plaguey beast with madness in its eye and the devil in its heart…

She took a deep, steadying breath. She must learn not to think of this as an imposition, but as part of her duties as the duchess. Marcus was right. If the tenants had not seen the lady of the house in some thirty years, it was important that she set things straight. She might not have to make too many more visits, until her riding improved.

She turned in surprise to see the duke not on a fine stallion, but on top of a most sensible carriage.

'I apologise,' he said, 'for not meeting you at the front of the house, but there were things I wished to see to here.' He glanced down at the habit. 'I've had them harness the barouche, but if you would prefer to ride…'

'Oh, no,' she interrupted. 'Really. This is much better.'

He nodded. 'Some men would say otherwise, that life's greatest joy is a spirited mount and the space to run him. But I've always thought that horses are a necessary evil and better managed when they have a desire to pull and not take fences at the gallop.'

Then why had she spent an afternoon sitting on a pillow with her ankle elevated? She made a mental note to fetch St John a swift kick for it, and several other things when she saw him next. She allowed the groom to help her up into the seat beside her husband and he coaxed the team to life.

He set off at a brisk pace down the road and the team responded to his commands. After a while he fell into easy commentary on the passing sights and the names of the cottages they were driving by and she found herself listening with interest. When he was not raging about something, or staring at her with those stormy grey eyes, he was good company.

'And there is the tree where, it is said, they hanged Blackjack Brody the highwayman,' he said, pointing to the old oak on their left.

'I know,' she replied. 'At least, that is what St John said, when he took me riding last week.'

He tightened on the reins, causing the horses to start and whinny, before he relaxed and regained control. 'St John was here, while I was gone?'

'Why, yes. He returned soon after you left.'

'I expect he did.' His voice was colder now than she had heard it before. 'I had no idea, madam, that I was boring you with a repetition of information that you'd heard before.'

'Oh, no. Really. What you have been telling me is of great interest, and not at all what I talked about with St John.'

She hoped that the colour was not rising in her cheeks to betray her. 'We discussed nothing of import, truly. Just idle chatter to pass the time.'

'I can imagine,' he replied in the same cold tone. 'In the future, Miranda, there will no doubt be other instances when I am called suddenly away from home. While I am gone from the house, I would prefer it if you did not entertain men in my absence.'

'But I thought, since he was your brother—'

'Perhaps I did not make myself clear. I do not wish you to entertain men when I am not here. My brother is a man, is he not?'

'Well, yes.' She resisted an urge to rub the back of her hand across her mouth, to clear it of any guilty traces of the kiss.

'Then he would be included. Do you have any problems with my request?'

Other than the fact that it was not a request, but an order? 'No, your Grace.'

He did not stop to correct the formality of her address. 'Good. Then we have an understanding.'

And the crushing silence fell again between them.

On the road ahead of them, a man was waving down the

carriage and he slowed and stopped. 'Master Marcus, thank the lord you come by.'

'Whoa. Steven, what is the matter?'

'Young Maggie. It's her time. And the women folk are visitin' elsewhere, but she's come early.'

'Maggie?' He was clearly searching his mind to attach a face to the name. 'Is with child?'

'Aye, Master Marcus, my granddaughter. Her husband is dead these six months and both her parents away, too. It's just me alone with her, and it's not goin' well at all.'

'Maggie already a widow? She was but a girl when I left. I've been away too long,' he muttered as he stepped down out of the carriage and helped his wife after him.

'But you're back now. Let us see what's to be done.'

From the tone of the screams, Miranda had a pretty good idea of how things were going before she was fully into the cottage.

'You see,' whispered Steven. 'She's been goin' on like this for some time and I don't know what to do.'

'Leave me alone, you old fool. There's naught for you to do now.'

The red-faced girl in the bed had managed the words on one breath, and followed them with a long full-volumed wail. 'Just a minute, Maggie, after I sort out the men, I'll be there to help you.' Miranda grabbed the duke and Steven by the arms and shoved them back out of the cottage, shutting the door behind them.

'And who the hell are you?' The volume was diminished, as Maggie reached a lull between contractions.

'My name is Miranda, Maggie, and I've been at the side of many birthing beds. Now, let's do what we can to make you more comfortable and then I'll have a look at things.'

In a few minutes, she broke away from the bedside to return to the men.

'If there's aught I can do to help,' muttered Steven, 'just say the word. I've been at many a foaling and a calving, and I'm right good with sheep, but I never seen or heard nothing like that before. Maggie was always such a meek and gentle girl. Not a cross word to anyone.'

'If cattle could talk,' she responded, 'I expect they'd be much the same way. Why don't you get up on the wagon, Steven, and his Grace will take you with him as he fetches the doctor.'

'Doctor? Surely we won't be needing…?'

'It would be best, just to be safe.' She gave him a gentle shove towards the carriage.

Her husband looked down at her and ran a worried hand through his hair. He was white about the lips, she noticed, and looking nervously towards the house. 'If it's difficult…will she…? Perhaps we'd better… My wife…' He reached out to touch her sleeve with an unsteady hand.

His wife. Miranda's heart swelled with pride at the words. 'I'll be all right.'

And she looked into his eyes, which were haunted with sadness, and realised that he was not with her, but in the past, at the side of a different birthing.

She gripped his arm and he focused again on her. 'You needn't be concerned. I've experience in these matters. She's already through the worst of it and it's simple from here, but it's Maggie's first. She doesn't need her grandfather, or a special visit from the duke to ease her labour. She needs her women around her. If you can't find those, then go to fetch the doctor, but take your sweet time in doing it. Just keep out of the way for a while and let nature do the rest.' She glanced at Steven. 'Sheep, indeed.' And she went back into the cottage and slammed the door as Maggie began a fresh round of curses.

Marcus looked after her in stunned relief. Of all the situations he was least able to deal with… He couldn't bring himself to cross the threshold of the cottage again, much less be of use when he got there. And she seemed so unafraid of the outcome. Didn't she know how it would be? He shook his head to clear the dots dancing before his eyes. 'Come on, Steven. Let's see if we can find your daughter, shall we?'

'Aye, Master Marcus. But who's the great lady we left with young Maggie?'

'I have no idea,' he muttered.

'Eh?'

'It's my new duchess, Steven.'

'Your mother, is it?'

He sighed. Steven sometimes got confused about things. No wonder Maggie had been screaming. 'No, Steven. I'm duke now; remember? And the fine lady with Maggie is my wife.'

'Ah, yes. Congratulations, your Grace. But I thought the Lady Bethany was with child as well.'

He was catching up, but still not in the present. 'Not Bethany. That was ten years ago. The Lady Bethany died…' the air became thick and caught in his throat '…died in childbirth.'

In his mind, he could still hear the screaming. They'd sent him away from the bedroom, but the sight of her, struggling for breath and screaming, had followed him as he wandered through the house. And the screams had echoed in the distance, as he sat on the stairs. He'd prayed, 'Let it be over. Dear God, let it end. I can't do this. I can't. There must be a way out.'

Then the screams had stopped. He'd listened for the cry of the child, but none had come. And he'd gone to the room. But there'd been so much blood. Too much blood.

'Your Grace?'

He snapped back to attention. His hands were slick with sweat on the reins, and he was urging the horses. He relaxed his grip. 'Where is it we're going, Steven? To find Maggie's mother?'

She'd been at a neighbouring farm, and had gathered her things and run for the wagon she'd come in. Then he'd driven on to the inn with Steven, and sunk down at a table in grateful silence, with ale in front of him, and listened to Steven brag to the other men there about the great lady who had come to see his granddaughter.

How long should they wait? For Bethany, it had been many hours. All day. And it was late in the evening when…

He shook his head to clear the image. He was a fool to attempt marriage again. And to wander into one as ill omened as the last.

Perhaps the results would be different, this time. By next year, he could be holding his son. With Miranda, smiling down at him as he did so. He tried to imagine her, straining and afraid, as Bethany had been, but could see only that confident chin come up, defiant of the pain. She'd swear like Maggie had done and she'd never let death take her or their child.

'Steven, are you ready to go back to your house, man?'

They pulled the carriage up in front of the cottage as the sun was setting, and Steven's daughter rushed into the yard to meet them.

'Oh, your Grace, thank you for bringing your wife to us.' She'd dropped into a curtsy.

'It was luck that we happened along when we did,' he mumbled, not sure what he'd done to receive the thanks, other than running from the problem as fast as he could.

'With your permission, Maggie would like to name the boy Marcus, in your honour.'

'Thank you…' He struggled to remember her name. 'Thank you, Jane. But surely the father…'

'The father run off, the fornicating bastard,' said the ringing voice of the meek and gentle Maggie. 'And deserves no credit since he had the pleasure and I'll have the work.'

'Would you like to come in, your Grace, and see the little one?'

He nodded cautiously, and was led into the freshly scrubbed room to see the mother and infant.

'My wife?' He looked around.

'Is out back, your Grace. Washing.'

'Here, your Grace.' She'd stepped beside him, without his noticing. 'It went well,' she murmured. 'No problems. You needn't have worried. There's screaming and mess, but these things usually sort themselves out just fine.'

He glanced down at her. She'd noticed, before, when he couldn't stay. Her face was bland, unaccusing. Matter of fact, about an area where she obviously knew more than he.

'Fine. Let us go, then, and leave these people to themselves.'

They walked back to the carriage, followed by many thanks and offers of a smoked ham and some preserves delivered to the kitchen of the great house, and were on their way.

He looked over at her, fading next to him in the gloom. 'Thank you for assisting them.'

'It is my duty, is it not, to help those in need?'

'But many women would have shirked it. Or been unable. Or worse, useless.'

She shrugged. 'I'm sure there are many things that the last duchess could do that I'll have no skill at.'

'Like embroidery and watercolours?'

She smiled.

'My late wife had a lovely singing voice, and a beautiful face. I thought, at the time, it was enough. But they meant nothing in the end.'

'I sing as well as any crow.'

'But you are a most handsome woman.'

'Not the great beauty that she was,' Miranda pointed out.

'Few are,' he replied. 'And she had the good sense to die young, so as not to spoil the effect with age.'

She started next to him, and then kept still.

'My mother was also a great beauty, but with a heart like a block of ice and a tongue like a razor.'

'I doubt, if she'd lived, that she would have approved of me,' Miranda muttered.

'Then we would have had much in common, for she never approved of me, either. On the whole, she preferred St John, who favoured her. I was too much like my father.'

'You are very unlike your brother,' she said softly. 'In many ways.'

'I have a foul temper and a sour disposition,' he stated. 'And have been told frequently that St John is more pleasant company.'

'He has not the worries that you do, nor the responsibilities.'

'Responsibilities I have been avoiding for ten years,' he corrected. 'These people are still strangers to me. I stayed away too long, and now there is much to be done.'

'I think it is best not to focus on the mistakes of the past,' she remarked, 'but to continue as you mean to go.'

They'd arrived at the front of the house and he helped her down, reaching to circle her with his arms, but she slipped away.

'Careful, your Grace. I do not want to ruin your suit.'

'What?'

'Childbirth, at its best, is a messy business. I've already ruined the lovely habit you've given me.'

He looked down, and noticed, for the first time, the fresh bloodstains on her dress and jacket. And, despite himself, he pulled away from her. He steadied himself, and moved closer, but not before she'd noticed his flinch.

She touched him on the arm. 'I am very tired, although I was not the one doing the work. And I'm sure, after your journey, and this day…'

'Yes,' he agreed. 'We are both very tired. But I look forward to tomorrow.'

'As do I. It has been a most interesting and informative afternoon.'

'Indeed,' he said to her back as she preceded him up the stairs to their rooms.

Chapter Seventeen

Strange, she thought, how much things could change in a day. Polly was hooking her into one of her many new gowns, a sprigged muslin day dress, and she was preparing to meet her husband for breakfast. A husband who hadn't shouted at her in almost twenty-four hours, she thought with a smile.

She'd inquired about the whereabouts of her brother-in-law, and been told that he'd left as soon as his brother arrived. 'Not unlike him,' admitted Polly. 'He and his Grace don't get on the best, and he tends to up and disappear on a regular basis no matter the location of the duke. He was about due if you ask me.'

Relief flooded through her. There was enough to worry about, without fending off the unwanted attentions of St John.

She quizzed herself. Had they been unwanted?

She did not wish to dishonour her husband, she told herself.

But his conversation had been pleasant. And the touches, however brief, had been exciting and she'd longed for more after each meeting.

And he'd given her more each time, she reminded herself.

A little and a little and a little, like a goose walking to the chopping block by following a trail of grain. St John was not as innocent as he appeared. And she'd ended, barricaded in her own room while he'd laughed and teased from the corridor. God knew how many servants had seen. Polly certainly, judging by the worried look she'd shown when Miranda had asked after the young lord. And the relief that was obvious when Miranda had cautioned her to take extra care with her hair, so that she could look her best for breakfast with her husband. She'd better be on her guard, then, lest she sink the marriage before it got out of port.

Marcus was dividing his attention between a plate of kippers and the morning's post, when the door opened and his new wife entered the room. He caught his breath at the sight of her. Surely a new dress and a good night's sleep could not work such magic. Her gown was apricot and set off her skin. He let his eyes trail from her face to the curve of her neck and lower, admiring the way her flush disappeared into the neckline of her dress. Images of ripe fruit flooded his mind. Sweet and succulent. Ready to touch and to taste.

He shook his head and smiled at her, wondering if she noticed his discomposure. 'Good morning, Miranda,' he said, helping her to her chair.

'Good morning, y—Marcus.' She'd caught herself before the formality slipped out.

'What are your plans today?'

She hesitated. 'I thought I would supervise the hanging of the silk in the dining room and make a list, for your approval, of other projects that need doing.'

'Very good.' But the plan annoyed him, and he realised

he'd hoped to find her idle. 'And tell me, my dear, what room is next on your schedule?'

She looked away. 'The bedrooms.'

'Perhaps we could look at them together.' There. That must be plain enough.

Her head dipped still lower. 'If we must.'

'Must?' He bit his tongue against the outburst that was forming in his mind. Now, of all times, he must not lose his temper. 'Miranda, I do not wish for you to feel that you *must* do anything to please me. As yet, you barely know me. If it would be easier if we postponed…'

'For just a few days. A week, perhaps?' she said.

He nodded, forcing the images of ripe peaches far from his mind.

And she continued, 'Of course, I understand if this is not convenient for you… I know that you must have certain…needs,' she almost whispered the word. 'If you might wish to visit your mistress…I would not blame you for it.'

He choked on his tea. 'There are a few things we need to make clear, lady wife. Firstly, I do not wish you to discuss such things at all, but, if you must, you will not do so over the breakfast table. Secondly, if and when I seek to visit my "mistress" I will not ask, or for that matter, need your permission to do so. Thirdly, you should not even know of such things, and, if you do, I'll thank you to keep the information to yourself. The last thing I want to do is discuss "my needs" with my wife.' The last seemed to him so ridiculous a statement that he was momentarily struck dumb. No wonder, with an attitude like that, he'd sought to avoid the married state for so long. He looked at her, expecting tears at his outburst, or a knowing laugh, but was met instead with a militant glare.

He could feel the temper rising within him again and started a fresh harangue.

'Visit my mistress? My God, woman, what gave you such a crack-brained notion?' Probably her own father. 'You think I can't control my animal lust for a few days without seeking release? Go to my mistress? And where am I keeping this woman, since you seem to know so much about her?'

'I thought, when you went to London...'

'Business,' he snapped. 'I went on business. That is all you need to know, and probably more than you would understand.'

'A vague answer, your Grace.'

He threw his hands into the air and bit his tongue. Now was not the time to announce to her, in a towering rage, that he knew all about her past. 'I return with a carriage full of gifts for you, and still you are not satisfied?'

'It makes me ask myself why a man with a clear conscience would waste the time on such extravagances.'

He looked into her eyes and saw something unrecognisable. And then it hit him. Jealousy. Certainly not an emotion he'd seen in his first wife. When he'd finally turned in desperation to a mistress, she'd been relieved, not jealous. But he recognised the glint in his wife's dark eyes from his own face in the mirror.

He paused, savouring the novelty of it and trying not to smile in triumph. She was not ready for the bedroom, but she already cared where he'd been and who he'd been with. Cared enough to reject his gifts yesterday and to press him for details today.

He walked slowly towards her and stood next to her chair. And she pretended interest in her breakfast, which had grown cold on the plate.

'I can think of many reasons why a man might buy gifts for his wife. As a reward, perhaps, for a memorable wedding night.'

She flushed.

'It was certainly memorable, but not deserving of reward, I think.'

She was hanging her head now, in embarrassment. But her lip still jutted out in a pout.

'As a sop to a guilty conscience. Hmmm. The idea certainly has possibilities. After spending two weeks in the arms of another woman, what kind of trifles would I bring to silence my new wife?' Now he saw another emotion on her face. Curiosity. And a heat rising that had nothing to do with embarrassment. 'It would be a shame to purchase one set of expensive gowns for the mistress, and be required to bring still more home for the wife. Perhaps since they were never to meet, it might be easiest to duplicate the wardrobes, and have the dressmaker make the same styles, but in two sizes. But one does become jaded, after a while, of falling to sleep spent on the pillow of perfumed breasts spilling from an indecent décolletage, and when it is time to come home, one wants one's wife properly attired. The sight of a woman wearing a corset, after so much time spent with the sort of woman that doesn't bother with stays is rather refreshing.'

She was watching him intently now; the fork paused halfway to her mouth.

'I would certainly buy a collection of decently plain fabrics for my wife. None of this nonsense with damped petticoats and sheer gowns. Of course,' he drawled absently, 'the sight of rouged nipples displayed behind transparent gauze is rather intriguing the first time one sees it, but annoying in practice.'

He cupped a hand over an imaginary breast. 'The rouge gets everywhere and stains the fingers. And the teeth, of course.'

She dropped her fork with a quick intake of breath.

'If I had spent the week with a mistress, I would, no doubt, bring you a most sensible wardrobe, well suited to your tastes, I'm sure. High necklines. Fabrics that don't show wear. And a bracelet, perhaps.'

He looked seriously into her eyes. 'But, as I do not, at this time, have a mistress, or plans to acquire one, I contented myself with bringing the silks and satins home to my wife, since I noticed on leaving that she was most sorely in need of clothes.'

Her mouth set in a prim line, disapproving of the joke he'd played. And then it changed to wonder as the words sunk in. And anger again, although he was not sure it was for him. Strange woman, his new wife. He leaned close to her and she turned her head away, refusing to meet his eyes. He let an idle hand drop to rest at the back of her chair, brushing the skin of her throat as he did so. And then he leaned low over her, so that his mouth nearly touched her ear.

'I seem to have the selfish and foolish desire to know that my wife is dressed from head to foot in clothing that I have given her.' His voice went husky. 'And I suspect it would give me equal pleasure to see those clothes removed at the end of the day. If that day is a week from now, or a year, I will wait for it.'

He could feel the breath catch in her throat, and wondered what her response would be if he leaned forward another inch and caught her earlobe in his teeth.

And, as if she'd read the thought in his mind, her breath escaped in a shuddering gasp.

He leaned away from her and laid a hand on her shoulder.

'Does it surprise you to think that I might want to see you

happy, Miranda? And that I might look forward to knowing you better?'

'I never thought…'

'Evidently. What did you think that marriage would be like? What did you expect when you came here?'

She thought for a moment and said carefully, 'I tried very hard not to expect anything.'

'You had no hopes? No dreams? No girlish fantasies?'

'I suppose…' She paused and began again. 'I left girlish fantasies behind long ago. It was quite plain that I would marry the man who would have me and make the best of it in any case. One can aim high, hoping to hit a star, and miss the target entirely.'

'But if one aims too low?' he asked.

'At least one does not lose the arrow. It seemed foolish to hope for a particular type of husband, when I would be saying yes to the man who offered, regardless of his features, his wealth or his personality.'

He laughed and she looked up at him, worried.

'If you were willing to settle for anyone, then I cannot be too great a disappointment.'

'A surprise, perhaps. But not a disappointment. And you, Marcus? Did you give thought to the sort of woman you might marry?' Her gaze was level, but tinged with apprehension. 'You say you have no mistress—'

'Because I have none.' He tried to keep the reproof out of his voice.

'Was there anyone else? Had you any plans before I came here?' She hesitated. 'When we met, you told me yourself that you were a notorious rake. Why should I not take you at your own word?'

He looked levelly back at her. 'A man does not reach the age of five and thirty without knowing women. Of course there were others, but none recently and none I intended to take as wife. While it is true that I had no desire to marry you when you arrived, and I had done my best to avoid my mother's scheme, it does not mean that your arrival spoiled any immediate plans. My mother was right in one thing: it was time that I was settled. I married once for love. It is a thing best got out of one's system in youth. It did not end well. If this time I married for honour and for expediency, I cannot be faulted.'

Her back stiffened and she looked away from him. 'Expediency.' The word was harsh as she said it, and she paused. When she began again, her voice was controlled. 'Of course. And I will do my best to be your helpmeet in all things and be a fit wife to you.' Her gaze was riveted on the plate before her and she began cutting her kipper with more violence than necessary.

He reached across the table to her, touching her hand, and felt her flinch before the rigid control dropped into place again and her hand was still under his. 'I think you lie to me, Miranda. You had hopes, right enough, though you won't admit it. Is your heart promised elsewhere, or did you enter into the marriage freely?'

He stared at her, looking for any hesitance. 'Truth, madam. There is still time, you know, if you are drawn elsewhere.'

'Time?' She looked at him curiously.

He reached into his pocket. 'Here is the reason for my trip. When I was in London, I took pains to get the licence that our marriage lacked. For it to truly be legal…'

She leaned back in alarm. 'And all this time we were not truly wed.'

'In the eyes of God, certainly, Miranda. I swore to you before God. I do not give oath lightly. But, in the eyes of the law, our names must be on the paper for the union to be real. I wanted to know that you understood that, should you have wanted to, you could have demanded a settlement at least.

'It would have been impossible to obtain a licence so quickly unless I had been expecting you and arranged it in advance. And, considering the circumstances, I felt that it would be better to act quickly and smooth the legalities later.'

'And that is what you went to London to get?'

'It was not quite the way I'd planned, but it was better, was it not, to get the licence before coming to your chamber? And the two weeks alone has given you time to think. To decide if you might be happy here.'

'Happy?' She looked puzzled, as though the thought had never entered her head that she was entitled to happiness, and his heart tightened in his chest. 'Why should I not be happy, your Grace? You have honoured me with your name and—'

He waved his hand. 'And you mean to be a good and dutiful wife to me. Yes, yes. We've been through all that. You are succeeding admirably. But I do not want you to feel coerced or trapped into this union. I'm sure, should you wish to leave now that you have seen the way of things here, that there are other men—'

'There are no other men,' she said hurriedly and he looked sharply into her eyes. Was she afraid of something? Of revealing something that he was not supposed to know?

'I meant only,' he stated, 'that you are an attractive woman.' He sucked in his breath and said, with sincerity, 'A damn attractive woman. And should you not wish to sign the paper that will bind you irrevocably to me, there might be other suitors in your future.'

She thought for a moment before speaking. 'When I entered the chapel, I went intending to keep the promises I made. It would be wrong to break them now, because of a lack of paperwork. If you wish to keep me, I wish to stay.'

He tried not to feel disappointed at the way she spoke. She stressed loyalty, above all else, but there was nothing in her tone to make him believe that he could ever expect more of her.

'Very well,' he said. 'Let us go to my study and finish this.'

She followed him out of the room.

When they reached his desk he sat down before it and spread the licence on the blotter in front of him. Dipping a quill in the ink well, he signed with a flourish. Then he offered the chair to her.

She sat on the edge, looking for all the world like she expected him to throw her bodily out of it, and took the quill in a shaking hand and wrote her name.

He scattered sand over the ink and they watched the licence dry.

'There. It is done. I will send it to the vicar, so that he may sign it as well.'

She sighed in what he hoped was relief.

He reached into his pocket. 'In the hurry, I forgot. There was an additional purchase I made while in London. I needed to correct an oversight.' He pulled the small square box from his pocket. 'In the hurry of the ceremony, I never thought to find you a proper ring. There must be many in the house, my mother's jewel box is full to bursting.'

'Really. It was—is not necessary,' she said, but her eyes were downcast.

'It is,' he assured her. 'The job is not complete without the ring. And in London, I sought something that might remind me of you. Perhaps you will not like it. I will let you choose another, if you wish.' He pulled the tiny signet from the box, kissed it and reached for her trembling hand. 'In the chapel, I promised you everything. My house, my home, my land, and myself and this ring is a symbol of that.'

She stared down at it and said nothing.

'And, it will not slip off your finger if you relax enough to stop clenching your fists in my presence.'

She still stared at the ring, but now a tear gathered at the corner of her eye and trickled down her nose. Dear God, he had made a misstep. 'There were diamonds,' he said quickly. 'Pearls, perhaps. Or an opal. No. No opals. That would not be a lucky stone for a wedding ring, for they are said to steal the soul of the wearer.'

Her face tipped up towards him as the tear slipped the rest of the way off her chin and was quickly followed by another. 'It is the most perfect thing I have ever seen.' She was still crying, but her face lit with the first true smile he had seen from her. 'I will never remove it. Thank you.' Her hand caressed the ring as she spoke and she laid it against her cheek before bringing it down to stare at it again.

'And now, madam, if you wish to rest for the afternoon, I have work I must do.'

She looked around as if noticing for the first time that she occupied the chair in his study. 'Yes. I…I think I will go to my rooms. Thank you,' she said again and drifted out of the door.

He thought of the mountains of satin and ribbon that had

brought such a storm down on him yesterday and compared it with the simple ring on her finger and the smile on her face. And he shrugged. A most curious woman, his new wife.

Chapter Eighteen

An afternoon's rest had done wonders for her mood. Of course, discovering that St John had lied in nearly every conversation they'd had might have done something to ease her worries. Her husband had no mistress. And hated the silk in the dining room as well. He taken time to show her, before the footman removed it, the place where, as a boy, he'd made charcoal alterations to the anatomy of one of the shepherdesses and expressed some relief that the evidence would be permanently removed by the redecorating.

She touched a curl. And Marcus liked her hair. She glanced down at the ring on her finger and smiled again. He hadn't abandoned her at all, but had been thinking of her while in London. And he'd remembered the ring. It was a sentimental choice for a man she'd thought cared only for obedience and appearance. And he'd kissed it as he had the ring he put on her finger the day they were married.

She hid a blush. Perhaps it was foolish and courting disappointment to spin fancies about her husband's motives. They were all so practical and yet they seemed those of a lover. She remembered the feel of his breath against her face and felt a delicious shudder run through her body. Perhaps he had come to see more than anger when he looked at her, and forget the frustration of the trap she'd caught him in.

And she meant to keep it that way. The talk she was imagining, where she admitted how she had come to him, must wait for a very long time. There was no point in marching across the fragile bridge they were building between them, to give him information that he did not want to hear.

She walked out into the hall, went over to the banister and stared up at the cobweb hanging from the ceiling. The spider had lived here much longer than she had, and the fact irked her. And would live there longer still. It might take months before the staff finished the bedrooms and worked their way to the top of the house.

If she left it for the staff, she thought. The spot was almost reachable from the third floor hallway, if she leaned over the banister a bit. She walked up the stairs, forming a plan of attack. It would be dangerous to lean too far, of course. But she could gauge the distance. Perhaps, with a rag at the end of a broom, she could swipe at the thing and knock it down. Or send a footman.

She laid a hand on the rail and leaned forward. No, not quite. There was a low bench on the opposite wall. She pushed it across and stepped up. The height was right, but she would need the broom to do the job, and someone to steady her as she stood.

Suddenly an arm gripped her waist and dragged her back off the stool and into the hall.

'What the devil are you playing at?' Her husband stood

before her, all signs of the recent truce evaporating, as angry as she'd ever seen him.

She struggled out of his grasp. 'I was just trying to find a way to take care of the spider's web there in the corner.' She pointed.

He ignored her hand and grabbed her by the shoulders. 'Trying to break your neck, more like. Do you have no care for your safety?'

'What utter nonsense. I was in no danger.'

'You were standing on a bench three storeys above the ground.'

'And well back from the edge.'

'Trying to do work that is best left to the servants.'

'I am perfectly capable—' She stopped in mid-sentence.

'Of working below stairs? I do not recall hiring you as a maid. You are a duchess and would do well to act like one.'

'Then you would do well to treat me as one, your Grace, instead of shouting at me like a servant and manhandling me in the corridors.'

'Am I some lecherous beast, then? Will you tell me that the cobwebs hang because the maids are afraid to come upstairs?'

'I never—'

'Nor did I.'

'Your Grace,' she whispered, 'we are in a common hallway. Anyone may hear…'

'There is not much that would shock the servants here, Miranda. They know to hold their tongues and they will obey me to the letter, should I choose to give a command. For instance, should I insist that they lock you in your room to prevent any further foolishness on your part, I am certain I will have their co-operation. I expect you to go to your rooms and take off that damn apron and try to behave like the mistress of the house and not the housekeeper. You said you wished to rest, and I expect you to do so. Is that clear?'

'As crystal, your Grace.' She shrugged out from under his hands and stalked down the hall towards her room.

Marcus reached for the brandy decanter, and then withdrew his hand. Locked in his rooms and drinking during the middle of the day, again? If he made a habit of that, the current marriage really would remind him of the last.

As it was, seeing Miranda balancing near the banister where Bethany had so often threatened to hurl herself into space had unhinged him. Would it have been possible to make a bigger fool of himself in his new wife's eyes? He thought not.

Had he put words in her mouth, or did she suspect him of bothering the maids? Where had she got such an idea?

Probably from previous employers. No wonder her father had been so eager to get her married and away. No wonder she was afraid to come to his bed. And, when he'd announced that the help could keep his secrets, he'd implied that there were secrets to keep.

Which, of course, there were. He tried to remember how much of the help had been there during the reign of his first wife. They might have heard Bethany, as she raged at him in the halls. And the maids had run from him then, convinced that the sweet duchess spoke the truth.

His mother, when she'd realised the volatility of the union, had removed to London, and let the rumours rage around him.

He ran a hand through his hair in frustration. Enough of the past. How best could he repair the present damage? Had he really shouted to her about deportment? Where had he obtained such definite ideas about how a duchess should act? Certainly not from Bethany the shrew, or his idle, negligent mother. While Miranda was rather outlandish in her desires to personally right all the wrongs done to the manor, he supposed there was no harm in it. And she was not complaining about the onus, or berating him for the work. Instead, she seemed to thrive on it.

So in his infinite wisdom, he sought to deny her the pleasure of setting her stamp on things. He shook his head in amazement at his own foolishness.

And then a thought occurred to him. He rang for Wilkins and sent him to the dowager's room for her jewel case.

It was as he remembered it, and he scrawled a hasty apology on it before handing the thing to Wilkins to relay to his wife's maid.

But he'd called Wilkins back before the old man had made it to the door. Marcus rummaged in his desk and produced his ring of keys, seldom needed as he trusted the servants to see to the locks. He added it to the peace offering and he prayed that he wasn't about to be shut out by his angry wife.

Miranda lay on the bed, glaring up at the hangings. The spiders were still there, too. She wondered—did she dare knock them down, or would her husband come raging into the room and insist that she might hurt herself on the sharp edge of the pillow? She was nowhere near the banister when Marcus had plucked her off the bench. Surely he didn't think her such a ninnyhammer as to fall over the edge. Or worse yet, jump. If it came to that, she'd choose a less messy end, considering the amount of time and boric acid it had taken to return the entry hall marble to pristine white.

She punched the offending pillow in frustration. It needed airing. As did the hangings.

She'd tried not to think that way. But there was so much to do. If he wanted her to be idle, she'd learn how.

And then she guiltily took the pillow and walked with it to the open window, pounding it on the sill before leaving it to hang in the breeze.

'Your Grace?' There was a faint knock and the door opened to reveal a hesitant Polly.

'Yes, Polly? Come in. You needn't linger in the hall like that.'

'Wilkins says that his Grace says you might be in a temper.'

'Does he now?' Marcus's belief that the servants could keep secrets was sorely misplaced.

'Yes, your Grace. But he told Wilkins, and Wilkins told me, that you was to have this, with his compliments.' And she dangled something towards Miranda, as though expecting her to bite.

It was a heavy chain, but it needed to be to support the many dangling attachments. There was a tiny pair of scissors, a needle case, and a small ivory tablet with a silver-plated pencil chained to it. Scrawled on the ivory, in a hand that was growing familiar to her, were the words 'I'm sorry'. And, to the last extension, he had attached a large ring of keys, which spoiled the grace of the thing but not the message.

'It's the dowager's chatelaine, your Grace. She couldn't be bothered with it, and I don't hear tell that the second duchess wore it neither. But his Grace says it's to be yours now, if you still wished and you could make what you will of it.'

* * *

She opened the door to the picture gallery, hesitating on the threshold. She shuddered. If only the room were not so full of ghosts. His mother was bad enough, although they had never met; Cecily's stories had been enough to colour her perceptions there. But to have to face the late duchess, larger than life before her, was a disconcerting mockery of her own position here.

Her husband stood transfixed in the gloom by the portrait of his late wife. Damn the marble of the floors, she thought, for her first steps echoed and he looked up, and she had to abandon the idea of creeping away unnoticed.

'Excuse me, Marcus. I didn't mean to interrupt...' She faded. What was she interrupting?

'Oh.' He stared at her as though he didn't recognise her; then seemed to come to himself. 'It is nothing. I come here sometimes, because it is quiet.'

She moved closer to him. 'I came to thank you for the gift.' The chatelaine jingled at her waist. 'And to tell you that there is no need to be sorry. The fault was mine.'

He sighed. 'You are too quick to take the blame for my mistakes. I looked up the stairs and saw you in the hallway and it reminded me of an old quarrel. One in which you played no part. I will try in the future to be less of a fool.'

She nodded. 'And I will try to behave more like a duchess.'

'Be who you are, Miranda, and if it makes you happy, I will be glad of it.' He slipped an arm around her shoulders and drew her closer to him, pointing to the portrait of himself. 'Look at that young idiot. It pains me to see him. More bluff than brains in me when they painted that. I was five and twenty and just married. No idea what I was up to. None at all.' He looked at her appraisingly. 'We shall have to find an artist who can do you justice.'

'What do you mean?'

'Not some idiot that would wrap you in lace and seat you next to a piano, or, God forbid, holding a lap dog. Of course, wearing an apron and holding a mop might be appropriate…' he touched the sensible cap that she was wearing to protect her hair as she worked '…but most unconventional for a formal portrait.'

'Whatever are you talking about?'

'When you married me, you earned your place on the wall, my dear. You belong at my right hand.'

She looked up at the portrait in front of her and said softly, 'The place is already full.'

His teasing ended, he grew silent and stared back up at the portrait in front of him.

'She was very beautiful,' she supplied.

'Yes.' His voice was expressionless.

'I should go,' *and leave you alone with your dead wife*. She felt a stab of jealousy at the thought.

'No. Stay.' He looked back to her, then back to the portrait, then back to her.

She cringed under his gaze.

Bethany remained in beatific imperturbability, smiling down at them.

'I wish you would not look at me so,' she muttered. 'I do not like to be compared to her, for I know I will be found wanting.'

'You are very different,' he confirmed. 'But I am not the man I was when I married for the first time. Bethany was a young man's choice.'

'And I?'

'An acquired taste,' he said bluntly.

'You acquired me, right enough. And had little choice in the matter.' But you wooed her, she thought, and the jealousy pricked her again.

'I had even less choice with Bethany. Mother arranged our meeting, and I was besotted from the first. She had the voice of an angel and the painting does not do justice to her beauty. We were married as soon after. And she was dead within the year.'

She remembered what St John had said. 'You must have been very sad.'

'Not really.' His tone was banal.

'If you do not miss her, then why do you come here?' To expiate an old guilt, as his brother had said.

'It is rather like the desire to pick the scab off an old wound. I can't seem to leave it alone to heal.'

'A wound?' To conscience?

'To pride. It did not take me long to realise that she wanted my title, and little more to do with me after she had it. Her mother had bred her and trained her to be an ornament and she did it well. But behind the façade…' he shook his head '…there was such emptiness there that I could never hope to fill it. And a heart of marble.' He reached out and took her chin in his hands and tilted her face so that he could look in her eyes.

'You are quite different from her. For when I look into your eyes, I suspect that there is more behind them, not less.'

She looked away. 'There is nothing. Nothing that I am hiding.'

His smile was sad when she met his eyes again. 'Oh, really? I think we all have something to hide. Even in the void that was my first wife, I found secrets. And there is much that you do not know about me.'

He stared down at her. 'I was not happy in my first marriage. It was a mistake I recognised soon, but too late to save myself.'

'But was she? Happy, I mean.' She blurted it out without thinking.

He smiled. 'Was she happy? From your perspective, that would be a sensible question. I was not always the man you married. Not so grim. So prone to bark and shout.' He pondered the question. 'Was she happy? I think there are some people who are happiest when the people around them are most unhappy. Does this make sense? I know my mother was such a one. Vain and empty headed. She sucked the joy from my father, certain enough. He'd have drunk himself to death to avoid her if the horse hadn't broken his neck. I never saw him so peaceful as the day he lay in the coffin, waiting for us to nail down the lid.

'And my wife was such a one as my mother. Was she happy? Certainly not with me, and she made no bones about telling me so. The title was enough for a while. She enjoyed the money and the spending of it. I was just the vessel, the vehicle. She needed more. She always needed something. I tried at first to satisfy her whims, but could never be enough. Could never do enough. No man could. It was like throwing pennies down a well, trying to keep her happy.'

He looked down at her again. 'I was afraid, when you came here, that my second marriage would be a repeat of my first. That does not seem to be the case.'

She thought of the quest for land and money that had brought her to this place. If it truly were not a repeat of his first marriage, then he would have to have wed someone free of avarice. 'I do not know. Were it not for the title before your name, I never would have come here. And I did not stay for love of you. After our first meeting, I would not have sought you out again.'

'Unless I was very rich,' he prompted.

'Even if you were very rich. If I'd have had a choice, then I'd have run from this house and from you, if I had but known where to go.'

'Then you are very different from my first wife. For she would have married me, no matter what. She filled my head with pretty lies and soft glances and led me to the altar by my nose. And despised me for being a fool.' He turned away from the portrait and stared at her again.

'And you, Miranda. Now that you are trapped here, you offer me service and obedience, which is something, I suppose. If you cannot offer me more than that, I will understand. But promise me that you will not ever pretend to more than you feel, for it is a cruel awakening to find the truth later when you have given your heart to one that has none.'

In the dim light filtering through the drawn curtains of the room, he was not the fierce noble that she remembered from the first day. He looked more like the man in the picture, but wary and tired. He wanted truth from her and there was still so much she hadn't told him. But at least she could promise not to deceive him in the contents of her heart. If only she could figure out what it was she felt when she looked at him, she would gladly share it. She reached out and clasped his hand in hers. 'I promise.'

He tucked her hand into the crook of his arm and drew her to his side. 'Very well, then.'

Chapter Nineteen

She toyed with the keys on her chain, watching them shine in the morning sunlight. It had been a lovely gift, but what did it mean? It made her happy to look at them, but was Marcus happy that she wore them?

Perhaps she should be more like Bethany. He'd never suggested it, but if he could have a happier, kinder, more devoted version of his first wife, Marcus might not look so sad and brood so on the past. If she were someone who could embroider useless frills and paint inferior watercolours, and sit at the spinet in the evenings, singing tedious songs in bad French, someone who could display her good breeding to the best advantage of her husband.

She sighed. If she could be someone she could never be. The servants in this house knew their place better than she did. Of course they hadn't known it until she'd arrived and taken charge of them, but what did that prove? That she'd make a better housekeeper than a duchess, she supposed. And what was left to her now?

Gardening, perhaps. She grabbed scissors and a basket from the still room. She could clip some roses for the dining room. Her husband could find no objection to that. If she did it gracefully and inefficiently enough, she might make a duchess after all.

But once in the garden, she discovered yet another area of the house that needed work. The park around the house was extensive, but only small areas of it were kept up, and in no particular plan or theme. She glanced towards the house, shading her eyes and counting windows. The dowager must have been confined to her room for the duration of her illness. And the gardener was underpaid and short of staff. He'd groomed the areas that could be seen from the bedroom windows and let the rest go to seed.

She strolled around the house, making notes in her head about the work that needed to be done, resisting an urge to begin the weeding herself, before preparing a plan of action. But when she got to the kitchen garden, she could not help herself. The herbs and salad greens were in order, but the fruit trees had not been pruned in ages. The year's harvest would not be what it should, and they would be buying apples in December, when, with a little care, they could eat happily from their own trees through the winter months. And at the back of the garden, the raspberries were an overgrown tangle, and the birds were stealing the last of the summer's crop.

She flapped her arms, and the flock took flight, squawking at the interruption. Then she used her rose shears to cut a hole through the brambles, so that she could reach the best of the fruit. She filled half a basket, then turned to the gooseberry bushes which were also heavy with berries.

* * *

She was busy for over an hour before she stopped and considered her work. Her fingers were stained, her dress had been snagged by thorns and, without a bonnet to protect her, at supper her nose would shine with evidence of a morning spent in direct sunlight. She had proved again that she was not the type of woman he'd expected to marry, not a fit duchess for Haughleigh.

If she was discovered. Hands could be washed, the dress could be mended or disposed of. There was powder in her room that could disguise the sunburn. If she was crafty. If she was not seen. He need never know. She crept down the hall from the gardens to the kitchen. She would leave the berries with the cook, sneak up the back stairs, and swear Polly to secrecy. By lunch she could claim that she had spent the morning taking a nap, and he would be none the wiser.

'What are you doing?' She almost dropped the basket of fruit she was carrying.

Her husband stood in front of her, blocking the way.

'Nothing. Really.' She made to step around him.

He countered her movement to block her again, glanced down into the basket and plucked a berry from the top of the pile. 'Nothing? It looks to me as though you've been working in the garden.'

'H-hardly working. There were some berries left on the bush. And it seemed a shame to leave them for the birds, if there were enough to make preserves or a pudding of some kind.'

'And you took it upon yourself to go picking?'

'It was no trouble.'

'Couldn't send a footman for them? Or tell cook that you wanted them picked?'

She raised her chin in defiance. 'It so happens that I like berries.'

He snatched another out of the basket. 'As do I. Tell me, Miranda, how do these berries taste?'

'Taste? Like berries, of course.'

'But are they sweeter than usual? Tart? A bit past their prime? It is late in the season, you know.'

'I…I haven't taken the time to try one,' she admitted.

'You pick them because you like them. And yet, when you were surrounded by them, you didn't think to pop one in your mouth?'

Her minded clouded with the memories. She'd learned, when young, that you did not eat as you picked from the wild patch near the cottage. It meant that you ate well and had a belly ache for your pains, but that the rest of the family went hungry because of your greed. It was better to wait until you got home and were sure that the bounty could be shared.

And picking at the great house? You did not eat if the berries did not belong to you. Her mind flashed back to another corridor, and a smiling man standing too close to her.

Of course, great men in great houses had no problems taking things that did not belong to them.

'No,' she said. 'I did not.' And she stared into her husband's eyes.

He sighed. 'What shall I do with you?' He put a hand on her shoulder and backed her against the wall.

She felt the cold of the stone at her back, and she remembered the vile whisperings and the taste of strawberries. And her expression changed to one of alarm.

'Close your eyes, Miranda. No, dear. I didn't say, "Stare at me as if I am about to eat you." I said, "Close your eyes."'

She closed them tight, and tensed, waiting for the hand on her body.

Instead she felt the lightest touch of a finger, tracing the straight line of her closed lips.

'Open.'

She felt his finger smooth over her mouth again, as the rest of the hand settled under her chin, and stroked. She unclenched her jaw with effort, and his fingertip dipped into her mouth, touching her lightly on the tongue.

'Taste.'

There was the barest hint of raspberry juice, on the tip of her tongue, sweet and wonderful. Without thinking, she licked at his finger as it slipped away.

'Again.' And he slipped a berry between her lips and let his fingers linger as she nibbled the fruit from them. When he spoke again, his voice was close to her ear, whispering, 'This is what you're missing, Miranda. Pleasures all around you, for the taking. Sweet as the berries. And all I can get you to do is work.'

He brought another fruit to her lips and she reached out and steadied his hand with her own as she ate, and heard his little intake of breath as her teeth grazed his fingers.

And suddenly he pulled her close with his other arm and she felt the basket slip between them as she lost her grip. She opened her eyes to see berries cascading down his linen shirt and smashing between the basket and his cravat.

And she felt her resolve slipping as the old desires swirled in her and she pushed him away, scooping the berries back into the basket. 'Lord, what a mess. Quickly, Marcus. Go upstairs and give that shirt to your valet before the juice ruins it.'

His eyes were darker than usual, and there was a moment that hung between them, where she was sure he was about to yell at her again, for being such a goose. And then he laughed. It was a sound that she couldn't remember ever hearing from him. And he took his juice-stained hands and brought them up to cup her face, pulling it close and kissing it, fast and firm. And his tongue darted between her shocked open lips once before it disappeared. Then he grabbed a handful of berries, and smashed them against his shirt front, popping the last one into his mouth. 'Sweet, Miranda. Very sweet. And well worth the cost of the shirt.' And he walked down the hall and away from her, as if nothing had happened.

Sweet, indeed. But did he mean the berries or the kiss? And without thinking, she took a handful of berries out of the basket and ate them one by one as she proceeded to the kitchen.

Miranda fidgeted on the divan in the drawing room and tried not to look as restless as she felt. This was to be a typical night at home with her husband, and she must learn to enjoy it.

The word caught in her mind like a lump in her throat. Home. This was home, she told herself. The memory of the place that had been home was already becoming indistinct at the edges. She remembered much happiness, of course, and she missed her father and Cici, but she must not forget the rest of it and be grateful for what she now had. This room was comfortable and quite pleasant, now that it had been cleaned and aired. Warm and quiet and spacious and the sound of the rain outside was distant and comforting. She did not have to empty the pan in the corner that caught drips from the hole in the roof, as she had at home. She was not sitting in a draught.

And despite the prickle of sunburn on her nose, she was not bone tired from a day's exertions and ready for bed. Strangely, that was part of the problem facing her tonight.

Her blood was still humming from the kiss in the hallway, but Marcus had been quiet all afternoon and distant at dinner. Perhaps some part of his mind, the part that had led him to the portrait hall, was still dwelling on the past and his first marriage. If so, it was one more lie that St John had told her, for he did not act like a man overcome by guilt but like one that had been deeply hurt and was afraid to reopen the old wounds. When he had suggested, after dinner, that he often retired to the drawing room in the evening and that, if she wished, she might join him there, she had jumped at the chance to do something that might relieve some of the strain on his face. But he had neglected to suggest what she might do to occupy herself when she got there.

She stole a glance at him over the book that she had been leafing through. He seemed comfortable enough, although he often looked up and stared into the fire before sighing and turning a page.

There was a pianoforte in the corner and she wondered if Bethany, who she was continually reminded was a most talented lady, had entertained her husband evenings by playing and singing. He had not mentioned any fondness for music to her. He had not suggested that she try her hand, for which she was most heartily grateful. The scales she'd practised in the schoolroom would not be enough to make for pleasant entertainment.

She glanced at the other chair near the fire and imagined Bethany, with silks and hooped linen, knotting and embroidering, the firelight glowing on her soft blonde hair. She was, no doubt, talented at that as well. But he did not want another Bethany, she reminded herself. This glowing vision was created by St John and the artist of the damn portrait. It was not the grasping shrew that Marcus had described to her.

But neither picture made it any clearer what she was to do to fill the evenings alone with her husband. She glanced down at her own hands and flexed the fingers. They were skilled enough, and could no doubt manage fancy work, if she had the patience for it. And there was the problem. They'd learned in the bone to do things that were necessary, and things that were practical. Straight seams and buttons. Mending. Sturdy unornamented garments. The most complicated sewing she'd managed in years had been turning Cici's cast-offs into the tired garments that she'd worn to Haughleigh. And there had been no comfort in that work, as there was in the ordinary mending. No sense of accomplishment.

She wondered what her husband would think if she stole mending from the servants to do of an evening, or perhaps demanded his valet to release his Grace's worn linen so that she might darn. He would think her mad.

She rose quietly, so as not to disturb Marcus's concentration, and walked to the window, watching the rain spatter against the glass, fondling a chess piece from the set on the table there.

'Are you tired, Miranda?'

She turned, clutching the pawn she was holding to her chest.

He had set his book aside and was watching her. 'You seem restless. And I heard you sighing before. If you are tired, you needn't wait up with me.'

She searched his face for any sign of anger or displeasure

and quickly returned to her seat. 'Oh, I'm sorry. I didn't mean to disturb you. No, I am not tired. Not at all. Just fine. Really. Thank you.' The words were spilling out of her and she closed her mouth with a snap to stop them. And glanced down into her lap to see that she had brought the pawn back with her. She cursed it, for now she would have to walk back across the room again to return it to its board and would be forced to create still more disturbance in the silence of the room.

'I see you admire the chess set. Hand-carved alabaster. A family heirloom.'

She looked down at the pawn and wondered if this meant she should return it immediately to its army.

'If you like…' he hesitated again '…I could teach you to play.'

'I already know.' She wished she could call the words back. He had offered, so gently, to teach her, and she had ruined it by confessing her knowledge. Bethany would probably have smiled and feigned ignorance and her husband would have had an entertaining evening demonstrating his superiority.

But lying about so simple a thing as chess would have added one more sin to her already onerous burden, and he would have caught her out after they'd played for a while and she progressed too rapidly. And she had promised, had she not, to be truthful? Her new husband seemed too sharp to let his own vanity interfere with his observations.

'My family had a set as well, although not so grand as this.' Hand carved, of course, but from scrap wood, with an oilcloth board and one army coloured dark with ink. 'My father used to play with me.' Because he thought it a much better occupation than cards once the fortune and house were gone.

Marcus stood and pulled the matching chair closer to the fire. 'Come. Bring the set and the table. We will have a game.'

She played cautiously at first, vowing to herself that she might still salvage the evening by losing. And he did beat her, after she made a rather stupid move that left her king exposed.

'Shall we play again?' He sounded neither pleased nor bored.

'Thank you. Please.'

'And if you insist on holding back your abilities, please try harder to conceal the fact. It insults me that you resort to such feeble play so that I may win. And remember your promise. I meant what I said. Do not hide your true self from me. Take pleasure in your surroundings.'

She stared up at him and saw, not a face clouded with sadness or anger, but cool calculation. In the firelight, his eyes seemed to sparkle as he set up the board for another game.

It was harder, now that he had some idea of her level of play, and she felt no need to resort to subterfuge to keep the game interesting. She lost several pieces before taking any of his and lost when he laid a trap and she rushed in to take his queen.

'Shall we retire, madam?'

'When I am so thoroughly defeated? How convenient. I have the energy for one more game if you are not too tired.' The challenge she issued surprised her, even as it left her lips.

His response was a sharp bark of laughter. He began setting up the pieces and said, 'Perhaps I am tiring and you are planning to use it against me.'

'Do you think it will work?' she inquired.

'Perhaps. You are an exceptionally good player when you make the effort. But you have other weapons with which to distract me if you want to win.'

'And what might those be?'

His voice was silk against her skin. 'The firelight shining in your hair as you bend close over the board. The way you bite your lip when you concentrate. And the catch of your breath when you discover an opening does the most incredible things to the neckline of your gown. I am tempted to play poorly, just to see the flush of your skin when you take my king.'

She swallowed. 'I swear, sir, you are saying these things just to distract me, so that you may beat me again.'

'And what will you give me if I do?'

The air seemed thick between them. 'I don't intend to let you beat me a third time, so I will not concern myself with your reward.'

He laughed again and moved one of his pawns and play began in earnest. Her concentration was not improved by the realisation that he was observing her so intimately as she chose her moves. But she struggled to convince herself that this was his problem and not hers. And in the end it seemed to work for, after an hour and a half of intense play, she shouted, 'Checkmate.'

And then stifled her triumph and waited to see his reaction.

He leaned back in his chair and steepled his fingers, looking over them at her. 'And now, if you apologise for beating me, as you seem about to, I shall throttle you, you impudent wench. I swear my mother would have looked elsewhere for my wife if she'd known what a delight you are to me. And now you blush to hear the truth. What would you have as a forfeit from me for losing this game?'

'Nothing. Really. I had not intended to play for stakes.'

'Because you feared what you might lose. But you won. Take your prize, whatever it may be.'

She stared at him for a long time, in a kind of horrified fascination. She knew what she wanted. It was a kiss. A kiss like St John had given her before she'd had to lock herself in her room to escape. Only she did not want to have to escape from this man. She wanted the same uncontrollable seeking that had made her lie passive in the arms of another. And the thought made her skin flush with shame and a strange indescribable heat.

She had promised to be truthful to him. What was she to say? Take me in your arms and kiss me like your brother did? She had promised him the truth. And there was no way she could give it to him.

He was unnaturally still, watching her for any sign. And she could see by the tension in him and the heat in his eyes that he would give her everything he had, if she would but ask for it.

Her eyes fell. 'I do not know what I want.'

'I think you do.'

Her blood chilled. Could he see into her thoughts? A true lady would not want to be taken before the fire in the drawing room. Would be innocent of the shameful desires rising in her now. Images came to her head, of the things Cici had explained to her, things no decent woman would know. A wife should be an ignorant but willing pupil when she came to her husband's bed. A proper woman would not feel her blood heating after a simple game of chess.

'You are mistaken.' The lie was shaky on her lips. 'I do not know what I want, other than to do whatever will please you.'

'Whatever will please me?' He leaned closer to her and her breath caught in her throat. What had she just offered? Cici had told stories of silken scarves and honey and hinted that there were many strange games for jaded pallets. The thought should repel her, but instead curiosity burned inside her.

'Yes. Marcus.' She'd almost stumbled over his name again.

'Ah, woman, there will be time, all the time in the world, a lifetime's worth, to take my pleasure in you. But to begin, I wish to let you choose.'

She trembled. 'And I swear to you. I do not know what I want. Do as you will with me.'

He sighed. And when he spoke his voice was gentle, but tired. 'Very well. Perhaps it is still too soon for you. There will come a time when you will understand, when your heart and body will give you no choice in the matter. You will be sure of what you want. And it is then that I want you to come to me. And you will tell me when you know?'

'Yes.'

'Very well. Then goodnight to you, my darling.' And he reached for her hands, taking them gently in his. His thumbs rubbed against her palms and he smiled and brought them to his lips, kissing the backs of them before turning them over to kiss her lightly on each wrist.

'Sleep well.'

Her hands slipped out of his and she said a hurried goodnight before running into the hall. His kiss seemed to seep through her skin and into the blood beneath and course through her body until it reached her heart. It warmed her, and she felt that she was carrying him with her, deep inside. Sleep well? She had never felt so awake.

Chapter Twenty

⁓⸺⸎⸎⸎⸎⸺⁓

When she seated herself at breakfast, her husband was, as usual, working his way through a stack of letters. He glanced up and passed an elegant engraved card down the table to her.

'Did you sleep well?' he inquired.

'Yes. Thank you.' And it was yet another lie. She had tossed and turned all night. Thinking of him.

If he was aware of her troubled mind as she drank her coffee, he concealed it well. 'It seems we have been invited to our first ball. An old family friend. I am sure he and his wife are most eager to meet the new duchess. Please see to the response.'

She stared blankly down at the invitation. 'I suppose we must attend?'

He glanced back at her, arching an eyebrow. 'I swear, madam, that is not the expected response. You are supposed to go into raptures at the chance to finally have a social life in this Godforsaken backwater. You will answer immediately in the affirmative, and then return to me at lunch to beg and wheedle and cajole until I agree that you must have a new gown, new ribbons, gloves, jewellery, and whatnot, and perhaps a trip to London for yet more shopping, until I cannot stand the din and agree to spend a small fortune for one night out.'

'That will not be necessary, I am sure.'

'Are you, indeed? Have you not gone through your wardrobe and found that it lacks solid gold stays, or a diamond-encrusted shift, or some such feminine nonsense?'

'No, Marcus. I am sure what I have is more than sufficient.'

'Hmmph. You are a most unusual wife, Miranda. How can I spoil you if you are always content? I hardly know what to do with you.' And he went back to reading his paper, but there was laughter in his eyes.

She retired to her desk after breakfast and began the first of several false attempts at a reply. The sheets of paper littered the fireplace before she was through and she hoped that her husband was as well-heeled as he claimed to be, for the waste of stationery to get a single satisfactory letter was most prodigious.

She damned Cici and her father for neglecting so much for so long, and then expecting her to jump with both feet into the deep water of her new life and stay afloat. How was she expected to manage penmanship, after years with little paper and no reason to write? She thought her spelling adequate to the task of writing the two or three sentences necessary to thank his lordship and her ladyship for their gracious offer of hospitality, but her hand was cramped and slanting. By the fourth attempt, it looked only slightly rushed and careless, rather than like she'd written with the pen in her teeth. It would have to do.

* * *

The next task, as her husband had pointed out, was to make sure that her wardrobe was in order for an evening out. When she told Polly what they were about, the girl's smile was so broad that it almost inspired Miranda to confidence in the endeavour. Polly produced not one, but a choice of three ball gowns from the selection that Miranda had been afraid to examine some days ago, each with matching shoes. There was a wide selection of evening gloves, a variety of headpieces, caps and turbans and a silk shawl to wear on the journey.

'Definitely the white and gold, your Grace.'

'Not the green?' She touched it carefully, as though the dress belonged to someone else.

'Not for this ball, ma'am. He'll give you the emeralds and then there'll be too much green.'

She looked at Polly, in surprise. 'Emeralds?'

Polly grinned. 'Look about you, your Grace. The only thing missing from your gifts is the jewellery. It's not likely that the duke has forgot 'em. He don't miss a trick, that one, and he's been married before. He knows what's expected and he'd not let you go bare necked to a fancy ball. It'll be the emeralds as they match the house livery, and go well with the suit his grace usually wears to these parties. If there's a doubt, I'll ask Thomas, but trust me. It'll be the emeralds, and the white and gold dress.' She held it up to the light. 'See? It's not a true white. There's a bit of colour in it, and the flowers in the lace have a green leaf.'

The words faded away. Emeralds? She remembered the necklace in the portrait, glittering at the throat of the last duchess. And now, she was to wear those jewels. She swallowed to clear the lump forming in her throat. A cursed necklace for a cursed evening, destined to showcase everything she did not know about being the lady of a great man. She picked up a fan from the pile of accessories before her. She tried an experimental flutter and snap and it slipped from her fingers. Perhaps no fan, or she would display her ignorance in yet another area of etiquette.

And she had been doing so well, she sighed to herself. Here alone in the house, if she had eccentricities, no one noticed. At least her husband showed no desire to comment on her strangeness.

But at a ball there would be worlds of rules that she could break. From which fork to use to what man to dance with. And the dancing.

She perched on the edge of her bed, toying with the fan. She had never learned. There had been no time for balls, when living with her father and Cici. And since this was to be her introduction to local society, there was no way she could manage on the few country dances she knew. With the fine gown, the Haughleigh emeralds, and the duke on her arm, she would be the centre of attention.

And revealed for the fraud she was.

He was lying in his grave again. Alive and struggling, although the mourners gathered around the hole and looked down at him as though nothing was wrong. St John leaned over him and laughed. And then he moved away and Marcus heard tools digging into the earth, and felt the cold slap of the first pile of dirt as it hit him in the face.

He coughed and muttered a weak 'no', spitting soil from his mouth. And when he looked up again, his mother was there, and Bethany, and they were the ones holding the shovels. And he heard the cutting noise again, as the metal blades dug in and stuck stones. And the earth, showering in on him, faster than he could dodge. And it lay heavy on him as he tried to raise a hand to cover his face, struggling to keep his nose clear so he could breath, his mouth clear so he could shout. And suddenly, Miranda was there, standing over him, leaning on her shovel and watching him struggle for air.

He screamed, 'Miranda! No!'

But her face was dispassionate. 'Why must you always shout at me, Marcus? Because you are afraid of shadows? You are a coward. And a fool.' But then she leaned forward, and light seemed to surround her in a nimbus. And instead of throwing dirt on him, scooped at the earth on him, freeing his legs. 'The hole is not so deep, if you had the sense to stand up. Stand up, Marcus. Stand up.'

'Wake up, Marcus. Are you awake?'

And he realised that his eyes were already open, and he was sitting up in his own bed and staring at her, standing in the connecting doorway to her room. 'Miranda?'

She repeated patiently, 'Are you awake? You called out in your sleep. Shouted my name. But when I opened the door you did not recognise me.'

'I was having a nightmare.' He swallowed and was relieved to find his voice steady though his heart was pounding in his chest. 'I am sorry if I disturbed you.'

'That is all right. I was unable to sleep.' She hovered in the doorway, obviously unsure whether to come closer or return to her room. 'I did not know if it would be wise to wake you. They say that to wake someone from a dream before it is finished is dangerous.'

'No harm done, I assure you.' He smiled at the sight of her

dishevelled curls. 'In the dream, you were berating me for my foolishness.'

She stiffened. 'I am sorry. I would never…'

He smiled again. 'Miranda, are you apologising for what you did while in my dream? Because I doubt you have much control over the workings of my sleep-addled brain.'

She shifted from foot to foot, and the light shone through the gown she was wearing. It was one he had purchased for her, he noted. The fabric was fine, almost transparent in the light from behind her. 'But how you must think of me…'

'You appeared like an angel when the dream was at its worst and tried to show me that the terrors were nonsense.'

'I did?' She stilled and he could see the outline of her body through the gown. High, round breasts, smooth belly, the curve of her hip and the dark place where her legs parted.

'Much as you appear now, darling.' He turned towards her and the covers fell away, baring his chest.

She took a hesitant step back into the light of her room and he lost the view of her body. 'Well, that is all right then. If you do not need anything else?'

He considered a moment, and smiled at her. He had need of her; that was certain. He could feel it growing in him like a slow fire in the blood. A delicious ache, when he looked at her. And he grew hard, seeing her body, almost bared before him.

'Yes. There is.'

He could see her tense, as though this was the last answer she had hoped to receive.

He patted the edge of the bed. 'Come. Sit with me a while.'

She hesitated, then walked forward like it was a march to the gallows. And sat on the outmost edge of the bed.

He patted a spot beside him. 'You do not have to be afraid of me, Miranda. I will not take more than you are ready to give. Come closer, so that I may hold you.'

She slid up the counterpane to a spot next to him and came stiffly into his arms.

She smelled like violets and sunshine. Was this something he had bought for her, he wondered? A scent included in the London purchases, something she had found in the village or just the way she always smelled? Unlike any other woman he had lain with. He buried his face in her hair and breathed deep.

She edged away from him and laid her hand on his heart. The pounding was receding, but still so noticeable that she had felt it through her gown. She looked inquiringly up at him.

'Yes.' He laughed, but the sound was tired. 'You must come to my bed and soothe me to sleep like a frightened child. Not the devilish seducer you were expecting, am I?'

'I was not expecting…' She must be giving him an obvious lie. 'I never know what to expect when I am with you, Marcus. You are always a surprise to me.'

He pushed a hand between them and pushed the bedclothes away. 'As are you to me. Lie with me, Miranda. Let me hold you tonight. Perhaps we will both sleep easier if we are not alone.'

She crawled beneath the covers, still hesitant, but more relaxed than she had been before. He felt her tense again when she realised that he was naked beneath the sheets, and felt her thinking before settling her arm around his waist and letting her body melt into his.

He sighed as his pulse slowed to normal with the touch of

her body, and kissed her violet-scented hair. He had forgotten how it felt to lie like this with a woman. Perhaps he had never known it. Bethany was careful to always return to her room after the act, and he had never felt welcome there. And a mistress's bed felt like a temporary resting place, even though it was his to rest in by right of ownership.

Miranda snuggled closer to him, trying to find the most comfortable place against his body, and he could feel her begin to doze. He thought of rousing her with a kiss, and then relaxed and closed his eyes. This was the first of many nights with her and he would savour it for what it was. He did not have to rush if he had a lifetime.

Chapter Twenty-One

She woke the next morning in a fog of confusion. Even before opening her eyes she realised that things were different. The smells were wrong. And she was warmer than she had been in her own cold white sheets.

Then she remembered. And opened her eyes. He was already awake, leaning against one arm and smiling down at her. Outside the hangings of the bed she could hear the valet moving around, readying to receive the duke.

'Good morning,' he whispered. 'Did you sleep well?'

'Yes, thank you.' She had, she realised, and the fact surprised her. She had been restless ever since coming here, and her easiest nights had been in the first weeks, when she'd worked herself to exhaustion and fallen into bed. But last night, after forcing herself into his bed to grant his request, she'd found more peace than she'd felt in a long time. It seemed there was even less to be afraid of than she thought. 'And you? Did you sleep well?'

He stretched and yawned. 'That was the best night's rest I've had since returning to this house. If I'd known that all that I lacked to achieve peace with myself was to have you at my side...'

'You'd have married me sooner?' She smiled at the impossibility of it.

'I'd have coaxed you into my bed long ago. I'd have never left your side to go to London.'

And before she could move he'd leaned forward and kissed her hard on the lips. 'And, now, my dear, I must rise and attend to business so that I may have my evening free to escort you to the ball. Shall I send for your maid?'

'I think I can manage to walk back to my room, thank you,' she said. He reached for his dressing gown at the foot of the bed and wrapped it around her shoulders. 'So you do not catch a chill on the way.' Then he slipped out of the bed himself, not fearing the cold air on his own bare skin.

She hurried back to her own room to find Polly already laying out a day dress and chattering on about preparations for tonight's ball.

She smiled to see the girl so happy about it. And tried to push the thoughts that had kept her awake the night before to the back of her mind. There was still a gap in her preparations, and she saw no easy way to remedy it.

After breakfast, she checked the books in the library, but found nothing to help fill in her education on the subject. She thought of asking Polly for help, but decided against it. At best, she would know only a little of what was necessary.

Perhaps she could feign illness. But she doubted that anything but a convincing display could change the duke's plan of attending. No fits of vapours or delicate megrims. He would want proof.

A sprained ankle, perhaps? A small fall down the stairs that would leave her incapacitated. And postpone the inevitable for how long? She might be able to beg off tonight's invitation, but there would be others. And the more she tried to avoid them, the more they would persist in trying to woo her from the house. And then she would be expected to throw balls and parties of her own.

She had no one to turn to. Nowhere to seek help.

Except…

He had said that he would be busy today, and she would no doubt be an unwelcome interruption. But she remembered the feel of his body next to hers during the night and a feeling of calm crept over her. If she could not turn to him for help, then she had nowhere else to go.

She approached her husband cautiously, as she always did. He was in his study, seated behind the great desk, poring over ledgers and nibbling on the end of his quill in a way that, if she hadn't been intimidated by her surroundings, she might have found rather endearing.

She cleared her throat.

He looked up. 'Yes, Miranda.'

'Your Grace…'

His eyebrow raised.

'Marcus. There is a problem. About tonight. The ball.'

'Missing some frill, m'dear? Is your gown too plain? Not plain enough? Need more ostrich plumes?'

'No,' she snapped. Her cheeks were burning with shame. Now he would realise what a fraud she was. 'I cannot go to a ball tonight. I don't know if I will be able… I can't.' She spread her hands in front of her in a gesture of defeat.

He was around the desk in a flash, his hands reaching out

to take hers, his eyes staring in to hers in concern. 'What? What is it that bothers you so?'

A single tear slipped down her cheek before she could call it back. 'I cannot go tonight, because I have never been to a ball before. I do not know how to dance.' Her voice fell to a whisper. 'And I am afraid.'

His arms were around her, and he pulled her close, and she sobbed into the wool of his coat.

She felt his breath ruffle her hair when he spoke. 'Ahhh. See. Now you are crying and I am undone. For I find a woman's tears as terrifying as you find tonight's ball. Now what can I do to save myself from them?' He squeezed her once and then set her gently away from him as he rang for Wilkins.

The butler appeared in record time, his back straight as a ramrod, she noticed with approval. She had done some good here, even if she would be more suited as a housekeeper than a great lady.

'Wilkins. I need servants. Six couples should be more than enough. And you. Pull them from their duties. The routine can wait. And anyone that can play a musical instrument. A fiddle, perhaps? Or we can hum, I suppose. They are to meet us in the ballroom. I am much out of practice when it comes to the dance, and fear I will crush her Grace's toes, should I dance with her tonight.' He smiled to give her confidence. 'A short rehearsal should be all that is needed.'

Wilkins disappeared. And Marcus frowned back at her. 'I am most disappointed in you, madam.'

'I'm sorry,' she stammered. 'My education is most woefully lacking in some things, but I will try…'

'In the future, when you find yourself in such a circumstance, you are to come to me immediately, and not work yourself in to a state over a trifle. We could have hired a dancing master.'

'I'm sorry,' she apologised again. 'For waiting so long, and taking you away from your work. You are right. It could have been handled without troubling you.'

He laid a finger against her lips. 'Miranda, you mistake my meaning. When you have a problem, you are to come to me, and not hang about in your room, worrying what my response may be. I will not guarantee that I will never be cross, for you have seen me so and won't believe it, but I promise: I bark but will never bite. And I am sworn before God, if you remember, to love and protect you.' And without taking his eyes from hers, he caught one of her hands in his own and raised it to his lips.

How strange, she thought as he kissed the back of her hand, that there should be so much feeling there. That she should feel his lips, pressing warm against her flesh, and the gentle roughness of his skin, not just in her hand, but deep inside her. His thumb rubbed at her palm, feeling the places where the calluses used to be, and the newly sensitive flesh tingled. Then he turned her hand over, pressing his lips on to her palm and running his tongue along the lines in her hand. His eyes were dark when he looked up at her, and his voice rough. 'Go to the ballroom. I will meet you there shortly.'

When she got to the ballroom, she looked at it with a critical eye. One more space that had not been cleaned in ages. Obviously unused, possibly since Marcus's first marriage. Turning back the Holland covers, she found delicate gold-legged chairs and small tables, music stands. The chandeliers were beyond dusty, and covered with candle drippings. The ceiling was smoke stained, and cobwebs hung from the ornate gold cherubs and plasterwork vines on the walls. It could be magnificent, she thought, after a good cleaning. Decorated with fresh flowers. Candlelight. Delicate treats on a buffet for the guests. Little cakes, lemonade and champagne. She'd imagined the scene many times, while preparing great rooms such as this for someone else's ball.

Behind her, one of the footmen was tuning a fiddle and a groom had produced a penny whistle, which he was tooting experimentally. Servants were gathered in a curious crowd, whispering amongst themselves.

And then the doors opened wide and her husband strode into the room, carrying a small box. He smiled at the assembled staff. 'I see we have more than the required number for a quadrille. Is everyone shirking, then? I trust no one was left behind to turn a spit or polish the silver.'

The servants looked doubtful.

'If they were, then run to get them now. Let the house have a holiday, at least for a few hours. I swear my wife must work you hard, judging by the startling transformations I've seen in my home these last weeks. Never fear. I plan to keep her busy for a while, and she will not be able to set you to task for not mopping this floor.' He turned to her. 'And you, my dear. If we are to play at going to the ball this afternoon, I thought you might like a costume.'

And he opened the box that he had brought with him and withdrew the emeralds, just as Polly had predicted.

'The necklace from the portrait,' she said.

'The stones,' he corrected. 'But not the necklace. When I was in London to retrieve them, I had them reset.' He ran a finger along their length. 'They are not so common and flashy as they were. The gold is fine and graceful as the throat of the wearer, and diamonds were added to match the sparkle in your eyes. May I?'

'Yes.'

He stood behind her, reached around to position the necklace between her breasts, then trailed his hands along it to the clasp at the back. He joined it, and his hand lingered on her shoulders as he pulled her close and whispered in her ear, 'I hope to make you say yes to me many times before the night is through, and I swear you will not be sorry for it. What say you to that, madam?'

She blushed crimson. 'Yes.'

'Very good.' And then he said loud enough so the servants could hear, 'Let us start with something easy that we all know. The Sir Roger de Coverly.'

And with the help of the fiddler and the flute, tapping time with his foot, he marched his wife and the staff through it, then a quadrille, a minuet and several country dances, until they were all laughing and exhausted.

'There is one final dance that I would teach you, although you will not need it for tonight.'

'Not need it?'

He smiled down at her again, and her blood warmed in her veins. 'Yes. They dance it on the continent, but it is much too wicked for an English country ball.'

'Too wicked?'

'Very. For a man must put his hands like so,' and he wrapped them around her waist and pulled her close to him.

'That does not feel too wicked,' she murmured. 'When you do it, it feels quite nice.'

'Very good, then, let us proceed. Fiddler, three-quarter time. A waltz.' And he swept her away.

It was hard at first, trying to decipher the step even though it was simple. But he held her even closer to him, and she felt his legs moving against hers and his arm at her waist guiding her, and suddenly nothing seemed more natural than to go where he went and move as he moved. He looked into her eyes, and she felt her heart wanting the same, to be moving and beating in harmony with his.

The music ended, but she wanted more. She sighed. 'And we will not need to do this at the ball? How sad.'

'Not at all. For then I might have to share you with other partners.'

'Perhaps some other time, then?'

He leaned close, and whispered in her ear. 'Tonight? If you come to my room after the ball I will dance with you all you wish. And teach you other steps that will give great pleasure to us both.'

'Yes.'

'Go upstairs and ready yourself, wife. Rest. For there is a long night ahead of us.' And he dipped his head forward and his lips touched her neck before he released her.

She hurried to her room, requesting that Polly deliver a light meal, and make arrangements for her bath and *toilette*.

She tried to rest, but sleep was impossible. Her blood sang in her veins. The ball and the accompanying worries were all but forgotten. It was only a place that she would spend the intervening hours before returning home with her husband. Any fears associated with that had burned away as he'd danced her around the floor. His touch was firm but his voice was soft, and the kiss on her neck had been warm and promising.

She no longer worried about not finding pleasure in the

marital bed. He had been nothing but accommodating in all other things, and attentive to her moods. And he would be so tonight as well, she was sure of it.

She still wore the heavy necklace that symbolised her house, but it was not such a great burden, if Marcus had placed it there. He could remove it later.

Chapter Twenty-Two

Polly supervised her dressing, which was just as well since Miranda was in such a state as to hardly know her own body. Every part of her felt new and tingling. The gown set off the emeralds. Her hair was piled high on her head and dressed with tiny diamond clips that sparkled in the firelight.

When it was time to go, there was a knock on the front door of her room. Polly opened it and her husband stood, framed in the doorway, staring at her.

She turned in a circle before him. When she faced him again, his eyes devoured her. 'Magnificent.'

'Do I please you?'

'Very much so.' He took her hand and stroked it before bringing it to his lips. Then he escorted her to the carriage, handed her in and seated himself across from her.

She glanced at the seat beside her and wondered why he chose to be so far away.

As if reading her mind he answered, 'Polly's handiwork will be safer if I keep my distance from you, my dear.'

'In what way?'

'In the privacy of this carriage, I do not trust myself. Given the chance, I would pull you into my lap and show you what I think of my new wife, and we would have to turn around before we ever reached the ball.'

'And what do you think of me?'

'I think you are overdressed.'

She looked in alarm at her gown. 'Is it too much?'

He laughed, low and sensuous. 'Any gown is too much, my dear. You are lovely as you are now, but to see you stretched naked across that seat would be infinitely better.'

'Naked?'

'Perhaps I shall let you retain the emerald necklace, for warmth.'

'And what will you be doing, while I am freezing to death?'

'I shall lie close to you, so you do not get cold. And I will tangle one hand in those fine curls at your neck, and another in the fine curls between your legs and warm everything between them with my lips.'

She trembled at the thought of him, taking her in the carriage on the way home this very night.

'Is that the way it is to be with us, sir?'

He nodded. 'With me utterly besotted and glaring at any man that will partner you this evening. Barking in a rage at the young puppies that will be crowded around, plying you with champagne, frightening off your admirers and making an ass of myself. And the other ladies laughing behind their fans at how you have me so thoroughly under your spell in such a few short weeks.'

'I have bespelled you?'

'Most completely. I find I can think of nothing else but you in my arms, and you by my side. I am yours to command, Miranda, whether you want me or no. I hope that the vicar and his wife are there to see. They will be most disappointed to find me reformed.'

She smiled. 'Do we have to stay so very long this evening?'

His eyebrows arched. 'You would rather be home?'

She smiled. 'With you. Yes.'

'Oh, Miranda, you were put on this earth to tempt me from my duties. Courtesy demands that we put in an appearance. We shall stay until midnight and then slip quietly away before supper. I shall tell the host that, since I am newly married and madly in love, I cannot bear to share you.'

'Madly?'

'Most certainly.'

She smiled again. 'And I shall tell the hostess that if I am not good company it is because it pains me to be away from your side, even for an hour.'

He grinned at her. 'Then we will steal away home as soon as possible and create as much scandal as possible while we are there. Perhaps I will kiss you on the dance floor.'

'Perhaps I will kiss you back. That will most certainly shock the vicar and his wife.'

He laughed and blew her a kiss as the carriage drew up in front of the great house where the ball was to be held. He took her arm, led her to be announced and escorted her to the receiving line to meet the host and hostess, a local lord and his wife who had known Marcus since he was a child.

The rosy-cheeked old man smiled at her and demanded, 'Where did you find such a lovely young thing, Haughleigh? Not on the continent, surely.'

'She was blown to me on that storm a few weeks ago. And a fair wind that was. I knew at once that I must have her.' He smiled down at her with such obvious pride that she couldn't help but smile back.

He led her out in a dance and then left her, kissing her hand as a crowd of young men surrounded her, vying for spots on her dance card and wondering aloud whether she might have a sister half as pretty.

To her surprise, she found the ball enjoyable, despite the absence of her husband. As she whirled around the dance floor in one set or another, she caught occasional glimpses of Marcus in the crowd, smiling with obvious pride at the success she was having. And her dancing skills were quite up to the abilities of many of her partners. She was spinning down the line in a gallopade and laughing at the number of times that her partner had almost trodden on her own toes when the man at the bottom of the set caught her and spun her.

'St John.' She mouthed the name as he smiled into her eyes.

She stumbled and caught herself, and was dancing unsteadily with her own partner again, mind whirling faster than the dance.

Of course, she was to see him again. He had been banished from the house, and she had hoped that that meant he was nowhere around. But it only meant he was out of sight of his brother. That was no reason to believe that he wasn't close by, and no reason why he might not appear at the home of an old family friend.

Had Marcus seen him? Had they spoken? She doubted it.

The last time she had seen Marcus he appeared relaxed and happy, not in the least like the man he was whenever St John was present. Or even mentioned in conversation, she remembered. The hatred between them, whatever its cause, ran so deep that they couldn't be in the same room together without incident. She must warn…

Who? She could not very well suggest to her husband that he leave before meeting St John. It would look too much to his proud eye like a retreat.

And St John? If she spoke to him at all, the results could be disastrous. What if he took it as a show of interest? What if Marcus saw them together? Or what if St John spoke to Marcus about the two weeks he had been gone. More for St John than for her, even a hint of what had transpired between them would be worse than disastrous.

The flush of guilt that swept through her when she thought of the last encounter with her brother-in-law was enough to verify the danger of the situation. She could not talk to either of them on this without ruining what she'd hoped would have been a perfect evening. She scanned the ballroom, but saw no sign of her husband, or of St John.

It would be a lie, and she had promised not to lie to her husband, but it must be done. It was almost midnight, and he had promised that they could go. She had but to whisper in his ear that she could bear no more and they would be in the carriage and on the way home.

After the set, she fanned herself and confessed to her partner that she was feeling faint, and in need of air. She declined his offer of company, but suggested, should the young man see the duke, that he tell him she was ready to depart. With that, she slipped out of the ballroom and on to the terrace, scanning it for signs of her husband. If he was not dancing, then he was here, or perhaps in the card room. A systematic search would be necessary.

'Seeking privacy, Miranda? Or seeking me?'

'St John.' She whirled to see him standing in the shadows next to an ornamental shrub.

'Of course. You did not think I would be gone for long, my dear, with so much unfinished between us.'

'There is nothing unfinished. I thought, when I slammed the door in your face, that I made my opinion plain.'

'Not plain enough by half. In my experience, a slammed door is an invitation to try harder the next time. If we were truly done, you would have told Marcus. And he would have called me out as he's been longing to for years.'

He stepped closer and she stepped back, running up against the terrace balustrade.

'But you didn't tell him anything, did you, Miranda? Why not? Are you ashamed of the way you acted? Because of the way you encouraged my advances while your husband was away?'

'I did not encourage you.'

'You did not discourage me, as you should have if you meant to be faithful to my brother. Perhaps I am just saving him the trouble of discovering later what a faithless wench he married.'

He leaned into her, and she scrambled away from him, pressing her back against the balustrade. 'You are afraid, now that your husband is close, of what might still happen between us?'

'Nothing will happen between us.' She tried to pull away, but he trapped her between his arm and the planter beside her.

'Too late, my dear. There is already something between us. You felt it. Don't deny it.'

'I'm sorry if I gave you the impression that I was interested.'

'Gave me the impression?' He leaned closer and his soft laugh stirred the hair near her ear. 'Your eyes darkened when I got close. And your breath quickened. You tugged at my lip with your teeth as I kissed you.'

'Stop it.' She pushed hard against him, shoving past him to go back to the dance floor.

He caught her wrist as she passed and held her firm.

'Let me go,' she whispered. 'People will see.'

'And why would I care?'

She noticed with shock the wolfish, predatory look he had about him.

'Your reputation would suffer. Mine would increase. Ask your husband. It is no less than the sort of behaviour that everyone expects of me.'

'What do you want?' She glared at him. 'What must I do to make you let me go?'

'Let you go?' He puzzled over the phrase. 'I have no intention of letting you go, now that I have you where I want. Perhaps, someday when I am tired of you, when the game becomes boring, but I'm sure there are many things we can find to do before that day.'

'Let me go this instant, or I'll—'

'Tell your husband? Let's tell him together and see whom he listens to. I'll tell him all about the two weeks we spent together. I won't even have to lie. I know my brother better than you, darling. I assure you, the truth will be quite damning enough.'

'Then what must I do—' she gritted her teeth '—for your silence?'

'Simply be a generous sister.' He leaned forward again and licked the shell of her ear.

'You disgust me.'

'With the lights on, perhaps. But in the dark, you will find me charming. And with my brother busy, putting the estate in order, we will have plenty of time to know each other better.'

She shuddered. 'He'll kill you.'

'Only if he catches us. He'll kill you as well. A very jealous man, my brother is.'

'But suppose…?'

'That you bear my brother a litter of blond-haired bastards?' He laughed. 'For that is my brother's worst nightmare, you know. Kind of an obsession, really.' He reached around and dug a fist into her belly, searching for telltale hardness. 'Not increasing yet, are you? Then, for now, we'll have to be careful. My brother can have the womb and good luck to him. It's all he's really interested in. But I demand right to everything else.'

'No.'

'Really? Are you sure? It's not an unpleasant thing I'm suggesting. Quite pleasurable, really. But you know that already, don't you?'

She stiffened. 'Whatever are you talking about?'

'Only that I know where you came from, my dear. A skilled pupil of Lady Cecily Dawson, aren't you? How much did she teach you, I wonder, before sending you off to my brother to play at being a duchess?'

'I have no idea what you mean.'

'Of course not, Miranda. You will no doubt claim that you had no idea that your guardian was a notorious courtesan. My mother told me everything, before she died. But nothing to my brother, or he'd never have had you. And he need never know anything about your past, just as he need never know that we've been together, if we are careful. I know tricks you'll never learn from my brother, not even from the infamous Cecily. And I'll share them all with you.'

'For the sport of cuckolding him?'

'Well put, dear lady. It will add that certain fillip to the encounter, knowing that the things I am doing are with my brother's wife.' He leaned against her leg and she pulled away, trembling.

'Don't touch me.'

He sighed. 'So cruel. So heartless. You would leave me to suffer?' Suddenly his voice was all business. 'You don't want to be seen alone with me. I'm going to take a refreshing walk in the garden. And in fifteen minutes, I will make my way to the library, which is down the hall and to the left of the ballroom. Meet me there, and we can spend the first of many delightful times together.'

'And if I don't?'

'Then I will go back to the ballroom and tell all and sundry how you were raised by a whore and broke my heart when you gave me all and then returned to my brother. Choose. And I trust you'll choose wisely.'

He hopped over the low balustrade and moved down the garden path, whistling softly, and she turned back towards the house, mind racing.

Everything had been going so well; the evening was not going to end thus. There had to be a way to stop it. She would find Marcus and beg him to take her home. She doubted that St John would bother to ruin her if her husband was not there to hear the story.

She searched the ballroom, the card room, and other surrounding rooms, but Marcus was nowhere to be found. Time was running out. She must come up with another plan.

You could meet him, suggested a small voice in her mind, and let him do his worst and be done. No one might be the wiser. It was what Cici would have done.

'No.' She said it aloud. She would not meet him, not to preserve any more secrets from her husband. She would die first.

If someone must die, why must it be you? said the matter-of-fact voice in her head. *You are only a foolish girl, trapped in circumstances. But St John—he is the one who trapped you. He is evil. And while he lives, he will be a danger to you, and to your husband, the man he longs to destroy.*

She continued to scan the crowd for Marcus, as the idea blossomed in her head. She could go to the library. She could call his bluff and tell him that there was no chance that she would let him touch her. And she could walk towards the fireplace as she said it. There would be a poker beside it. One swing might permanently solve her problem.

She shuddered against it. It was horrible. Too horrible to contemplate. She would have his blood on her hands.

But she could not be faithless to the man she loved. No shame was worth that.

But what if St John sprang upon her as soon as she entered the room?

Not likely, she told herself. He preferred to toy with her. He would not force. He would try to goad her to walk into his arms. And it would give her time to find a weapon.

And what if one blow isn't enough?

If he survived, or even if he died and she was discovered, she'd claim she'd done it in defence of her honour. Her lies couldn't be any less believable than his.

* * *

The clock in the hall said five minutes to midnight. Perhaps, if she arrived in the room before him, she could position herself next to a weapon before he came. She proceeded down the empty hallway. What if she was discovered now? Then the witness must realise that she was only looking for her husband. She opened the door of the darkened room and called softly, 'Marcus?'

It was very dark. She had not planned on this. There were no candles lit and the fire was banked low and revealed only outlines of furniture and dim shapes in the gloom. She stepped into the room. And then she felt the man behind her, pushing her forward and shutting the door.

And he was on her before she could act, pinning her tight against the wall with his body and tangling a hand in her hair.

'Oh, no,' she managed before his lips closed over hers. The element of surprise had fallen by the wayside. His arms drew her closer, and he whispered, 'My darling Miranda. I've waited so long.'

Then his lips were on hers again, moving over her as his hands roamed her body. And she remembered the real reason that St John was a danger to her. When he wanted to be, he was sweet, unbearably sweet. Sweet as the kiss he was giving her now, which settled into a gentle exploration of her mouth and built, when she sighed, to probing between her lips and thrusting into them in a rhythm that built again to a frenzy. Her mind screamed for her to push him away, but her body screamed for another kind of release. The compromise between the two was a useless push of her hands against his chest, and a 'No, we mustn't', which sounded far too much like a plea for more.

He gathered her tighter to him. 'Oh, yes, we must. Here. Now. Quick, before someone finds us. No more waiting.'

'My husband…' She tried to gather her wits as a defence against him, as his lips trailed down her neck and settled on her shoulder.

He groaned, and his hands reached lower and tugged up the hem of her gown and found the soft flesh of her bottom, to knead her and crush her to the hardness of him. She felt as his hand slipped between them to the buttons on his breeches, and she knew what was about to happen and she fought.

'No! St John. Let me go. You promised you wouldn't…'

'What?' And he stiffened against her, pushing away. And the door opened and she struggled to stay upright. She saw the silhouette of the man in the doorway, as he stepped into the room, shut the door and struck a match. 'Well, I must say, this is an interesting picture. I arrive a few minutes late and find you've started without me. And such a choice of partners.'

St John strode around the room, while her eyes were still adjusting to the light, and touched his flame to a candle, filling the room with flickering shadows. 'Are you enjoying her as much as I have, Marcus?'

She looked in horror to the face of the man in front of her.

His arms still circled her, pinning her in place in front of him. But the body that had been moving against her moments before seemed to have turned to stone, trapping her to him. Perhaps it was a trick of the light, but his face seemed to harden as she watched, passion and pain draining out of it to leave an impassive granite mask. He looked from her to his brother standing beside the fireplace, and let out a strange barking laugh. 'If you think you can hurt me this way, St John, you are mistaken. If I cared, I would call you out over this. But the blood that ran in my veins when I shot you would be cold, not hot. In truth, I haven't the time or the energy to battle to the death over every damn game you play. It hardly seems worth the trouble to put a bullet through your brain just because you are a damned nuisance.'

St John's laugh was not strange, but genuine. 'Oh, Marcus, what an actor you are. You will not call me out because you are soft and weak and do not trust your hand to finish the job, when the time comes. And I have no desire to kill you outright at dawn. I prefer to wound. What is it they call the torture in the adventure stories we read together as children? The death of a thousand cuts. That is what I want for you. I want to watch you bleed. To suffer as I have suffered.'

'Then I am sorry to disappoint you. Is that all, St John?'

'For now, Marcus.'

'Then good evening.'

St John swept a deep, mocking bow to his brother. 'By your leave, your Grace.' And sauntered through the door of the library, leaving them alone.

Only then, when he heard the door latch, did he push away from her, as though she were on fire and the contact burned him.

'Marcus,' she said urgently, 'I can explain.'

'I've heard more than enough from you this evening. I am going to take my leave of our host. I will say you are indisposed and we are returning home. Wait here, until I send a servant to fetch you to the carriage.' He looked down at her with loathing. 'In the meantime, try to compose yourself to look more like a duchess and less like a whore.' And he strode from the room.

* * *

They rode home in silence. He stared ahead into the darkness, and she was afraid to disturb him. She made a few tentative attempts at apology and he stared down at her, as though he was unsure where the noise was coming from.

When he pulled the carriage into the drive, he dropped the reins for the groom and strode into the house with her following in his wake.

He tossed his greatcoat on the bench in the hall, not waiting for the servant to take it, and turned back to her. 'Madam, attend me.' Then he turned way again and strode to the stairs and up them.

There would be a scene. It was better, when it came, that they were alone. There was no point in the servants knowing what a disaster the night had been.

And would that it were just words he was bottling up. The line of his back as it advanced up the stairs in front of her was as rigid as an iron bar.

What if she had provoked Marcus to violence? It was too late to claim that it was no fault of hers. That she had been tricked into it. That she had never meant him harm or disgrace. Who would he believe? Perhaps her, if she had not made it plain, in the library, that she thought she was in another man's arms. It would be impossible, now, to make him believe that she was an innocent victim. She stopped at her own door with her hand on the knob.

'Dismiss your maid.'

'But…' She reached to her bodice.

'You will not need her tonight. Dismiss her and come to my room.' He stalked past her to his own room and closed the door behind him.

She went into her room and told a sleepy Polly that her services would not be needed, and the girl grinned at her and hurried away. If she saw the look in Miranda's eyes, she mistook it for anticipatory nerves and not dawning terror.

Miranda glanced around the room, looking for a solution. It would not do to lock the doors. To ignore his order tonight would make a bad situation even worse. Her knees felt weak.

'I await you, madam.' He was standing in the open door between the two rooms.

She reached for the dressing gown draped over the foot of the bed.

'You will not need it. Let it be and come to my room.'

He turned and disappeared through the doorway, and she followed after.

He had shed his coat and waistcoat, and his white shirt gleamed at her in the candlelight. She stepped in to the room, unsure of what was expected of her, but he ignored her to sit on the bed and pry off his boots and hose, which he tossed into a corner. He ripped at the cravat and pulled the shirt over his head, sending the linen sailing after the boots. Then he looked up at her expectantly.

She stared at his body in the dim light. His chest was broad and smooth, the muscles bunched in his arms as he reached for the buttons on his breeches. Every move he made revealed the strength in him, as though a great energy lay waiting to be unleashed.

He paused and glared up at her. 'Well?'

'Wh-what do you want from me?'

'Nothing that you have not given freely elsewhere. The time for talking and waiting has ended. Take off your dress.'

'I can't. I can't reach…' She gestured to the closures and he sighed in impatience and strode across the room to her.

She turned her back to him and felt the hairs on her neck rise. She stood still, holding her breath and felt his hands on the hooks, felt each one pop open and her bodice loosen and slip down her body. He laid a hand on the corset beneath it, and then wrapped one hand around her waist while the other tugged at the knotted laces and worked them loose with a series of sharp yanks. Then the tugging stopped and she heard him walk back across the carpet to the bed.

She kept her back turned from him and eased the gown off her shoulder, stepping out of it. She picked it up, straightening the fabric with her hand. She looked around the room for a place to hang it, perhaps a chair to drape it over.

'Leave it.'

She dropped it and stepped away, removing her slippers and stockings and leaving them beside the gown on the floor.

'Turn around.'

She turned towards him, eyes still focused on the ground.

'Look at me when I'm talking to you.'

Slowly, she raised her eyes to his. The breeches had followed the rest of his clothing and he lay on his side, head resting on an upraised arm. The muscles of his chest flowed gracefully to meet the muscles of his abdomen. And lower.

'What are you waiting for? Take off the corset.'

She made to turn away from him again and he said, 'No more ridiculous displays of modesty. They do not impress me. If you are shy of me now, soon you will have no reason to be. Take off the corset.

'I want to see you.'

She loosened the laces the rest of the way and let it fall,

fighting the urge to throw an arm over her bare breasts. She could hear his breathing change as he stared at her, and she looked into his eyes again.

'And the rest. Take it off.'

She reached behind her to loosen the clasp of the necklace.

'Leave the emeralds on. And remember who you are.'

Who she was? Even she didn't know that any more.

She loosened the tie on her petticoat and let it fall.

'Come here.'

She walked towards the bed and stood in front of him. Maybe if she told him now, that she had never done this, that she was sorry, that it was all a mistake, he might be gentle.

'Tonight, I—'

'Don't speak! Not another word. Lay on the bed beside me.'

She climbed on to the bed and lay next to him on her back. She reached with one hand to pull the covers up and he pulled them out of her grasp and tossed them towards the foot of the bed, leaving her vulnerable.

And then he was touching her.

Her flesh had been tensed for a blow. When his touch came it hardly registered. He ran a hand up and down the length of her bare arm, and she felt the hairs stand and the flesh prickle. The stroking ended and he ran the hand over her shoulder and down to cup first one breast and then the other. Her nipples tightened and grew hard against his palm.

She stared up at the ceiling, afraid to look at him. This was a trap to lull her to stillness before the harsh words, before the beating, before...

His head dipped to where his hand had been and pulled a nipple into his mouth. And she forgot everything but the moment and the feel of his mouth on her breast and the blood pounding in her ears as the world spun under her.

His hand slipped lower, caressing her abdomen. And lower to tug at the curls between her legs. Without meaning to, she relaxed and her legs opened and his hand slipped between. He stroked her and she could feel herself grow wet, feel the heat between her legs and a want inside that made her arch her hips to press against his hand. And when he slipped first one finger, and then two inside to stroke deeper, she knew what she wanted, and rocked against him, a moan escaping her lips.

He raised his head, and his other hand touched her chin, turning her face until she looked into his eyes. And she lost herself in his gaze and his touch, on her and inside her, and felt the strangeness and need building within her body until she could stand it no more. And, when she thought she must scream that she was his, and could deny him nothing, he took her further until the passion broke her and she lay spent and trembling against him.

Then his hand stilled and he shifted his weight, and lay on top of her. He entered her slowly at first and it seemed that there was no way that her body could hold him.

And he withdrew. And pushed again, harder this time, and she gasped against the pain and turned her head into the pillow, gripping the sheet beside her in her balled fists.

And he swore in surprise, burying his face in the curve of her neck as he pushed again, and again.

It was over quickly. He shuddered against her, let his weight rest on her body and then rolled off to lie beside her. She felt his hand slide between her legs and she trembled, but he laid a steadying hand on her shoulder, rolling her to face him. He brushed his fingertips against her and examined the blood on his hand, wiping it in a red smear across the white sheet.

Then he reached out and clutched her convulsively to him, his breath ragged against her ear and whispered, 'Sleep.'

Chapter Twenty-Three

He was damned. He knew it in his bones. It wasn't the misery that ate at him, or the loneliness. He'd grown used to it. It was the feeling that a change was coming. The sense that something wonderful lay just around the corner, only to see his hopes dashed and to find he'd given his heart to a woman who did not want him.

'Good morning.' She'd come into the breakfast room so quietly that he hadn't heard. And her voice was hoarse, as though she'd cried herself to sleep after creeping back to her room in the night. Unable to rest, he had gone to the library in search of the brandy bottle and when he returned she was gone from his bed.

'Good morning,' he responded. What else could he say to her? What apology could he offer? What explanation could he give that would take the bitterness out of this morning?

She'd come into his life, unwilling. He'd laughed to himself that his mother had chosen the perfect bride, a woman just as unhappy as he was. It would be a case of like drawing to like and they could live ever after in the gloom of this house, raising a pack of pitiable brats in stony silence.

And he'd learned her story and been moved by it. And watched as she'd blossomed, changing the house and her surroundings and giving him reason to hope that things might be different. Different for him. Different between them.

'Coffee?'

Before he could decline, she was filling his cup. She would do the same with his afternoon tea, adding the milk and lemon that he liked. He could never remember telling her his preferences, but she knew them, none the less, and went out of her way to see him comfortable. The coffee burned on his tongue like bile.

He'd looked at her across the ballroom, last night and been dazzled by her. The gown that he'd bought her, the jewels that he'd given her sparkling against her neck. And she'd smiled to him as the crowd swept her away. He heard the sighs of the young men as she passed and the curious whisperings of the dowagers, and he'd basked in their envy.

The wine at dinner and the brandy after had been too much. Odd that the drink would affect him so. But he suspected it wasn't the drink. He was drunk with the sight of her, the joy of knowing that she was his. His body hummed with it. Anticipation. He felt like…

A bridegroom. And he'd grown tired of the knowing smiles that the other men gave him, the too-hearty pats on the back, when he saw her searching for him, calling his name and sneaking in to the darkened library.

And, unable to wait a moment longer, he followed her. Excited beyond all reason at the scandal of it. Hurtling towards the inevitable and would have taken her there in her gown on the library floor if only…

He pounded his fist into a palm to bring himself back to the truth. And she jumped in alarm, dropping the spoon she'd been holding and letting it clatter to her plate. Then, with deliberation, she picked the thing up and went back to her breakfast, not eating but moving the food around on her plate in a credible simulation of someone enjoying her meal.

If only she'd known who he was. The kisses she'd given him were meant for someone else.

And when they'd got home…

The woman who had smiled so at the ball could hardly bring herself to look at him. And he'd silenced her, afraid of what she might say.

'I never loved you.'

'Release me.'

'Let me go to him.'

He'd lost himself in the alabaster of her skin, the curve of her throat. A body made to love and be loved, even if it held a faithless heart.

But at least what had happened between his wife and his brother had not gone so far as to cast doubts on legitimacy. She'd come to his bed a virgin. There were ways of tricking a man, he well knew, if a woman chose to go to the trouble. She'd had no time to prepare a deception and he'd felt her body respond with pain, not pleasure, when he'd entered her. In his carelessness, and jealousy, he'd hurt her.

He pushed away from the table and went to the window and stared out over the garden. The sun played in over the flowers, mocking them with the illusion of peace and happiness.

'St John is gone.' She had come to stand beside him and was looking out of the window as well.

'I know.' That was his way, after all. It always had been. Cause as much chaos as possible, and then disappear, leaving the shambles in his wake.

'The grooms said he rode out shortly before we got home.'

So she'd gone to find him first thing this morning. He twisted a hand in the velvet draperies and felt the rings giving way under the pressure of his hand. He willed himself to relax before answering. 'I know.'

'Last night, at the ball—'

'Let us not speak of last night,' he cut in. 'I do not wish to hear the details. I am willing to forget last night ever happened—' *God how I want to forget.* '—if you can promise me—can swear—that any child born to you will be mine.' He turned to her, awaiting the answer.

'I swear.' Her voice was almost inaudible.

'Very good, then,' he said, untangling himself from the curtain. 'I have business to attend to today. I will see you this evening.' He strode from the room.

Miranda watched the tension in her husband's retreating back, as though the weight of her gaze was too much to bear. She sank on to her chair and toyed with her breakfast. She'd hoped, with St John gone, to have a chance to talk things out with her husband. Of course, she'd hoped to be free of the secrets she was already keeping, and now he'd insisted on making it worse. After last night, there was yet another on the list of things that she must never discuss.

Damn St John for knowing his brother too well. It was a strike at his heart, as well as his pride. She was sure, before last night, that he had warmed to her and that things were to be easier between them.

And he had responded, when she'd found him in the library. He'd responded with enthusiasm. She shuddered as desire flooded her again. If it had been St John, would she have reacted as she had?

St John's expertise could never have overcome the hatred she felt for him. When she'd found Marcus, her heart had known what her mind did not, and she'd responded to his kisses. But how could she explain if Marcus wished to pretend that nothing had happened? And he still talked of children.

It's all he's really interested in.

Perhaps so. But if not love, there had been warmth before. And the sense that there could be more than breeding in the time they spent together in his bed. Last night had been brief and there had been pain, but he had not used her in cruelty. She remembered the touch of his hands, and his lips, on her body, and felt need growing inside her, driving out the fear. She would go back to him tonight, without the shadow between them and see if he truly meant to forget the ball.

He kept good his promise and stayed away all day and into the evening, leaving her to dine alone. Perhaps he meant to forget by avoiding anything that reminded. Perhaps he intended to stay away for months at a time, visiting occasionally to try to get her with child.

She gritted her teeth. Cici was right. The only way her position would be secure in the house was with a babe in arms. And if he intended to come home at all, she would be ready for him. She summoned Polly and requested a bath and her best nightrail. Then she sat at the edge of her bed and waited, listening for the telltale sounds from next door.

The clock crept forward, hour by hour, and it was almost midnight when she was ready to give up. Perhaps, if she crept into his room through the adjoining door, he could find her in his own bed, if he came home.

If.

She would have to do something, she realised, or she would go mad wondering. She tested the doorknob and, as it had the first night, it gave in her hand. She pushed.

He was already there, sitting on the edge of the bed with a brandy glass in his hand, staring out of the window.

'Marcus?' She stood in the doorway, hesitant to continue without an invitation to enter.

'What do you want, Miranda?'

What did she want? Why must he make everything so hard? 'I thought… Did you want…? Will you be needing me to-night?' Wonderful. She felt like a servant, waiting to be dismissed.

He swirled the brandy in his glass. And smiled as he spoke. 'I did not expect you. But if you persist in standing in the doorway like that, I will most certainly be needing you. The light from behind you renders that nightdress transparent.'

'Oh.' She took a step forward out of the light, closing the door behind her and then stopped, confused. He had been admiring her, which was a desirable result, and she'd put a stop to it by closing the door.

'Is there something I can do for you, Miranda?'

Yes, there was, but she was unsure exactly what. Cici would know what to do to work her charms on a man, but she'd never explained in any detail. She'd hinted that, once things got to the point of being in the bedroom and available, no further magic was necessary. 'I thought, perhaps, if you were eager that I should conceive that it would be wise to try more than once.'

The words struck him as funny and he roared with laughter, flopping back on to the bed, spilling the last of the brandy into the sheets. 'Do you, now? Well, then, madam. I wish that I hadn't got foxed at the inn, for I can hardly manage my own boots. Lord knows how I'll manage with you.'

'What of your valet?'

'Dismissed him for the night. Not fair, keepin' the servants up all night because I've not got the sense to come to bed.'

At last, this was something she understood. She stepped forward and knelt at his feet, tugging the boots down over his calf and off, and setting them aside. Then, she climbed up into the bed and retrieved the brandy glass, setting it on the bedside table. He sat up to watch her and she slipped her arms inside his jacket, pushed it down his shoulders and off, carrying it to the wardrobe to hang.

When she came back to the bed for the waistcoat, he eased away from her, so she had to crawl on to the bed to retrieve it. She carried it away to hang with the coat, feeling his eyes on her, as she walked. When she turned back to the bed, he'd moved to the centre, and was leaning against the headboard with his hands behind his head in feigned nonchalance. She sighed and climbed on to the bed after him, undoing the elegant knot of his cravat and his shirt.

He caught her hands, when she reached for the buttons on his breeches, and rolled, trapping her beneath him with her hands at her head. 'What are you playing at?' He stared down into her eyes, his expression hard.

'It is past midnight, and you are sitting fully dressed in your bed. I assumed you needed assistance and am providing it.'

'I'm not as drunk as all that. You make a most efficient valet, madam. Do you have much experience?'

She glared back at him. 'Yes, from dressing and undressing the infirm. I can undo a button as well as any of your servants, your Grace, although I'd not be able to tie as fine a cravat as your valet. But, that is not what you mean, is it? I came here tonight because I thought you meant for us to start fresh. Last night at the ball—'

'I do not wish you to speak of it.'

'No, but you plan to reproach me with it for an eternity without hearing a word in my defence. Last night at the ball, your brother requested that I meet him in the library, or he would reveal certain facts to you.'

'And you went to the library…'

'I did not know what else to do. I thought perhaps there would be a candlestick, or a letter opener, something that I could strike him with to make him leave me alone.'

'And you found me there instead?'

'And I quite forgot, for a moment, my reason for coming to the library in the first place. Your kisses are most…' she paused, blushing '…distracting.'

His eyes went dark and she heard his breath quicken. 'And what are these facts that my brother knew and you were so afraid to tell me?'

She closed her eyes and began. 'While you were in London—' she felt his body go tense against her '—I did not know where you were or when you would be back.'

'But, in my letter—'

Her eyes flew open. 'What letter? I received none. I had no idea where you'd gone or why.'

His body was still tense, but the grip on her wrists relaxed. 'I think I begin to understand. Go on.'

'Your brother befriended me. He was kind. I was flattered. And I didn't notice at first that he was becoming too familiar.'

'And just how familiar did he become?'

She took a deep breath and felt the tension in him. 'He touched my hair. My ankle. He kissed me.' She hurried over the last bit, hoping that he might not notice. 'And I locked myself in my room, and would not see him again. The next day you were back and he was gone.'

'And this is what happened between you, that you were afraid to tell me.'

'He said that you would believe the worst, and that you only wanted me for the child I could bring, so that it should not matter to me how you felt.'

'He said that I did not desire you?' He laughed again, and she looked up, startled.

'He is your brother, and I am new to this house. How was I to know truth from lies?'

'So my brother deceived you, and you put your honour at risk trying to conceal the fact. I asked you once, Miranda, to not lie to me about the contents of your heart. Is there anything else you wish to tell me?'

She bit her lip. If the truth was too much for him to bear, then so be it. She began. 'When I was ten, my mother died and my father lost the family home.' She proceeded methodically through their fall in circumstances and told him everything, up to her arrival at his doorstep.

And she felt his body relaxing against her, and her own nerves unknot as the truth came out and disaster did not strike.

His voice was level, when he spoke again. 'Now I charge you, tell me the truth. You were sent here against your will to make a match. And it is much the same to your family who your husband is, as long as you are settled. I find no pleasure in fighting to keep a woman who has given her heart elsewhere. If last night had not happened, if I had not touched you, if you were free to go and he would have you—would you go to St John?'

'No.' It was barely a whisper. 'I was a fool and he took advantage of the fact. Turn me out if you must, Marcus, but don't make me go to him. He is wicked and I would rather go to the workhouse than to your brother.'

His tone was dry. 'Very well. You do not prefer my brother to the workhouse. And where do I stand? My brother thinks I've spent ten years in the fleshpots of Europe without learning to appreciate a beautiful woman when I find one under my own roof.'

'Beautiful?' The word echoed in her mind.

'Miranda.' He smiled and touched her lip. 'There is a statue in a Paris museum, of a Greek goddess. I visited her often, since the sight of her made me want to climb the plinth and lick the marble. And when you stand in the doorway with the light illuminating your body, I detect a startling resemblance.'

'Oh.' She squirmed under his weight.

'Am I making you uncomfortable?'

'No,' she murmured.

He released her wrists and slid off her body to lie beside her, his hand resting on her hip so that she could feel the warmth of it through the fabric.

'Of course, you have many other qualities that I find admirable.'

'Really?' She suspected that he was teasing, but was at a loss as to why.

'You have a quick wit and a keen mind. A firm hand with the servants. You understand what it takes to manage a great household and do it better than my mother ever did. You do not respond in fits of tears when I bully you, but have a fine temper of your own.

'If it weren't for an annoying tendency on your part to keep secrets from me for my own good, and always put your wants and needs last, I would say you were near perfection in what I would seek for in a wife.'

'Oh.'

He ran a thumb along the bow of her lip. 'And you say you find my kisses distracting?'

She could feel her skin going red with heat. 'I was unable to think of anything else.'

He leaned forward and brushed her lips with his. 'But surely they are common if you can confuse my brother's kisses with mine.'

She bowed her head. 'I had so few of your kisses with which to compare.'

He leaned forward again and this time he lingered, and she parted her lips to him. The kiss seeped into her like water into the soil. He tasted her lips and her tongue, and she sighed into his mouth and reached out to him, pulling herself close to his chest to feel his heart beating close beside hers.

'Better?' He breathed into her ear.

'Yes. But…' How could she say it without hurting him? She stopped.

'No more secrets, wife. Say what you are thinking.'

'But not the same as yesterday.' She stopped again. 'And you did not kiss me at all, when we—'

'I could not kiss you then. I did not dare. I wanted you beyond reason. With a word, you could have ripped the heart from my body and left me dying. I looked at your body and knew I could not help my reaction to it, but I was afraid to share my soul with you. As I do now.' And his lips came down upon hers and swept away all thought, and she clung to him as he took the sweetness from her mouth and left her hungry for things she didn't know or understand.

And the kiss moved down her throat to her shoulders and the swell of her breasts, and she struggled against the fabric of her nightdress until he pushed it out of the way and covered her nipple with his mouth and stroked with his hands and his tongue until she moaned.

He pulled away to kiss her temple, and she whispered, 'Yes. That is you. That is what I want.'

'And is that all?' He was laughing at her again, but she didn't care. 'If there is more than that?'

There is, her body urged. *There is.*

'Then I want you to give it to me.'

He framed her face in his hands, and smiled again. 'I was a fool to leave you alone, even for a moment.' He stroked her body through the nightdress and down the side of her leg. His smile faded, but the glint in his eyes was pure devilment. 'And my brother touched only your ankle?'

'Through the stocking,' she responded. 'I fell. And he said he was checking for injury.'

'Of course. I'd say some fustian like that myself to get a hand under your skirt.'

'Under my skirt?'

But he'd slid to the bottom of the bed and held her ankle between the palms of his hands. 'And which would it be, this injured ankle. The left or the right?'

'I don't remember.'

'Both, then.' And he was kissing her insteps and her arches, swirling a tongue over the little knobs of bone. Running hands up the length of her legs to grasp her behind her knees and spread her legs to straddle his face.

And his kisses had reached her knee caps, which was interesting, but not as interesting as what his hands were doing to the sensitive skin on the inside of her thighs. And his tongue was gliding along her skin, but his fingers had reached the place where her legs joined, and…

'Oh, Lord.'

He stopped. He stopped and raised his head to look at her. And he was smiling again. 'Did you say something?'

'No. Well, yes. It's just…very good.'

'Good.' And his hands resumed their movement, and his thumbs began doing something incredible, and his fingertips grazed the opening of her and dipped inside, and she twisted against him, unsure whether she needed to be closer or further away.

And his kisses continued to climb her legs until she thought perhaps he meant to kiss her…

'Oh, dear God.'

He paused, with a finger still inside her, stroking gently, and looked up into her eyes. 'I'm sorry. Did you speak?'

'It was nothing. It's just that I've never felt anything like this before.'

He wasn't smiling any more. And his face disappeared

from view, as he returned to kissing her, and his lips reached their goal as his hands slid beneath her to draw her closer.

And her hands were twisted in the bedclothes as they had been the night before, but in fear that she would be carried away by the waves of feeling crashing through her body, and she felt the muscles that had resisted the night before, clenching and pulsing, and the confused empty feeling was gone and replaced by chaos and triumph and she thought she must have cried out for joy, but the room seemed too far away to hear the sound, and then she was floating back to it, and the sensation of her husband's head resting on her belly and his hand laying between her legs.

'Well.' The last of her breath left her with a whoosh.

She could feel him smile against her, and she smiled back, amazed.

'Well?' His voice was deep and the sound rumbled against her skin and made it tingle. He ran fingertips along the length of her leg and she shuddered against him.

'What happens, now?'

'You honestly don't know?' His voice was light and she heard amazement, and a touch of smugness. 'What happens now is what you choose, my love. I am at your command.'

'Do you want to…what we did last night?' She could feel that he was hard, but there was no tension in the rest of him.

'We could.' There was a touch of doubt in his voice. 'If, after last night, you are not sore. I was not as gentle as I could have been. And I would not hurt you again in a quest for pleasure.'

She felt a yearning, building within her, to be closer to him. To be held in his arms, even as she held him in her body. 'I would like to try.'

He slid up the bed to lie beside her. 'A different way,

perhaps. Easier for you to decide what is right.' He stroked her with his hand as his lips settled against her breast, tasting and teasing. She could feel her body starting to glow again and wondered, how long? How often? How much pleasure could she stand without dying from sheer joy? She ran a hand along his side and felt the muscles and the strange angles and hardness of her husband's body. The unexpected planes and smoothness and the roughness of old scars. And, ever so gently she let her hand drift lower, to stroke him as he was stroking her.

His hands went hard on her and pulled her closer, and his mouth found her neck and bit, sucking the skin until she felt the pull inside her. He took her mouth and it was rough and wonderful and she revelled in the taking.

Then he trapped her hips in his hands, pushing himself against her, and she braced for his entry, but instead, he rolled over on his back, dragging her on top of him.

He whispered, 'Do what you want.' And took the imprisoning hands from her body.

She kissed him. Cautiously at first, then building to the intensity that he had given her, thrusting her tongue into his mouth, trying to take him all into her. Then she pulled away to slide a hand between them to find him again, and feel the skin, so unlike anything she'd felt on her own body, and to stoke until his breath came in tight gasps, and she felt a drop of liquid smoothing the path of her fingers.

And she listened to her body, calling to be filled. Telling her what must happen next, and she straddled him, and guided him until he was inside her and she could stroke with her body as she had with her hand.

He moaned under her, and cried out, 'My love', and the

sound gave her power to quicken the pace, and then he shuddered and she felt the rush of him against the building tension in her own body, and she stroked again until the tension broke and she lay spent on top of him.

He was murmuring in her ear, again. Calling her his darling and his heart, speaking haltingly in French, which tickled her ears, but which she did not understand.

'I'm sorry, your Grace' she whispered, as she licked his throat, 'but I have no idea what it is you are saying to me.'

'I will teach you, then,' he whispered back.

'I am glad…' she kissed him again '…for you are a most amazing teacher.'

She reached out to touch him and felt him go hard in her hand.

He smiled. 'And I think it is time for another lesson.'

His Grace's valet returned to below stairs shortly after breakfast and sat at the table in shock. Never in all his years with the duke had he seen the like. He'd arrived at the usual time, to wake the duke and lay out his clothes for the day, only to find him wrapping a dressing gown around himself and shutting the bed's hangings behind him.

And he was smiling.

Not the knowing smiles he'd seen in Paris or London, or the glares he was accustomed to, when his Grace was in residence at the manor. This was the look of a man drunk on pleasure.

His Grace, the duke, raised a finger cautiously to his lips. 'Shh.'

When he went to the wardrobe to select the day's clothes the duke waved him away. 'That won't be necessary, Thomas. I think I will be spending the day in my rooms.'

'Are you ill, your Grace?'

'Exhausted.' His tone rose. 'Too spent to consider leaving my rooms. Almost too tired to rise.'

Thomas distinctly heard a feminine giggle from behind the hangings of the bed.

'I expect my wife would also like to remain in bed. Send Polly away today, for I doubt she'll be needed.'

Thomas nodded dubiously. 'And breakfast, your Grace?'

'Leave the tray outside the door, Thomas. And bring enough for two, for I am most uncommonly hungry today. Lunch as well. Possibly even supper.'

There was another giggle from the bed and his Grace the duke positively grinned.

Chapter Twenty-Four

Miranda stared up into her husband's face as he sat before the fire, sipping his port. Evenings were her favourite time of day, when the house was putting itself to bed and the day's duties were done. She thought back to how worried she'd been, when the silences between them had seemed so oppressive.

As time passed, and they'd found happiness, the silence had grown richer than words. He could sit for hours staring into the fire, but now he smiled instead of scowled, and closed his eyes, at peace with her and with himself. And she sat beside him, dozing with her head on his shoulder or in his lap, while he stroked her hair.

She hated to break the silence tonight, but it was time, she thought, to ask the things she wanted to know. And it would be better now, when he was relaxed and happy, than waiting until he might be less receptive to her. 'Marcus?'

'Yes, my love.'

'There is something I would ask of you.'

'Anything, Miranda. Anything for you.'

She sighed. 'I am not so sure if you know what you are saying. Promise me you will not be angry.'

He ruffled her curls. 'You are wheedling, wife. Trying to be coy. It does not become you. Plain speaking between us, remember. What is it you want?'

'I want you to tell me about St John.'

His hand stilled on her hair and the room seemed to get colder around her.

She pressed on. 'Why does he hate you so? Is it just that he is jealous? Has it always been thus?'

He was silent, and she felt his body grow tense. 'Why do you ask about things that are in the past?'

'Because I know how damaging secrets are, for the person who keeps them. I want to be a part of your life, Marcus.'

'You already are, Miranda. Not just a part. You are my life.'

'All the more reason for you to tell me about your past. I want to know all of you.'

He sighed. 'How much has he told you already? When you were alone with him, he talked, didn't he?'

'But he lied, Marcus. About so much. I don't know if I heard two words of truth out of him in two weeks.'

He stared into the fire as if puzzling out the answer. 'His truth and mine are not the same, Miranda. And that is the problem.'

'What is your truth, then?'

'That our relationship was doomed from the start. Father favoured his heir. Mother favoured her younger son. And they played the two of us off against each other, letting us quarrel as they quarrelled with each other. Neither of us was happy with what we had. He had the affection but I had the respect.

'We competed in all things. I almost broke my neck trying

to jump a fence. He is the better rider, and Father forbade me to follow him. And St John laughed and called me coward. He was always wild, and I envied him for it. I had to be the sensible one. Especially after Father died and the title came to me. He spent the allowance Mother insisted I give him and threw my charity back in my face.

'Finally, we quarreled over a woman. We were rivals, and against all common sense I won her, and found no happiness in winning. He has never forgiven me.'

She spoke the word she was afraid to hear him speak. 'Bethany?'

'Yes. And you, Miranda, wandered into the thicket with us, and the whole thing began again.'

She moved closer to him and whispered, 'But it ended differently, I hope. Are you happy with me, husband?'

He smiled down at her, a sad little smile. 'Most happy with you, wife.'

She smiled back at him and wrapped her arms around his waist. 'Then I will never leave you.'

He kissed the top of her head. 'I will ask you to leave me now, darling. It is bedtime, I think. Go up to our rooms and wait for me. I will be along shortly.'

She kissed him back, and left him staring intently into the fire as though the answer to all of life's questions was written in the flames.

She hurried up the stairs, hoping that it would not be long until he came to her. It was worrisome to see him like this, so deep in thought that he could not be roused away from it. Knowing that she had forced him to it made things all the worse. Still, it was better than when he had been angry all the time. Or filled with the all-encompassing sadness that had held him so much of his life. To mourn occasionally for the life he never had, to be sometimes moody, was natural, she supposed. At least it was not the unbearable weight on his soul that it had been.

And when he came to her later, his mood would change fast enough. She shivered in anticipation, so glad that he wasn't the bookish scholar she had hoped for, or the tired older man, or even the dashing young one, but instead the temperamental, brooding, stubborn man that she had married. A man capable of more love and tenderness than she had ever imagined on that first day when he'd stormed and sworn at the prospect of marriage.

She entered her room and closed the door out of habit, even as she realised that something was wrong.

There was someone there. She could feel it. Could feel eyes staring at her at the edge of the candlelight.

She turned slowly, back still against the door, to see St John, lounging there on top of the coverlet of her bed. With disgust, she noticed that his boots were muddy and staining the bedclothes. In his hand, he held a cocked pistol, pointed at her.

'What are you doing here?' She tried to keep the quaver out of her voice.

'Waiting for you.'

'How—?'

'—Did I come here? How did I get in?' He smiled, and it was the same cheerful grin he'd used to woo her. His tone was light, but the glint in his eyes was deadly serious.

'It is not so hard, once you have the keys. Mrs Clopton still hates you, you know. But she was always quite fond of me. She's working at an inn on the main road. When you let her go, you should have thought to ask for the second set of keys. She was most forthcoming with them when I wanted them.'

'And what—?'

'Do I want from you? Why don't you stop asking questions and let me finish, Miranda. For that is what I want. To finish the business between us.'

'There is nothing between us. We are finished, St John.' Her voice gave lie to the words.

His held the same annoying confidence. 'I beg to differ. We are finished when I say we are finished.'

She turned to grab for the door handle and saw, out of the corner of her eye, the pistol barrel following her movements.

'Uh, uh, uh.' He wagged a finger at her as though she were a disobedient child. 'It is far too early to think about leaving. Relax, my dear. Why don't you have a seat at the writing desk? And go slowly. I'm afraid sudden movements or screaming on your part might startle me and cause an accident.'

'You don't seriously mean to shoot me, do you?' Her voice was not as steady as she had hoped.

'I don't mean to, no. But I could. For now at least, make yourself comfortable. Now remove some stationery from the desk and write what I tell you to write. Then we are going on a little trip. If all goes according to plan, you will be released unhurt.'

'When?' she demanded.

'A few days. A week perhaps. As long as it takes for your husband to realise that you are gone. And to realise who you are with and what you've been doing.'

'What I've been doing? If this is some crude attempt at seduction… Kidnapping and rape?' She managed a frail laugh.

'Really, St John, you might as well leave now. Or prepare to use that gun you're holding—I'll die before I let you touch me.'

'Let me?' His laugh was hearty and confident. 'You have a very lopsided view of the circumstances as they present themselves, my dear. I'll shoot you if you try to escape, of course. And as for the rest? If I choose to have you, the gun will hardly be necessary. I outweigh you by several stone and am perfectly capable of forcing you to do what I want.' His eyes travelled over her body. 'Of course, it would be much more pleasant for both of us if you came to me willingly, as my brother's first wife did.'

She stared at him in disgust. 'I don't care what is in the past. If you think I plan to repeat the infidelities of my husband's first duchess…'

He waved a dismissive hand. 'It is unnecessary for you to decide anything at this point. I would not dismiss the possibility out of hand. I know my brother better than you. You may not care what is in the past, but it is very much alive to him. The knowledge that you spent a week alone in my company, whether willing or unwilling, should be sufficient to accomplish my ends.'

'And just what are your ends, St John?'

'To ruin, once and for all, any happiness that my brother might have on this earth. To make him wonder for the rest of his life whether his first child looks a little too much like me. To destroy his trust in you, now that it is too late to cast you off.' He stared at her. 'It is too late, isn't it? You are not the unknowing girl I met a few short weeks ago, but his wife for good and earnest. And my brother has no doubt formed an attachment to you. Marcus is too soft-hearted by far when it comes to women. That was what made it so easy for Bethany to come to me, once they were married. He trusted her, despite evidence to the contrary. At first he did not want to believe, and, when his face was rubbed in the truth, things had progressed too far for him to see a way out. His precious honour would not allow him to divest himself of a wife that loved another. Let us see how he handles the thing this time.'

'But it is not the same, St John,' she protested. 'I do not love you. I loathe you. And Marcus knows this.'

'But that was not always true, was it, Miranda?' There was a trace of hope in his voice. 'I remember the look in your eyes those first weeks. You did not loathe me then. And if Marcus had not returned when he had, you'd have been mine. Can you look in my eyes and lie to me? Tell me that it is not true.'

She stared straight into his eyes and through him. 'St John, you are beautiful to look at. And charming. Perhaps I could have loved the man I thought you were, when you were kind to me. But that was all a lie. Every word you said to me.'

'Not every word, perhaps,' he murmured.

Her temper flared. 'You have the nerve to come to my room, talking sweet words, but with a pistol in your hand. Your present actions prove to me that the sweet, funny man I knew is not the real you at all. There is something twisted in you, St John. Something ugly and broken. And it repels me.'

The smile twisted on his face as her words hit home. 'Fortunately for me, your approval of my character is not required.' He waved the pistol at a blank paper on the desk. 'You are going to write a letter to your husband, now, explaining our elopement.'

'I most certainly will not.'

'You can write it in ink or I will write it in blood on the

walls.' His voice was cold and angry and the hand holding the pistol was rock steady.

'Marcus will never believe that I went with you willingly.' Her voice was losing its bluster.

'It will not matter whether you come willingly or are dragged out of this room by your hair. When you return to him, Marcus will say he believes you. Perhaps he will even believe he speaks the truth. And he will welcome you back with open arms. But he will wonder. He will lie awake beside you at night, wondering what truly happened while you were with me. And the more you protest, the less he will trust. Of course, I will assure him. Lay his fears to rest.' He laughed. 'Much as I did when he was married to Bethany. It will not matter if I leave you untouched, and say in all honesty that nothing happened. Honesty from my lips rings more false in his ears than any lie I could produce.'

'But I am not Bethany, St John. Things are different from how they used to be. Marcus is different. And he will trust me when I tell him the truth.'

I hope. The voice rose small in her. *Although I was untrustworthy before, he will trust me now.*

St John stared into her eyes. 'You really think that he will trust you? And how much does he know about you, really? Does he know about your guardian, for instance? The notable Lady Cecily?'

She stared at him in amazement. 'You truly are the most horrible person I have ever met. And deluded, if you think that you can hold me against my will and ruin your brother so easily. You are right, St John. We are well and truly married now. He knows the truth. And as for your pathetic little scheme?' She shrugged. 'It did not work the last time, when you so obviously compromised me at the ball. Yet you try the same thing again. Will you never learn, or must I go through repeated blackmail and kidnapping until we are all old and grey?'

There was a flicker of doubt in his eyes and she pushed on.

'You could kill me, and drag the body downstairs to lay it at your brother's feet. But I don't think you have the stomach for it.' She prayed she was correct. 'They'd hang you for a cold-blooded murderer. A rope around the neck is not nearly so fashionable as your cravat.

'Your brother, however? When he finds you, I doubt he'll have any compunction about putting a ball through your heart. And he'll be doing it in defence of his wife's honour. Are you sure you want to continue with this?'

His eyes were hooded, but she noticed the muzzle of the pistol droop.

'Go now, St John. Marcus has done nothing so terrible to deserve such hatred as this. And if he did, it is in the past. Do not let it destroy what is left of both your lives. Let it go.'

The gun was pointed towards the ground, now. Her argument was succeeding. She could see the tiredness in his eyes. He opened his mouth to speak.

And suddenly the connecting door burst open and Marcus strode into the room. There was a look of murder in his eyes.

'I can explain,' she began.

'You don't have to explain. I can guess what happened,' he growled. 'Stand aside.' His eye on the pistol, he stepped in front of her. 'Keep out of the way, Miranda. Go into my room and wait for me there. This will be over soon enough. St John, get down off the bed and let us settle this once and for all.'

'Marcus, no.' She tried to step in front of him, but he pushed her back. 'I will not leave you.' Not while St John still held his pistol and her husband stood before him unarmed.

'Brother, I didn't expect you so soon.' St John's arms opened wide and he smiled as he swung his feet off the bed. Marcus's eyes followed the pistol as it veered off target.

'You invade my house and force yourself into my wife's bedchamber and do not expect that I will find you? The servants have been warned. If they value their jobs, they will tell me of your presence. I am not the fool I once was, St John.'

St John's smile was triumphant. 'How do you know I am not here by invitation?'

Her heart stopped in her throat, for barely a beat before he answered, 'Because I know you. And because I know my wife. You may think me a fool, but she knows I am not.' He smiled coldly. 'If she invited you here, then she would make certain you were not caught.'

'Really? I suppose that is true. She is very good at keeping secrets, is she not? Do you know she was raised by a whore and a drunkard?'

'Is that the revelation you've been holding over her head? It has no legs, St John. I've known from the first. When I went to London after our marriage.'

St John seemed to deflate a bit, and Marcus shot her a quick encouraging look. 'And don't think that you can threaten her with exposure. I'll stand by her. It matters not to me, one way or the other. I imagine the family that can hold you can stand one more scandal. And it is a very old scandal, is it not? And now that her father's debts are paid…'

'Paid?' Her legs buckled under her and she collapsed into the chair by the desk.

'I was saving it for a Christmas present.' Marcus's smile was sincere as he looked at her. 'My idiot brother has spoiled my surprise.'

Her father was free. She could rest easy, knowing that he was safe. If she survived the night, of course. She smiled weakly back at her husband.

St John growled low in his throat, frustrated that his threat was not being received in the intended light. Then he grinned. 'Very well. So it doesn't matter to you if you drag your own name through the mud marrying the student of a whore. How well does she know our old family scandals, Marcus?'

'She knows enough, St John. The rest is better left dead and buried with the people concerned, where it's been for ten years.'

St John raised the pistol again and pointed it towards his brother. 'Dead for you, Marcus. You never suffered for it.'

'Oh, I suffered, St John. Much as you wish to believe otherwise.'

'Suffered tragically, I'm sure.' St John turned to her and gestured with the pistol in his hand. 'Your precious husband, your duke, who had had everything his way since the moment of birth. The title, the land, the woman, the heir. All falling into his lap, and still he wasn't happy. Not even when he had taken what little belonged to me. Did he tell you, then, how he came to marry Bethany? Despite the fact that she was engaged to me?'

'Engaged?' She looked to Marcus.

'Abandoned, more likely,' Marcus countered. 'And already with child. And I knew nothing of it until too late.'

'You lie. You wanted her because she was beautiful. And because she was mine. You always were a greedy bastard,

Marcus. Never satisfied with the best and the biggest share. You had to have it all, didn't you? I went to London. I was coming back with a ring. You waited until my back was turned and took her from me.'

Marcus held out a hand in supplication. 'As I told you at the time, God help me, if Mother had told me the whole truth before the wedding, I'd never have married the girl. She couldn't find you, for you'd run off yet again. Bethany's family wanted justice to be done and honour restored. They came to Mother with the story and not to me.

'And she made her plans as she always did, not caring a whit for what it would do to the family. Mother threw us together. Bethany was beautiful. She was talented. I was besotted. How could I not be? I knew there had been something between you, but she gave no sign that it was serious.'

'You could have looked for me. You could have asked me for the truth.'

'I didn't want the truth. I wanted the woman. And she didn't want you, St John, if there was a duke to be had. An eighteen-year-old, younger son is no prize when the peer is handy and gullible. And our dear mother cared not that I was not to father my own heir. If you, her favourite, could not have the title, then your son could be duke after me. It was a tidy plan. But then, our mother always was good at those things.'

'History repeats itself,' St John spat back. 'Our mother has chosen you another bride who arrives on the doorstep without her honour but eager for a title. And you are just as gullible as you ever were.'

'And you think that you can steal my wife away from me, as easily as you did ten years ago?'

'If your first wife had lived, she would still be mine.'

'And your child my heir.' It was Marcus's turn to spit. 'If she had lived, she would have led us both a merry dance, and my heir could have been a coachman's son. Mother was as big a fool as either of us to believe the girl's story. Even on our wedding night, Bethany knew more tricks in the bedroom than she could have learned from you.'

'Liar.' The word exploded out of St John like a pistol shot.

'Swear to me that she was innocent when you first came to her, and that you were not a boy, green with love and as gullible as I was.'

'Damn you, and your title and your land. You married the woman I loved and you let her die.'

'And she loved neither of us. Let her stay dead.' Marcus held out a hand to his brother, all the time watching the pistol.

'No.' It came out as a howl. Then St John threw the gun aside and lunged for his brother.

His fists landed again and again against Marcus, who grunted and received the blows. Blood was trickling from his split lip and he gasped as a fist connected with his stomach, but he was the bigger man and stayed upright. He forced his arms up to shield himself against his younger brother and pushed to separate them. And then his hands closed on St John's throat.

The younger man continued to thrash, but his blows weakened.

Her husband's eyes were distant, and sorrowful, but his grip remained steady.

'Marcus. Enough. Let him go. He is your brother,' Miranda pleaded with him, as the contest, so obviously unmatched, headed towards a murderous conclusion.

With an oath he threw his brother's body away from him, and St John lay panting on the carpet. 'You were right, St

John. I am too soft to kill you. You are my brother, worthless wretch though you are.' He looked hopelessly at Miranda. 'But what am I to do with him? He will try again to hurt you, if he thinks by doing it he can hurt me.'

'Why stop him, Miranda? Let him kill me. Make him finish the job he started years ago.'

She looked down at St John, still panting on the carpet, eyes full of death and despair, the red marks of his brother's hands on his throat. Then she rose and walked to her jewel case, and got what she sought.

She walked back to him then and stood over him, unafraid. 'St John, it is over. You have lost. You cannot use me to hurt Marcus. I will not let you. Even if you find your revenge here, you cannot bring Bethany back. Nothing will change the past. If you cannot live with that, if you truly wish for death, you must find it some other way than at your brother's hand, for I will not let him hurt you.'

Marcus stirred next to her and she wondered, if the circumstance were repeated, whether she would be able to do anything of the kind.

Then she opened her hand and dropped the Haughleigh emeralds on to St John's heaving chest. 'When I came to this house, you befriended me. Tell me now, was it all a lie?'

He looked at her, and his face softened, but he said nothing.

'If there was some moment of kindness, some trace of warmth and friendship for me, aside from the plans and machinations you worked against your brother's wife, I thank you for it. I will choose to forget the rest and remember that you were kind to me. But I will not have you in my house any longer if you mean to come between my husband and I. Take the necklace. You cannot have the title, or the house, or me. But you can take this symbol of the family honour. You deserve some share of that. Take it and sell it. It is more than enough to buy yourself a commission. A fresh start, St John, far away from here. If you are so eager to throw your life away, do it in defence of your country, and not in some ridiculous scheme to die at your brother's hands.'

She offered him her hand and pulled him to his feet.

He paused, allowing the necklace to slip to the floor before snatching it and stuffing it into his pocket. Then he brushed off his clothes and rubbed a hand across his swollen neck. He wiped the sweat from his face with the corner of his wilted cravat and when his hand passed away from it she saw the same devil-may-care expression that she had seen on the first day drop into place like a mask. He turned to her and bowed, deeply and sarcastically. 'Thank you, your Grace, for being so free with your husband's favours, since you refuse to be free with your own.'

She saw Marcus tense to respond, and felt the relief flood through her as he checked himself.

St John turned to his brother and offered the same sarcastic salute. 'And thank you, Marcus, for my worthless life, much good will the sparing of it do either of us. I will no doubt squander it and the money I'll get for this trinket. Whether I go to the Peninsula, or some whore pit in London, is yet to be decided, but you can be comforted with the fact that, when I die, your hands will be free of blood.'

She looked to her husband and saw only a glint in his eye to prove that the last barb had struck home. 'I cannot save you from yourself, St John. Only you can do that. If you cannot find happiness, then may you at least find peace.'

And with a bitter laugh, St John strolled from the room and his footsteps died away as he retreated down the hall.

Chapter Twenty-Five

Miranda looked down the table at her husband as she had done so many mornings in the past six months and smiled. He was reading his mail, and when he sensed her eyes upon him he took the letter before him and slipped it to the bottom of the stack and out of sight.

'Is there anything interesting in today's post?' she asked pointedly.

'Hmm.' He looked down at his mail and pretended ignorance, but she could see the smile playing at the corners of his lips.

'Something that you don't want to tell me about?'

His smile broadened to a grin. 'Not yet, anyway.'

'Some part of the great Christmas surprise you've promised me. No,' she corrected, 'have taunted me with for weeks without revealing anything.'

'That would be the definition of surprise, would it not? Something I know which you do not. And which I will reveal to you soon, even though it is still a week to Christmas.'

'How soon?'

'Very soon. Today, perhaps.'

'If I am very good?'

His eyes darkened as he gazed down the table at her. 'You are always very good, my darling. And, no, your behaviour will not affect the timing of the revelation.'

'But you might tell me today. Or will you show me? Is this an event? Or a physical thing?'

'Are we to play "yes and no" while you try to guess what I have no intention of telling you?'

'Will it work?'

'No. And my eggs are getting cold.'

'Then eat them, sir.'

He forked up a mouthful and muttered around it, 'And did you receive anything interesting in the post?'

'Christmas greetings from the neighbours. Several more acceptances for our ball.' She touched her stomach. 'The women have all assured me that dancing will not hurt the baby, now that I am well along. But I tire easily.'

'Then you must not overwork, darling. And at the ball you must only dance with me.'

'Are you looking out for my welfare, Marcus, or is this merely an attempt to keep me to yourself?'

'Both. If successful, I would have persuaded you that any entertaining would be too stressful, and that you must remain alone with me at all times. But I suppose we must have all these people traipsing through our home, eating our food and breaking up the peace until the wee hours.'

'Indeed. We owe many invitations, since everyone in the area has opened their homes to us. I can no longer use the excuse that the house is not fit, for we scrubbed the last crystal on the ballroom chandelier several days ago and the decorating is complete. The footmen have been gathering greens and hanging mistletoe.'

'And chasing the maids,' he added. 'How you get any work out of the staff at this time of year is quite beyond me. But you are right. The house looks splendid and we must open it to our friends. This is quite the nicest I've seen it since my father was alive.' He toasted her with his coffee cup. 'You have done well, Miranda.'

'Thank you.'

'Thank *you*.'

She returned to her own mail with a contented smile. The last letter in her stack was a strange one. It was lumpy and stained and appeared to have travelled a great distance to get to her, but there was no direction to indicate the sender's whereabouts. When she opened the envelope, it contained one sheet of tightly folded paper. She unwrapped it and a single green stone tumbled out onto the table. On the paper, someone had written the words 'Thank you' in a steady masculine hand.

She walked to the head of the table and set it in front of her husband.

'Do you think this means…?'

'That St John has written to let you know he is alive and well? It certainly seems so.'

'I am glad.'

'As am I. As long as the letter has come to us from far away.' He turned the envelope over. 'It is addressed to you, but that makes sense. I doubt a few months' time would be sufficient to cause St John to thank *me* for anything.' He held the stone up to the light. 'And it appears he has sent you the change from your gift. He must have landed on his feet before squandering all of the money.' He handed it back to her. 'Put this in your jewellery box for luck.'

'A-hem.' Wilkins had crept into the room and announced himself as discreetly as possible. If the single fidget and the raised eyebrow were any indication, he was in a state of extreme anticipation.

'Yes, Wilkins?'

'The package you were expecting has arrived, your Grace.' It was said with such significance that Miranda was certain it must hide a secret.

'Very well. It seems you are to know the answer to all your questions for breakfast after all, my dear.' He produced a clean handkerchief from his coat pocket and began folding it into a blindfold.

'Surely not?'

'Most surely. I have taken great pains to arrange this surprise and intend to wring every last ounce of suspense from it.'

'Very well, then. If you must.'

He stood behind her and covered her eyes with the linen. 'And now, if you will take my arm?' Her hand flailed in the air before she felt him catch it and squeeze. Then he raised it and she felt the press of his lips against the palm before he tucked it into the crook of his arm. He helped her to rise and guided her from the room. And into the hall, she noted, as the carpet changed to smooth marble beneath her feet.

'You really are the most impossible man.' She smiled.

'As well you knew before you married me. And yet it did not stop you.'

'I did not think it proper, at the time, to inform you of the fact.'

'No. Of course not. You waited until the wedding night to enumerate my faults and drove me from my home.'

'Drove you…?'

'To London. Which is where I got the idea for this surprise.'

He had taken her to the entry hall. She could hear his voice echoing off the distant walls and feel the cold draught from the recently opened door. She racked her brain. What kind of package could have arrived at this hour? Something come by a special coach from London, perhaps? She dreaded the thought that it could be a replacement for the accursed emerald necklace. Certainly he would not give that to her in the morning.

And if he did, she reminded herself, she would accept it with all good grace and a silent prayer that St John would soon return with empty pockets to be bought off again. Her husband had spent too much time dwelling in the past, and the emeralds were a sad reminder of it. It was time to cast off the old family traditions and make new ones.

'Are you ready?' he asked.

'Really, Marcus. You know you needn't have bought me anything. You have already given me everything I could possibly want.'

'Every thing save one.'

And he removed the blindfold and left her blinking in the bright light as Wilkins announced in his grandest voice, 'Sir Anthony and Lady Cecily Grey.'

She rushed to her family, for her father's frail embrace that she had missed for almost half a year, and the tears and kisses from Cici. At last, she turned to her husband, unable to express the feelings in her brimming heart. 'Thank you, Marcus, my love. I thought you'd already given me everything my heart could desire. And then you grant my fondest wish.'

'And now you must give me something as well, as must Sir Anthony.' He was beaming at her, but there was a shyness, a nervousness about him that was most endearing.

She looked to her father in confusion, and found his smile almost as broad as her husband's.

And then, to her amazement, her husband stepped forward and said in a strained voice, 'Sir Anthony. Excuse me. May I request the hand of your daughter in marriage?'

Her father paused, as if considering.

'I swear, sir, that she will have all the comfort she deserves, and all the love in my heart.'

When her father nodded, Marcus turned to her and went down on one knee before her, taking her hand in his. 'And you, Miranda. Will you give me this hand, and accept my heart in trade?'

She blushed at the sight of him, kneeling there, in sight of the servants and in the cold of the open door. 'Marcus, get up. Of course I give you my hand. I gave it to you before. We are already married, are we not?'

He looked up at her. 'In our souls, perhaps. But not as you deserved, my sweet. If you will agree, we can do it again, and properly, for the benefit of your parents, and the Reverend Winslow, who is waiting in the chapel. And all the world if you like, for I want there to be no doubt about what I feel for you.'

She took his upturned face in her hands and kissed him on the top of the head. 'Stand up, then, before you catch your death. Let us go to the chapel. For I would like nothing better than to give my life and my heart to you again.'

She could feel his body relax as she pulled him to his feet, and when she looked at him, he seemed every bit as excited as a new bridegroom.

He smiled down at her. 'Of course, this does create a dilemma in the future. I am most happy to give you everything I am and everything I ever shall be. But whatever shall I get you next Christmas?'

* * * * *

An Unladylike Offer

Chapter One

'If you're cold, Miss Esme, I could ask a footman to lay the fire.'

Esme Canville resisted the impulse to gather her shawl more tightly around her. 'No, Meg. I am quite comfortable. No need for a fire. No need for anything, actually. I am content.'

The maid continued to bustle around the room, straightening things that had been straight enough for hours. 'You're sure, miss? Because it seems a bit chill.'

'No, really. I am fine. You may go.' She tried to sound firm without drawing attention. 'I wish to spend the morning reading.'

Was the maid watching her with too much interest? It was so hard to be sure. Meg was new, and quite devoted to the master of the house. Certainly not someone Esme could consider an ally. But not an enemy, either, she hoped. Still, if her father had requested a report on any unusual behaviour, it was best not to provide fodder. She moved to the settee, and picked up her book.

Meg hesitated, and then said, 'If you're sure, then. But it is still quite cold.'

Esme gathered as much hauteur as she could muster. It would not do to allow her lady's maid to decide for her. 'I find it invigorating. And most economic. I am sure my father would not approve of me wasting coal in the morning, when the afternoon will be temperate.'

Meg nodded, approving of anything that Mr Canville approved of. 'If that is what your father wants, then of course, miss. But you'll ring…'

'If I need anything. Certainly. You may go, Meg.'

The maid let herself out of the room and Esme breathed a sigh of relief as she hurried to the fireplace. Meg took her new duties far too seriously. It had been better when Bess had held the job. But then, Bess had been too good a friend to Esme for her father's taste. And when service to her lady had smacked of disobedience to her master, that had been the end of her. And now, the much more cooperative Meg was trying to lay fires where none were needed.

Esme dropped her shawl carefully on the hearth in front of her and knelt on it, silently thanking the staff for the cleanliness of the slate. What ashes there were would hardly show on the shawl's grey wool. She opened the damper and leaned her cheek against the bricks at the back of the fireplace.

Voices travelled faintly up from the room below. Her father's study was just as cold and fireless as her bedroom, and it shared a chimney. Esme closed her eyes, trying to imagine the men below.

'…for coming here today. I am sure we can find an arrangement that is agreeable to all parties concerned.' Her father was speaking.

'But without even a meeting? Are you sure…?' The visitor's voice trailed off as he walked away from the fireplace.

Esme hissed in frustration. If they didn't stand still, how was she to hear?

'A meeting is not necessary.' She could almost see her father waving a hand in dismissal. 'She will do as she's told in the matter. And you have seen the miniature, have you not? I assure you it is a good likeness.'

Esme touched her own hair. The portrait was a fair likeness of her at best. And done several years ago. At twenty, she was hardly on the shelf, but she was not the wide-eyed innocent in the little painting.

'…lovely.' The man was walking back towards the fireplace again and his voice grew louder. 'Very much to my taste. And she will agree? You're certain of it?'

'I fail to see how it signifies. She will do as she's told, or face the consequences. And since it is you or no one, she'll soon see the wisdom of cooperation. It is more than a favourable match, milord. She would be a fool to hope for better.'

The voices faded away again as the men in the room

below walked towards the desk. Esme's mouth compressed to a thin white line. How could she hope for better? She was not to be allowed a Season. Ever. Or to travel unescorted by her father into any of the social circles that other young ladies were permitted to as a matter of course. Evenings were spent at home or in the company of her father and his friends, who were almost all as old as he. Certainly not marriage material.

She hoped.

'And I would be well pleased with one so young and lovely as your daughter.'

Young. He found her young enough to comment on it. This could not be good. She strained her ears, trying to guess the nature of the man from the voice that echoed up through the brickwork. His tone told nothing, although she could not say the sound of it pleased her. There had been no passion in it as he'd examined her likeness, only cool appraisal. He could as easily have been choosing furniture as a wife.

'She will be honoured by your suit, Lord Halverston.'

A lord. But of course. Her father would wish a match that would advance the family. But her future husband's rank did not signify if she could not find room for him in her heart.

The voices increased in volume again. '…and obedient, you say? Girls these days are too wilful by half, and I'll have none of that in a prospective wife.' They were walking away from the fireplace again as he continued his diatribe against youth, female youth in particular.

And there was the first emotion she'd heard from him, for his increased volume carried the words to her as he enumerated the faults of other prospective brides, compared with the agreeability of making a match without having to contend with the fractious personality of a girl.

Her heart sank.

Her father responded. 'I'm sure you will have no problem there. She knows her duty.'

'Or she soon will,' Halverston responded.

Both men laughed.

She stood up, heart pounding. It was inevitable, was it not? Of course, her father would find her a husband and make the decision himself. And he would choose someone of a like mind to his own. Someone who believed in the need to use a closed fist to explain one's duty. Someone who was sure that nothing refreshed the memory of a disobedient daughter or a wayward wife like the sting of the razor strop on her back.

She gripped the mantelpiece and tried to steady her breathing. It was possible that the situation was not as bad as it sounded. Without meeting Lord Halverston, it was unfair to judge him. And she was making many assumptions, based on what little she'd managed to overhear of a single conversation.

Her father and Halverston had come to an agreement and were moving out of the study and into the front hall. She brushed the soot from her skirt and hurried out on to the balcony, staying close to the wall so as not to be spied from the street. After a brief farewell, the man would call for his hat and stick and he would come through the door beneath her.

And then she would catch her first glimpse of the man her father intended her to marry. His carriage was already waiting on the street below and she admired the fine matched bays with silver on their harnesses. The body of the carriage was rich, and she could see the well-upholstered squabs, and almost smell the leather. Her future husband would be wealthy. And she would share in his wealth. It would not be all bad. She would have gowns, jewels, and a fine house to live in. Houses, perhaps.

She heard the door closing and watched as the driver and grooms straightened as their master approached. With respect, she hoped, and not fear of punishment for idleness. She would have servants, she reminded herself. Perhaps a maid that answered to her before her father.

Esme bit her lip. All that was well and good. But was it too much to hope that her husband would be gentle, as well as a gentleman? She forced the thought from her mind, trying not to let the snippets of conversation she'd heard affect her opinions.·

And then she saw the man step up and into the carriage and she moved forward for a better look.

He was old. She could tell it from the stoop of his

shoulders. His gait was steady, but stiff and measured, and his body tall and unnaturally thin, as though wasted by illness. The fingers that he spread on the dark leather of the seat looked bony and twisted, more claw than hand.

She stifled her disappointment. It would have been foolish to hope for a young man, after seeing the carriage. It must have taken time to get the wealth necessary to own such a fine thing. Of course, he would be older than herself.

But if he were as old as he appeared... She shuddered at the thought of him coming to her in the night, and could almost feel the bony hands as they plucked at her hair and touched her bare skin. He was older than her father. And she might soon be a widow.

It was horrible to think such a thing. Perhaps her father was right to punish her, for she truly was wicked.

But the voice inside her refused to be silent. *You are not wicked. You know you are not. He is old, but you are young. And your father is doing this to be sure that you never enjoy that youth.*

As though he sensed her eyes upon him, Lord Halverston lifted his head and spied her on the balcony.

She held still as he looked at her, and tried not to let the fear of him show on her face.

He held up a staying hand to the driver, and stared at her for what seemed like a long time. And she could feel his eyes, lingering on her body, travelling slowly over her belly, her breasts and her throat, before coming to rest on her face. Then he smiled at her, seeing her without acknowledging her, and there was not a trace of warmth in his face.

She watched as his hand began to twitch and then to stroke the leather of the seat, palm cupping the curves of the upholstery and fingers stroking and thrusting again and again into the crevices between the cushions.

Then he signalled to the driver in a voice that was harsh and excited, and the coach pulled away.

She sagged against the stone of the house and felt her knees trembling beneath her. Perhaps she was imagining his expression. It was the distance, the smells of the street, and the sun in her eyes, combining to overheat her imagination. He could have been thinking about other things entirely than marriage to her. He could have been searching for a key, or a coin, or some other small thing on the seat beside him.

And it was merely the devil in her, as her father had so often claimed, that made her feel that hand travelling over her body. Stroking. Grasping. Thrusting.

She gripped the balustrade and fought down a wave of sickness, taking in great gasps of air. She could not do it. She simply could not. Her father must listen to reason, just this once. Perhaps if she promised to be good, from now on. Not to anger him as she always seemed to. If she agreed to marry any man he chose. Any man other than the Earl of Halverston...

A sudden crash roused her from the waking nightmare of her future. A pane of glass had shattered in the

French doors on the balcony across the street. As she watched, a man threw the doors open and stood in the opening with his back to her. He had a military bearing, and, when he spoke, his pleasant baritone was loud without shouting and carried clearly to her, despite the distance.

'I believe this proves my point. Let us keep these open and spare the rest of the window glass from your little moods.'

A projectile sailed past him and into the street. Then another, which he turned and caught as it narrowly missed his head. He waved it in the air next to him, and she could see that it was a lady's silk slipper.

He spoke again. 'And what, pray tell, was the point of that? Even if you'd hit me, it would have done no real damage. Since you missed, you've lost one shoe and must hop home, for I'll be damned before I go into the street to retrieve the one you threw at me.'

The owner of the slippers responded with an angry tirade of what sounded to her uneducated ears like Spanish.

The man folded his arms in front of him and leaned against the door-frame, giving Esme a view of a fine profile and a sardonic smile. 'No. That would not be technically accurate. My mother assured me that I was legitimate. Not that my parentage has done me a lick of good.'

There was more Spanish and another crash of breaking glass, but this time from inside the apartment.

'And now you have broken the mirror, and are left to dance in the shards in your bare feet.' He tossed the shoe back into the room with no great force in the general direction of his opponent. 'Why I ever chose to keep such a goose-brained creature…' He looked into the room for a moment. 'Well, of course, it's plain why I chose you…but insufficient reason to keep you now. Cara, as I told you before, the apartment is yours until the end of the month. It should not be hard to find another protector, for you are a great beauty and quite charming when you are not breaking glass and throwing the expensive baubles I've bought you back in my face.'

The woman in the house released another torrent of offended and unintelligible speech.

Esme sank beneath the balcony rail, embarrassed by her own eavesdropping. But it was hard to look away from so interesting a performance. And so public a one as well. It was quite the most exciting thing she'd seen in years, and she did not even have to leave her room to enjoy it.

Her father had warned her about the new neighbour. The scandalous Captain St John Radwell, just back from the Peninsula. It had been rumoured that he'd bought his commission with stolen family jewels, on the run from one of his many disastrous affairs. If there was any truth to the story, it wouldn't have come from his brother, the Duke of Haughleigh, who, when questioned, refused to acknowledge he had a brother at all.

Captain Radwell was another of the many things her father railed about, and warned her against. And here was the devil in the flesh, casting off his mistress in broad daylight in a decent neighbourhood, and loud enough for the whole street to hear.

She peeped over the railing at him, unable to look away.

When the irate woman in the room opposite paused for breath, Radwell retorted, 'Then sell the bracelet. Or perhaps the earrings. They cost a pretty penny, as I well know, and should keep you comfortably until another fool comes along to take my place. But this interview is at an end.'

She could hear the sound of angry sobbing in the distance, followed by slamming doors.

Her own troubles were forgotten as she smiled wickedly to herself. It was nice to see that one of her father's irrational ravings had a basis in fact.

Without warning, St John Radwell turned to face her, and caught her staring.

He wasn't merely a devil. He was Lucifer himself, with his hair, golden in the sunlight, waved to cover his temple, a straight nose and a slightly crooked grin. His eyes must be blue, although she could not see the colour from this distance, for clear blue eyes would suit the face. The cut of his coat and smooth fit of his breeches accented a well-muscled body and straight back. He gave every indication of perfection as he stood framed in the windows of his apartments. The sight left her breathless.

And then he stared back, holding her gaze before turning his attention to the rest of her. He examined her at length and at last he smiled, and she felt the rioting in her stomach turn to the gentle flutter of butterflies.

He tapped the side of his nose and nodded significantly.

But significant of what? His gesture was strange. Not a scold at her rudeness, but an indication of something. She shook her head in confusion.

With a flourish, he pulled a handkerchief from his pocket, unfolded it with a snap and wiped his own face, then gestured to her.

Her hands flew to her cheeks, and she rubbed once. When she held them in front of her, they showed traces of soot. Not only was she eavesdropping on the neighbours, she was as dirty as a chimney sweep.

He waved the handkerchief in triumph, seeing that his message had been understood, bowed to her with a grin, then turned and re-entered his apartment, shutting the windows behind him.

Her heart was pounding as she stepped back into her own room and shut the balcony doors. Oh, the horrible man, to make such a scene and then tease her for her impertinence. He seemed not the least bit perturbed to be caught in an indiscretion, or to catch her as well.

It must be delightful to know such freedom, to not give a damn for society and do just as you liked.

The plan was forming in her mind before she even realised it. It was daring, and the most improper thing she had ever imagined. She was shameless, and now the world would know it. It would serve her father right, if his only daughter came to such. And it would certainly make marriage to the earl out of the question. It would be easier to accomplish if she waited for darkness, but in a few short hours, with the help of the scandalous Captain St John Radwell, she could be free of her father, this house *and* the earl. She would do it.

Chapter Two

'No, thank you, Toby. I'll not need you tonight. It's another quiet evening at home for me. Relaxing in front of the fire. And perhaps a brandy before bed. Don't bother. I'll get it. You should know, after Portugal, that I'm able to manage for myself.'

The valet left the room and St John threw himself into a chair, staring into the fire. Relaxing, indeed. It was damned boring. But considering the contents of his purse, or lack thereof, it was all he could afford. The risk of creating new debt at White's was greater than the chance that he'd win and refill the coffers. And his credit was stretched uncomfortably thin already.

He was due a reversal in fortune. It had been all but guaranteed to him—if he kept his nose clean, of course. When he'd been presented at court to be decorated, the regent had hinted that rich rewards would be given to those who'd served their country so well. If, that was, they could also manage to navigate society without embarrassing themselves and their patrons. How had Prinny put it?

'A man who can survive the French must also be able to survive a Season in London without getting himself shot by jealous husbands or his own brother for conduct unbecoming. Steer clear of trouble and Haughleigh. The Earl of Stanton is turning eighty, and not likely to get an heir at this late date. There is a nice little piece of land attached to that title and I'd like to award it to someone who can prove himself worthy of the honour.'

St John Radwell, Earl of Stanton. He said the words to himself on nights like this, when the old desires arose to tempt him. But he was not an earl yet. And he would never be one if he landed himself in scandal, or gambled away the entail before receiving it. Better to be circumspect in all things, at least for a while. He must remember that he was a respectable man about town, and a distinguished Peninsular veteran, ready to live a quiet life in the country. There would be no awards to the scapegrace brother of the Duke of Haughleigh, with pockets to let and a list of sins long enough to get him permanently banned from the family estates.

He sighed. After five years in Portugal and Spain, he missed home. He'd found that he even missed his brother, which was a thing he'd never have believed possible. He'd often thought, in the hours before a battle, of the things he might never be able to say to Marcus or his wife Miranda, should things go badly. And despite the end he'd expected and sometimes felt he deserved, he'd escaped with a whole skin. It seemed he might still have his chance to heal the breach between them.

And his apologies might ring with more truth, should he arrive at Haughleigh with his own title and perhaps a wife at his side. Lord knew, he did not want to marry. But it would be necessary. He would want heirs. A family of his own would be proof positive that he was no threat to his brother's marriage and that old rivalries over the Haughleigh succession might be permanently buried.

But he needn't worry about any of it now. The current plans might take years to bear fruit, and it did no good to wish on it. Until then there would be many more quiet nights at home, biding his time and letting the scandals die and his old reputation be forgotten. And with not even the solace of female distraction, now that he'd cast off Cara as too volatile and far too expensive.

Of course, the old St John would have appealed to his brother for funds to tide him over, offering his newly reformed character as collateral, oblivious of the reaction it would provoke from the duke. The thought was so amusing, he laughed out loud.

There was a discreet cough behind him.

'Yes, Toby.'

'You have a guest, sir. A lady.'

'A lady?' No lady, certainly, if she was visiting at this

hour. But there was no trace of irony in the word as Toby spoke it. 'Show her up, then. And bring that brandy after all.'

St John detected a hint of disapproval in the set of his valet's shoulders, at the idea of bringing the female upstairs. But, whoever she was, she must know full well what she was getting into, and if Toby cared more for her reputation than she did, he could keep his tongue in his head.

The door opened shortly and Toby announced, 'Miss Esme Canville.'

'Who?' It was rude, but he couldn't help himself. The name did not register in any corner of his brain, and certainly didn't match any of the discreet widows or straying wives he'd expected to darken his doorway at so late an hour.

She stepped into the room and curtsied politely and he was on his feet, offering her a chair and trying to conceal his confusion. It was the damned nosy chit from across the street. Whatever would bring her here? 'I beg your pardon, Miss Canville. But you quite have the better of me. Toby?' He'd hoped to keep the servant in the room, although it would hardly cover the impropriety of the situation, should the girl's father get wind of this. But Toby had left the brandy and retreated to the kitchen.

'No. Please, Captain Radwell. I would prefer that our conversation be private, if that is possible.'

Dear God, he couldn't be alone with her. But perhaps

if she said her piece, whatever it was, he could get her back out of the house before anyone guessed her whereabouts. 'All right. And I do admit to a certain curiosity on that count. Just what is it that brings a gently bred female to my chambers at this late hour? I don't believe we have even been formally introduced.'

'No.' She had the sense to look embarrassed. 'We have not actually met. Although earlier today...I couldn't help but overhear... And I certainly know of you, Captain Radwell. By reputation.'

'I suppose I should assure you, at this point, that the reputation is undeserved, but, alas, I cannot. I'm sure I've done most of the things attributed to me over the years. And if not? Well, I've probably done worse, but not been caught.' He almost smiled before remembering that there was no reason to boast. 'You understand, Miss Canville, that you put yourself in a very dangerous position by coming here alone?'

Her chin rose a fraction of a degree and she looked into his eyes without flinching. 'If I cared at all for my reputation, that would be the case. But circumstances force me to take drastic action on that front, Captain Radwell. I find myself in a difficult situation and had hoped that perhaps you might be able to help me.'

'Help you?' He straightened. 'Why you should choose me to aid you, I have no idea. But as an officer and—' he cleared his throat at the unfamiliar idea '—a...ah...gentleman, I will certainly do everything in my power to aid you.'

Her confidence was short lived, and he sensed that she must be near to telling him the reason for her visit. She removed a handkerchief from her reticule and twisted it in nervous hands. 'Well, yes. I was seeking your aid, after a fashion, but not precisely as an officer and a gentleman. I think the term I am searching for is protection.' Her eyes were full of hope as she looked up into his. 'If you could see fit to offer me your protection…'

At first he had the outlandish idea that she meant him to draw sword and stand between her and a foe. Protection? What did she need protection from? Certainly not her father, for he hardly looked the sort to do violence…

Protection. An ungentlemanly offer of protection?

He sprang from his seat to put as much distance between himself and the young lady as possible. 'I say. You can't mean… You don't think that I would…'

'I couldn't help but hear you arguing with your…' she searched for a word '—paramour earlier in the day. It was most plain that you were casting her off. And I assumed that that might mean that there was a position open…'

'Position? Dear God, woman. You are not hiring yourself out as a governess.'

'Well, I know that, of course. I could never have a job as a governess without my father becoming aware of it. Even securing the necessary references would be impossible.' She explained it as though it should be the most obvious thing in the world.

'I seriously doubt that you have references for the position you're inquiring after now.'

'Are references required?' She looked more alarmed by that prospect than she did by the situation, which he found more than alarming enough for both of them.

'Not references, per se. But I would hope that you are lacking in previous experience.' He sat down next to her, and looked gravely into her face. 'I mean, Miss Canville—'

'Please call me Esme.'

'Miss Canville,' he responded firmly. 'Do you really have any idea exactly what the duties of such a position entail?'

'Exactly?' She blushed. 'No. Not exactly. Is that a problem?'

'That a young lady such as yourself does not know… No. Definitely not a problem. I should be quite shocked if you did.'

She held out her hands in front of her. 'I had rather hoped that this was the sort of thing that one could learn by doing. Is there anything about me that would lead you to suspect I wouldn't be able to do the job, as required?'

It was as if he was looking at her for the first time. She had a sweet face, with soft, full lips, and pale skin that hinted at roses underneath. She'd thrown off her cloak and sat before him in a modest and rather ugly gown, but the plain fabric and high neck hid what appeared to be a fine bosom. He imagined the full breasts, the curve of her hip, the way her legs would rap around him, and feel of her flowing blonde hair as he ran his fingers through it to pull that mouth up to his...

He stood again and paced across the room. 'No. No. No, there is absolutely nothing about you that would make me think you unfit or unable. But that is not the point. What I think you might be capable of should be no concern of yours, for I am a rather base and untrustworthy fellow, and could eat a little lamb like you for breakfast and have no compunction about leaving you after.'

The girl said, 'But I seriously doubt that is the case. I watched you today, as you argued with the lady in your chambers. She did several things that might have provoked a lesser man to violence, but you were the picture of reason. You also made it clear that you'd left her with sufficient funds to care for herself, until she could find another position.' She smiled. 'And she was most unreasonable about the whole thing, I might add. You need have no fear, when the time comes to cast me off, that I will throw such unladylike fits about it.'

'Cast you off? Dear God, woman. I have no intention of taking you on, so I need never worry about casting you off.' He made a shooing gesture. 'Run home to your father, now, before someone realises you are gone, and we're both in the soup.'

She shook her head. 'That is quite impossible. I am not going back, no matter what you might say in the matter.'

'Then I shall carry you there myself.'

She planted her hands on her hips. 'You shall not. For if you do, I will tell my father where I have been, with the addition of certain colourful and inaccurate details, and you shall be the only one in the soup, Captain Radwell. I doubt it would be possible for *my* life to be any worse than it already is, but *you* would run the risk of being saddled with me, and society would require a more permanent union than the one I am suggesting.'

She was right, damn her. But the situation was even worse than she threatened. Should word of this get out, it would not matter if he married her or not. There would be no title in his future. And Prinny's displeasure would be the least of his worries. He could well imagine the look on his brother's face, if he tried to gain entrance to the family home with an empty purse and a broken reputation, out of favour with the regent and two steps ahead of Esme Canville's angry papa, but claiming that it was all a horrible mistake. 'You think, if I take you back, that I can be forced to marry you. But if I don't, you would permit me to do as I will with you, without the benefit of marriage?' And for a moment he was tempted. He shook his head. It mattered not that her charms were considerable—they would not outweigh their cost.

'Of course, I would expect similar compensation to the woman who left your employ earlier in the day. Not so much, perhaps, since I am inexperienced,' she reassured.

'No.'

'I do not eat much, and I am not vain about clothing or jewelry. Nor do I require much space to be happy. I dare say I shall be much less expensive to keep than your last mistress.'

'No!'

'Then perhaps you could arrange an introduction to one of your friends? Someone of a similar temperament, but also in need of female companionship?'

'And now you expect me to turn panderer? Oh, this is too rich, madam. I know that my reputation is black, but I never had anyone suggest that I should become a procurer for my friends.'

'I am so sorry,' she responded. 'I never meant to offend you.'

He shook his head. 'And a virgin, no less.' He reached for the brandy with a shaking hand and watched her eyes follow his movement. 'Would you care for a glass?'

'No, thank you. I do not drink spirits.'

'That you are able to come up with a hare-brained notion such as this stone-cold sober astounds me. Besides, I could never consider someone teetotal for the job you are seeking.'

She set her chin. 'Then pour me a glass, sir, for I assure you, I am serious in my request. Although I would much prefer it to be you, since I must admit I admire you greatly, I *will* find another willing man if I must.' Her voice fell to a whisper. 'Surely someone would want me. I cannot be so bad as all that. But, whatever the outcome, I will not return home.'

He poured a jot of brandy into a snifter and carefully added a few drops from the flask in his pocket, swirling the liquid to mix the contents.

She watched him with curiosity. 'What is that you have added to your drink?'

'Nothing you need be concerned about. I find it sometimes necessary to take laudanum to quiet my nerves, and I must say that your behaviour is quite shocking enough to unbalance a man stronger than myself.'

She laughed. 'What have you to be afraid of? You seem most steady to me. If you are as bad as you claim, than there should be nothing particularly fearsome in finding a woman in your rooms.'

She stepped closer to him, and his breath felt thick in his lungs. She was right, of course. There was nothing to be afraid of in the thought of a woman, soft and willing in his arms. And the night always passed more easily when he was not alone.

Her voice was husky and low as she said, 'As you have pointed out, it is I who should be afraid of you. For you know exactly what is to happen to me tonight, while I know only whispers and rumours of what goes on between a man and a woman at a time like this.'

She came the rest of the way to him, standing within easy reach, and he stood rooted to the spot, watching her in fascination.

She tilted her head to look into his eyes. 'Is it true that it can be both pleasant and painful? I've always wondered how that could be possible. I know much of pain, but very little of pleasure.'

He could certainly show her pleasure, if that was what she was seeking. It was late, they were alone, and no one would expect to find her here. He could give her what she wanted, and send her home and none need be the wiser. He could feel the offer forming in his mind and bit his tongue to keep from saying the words, but he could not bring himself to step away as she came closer still and the fabric of her gown brushed against his shirtfront.

'Since you are, as you say, an officer and a gentleman, I would hope that you take into account my inexperience as we proceed, and to be as gentle as possible, for I will admit to being somewhat frightened, now that the time has come. I suspect that my nerves are even more unsteady than yours.'

Without warning, she reached out and snatched the brandy from his hand and drained the glass, laudanum and all. She coughed once, and her eyes watered at the strength of the drink. Then she set it carefully on the table beside them, and stepped away from him to sit on the sofa, leaning back into the cushions.

'Dear God, Miss Canville.' He dropped his hands to his sides helplessly. Even as he cursed himself for a fool, he could feel his body missing the warmth of hers as she stood close. He'd seen only the woman, pretty and willing, and ignored the mind, sharper and more devious than he'd expected in one so young. And now the slip of a girl had outfoxed him, and there was little he could do to undo what had been done.

He smiled his best and most seductive smile and stepped closer to look down upon her. 'Very well, if you are intent on doing what you seem to wish, you are right that it could be a difficult and rather painful experience. It will go easier on both of us if we wait until you are fully relaxed.'

She looked at him with large, frightened eyes and said, 'Do as you will. I am prepared.'

And he hated himself for seeing her as such a bold temptress, only a few moments before. The girl was terrified of what was about to happen, and that he had allowed himself to consider her request even for a moment proved that he had as black a soul as others claimed. He sat down on the sofa near her and took her hand. 'Not yet, I think. A little while longer.'

St John watched as her limbs began to relax and the brandy brought a flush to her cheeks. 'How long? Before I begin to feel the effects?' Her breathing steadied and she moistened her parted lips with the tip of her tongue.

And to his shame, he felt his body stirring in response. He could feel the grasp of her hand relaxing in his as the drug took effect and gave it what he hoped was an encouraging pat. 'Not very.'

'That is good. And I'm sure you are right. It will be

easier this way.' Esme shook her head a little and smiled. 'Oh, how odd. It is as if I cannot feel my body. It is so wonderful not to feel any more.'

He smiled in sympathy. 'You understand too well, little one.'

She closed her eyes and murmured, 'If I had the contents of your little bottle in my possession before coming here, this might not have been necessary. Of course, I doubt I'd have stopped at a few drops.' And her head drooped to the side and she was lost to the world.

St John forced himself not to pace the marble floor of the entryway. In another house, he would not have been left standing in the hall. The servants would have had the decency to show him to a parlour somewhere, to wait before the fire. Of course, in most other houses, he was not total anathema. And he'd never arrived so late in the evening and with such an unusual problem.

The butler was returning with the lady of the house a discreet step behind him. When she saw him, her voice was low and full of warning. 'St John.'

'Miranda.' He bowed low, hoping that the she did not notice the look in his eyes. She had grown even lovelier in the five years since he'd last seen her. Marriage to his brother had been kind to her.

Jealousy flashed within him, and he crushed it. She was happy here. It was what he'd wished for her, certainly what she deserved, and he would not spoil it now.

'How much?' Her tone was all business.

'I beg your pardon?'

'How much do you need? To make you go away again. For I swear, St John, if Marcus realises you are here, this time I will not be able to protect you.'

'And how is my brother?'

'Well,' she answered without thinking. 'As are the children.'

'My nephew and my niece.' He smiled as he tasted the unfamiliar words on his tongue. 'I meant to congratulate you on their births, but was not sure it would be welcome.'

She shook her head in disapproval. 'You know well it would not have been. But you are not here, at this advanced hour, to enquire after the health of the family. How much do you need, St John?'

He snorted. 'I'm sorry to admit that I have a problem that cannot be solved by an open purse.'

He stepped to the side and revealed the bundle on the bench beside the door.

Miranda rushed to the girl, throwing back her cloak and touching her cheek, feeling at her throat for a pulse. She glared up at him. 'Oh, dear God, St John. What have you done to her?'

'Nothing. I swear. She is only drugged. And untouched. On my—' He stopped. Swearing on non-existent honour would be worse than useless in this house. 'On Marcus's honour, shall we say? Let me swear in a coin that has some worth to you. I brought her here because it was the most respectable place I could think of. I had barely a passing acquaintance with the girl before this evening. She arrived on my doorstep suggesting… I hesitate to say it to a lady.'

Miranda arched a sceptical eyebrow.

'In truth, she was suggesting I take her as mistress. And she was damned insistent about it, too. Said if it wasn't me, then it would be someone else, but that she couldn't go home. She chose to take the laudanum. I swear it was accidental. But there at the end, when her mind was relaxed and her speech unguarded, she was hinting that she'd do away with herself, given the opportunity. I couldn't take her home. Even being seen in my presence might be enough to ruin her. I couldn't talk sense into her. I couldn't even manage to frighten her. She took my glass and drank the drug without a qualm. Then she laid back on the sofa, ready to let me—' He broke off in embarrassment. 'It was dashed strange. When I was sure she was fully unconscious, I took her down the back stairs and brought her here in a closed carriage. I needed to find a place of safety for her. For her reputation's sake, no one must know I had anything to do with her condition. And I thought—'

'That your brother could dispose of the woman you kidnapped?' Miranda's voice was rising now.

St John shook his head. 'It was not a kidnapping. Not intentionally, at least. She needed to be rescued from herself.'

'Miranda, why on earth are you shouting in the hall?'

St John stiffened himself against what was to come.

Now, of all times, was not the moment for the tender reunion he had wanted with his brother. 'Marcus.'

'Pistols or swords, St John?'

'I really don't think that will be—'

'It was a statement, not a request. Choose a weapon. And choose your second.'

'No.'

'How dare you?' Marcus reached for him, ready to strike.

St John fought every instinct that had been honed for five years on the battlefield and stepped into range of his enemy's attack, holding his hands empty at his side. The blow caught him across the cheek, a backhanded slap that sent him staggering. And he let it connect, making no effort to block, fighting the urge to strike back, not allowing himself even the desire to grip his brother's shoulder to stay on his feet. St John let the force of the blow drive him back into the wall and dropped to his knees, waiting for the ringing in his head to clear.

He looked up into his brother's rage-contorted face. 'And I said, no. I will not fight you. If you strike me, I will not strike back. If you kill me, it will be in cold blood. Throw me into the street if you must. But if you do, let me go alone.' He looked pointedly at Miranda.

'Marcus, wait.' Miranda grabbed her husband's arm before he could strike again. 'He has a legitimate reason for coming to us.'

'You were always quick to defend him, Miranda.'

'Marcus, you ninny,' St John said in exasperation. 'if it makes you feel any better, then hit me again. But do not take that tone with your wife in front of me. She has never been anything but loyal to you, much to my disappointment. If it were just for me, I would never have come near you or your family. But I have here someone who needs the protection of an honourable man. And all the little fool could find was me. Take care of her, will you? But do not send her home until you have obtained the truth from her, for there is something there so horrible that she would die rather than face it.'

His eyes locked with Marcus's, and he waited for a moment to see what reaction his words would receive. His brother looked more tired than angry, as if the single blow had taken all his strength. And his expression held the same disappointment that St John had seen so many times before—the look that said St John had failed the family and shamed himself and now the duke must avert another scandal. And here was another proof that he could not manage his own affairs.

But then Marcus looked to the girl, and gave an almost imperceptible nod.

St John tasted gall along with the relief, and nodded in return. 'Now, if you will excuse me? I'll take myself out of your life and hers and trouble you no further.' And he turned stiffly, without glancing at Esme Canville, and walked out the door and into the street.

Chapter Three

Esme opened her eyes cautiously and looked at the canopy above her. It most certainly was not her own room, but neither was it what she expected to find in the bachelor's quarters of Captain St John Radwell. And she did not remember travelling anywhere else. She moved her head and winced. Ah, yes. The brandy had been drugged. He'd said she needed to relax, but she had not expected to be totally unconscious, when the moment came. Had it been pleasant for him, she wondered? She must have been almost corpse-like; if the Spanish lady from yesterday was any indication, he was accustomed to someone a trifle more animated.

Unless…

She frowned. She did not feel any different, other than the headache. She knew only the vaguest details of the process, but there was supposed to be blood, and pain. And she remembered neither. There was not even an indication that he'd disarranged her clothes, for she was sleeping *sans* shoes, but still in her gown.

'You are awake, I see. Let me offer you tea. Or would you prefer chocolate?'

The voice was pleasant and female and Esme craned her neck to get a look at the speaker. The woman had chestnut hair arranged in attractive curls, and the graceful posture of a swan. Her clothing was simple, but well cut and expensive. Esme scanned the room. Also expensive. Whatever she'd been expecting to see when she awoke, this was certainly not it.

The woman spoke again. 'You are, no doubt, wondering where you are. I am the wife of St John's brother, and you are in my home.'

Esme sat up quickly. 'But his brother is the Duke of Haughleigh. And you must be…'

'Miranda. That is sufficient, I think. You may call me Miranda. But what am I to call you? St John was most remiss on that point.'

'Esme Canville, your Grace.'

The woman laughed. 'Please, as I told you before, let us not bring my grace into discussion. I am Miranda. May I call you Esme?'

'Of, course, Miranda.' How strange. She thought carefully before she spoke. 'How came I to be here? You say Captain Radwell brought me, but I understood that there was an estrangement between the brothers. I certainly did not expect—'

'The estrangement was temporarily mended, because St John was concerned for your welfare. And rightly so. Perhaps you do not realise what risk you put your reputation in when you sought out help from him.'

Esme sat up and took the cup that was offered by Miranda. 'Oh, no. I was quite aware of it. As a matter of fact, it was precisely what I was looking for. When one wishes to be dishonoured, it makes no sense to go to a gentleman.'

'You wish for dishonour?' Miranda's own cup had stopped halfway to her mouth.

'I wish, just once, to be guilty of the crimes for which I'm punished. Does that sound strange to you?' She paused. 'I suppose it does. Let me try to explain. My father is a proud and upright man. He believes in living simply, not courting vanity or ornament, and shuns society as foolish and dangerous to the soul. And he believes that it is a suitable life for me as well. Silks and fripperies are a waste of money. Lavish dinners and dancing are merely an excuse to indulge the sins of the flesh and must be avoided at all costs.'

'Well…' Miranda was obviously searching for a way to proceed with the conversation without censuring Esme's family '…it is a noble aspiration to keep one's soul pure and avoid excesses.'

'Perhaps if we all avoided such excesses, the world would be a paradise. But I speak from experience when I tell you that it would be incredibly dull.'

Miranda's mouth thinned in disapproval. 'Boredom is not the worst fate that could befall a young lady.'

'No, it is not. I suspect that it will be far worse to be bound in marriage to a man I have never met, who is old enough to be my father. While I cannot be sure of the fact, judging by the look he gave me yesterday when I spied him in the street, he does not wish to spend our evenings together in prayer and reflection.'

'Oh.' Miranda chose her next words carefully. 'But there would be the benefit of marriage. And certainly the kind of life that St John would offer…'

'I have seen the life that St John might offer, for I have seen him with his mistress.'

'Surely not…?'

'In flagrante delicto?' Esme smiled. 'No. Merely in argument. She was throwing shoes and breaking glass, and he appeared to be bearing it with a great deal of patience and good humour. I did not see him strike her for uttering an impertinence, or beat her for imagined transgressions, or lock her in her room to ensure obedience. This is the life I am accustomed to, and I suspect that my father has chosen a husband for me who is much in the same mould.' She felt a tear on her own cheek and ignored it. 'Because he has my welfare for ever in mind.'

'And what of your mother? Can she do nothing to help you? Or is she no longer with us?'

'She is no longer with me, certainly, for she ran away with a dancing master when I was fourteen. I do not know whether she is alive or dead, but, wherever she is, I suspect she is happier than she was with my father. He is much older than she, and he treated her much the same way he treats me now.' There was another tear on her cheek, and she wiped it away, hoping that the gesture did not draw too much attention. 'I do not know whether my life might have been different, if she had stayed. But there might have been a chance for a Season, marriage, and escape if he had no reason to be ever vigilant of my character. Which, despite my efforts to the contrary, seems to need continual correction. He says I am much like my mother, and he will not make the same mistakes with me that he did with her and that what he does to me is for the honour of the house and my own good.' More tears were coming and she swallowed hard to drive them back. 'I swear, I never give him cause. I am not vain because I know I have no reason. I do not flirt. I do not seek the attentions of suitors. How can I when I am never in the company of anyone who might want me? And yet he punishes me and says it is for things I might do, if given the opportunity. I know you must think me horrible, but I would much prefer to live in comfort as the paid companion of a rake than to live another moment in the life set out for me. When I die, I will burn for my sins, but at least there will be a chance for a moment's pleasure in life.' She took a sip of tea and felt the cup rattle on the saucer as her hands shook, so she set it down. 'I am sorry to bother you with my problems. Indeed, I never intended it. But I cannot bear it any longer. I simply cannot.' She looked down at her hands, which were still shaking, and clasped them together in front of her.

Miranda's voice was strangely distant. 'And what was your plan, if and when St John turned you away? For that is what happens in the end, when you accept a *carte blanche*.'

'Then I would find another such offer, or throw myself into the Thames. It was my plan last night as well. It matters very little to me any more. If I go home, I will get such a beating that a quick end might be preferable.' Another tear fell. Once they started in earnest she would not be able to stop them. She raised her hands to cover her face, wishing she could force the emotions back into hiding.

She felt the cool air on her wrists as her sleeves crept up to reveal the flesh of her forearms.

There was a sharp gasp from the duchess.

Esme lowered her arms and tugged her dress back into place, but it was too late to hide the vivid bruises that were the marks of her father's hands upon her.

She hung her head. 'I was choosing a book from the study, and he wanted me to go back to my room. A guest was coming, and he did not wish me to be present. I did not move quickly enough. So he took me by the wrists to encourage me.' She lifted her head again, to stare into the duchess's concerned eyes.

'Please, do not tell anyone of this. The simplicity of my dress is not for modesty alone. Much can be hidden with high necklines and long sleeves. And I am so ashamed.' She closed her eyes so she would not have to see Miranda's expression turn from pity to disgust. She had hoped to hide the truth a little longer, at least from the fine lady sitting in front of her. She was marked by punishment, in body and spirit. Next to the Duchess of Haughleigh, with her graceful white throat, smooth unmarked arms, and serene disposition, Esme felt coarse and unclean. And now the tears were squeezing out from between her lashes, embarrassing her further.

Then, the strangest thing happened. She felt a weight on the bed, and the duchess's arms about her, hands stroking her hair and her melodic voice promising that everything would be all right and that she needn't worry any more. And Esme sagged in relief, laid her head upon Miranda's shoulder and wept.

Miranda looked at her brother-in-law lounging insolently in a chair, and her husband sitting in stony silence behind his desk. This might go more easily, if it were just she and Marcus. But for all his apparent innocence in the matter, it was St John's business, as much as theirs.

Even if St John did not see it that way. 'I do not understand why I have been called to account for this. The girl is better off, is she not, if I stay far, far away from her?'

'Much as you are better off if you stay far from me,' responded Marcus.

'I was endeavouring to do just that, brother, until your wife summoned me back this morning. Would you have me flout her wishes? Perhaps you would. And I should defer to the peer, should I not? I beg your pardon, your Grace.'

'And now you throw my title back in my face?'

'If you wish to play the role, then how am I to ignore it?'

'Enough!' Miranda stepped between them. 'St John, I did not send for you because I wished to listen to the two of you argue. Marcus, you as well should mind your tongue and listen to what I have to say. For we are all in a pretty pickle because of the young lady upstairs and it will take more heads than mine to get us out of it.' She looked to her husband. 'If the girl is to be believed, and I think she is, she had little to no prior acquaintance with St John before last night. What she knew of him was from reputation and from spying on his apartments across the street from her home. She sought him out because she believed that he was the sort who would stoop to ruining a young lady under the very nose of her father and might think it good sport to set her up somewhere…'

'And I disappointed her,' remarked St John. 'See, Marcus? I am not so bad as you paint me. Or as stupid. I have more honour and sense than that.'

'It is too late to brag to me about your new-found good sense. Bitter experience has taught me the depths to which you will stoop—'

Miranda glared at the interruption and spoke over it. '…until such time as he tired of her, whereupon she meant to find another or end her life.'

The two men fell silent.

'She does not want to return home, fearing punishment, and I must agree that it would be unwise. From what she describes, her father's response will be swift and severe. If we send her back, we can rest sure in the knowledge that she will be soundly beaten and locked in her room until such time as she can be married against her wishes to an elderly gentleman of her father's choosing.'

She noted, with some satisfaction, that the glances passing between the two brothers showed alarm at the girl's condition and had nothing to do with their previous quarrel. 'I am sorry,' began St John, 'to involve you in this. But last night I had no idea what to do with the chit, other than to return her to her home. She was spouting such a variety of nonsense that it did seem, at first, to be the best plan. But her talk was wild. It worried me. And then she took my drugged brandy and drank it before I could stop her. What if she ran away again when the laudanum wore off? Or did herself an injury? Or was found in her drugged condition by someone with even fewer scruples than myself?' He held out open hands to his brother. 'I did not want to be responsible for the ruin of an innocent. So I brought her to you. I thought that she would see reason in the morning, and her virtue would be intact. No father could argue that a night spent in so august a household could be anything but an honour. And her name would not be linked in shame with mine because all the world knows we are estranged. This must be the last place that I would bring her.'

Marcus nodded. 'It makes sense, when you explain it thus. This would be the last place she'd end up, if you were involved. But what are we to do with her, now we've got her?'

Miranda cleared her throat. 'I have a suggestion. It is rather unorthodox, and only a temporary solution to the girl's troubles. And it will require her co-operation and some time getting the story straight between us.' She looked at St John. 'If anyone asks you, last night, you retired early and alone. You saw nothing of Esme Canville. Do your servants gossip?'

St John shrugged. 'All servants gossip.'

She looked to Marcus. 'Then we must see that St John's are generously rewarded to hold their tongues. The Canville household must get no wind of her true behaviour last night. I suspect that St John is in no financial position to do this, and we will help him.'

Marcus hesitated for a moment, then nodded.

'Marcus, last night we were travelling by carriage in the neighborhood of the Canville home. It matters not why. And we found a strange girl, dazed and wandering in the street.' She snapped her fingers. 'And feverish. Which is why she cannot return immediately home. She was taken ill in the night and somehow wandered away from home in her delirium.'

St John grinned. 'I say, Miranda, that's a cracking good yarn. Have you considered writing for the stage?'

Marcus's eyes flashed at the impertinence and Miranda leapt into the conversational gap before he could respond. 'And you, Marcus, have managed to discover her direction, and will go to the Canville household with the sad news of the illness. You will assure her father that we will care for her until she is better. I think it shall be several weeks before she is fully recovered. It might be best done in Devon, where the air is clean and the noise of the city does not prey upon her nerves. Go in your most severe black suit, for Mr Canville disapproves of artifice and ornament. But go with full livery and the best carriage—I doubt his disdain will extend to your title.'

Marcus grinned, and she noted that the two brothers looked very alike when they smiled, although they would never believe it.

'All right. I frighten Lord Canville into giving us his only child, or bludgeon him into co-operation with my title. What are we to do with Esme Canville and her imaginary fever?'

'We will take her out of the city, far away from the loving attentions of her father and the suitor he has chosen for her. We entertain lavishly and introduce her to all the families in the area. Even in brief conversation with her, I find her to be a girl of surpassing wit and no little beauty. But her father has taken pains to ensure that she never meets with the opposite gender and so she has never been courted by them. We find a match to her satisfaction and she need never return home. She is nearing the age of consent. It is only her father's control that has prevented her from finding someone appropriate. If we find such a man, we lean on her father until he sees reason, or stall her return until she is of age. And thus we solve all her problems.'

Marcus's smile faded. 'While I agree that we must work to preserve the girl's reputation, we do not have the right to separate her from her family and reshape her future. If her father wishes to keep her apart from society, then who are we to say he is wrong?'

Miranda bit her lip. This had been a mistake. She should have spoken to her husband in private, revealed all and obtained his approval. She could not very well betray the girl's confidence and parade her bruises in front of the family to win the argument. 'Marcus, I understand we have no legal right. But we do have a moral obligation to do all we can for her. You must trust me when I say we cannot just make up some fustian to cover last night, and then send her home. While her father may have the right, he is not in the right. Not in the eyes of God or man. Even a few weeks apart from her may be enough to calm his temper and persuade him to see reason.' *At least it will heal the marks on her arms.*

Marcus looked into her eyes, searching for an explanation, and then said at last, 'Very well. I trust you in all things. If you feel this strongly about it, then be damned to society. We will do what you feel is necessary. But I will also consult our solicitor, so that we might raise a defence should this go awry.'

She nodded, relieved.

'Then it's off to Devon for you and the girl, and I am well clear of things, as soon as I gain control of the servants.' St John rose to go.

Miranda turned to him. 'There is some little dispute on that matter.'

He dropped back into his chair.

She smiled. 'While I do not begrudge helping her, you have caused much difficulty by bringing the girl to our house. I don't think you should get off scot free in this.'

'But what can I do to assist?' St John looked suspicious.

She looked from St John to Marcus and proceeded with caution. 'After a week or two, you might retire quietly to the country as well, St John. For your health. Or your pocket. The girl seems to have developed a small *tendre* for you, and the quickest way to cure her of it might be for her to get to know you better. Then she will see how hopeless a thing that is, and be more amenable to the suitors we will choose for her.'

He drew himself up in his chair, no longer the indolent young noble. 'Prolonged contact with me is so odious?'

Miranda smiled. 'Well, you must admit that it is quite easy to see through your advances, once one knows which way the wind blows. And Esme Canville might be sheltered, but she's no fool. When she sees that you are not interested in her—'

Miranda was pleased to see the shadow of doubt that passed over St John's face.

'—and that all you can offer is dishonour, but that there is a chance for a decent union with some respectable young man in the neighbourhood, she'll soon be set right.'

'I am not so easy to see through as all that.' St John seemed genuinely put out. 'I've a good mind to come down to Devon and show you just how charming I can be, when on my best behaviour.'

'But we do not need your best behaviour, St John. We need for you to be a fate worse than death. She must be disabused of any romantic notions she might have of a glamorous life in the *demimonde*. While I am fully capable of telling her, this is a lesson that will be better learned from you. I recommend that you do not break her heart, only damage it a little. Send her into the arms of a young man of our mutual agreement, and we all end happily.'

St John shook his head. 'This is a plot of surpassing deviousness, Miranda. I am surprised at you. Prolonged association with my brother has warped your character.'

Marcus darkened, but then smiled as he said, 'For once, I must agree with St John. It is a most convoluted plan, but I see no reason why it might not work.'

There was at least one glaring reason, and Miranda was pleased to note that the men had not noticed it.

'Very well, then. I retire to the country. In advance of you, I think—that will seem less suspicious. I will set myself up at the inn near Haughleigh. If you have no objections,' St John added, looking to the duke.

Miranda felt a brief flare of hope. The St John she knew of old had been quick enough to ignore his banishment from the family lands and would never have asked for the duke's permission before returning. His last comment had almost sounded like sincere respect for Marcus's wishes. Was it too much to hope that his service in Portugal had changed him for the better?

Marcus looked at the desk blotter, not his brother, as he said, 'If you retire to Devon, you might as well go straight to the house. No reason for you to pay an innkeeper when the family manor stands empty. I will write to the servants, informing them of the change.'

Miranda started, and concealed her smile. Her husband was being unusually generous of spirit, possibly because of St John's circumspect and polite behaviour. So they would all be staying at the house together? All the better, for she might kill both birds with one stone. If things went according to her plans, there would be a reconciliation between the brothers before the summer was through.

And Esme Canville would find a way out of her difficulties as well. For unless she missed her guess, Miranda had already found a suitor who would meet with Esme's approval, and he was sitting in the room with them.

Chapter Four

St John turned his face into the pillow, away from the spring sunlight streaming through the window. Things had changed at Haughleigh under the care of his sister-in-law. For one thing, he didn't remember it as being so damned bright when his mother had been in charge. He had come to his old home, hoping to nurse his dark moods in the gloom. But everywhere he turned there was sunshine and fresh air. It was most disconcerting.

He sat up and took his tea from the waiting valet. The food was good, as well. It was all too comfortable and it put him on his guard.

Not that he expected his brother to be laying traps for him. This was not the Peninsula, after all, with danger at every turn and spies in the bushes. Marcus was much more straightforward then that. If there was to be an attack from Marcus, it would be full on and from the front, not preceded by peaceful overtures and tea in his old bedroom. He was here at the invitation of the duke, and could take it at face value. Perhaps the blow in the hallway had been enough to settle the score between them.

But he doubted it. Letting his brother strike him had been enough to allow him entrance to the house. To allow him back into the family would take something more. Time, money and apologies. And while he had all the time in the world, he was at a loss as to how to carry on with the rest.

If he had to dance to Miranda's tune for a while, and get the Canville chit properly married, so be it. It was an odd scheme, but it fit well with his own plans for re-conciliation with his family. It would be much easier to demonstrate his repentance while living under the nose of his brother. The family was scheduled to arrive today and he had done nothing so far to arouse comment from servants or neighbours. He expected that Marcus would quiz the staff on his behaviour when unobserved by family. The report should be most favourable, since he had taken great pains to appear to be nothing more than the circumspect gentleman he was.

He could hear the carriages in the distance, and hurried with his dressing, not wanting to be caught unprepared when his host arrived.

St John wandered down the corridor to the sound of Marcus's voice booming orders in the hallway. It still had the tone of command, but with less bluster than when St John had last heard it. There was laughter in his brother's nature that had not been there before. And Miranda's as well, sweet and clear, happy to be home.

He froze at the next sounds. The laughter of children—a boy and a girl. Of course he knew of them, he'd read the announcement of the births in *The Times*. He'd just doubted he would ever be allowed to meet them. It was a shock to hear them so close.

St John walked slowly down the stairs, into the bustle of the homecoming, and felt it stop around him. Miranda, at least, appeared happy to see him.

'St John.' Marcus's voice gave nothing away. But his posture was alert and the laughter was gone from his eyes.

'Marcus.' What was he expected to say in return? He could hardly welcome the man to his own house. 'I trust the trip was uneventful?'

Miranda filled the silence. 'No trip with children is ever uneventful. And you have not met ours, have you? Come, children, and meet your uncle.' She gestured the two forward, a boy of about five and a girl who, if his memory served, must be almost four.

He continued down the stairs and to them and stooped to take the boy's hand. 'How do you do, Johnny?'

The boy was every bit his father's son and pierced him with a gimlet eye. 'My name is John.'

'John, then. I'm your uncle St John. Our names are rather the same, aren't they?'

'No, they're not. My father says we are not the least bit alike and he is glad of it.'

'John!' His mother laid a warning hand on her son's shoulder. 'And this is little Charlotte.' She nudged her daughter forward.

St John bowed low to her, and produced a penny from his pocket, handing it to the girl. 'Fair Charlotte, I am charmed to meet you.'

She smiled back at him and mumbled, 'Thank you, uncle.'

'You're welcome.'

'Where's mine?' Little John was glaring at him with a miniature of Marcus's commanding stare, and pointing to the penny.

'John…' Miranda warned again.

St John smiled back at him. 'Still in my pocket, Johnny. And your father is right, you are much more like him than me.' He produced the penny and handed it to the boy. 'Some time, when he is not watching, bring me the penny and I'll tell you stories of your father, when he was little.'

Marcus took a step forward, closer to his son, and St John could almost hear the frost forming.

'You've been remiss in the child's education, Marcus. Has he discovered how to get down to the kitchen and steal sweets without Cook noticing?'

Miranda shot him a warning glance, but little John was now looking at him with thinly veiled curiosity.

'There is a way. I learned it from your father, and you

shall learn it from me. And don't tell your mother or she'll give us both a hiding.'

He could feel Marcus relaxing.

What did you think I'd tell him, Marcus? I am not so bad as all that.

The children retreated to cling to the skirts of the governess, or so St John thought. As he looked up, he realised he was mistaken. The style was simple, but the blue wool of the travelling dress was too fine for a servant. And the face of the woman looking down at the children with such obvious affection was shockingly familiar.

'Miss Canville?' Her presence had caught him off guard. He had known she would be with the family. But he had been expecting the desperate girl who had come to his rooms.

The fashionable young woman who stood before him was hardly recognisable. There was no hint of hardship in her. Her lovely face was untroubled, her smile peaceful. He felt himself relaxing as he gazed on her, as one might when enjoying a fine spring day. She looked deceptively innocent, with her hair caught in a modest knot and the children tangling in her skirts, but the look in her wide blue eyes when she gazed at him was anything but maternal.

'Captain Radwell. How good to see you again.'

'And you, miss.' He offered a belated bow. 'Are you faring well with my brother and his family?'

'Certainly better than I fared with you.' He was

readying an apology when he noticed the slight quirk of her lips. She had him off balance again, and was enjoying it.

'Well. That is good to hear.' It was embarrassing, but he was suddenly at a loss for anything to say.

'The duke and duchess have been most kind to me. Thank you for placing me in their company.'

He nodded. 'Your servant, miss.' And then he remembered that he was only there to be a threat to her virtue. 'When it comes to something like that, at least,' he added and managed what he hoped was a leer.

And she laughed. There was no hint of embarrassed modesty, nor was it the knowing giggle of a mistress. She had laughed at him as though she knew his measure and did not believe his threats.

This was most irritating. Five years ago he could raise a blush on the cheek of any young thing, with much less effort than that. But after a drugging and a kidnapping that should have left her faint with terror, Esme Canville was laughing at him. His reputation as a danger to womankind was in need of polishing.

And then he remembered that he was no longer attempting to maintain the gloss on his infamy. He should be hoping it would fade into tarnished obscurity. But he would never manage to scare her into the arms of another man if she found his attentions a source of amusement.

He glanced to Miranda for help, but she was busy seeing to the children, and Marcus was his old pompous self, shouting orders to the servants in a right good humour. They were distracted and retreating down different hallways, too caught up in the business of homecoming to notice him.

And suddenly he was alone with Miss Canville.

She looked at him expectantly. 'It seems they have quite forgotten me. But that is rather easy to do, I suppose.'

'Oh, no. I find you most memorable, and I am a very good judge of these things.'

Damn. That had sounded positively sincere and in no way dangerous.

She should have responded by blushing prettily. Instead, she cocked her head slightly to one side, considering him, and then said, 'I suppose you must be, for you have quite a reputation as a lady's man. But tell me, Captain Radwell—how many women do you find memorable? In round numbers, I mean.'

He sputtered. 'Miss Canville, that is a most impertinent question.'

'I suppose it is, but I am, as you've pointed out, just a green girl. I can hardly be expected to know what to say to a man of your reputation. You claim I am memorable, but if you find all women you meet to be memorable, then your last comment is more a tribute to your good memory than it is to any great beauty or virtue on my part.'

He smiled, despite himself. 'Let us just say that I have trouble forgetting women who come to my rooms in the evening making such suggestions as you did.'

Again, she considered before speaking. 'Well, that does narrow the field somewhat. But not to an extent where I might be truly flattered. There have been quite a few women who have done that, if the stories I hear are true.'

He could no longer contain his exasperation. 'Esme, if you hear stories such as that, you are to pretend you haven't heard them and under no circumstances are you to repeat them back to me.'

'Just as you are not to address me by my given name without permission. And yet I could swear I just heard you use it.'

He stopped dead in his conversational tracks. She was correct. But just when had he begun thinking of her as Esme? 'That's as may be, Miss Canville—'

'Too late to redeem yourself, Captain Radwell. From now on, I must always be Esme to you.'

He sighed. 'Must you?'

She smiled. 'Yes, I must. And I will call you St John.'

'And I suppose it is too late to beg pardon and say that I merely forgot myself.'

'Scant moments ago, you confessed to an excellent memory. regarding me, at least. You remember my name, which is more than I expected. And if you can remember me, and forget yourself?' She smiled and he felt dazed by the flood of words. 'Then I think I will take that as a most singular compliment, indeed. And now, let us test your memory of the house. Perhaps you can give me a brief tour until my bags have found their way to my room.'

He shook off the effect of the smile and struggled to regain control of the conversation. 'It would not do for us to wander off alone. It is not proper for a young, unmarried lady to be seen in the company of a notorious rake.'

'Then there would have to be someone to see us.' She gestured around the room. 'In case you hadn't noticed, we are already alone. Hardly our fault, since it is the rest of the family that has moved away.' She slipped an arm through the crook of his elbow, and was leading him down the corridor and away from the hall.

The feel of her arm in his was most pleasant, as was the sensation of her standing at his side. She was neither too tall nor too short and when he looked down at her, their eyes met with no unfortunate slouching or craning of necks on either part. She fell easily in step beside him as they walked, so that no adjustment of his gait was necessary.

She smiled at him, and he smiled back, forgetting that ease and comfort between them was never meant to be the order of the day. That had not been the object in his being here, but he was at a loss as to why he would care. He was overcome with the feeling that he had fallen off a dock somewhere and was being towed out to sea by the current, further and further away from the safety of land.

'St John.' His brother's voice was as sharp as a rifle crack, and it brought St John to his senses. As a bad example to the girl, he was already a failure.

Marcus was standing in the doorway of the nearest room, his eyes dark with a gathering storm.

St John withdrew his arm from the girl's and said with as much composure as possible, 'And the first stop on our tour is my brother's study. Marcus, you are most remiss in treatment of your guests. Es...er...Miss Canville does not know the direction of her room.'

'And she certainly does not need your help to find it.' Marcus glared at him, before turning and bowing to Esme. 'I'm sorry, Miss Canville, I cannot think what my wife is about, abandoning you like this. There must have been some problem with the children or the servants.'

As Marcus rang for the butler to take Esme to her room, St John noted to himself that the situation was indeed most strange. The children seemed quite all right when they were in the hall, as had the servants. And yet Miranda had gone away and left the two of them alone. Surely she did not expect him to seduce the girl in the first five minutes.

The butler was leading a somewhat wistful Esme toward the front stairs, and St John sighed with relief. Whatever her plan had been, he was most happy to see it effectively scotched. The girl moved much too fast for his taste. He turned in relief from her retreating form, only to be faced by the still-angry figure of the duke.

'We will speak in my study, St John. Please.'

St John recognised the word 'please' for what it was—merely a placeholder for the word 'now'. A command from the duke, masquerading as a request from a brother to set the family and servants at ease. Very well, then. After five years he was used to following orders and obeying commands. It would be no different here. He shrugged indifferently and strolled after his stiff-backed brother into the study. Flinging himself into a chair in front of the desk, he waited for Marcus to speak.

'If you are to be here, then we had best set down a code of conduct. I do not want this visit to degenerate, until it is even worse than the others.'

St John smiled. 'I doubt that would be possible. I've set the bar low enough to be hard set to find conduct that could crawl under it.'

Marcus ignored the comment and went on. 'If you wish to remain under my roof, I expect you to maintain a level of decency, and I have written down some rules to that effect.' Marcus reached into his pocket and pulled out a folded sheet of paper, and stared down at it.

'You've written them down?' St John craned his neck to get a glimpse of the paper, and Marcus angled it away so that he could not read. 'Well, how very like you, brother. So organised. God forbid we should leave anything to chance or memory. Is your pen ready? If the nib is trimmed and the ink handy, you can check off the points as we cover them.'

Marcus's eyes rose from the paper to pin him to his chair, but St John smiled back at him, trying and failing to force some trace of amusement into his brother.

Then he waved his hand in dismissal. 'Read on, then. Let us get this done with.'

'First, you shall not harass the servants in any way: no chasing maids, no lingering below stairs, attempting to turn the staff to your will. No sneaking about the house like an intruder. You will enter and leave through the front doors, and if I tell you to be off, there will be no argument.'

St John examined his nails, indifferent to his brother's words.

'There will be no gambling, no whoring, no drinking.'

'Is that just in the house, or does it apply to the grounds, and the land surrounding? Because I know an inn just a few miles down the road...'

He looked up into his brother's glare. 'All right. I will have the deportment of a vicar, if you wish. But you'd best change the last to "no public drunkenness". I know the cellars in this house and I will not refuse a brandy, no matter what your list might demand.'

'Very well. Thirdly, you will not harass Miss Canville, or any of the other guests.'

'And what, exactly, is the definition of "harass"? If you wish me to break her heart, it is not as if I can avoid her totally.'

'Unwelcome attentions.'

'There again, you have me, Marcus. She made it quite plain that all my attentions were welcome, not that I chose to give them, mind you. This puts me in a damned difficult position.'

'One in which you have more experience than I, I am certain. You know from much practice where harmless flirtation ends and a true threat to honour begins. Do not cross the line. If she is as inexperienced as she appears—'

'There is no "if", Marcus. Of course she is inexperienced. The girl is a complete innocent.' His mouth snapped shut, as he caught his brother's searching expression. What did it matter what Marcus thought of the girl's character? They would both be rid of her soon enough. He began again. 'If she had any true knowledge of the facts, she would not have made the offer she did. And, yes, I probably do know more than enough to destroy her heart while leaving her virtue intact. But I don't have to enjoy the situation. Your next rule, please.'

Marcus looked almost sad, as he said the next words, 'You will avoid prolonged contact with my wife and children when I am not present. While the prospect of a truce between us pleases me, I find I cannot bring myself to trust you with those I hold closest to my heart. It is too late for you to be dear Uncle St John to my children, or to pretend brotherly interest in Miranda. If I think you are attempting to ingratiate yourself into the household, I will remove you myself, by force if necessary. Is that clear?'

St John bit back the desire to point out the difficulty of removing him by force from anywhere he chose to be. If the French army had not managed it… He took a deep, steadying breath. 'Very well. It is no less than I expected, or deserve, considering my past conduct...' he took another breath '...for which, I apologise.'

The phrase hung in the air, surrounded by silence.

And what had he expected, really? To come back to the house, say a few simple words and be greeted by his brother with open arms? It was foolish beyond reason to think that he could turn back the clock and undo any of it. And yet he had to try.

'I know that that is not sufficient. But it is all I can think to do. I will do my best to abide by the rules you have set down for me. You have my word, such as it is.'

And he held out his hand to his brother.

There was another long pause before Marcus took the offered hand in his own firm grasp. But there was no smile on his face and his eyes never wavered as they stared into St John's, searching his character.

Chapter Five

'This is the plan as I see it,' Miranda was biting the tip of her pencil, as she stared down at the paper in front of her.

Not for the first time, Esme wondered at the unusualness of the situation. The elegant woman in front of her was the last person Esme would have expected to take an interest in the problems of a nobody such as herself. And yet she seemed genuinely concerned.

Esme shifted in her chair by the morning-room fire, listening to the crisp rustle of her new gown. The clothing was another thing that Miranda had insisted upon. And matching accessories. When they'd left London, she'd had two trunks full of dresses, shoes, gloves, fans, bonnets and anything else she could think to ask for. And she was promised borrowed jewellery to suit any occasion, since Miranda had assured her that there was no want of such things at Haughleigh.

Miranda scanned her guest list again, as though searching for a name. 'You need a husband, and you need him with expedience.'

Esme hesitated, afraid to offend her exalted new friend. 'On the contrary, I do not want or need a husband. I merely need to get rid of the one my father has chosen for me.'

'The quickest way to do that is to choose another. Preferably one so high born as to be impossible for your father to resist. What is the rank and income of the man to whom you are betrothed?'

'An Earl. Lord Halverston. I am unsure of his income, but he must be nearing eighty and is respected in the *ton*.' Esme shuddered, thinking at the vile stare from the carriage beneath her window.

'So I need to find you an earl, or better. Or someone without title, but with a fortune that no sane father could ignore. I can ask Marcus's advice on the income, for he knows anyone who matters in Parliament. And he should be young enough to suit you, but old enough to suit your father.' She glanced over the paper at Esme and began writing down names. 'I can think of several candidates in the area who might suit. And a plan of attack—'

'You make it sound as though it were a battle.'

Miranda smiled. 'But it is, my dear. It is. Or perhaps it is only a game. The gentlemen think that they have the upper hand in all things, but on this field they are consistently outmatched, should a woman truly choose to play. I will be throwing a series of parties and soirées, to entertain my new friend from the city.' She gestured in Esme's general direction with the pencil. 'It would be unspeakably rude to turn me down. And the gentlemen will think themselves quite safe, knowing that there is only one of you and…' she glanced down the paper '…three of them. Should there be matchmaking afoot, when the lot falls, it must surely fall on one of the other two.'

'And I am to choose between these three gentlemen?'

Miranda laughed. 'Three is a broad enough choice, I assure you. Any one would be fine. I would not steer you false. And we might not get all of them up to scratch. Meet them and choose the one who chooses you. Or someone else. If there is someone in attendance that you'd like better, then set your cap at him. There is no reason to limit yourself to my choices. If you need help in the matter, I will advise.'

Esme looked back doubtfully. 'That is all there is to it? I meet them and one of them is sure to offer?'

Miranda walked over and stood before her, drawing her out of her chair and to the pier-glass at the end of the room. 'I should quite think so. Look at yourself, Esme. You are lovely.'

'In borrowed finery,' Esme retorted.

'Not borrowed. Gifts. I have more than enough clothes, and I fancied a trip to the shops. It was most enjoyable to outfit you.'

'If you had more than enough, then your cast-offs would have been sufficient for me.'

'With your fair skin and hair? I should think not. You would disappear in the colours that suit me, while I would look deplorable in the roses and pale blues that suit you so well.'

'But if most of the events are to be in the evening, surely it was not necessary to buy so many day dresses.'

'It pays to be prepared for any eventuality. One never knows who one might see during the day.'

And Esme's memory was flooded with a vision of St John, standing in the hall as she'd entered, and the look on his face when he'd seen her. She'd been warned to expect him, and apprised of Miranda's plans to use her début as an excuse to reconcile the brothers. But she'd thought that he'd be in bored attendance at some ball or other, or invited to the occasional family dinner. She hadn't dared hope that he'd be staying in the house with them, and waiting at the door for his brother's arrival.

The stunned look on his face as he'd seen her turned out properly was worth any amount of risk. As was his obvious discomposure at finding himself alone with her. It was doubtful that she'd be so lucky again, since Miranda showed every sign of being a diligent chaperon. She struggled to pay attention to Miranda's plans for the co-ordination of the Haughleigh jewelry with her new wardrobe.

'If we want these gentlemen to give you a second

look, it helps to display you to your best advantage. For-give me for saying it, but the clothing that your father allowed did not flatter you.'

'It was not intended to. It was serviceable, and inexpensive.' She could almost feel the coarse cloth against her skin, the heat of wool in summer, and the way the greys and browns hid the dirt as the shape hid her figure. She looked at her faint reflection in the window glass and saw a healthy glow to her skin and the curve of her bosom at the square neckline of the dress. 'My father would have found both these dresses and the person in them to be foolish beyond endurance. But I think I like them.'

'As will your suitors.' Miranda glanced down at the paper before her. 'Mr Webberly, not currently titled, but five and twenty and in line for his father's land. The Earl of Baxter, both titled and wealthy, and of an age that your father will approve: almost fifty. Not too old, I assure you. He is in excellent health and with a youthful demeanor. And Sir Anthony de Portnay Smythe.' She frowned. 'I am unsure of Tony's age or background. Perhaps he is not the wisest choice. But he is always a gentleman, and I must admit he is quite dashing. Should he fancy you enough to offer, he would be the one most likely to find a way through your father's disapproval.'

'And what of St John?' Esme tried not to appear too interested in the answer. 'Is he not single, and of an age to marry?'

Miranda looked searchingly into her eyes before saying, 'He is of an age, but not of an inclination. And it is as well for you that he has found some sense in these last five years, or we would not be talking now. He would have put you up in some *pied-a-terre* without benefit of clergy and then where would you be?'

Esme tried not to imagine where she might be, right now, if she were alone with St John, and the flush crept into her cheeks.

Miranda frowned. 'You must not romanticise the life of a courtesan, Esme. It is not glamorous. You would be jumping from the frying pan to the fire.'

'Perhaps.' But Esme had watched the look in St John's eyes change as he'd seen her in the hall. At first he'd scanned past, dismissing her as one of the servants. But his gaze had returned to her, when he'd noticed she was young and pretty, and there was an almost predatory gleam in the second appraisal. He'd liked what he was seeing. To be alone with a man who had that look in his eye would mean certain ruin.

But she remembered the shock and embarrassment that had followed the first roguish assessment, when St John's gaze had risen to her face and he had recognised her. And how quickly he'd looked away, only to glance back when he'd thought she wasn't looking. As though he had found his heart unexpectedly engaged.

Esme continued, 'And yet you said if I was to find someone I liked better, I should set my cap.'

Miranda looked stern, but Esme could detect the faint twinkle in her eyes. 'St John is much too wild, and shows no indication that he wishes to settle down. If you are still harbouring any foolish thoughts about becoming my brother-in-law's mistress, and if he shows any indication of the even more foolish idea of helping you to ruin, then I will do everything in my power to stop you both. Although it is of short duration, I value our friendship far too much, Esme, to allow you to do anything to jeopardise it. As St John's mistress, you would no longer be welcome in our home. I also value the bond of blood between my husband and his brother, and do not wish St John to destroy it by returning to his old ways.

'That said, if there is any chance that you can turn his head and bring him up to snuff on the subject of marriage and children—' she smiled '—then you would be doing this family a great favour and I would dearly love to call you sister. But, for now, I think it best to consider all possible candidates and not place all of the eggs in a basket so weak as St John's. Now let us go down to luncheon and show this list to my husband. Perhaps he can add other names.'

The dining room at Haughleigh was as splendid as all the other rooms, richly appointed in crimson silk and much too large for only three people. The servants had set the four places at an end of the great table, hoping to add intimacy, but without success. The duke sat at the head, which was no great surprise, with Miranda and Esme at either side. The place to

Esme's left, which must have been laid for St John, was empty.

The luncheon was exceptional, but the discussion of Miranda's plans and potential guests who might suit Esme lacked the ease of their week in London. At first, Esme feared it might be caused by the expense of the parties, or the duke's discomfort of having her still with them, an uninvited guest. Many men would resent such an intrusion in their own home that they might tolerate for a week in London.

But then she felt the subtle shift in the air as another course was laid and removed from the empty chair next to hers. It was as though, even without being present in the room, St John was controlling the conversation. The duke would pause every so often during his own meal to glare at the untouched food on St John's plate. Then Miranda would make some off-hand remark, or ask a question, that would serve as a distraction to him until something else reminded him of his brother's absence. And then the pattern would repeat itself.

When the door finally opened, midway through the fish, all three heads snapped up to follow St John into the room. He took his chair without explanation and began to eat.

'You are late.' The duke was at his most commanding. There was no question but the tone demanded an explanation.

'I am sorry,' St John responded, sounding anything but. 'I did not realise that my prompt attendance at meals was mandatory. If there are other house rules you wish me to follow, perhaps you could write them down.'

'Only to see you flout them later.'

'No need to worry, brother. If I wish to flout any of your rules, I shall make sure that you are not there to see it, and thus it will not bother you.'

'Is that where you were, just now? Breaking house rules since you knew my probable location.'

'Actually, no. I was in my room, taking a nap.'

There was a tink of crystal as the stem of the duke's glass snapped in his hand. Wine spattered the tablecloth. Esme noticed the drop of blood forming in his palm before he curled his fingers into a fist and stuffed the hand into his jacket pocket. 'If you must talk at all, the least you could do is speak truth in two words out of three. First that fustian apology in my study, and now this. A nap in your room? Surely you can do better than that.'

St John glared back at him. 'It matters not what I say, since you construe all my words to be lies. I was taking a nap in my room. I was alone, to answer your next question.'

'If there had been a next question, I would not be asking it here,' the duke snapped.

'Of course not. You would be lecturing me in your study while brandishing an extensive list of things I mustn't do.'

'Can you not keep a civil tongue in your head, even at luncheon? And in front of ladies?'

'Another thing that was not on your list. Perhaps this would go easier, Marcus, if you would simply write down the things I am allowed to do. It would save my time and your ink and paper, since your list of "do's" will be considerably shorter than the "don't's".'

The duke rose from the table, too angry to respond, and stalked to the door, his uninjured hand outstretched. It struck the door palm first, springing the latch without bothering to turn the knob. Servants retreated and swirled behind him like the wake of a boat.

Miranda rose halfway out of her chair as if to follow, then glanced back at the two of them still at the table and sank back, returning to her meal as though nothing had happened.

St John said, with a hint of sadness, 'I think my brother is not so happy to see me as you'd hoped.'

Miranda took a bite of her food, not bothering to glance up again. Esme noted she was giving more than the necessary attention to chewing and swallowing, as though she needed time to marshal her emotions before speaking. At last she said, 'Perhaps if you did not provoke him so.'

St John sighed. 'Perhaps if he were not so easily provoked. I did not come here wishing to goad him. My earlier apology was sincere. I had hoped that prolonged contact would prove my intent. But that will be most difficult, since he cannot abide my company for more than a few moments at a time.'

Miranda's tone was chill. 'It is not as if he has no reason. I doubt that a simple apology will be the solution to the problem at hand.'

'But it will be a start. And despite what he may believe, I mean to follow his rules to the letter. Eventually, he will rage himself out, and then perhaps we can begin again.' St John looked down at his own plate, pushing it away untouched. 'But how long might it take for him to spend his anger? I had hoped...'

And then he looked up, smiling, and reached into his pocket. 'But maybe this will help.' He produced a velvet box and slid it across the table to his hostess. 'Something concrete to demonstrate my intentions. I had wanted to give this to you with Marcus here to witness. But Esme can assure him that my intentions in giving the gift were not dishonourable. I have debts that need settling if I am to prove to Marcus that I have changed.'

Miranda reached in front of her, snapped open the box, and recoiled as if it had been full of snakes. 'St John. How could you?' She covered her mouth with her hand and fled the room.

Esme got up and walked to the head of the table, examining the contents. 'Oh, St John, they are magnificent. But why—'

'Would my sister-in-law be so upset by the gift of an emerald necklace? I suspect my family has decided that the best way to deal with the past is to ignore it. It is an easy thing to pretend I do not exist when I am in Portugal, but much more difficult to do when I am in their presence, a constant reminder of the history between us.

And this has upset her to the point of leaving us alone together. A very grave mistake, which I will now rectify.' He rose from the table as if to go.

'Wait. You cannot leave me here alone, and with only half the story.' She gripped his sleeve and tugged him back into the chair. 'What is it about the necklace that pains Miranda so?'

'The emeralds are very similar to ones that my sister-in-law once used to buy me off. A family heirloom, passed down through generations of Haughleighs. It should be gracing her neck, as it did my mother's and every other duchess of this house.' He grimaced. 'I used a pocketknife to pry the stones out and sold them, for drink and women. I treated it no better than dross. Came to my senses before the money ran out and used the last few gems to buy my commission.'

He held up the necklace and she took it from him, touching an empty setting at the centre.

'I sent the last remaining stone to Miranda for Christmas before I left for the war. That is the place for it. I kept the setting. I always meant to repay her.' He frowned down at the necklace. 'I saved every penny of my soldier's pay to buy new stones and have them reset. It is all I have left in the world. I was hoping to give it back and then we could be even. Better to start fresh with nothing than to live any longer with this debt. But it is still not enough. She is no more willing to accept it than my brother is to hear my apology.'

She placed the necklace back in its case. 'But what

could you have done that was so horrible that your only brother will not forgive it?'

St John took a sip of wine. 'I seduced his wife.'

Esme's jaw dropped.

He held up a finger. 'Wives, actually.' Then shook his head. 'No. Wife would be more correct. His first wife, only. I attempted to seduce Miranda, but was unsuccessful.' His look was almost wistful. 'When she first came here, she was not the great beauty that she is now. But lovely all the same. And my foolish brother left her alone. I hated him, and I thought it would serve him right had he lost her.' He shook his head. 'I hope, if I did nothing else, I taught him to appreciate his wife.'

'And did you teach him to appreciate his first wife?' Esme's tone was sharper than she meant it to be.

'No. I loved her.' His eyes were so sad, and so distant, that she was sorry she'd rebuked him. He stared back at her, empty. 'As did Marcus, I think. And Bethany loved no one but herself. She played us against each other. And then she died. We were young, and foolish. I was particularly so. By the time she died, I was mad with wanting her and knowing I could never have her. It took years for the madness to fade. When it did, I was in the army, a thousand miles from home. I swore, if I lived to see England again, that I would make amends.'

Esme smiled encouragingly. 'I knew, when I looked at you, that you could not be the man my father said you were.'

St John smiled sadly back at her. 'Oh, no, darling. I am as bad and worse. Because I no longer attempt to steal my brother's wife does not mean I'm incapable of stealing from another man. Only more selective.'

Esme hinted, 'Then perhaps you ought to find a woman who is not already attached.'

'And let her attach herself to me? No, thank you.' His smile turned cynical. 'Or is this another attempt to achieve ruination? You still do not understand.' He leaned close to her and let his breath touch her cheek as he whispered in her ear. 'You think, because you see a moment's softness of heart, and because I do not strike women, no matter how much they deserve a good beating, that I am some kind of saviour? A dark angel, come to rescue you? Well, think again, little one. If you let me, I will take everything you offer.'

She closed her eyes so that he could not see the longing in them.

His tone turned bitter. 'I will take from you things you do not know you have to give. And when you are empty and there is nothing left to take, I will be gone and you can go home to your father. Then you may look him in the eye if you are able, and explain to him why no decent man would ever want you. I have done it before, you know. There are worse sins on my conscience than cuckolding my brother. Do not ask me to ruin another innocent, even if it is yourself. It is too much.' And he pushed away from the table, turned and walked from the room.

Chapter Six

Esme stood in the doorway of the ballroom at Haugh-leigh before her introduction to Devon society, fighting the urge to run. It would be most ungrateful of her to bolt from a party at which she was the honoured guest. It had been quite amazing to watch her new friend, Miranda, effortlessly organise dinner and a ball for more than a hundred people, creating guest lists and menus from notes of the many past balls she'd given, and sending the majority of preparations on ahead before they'd even left London.

It was to be a welcoming event for Esme, and a celebration of the duke and duchess's return to their estate. Miranda assured her that the neighbours would be happy to attend, and were likely to reciprocate with invitations of their own.

Esme tried to quell the trepidation she felt at the prospect. She'd had no Season of her own, and what parties she'd attended were small and rather dull. And she'd never been the centre of attention at any of them. But this night she was in the receiving line as the guests filed past, and Miranda had introduced them all, occasionally leaning towards her and whispering, 'Eligible' 'Very eligible' or 'Eligible and rich.' It got to the point where Esme could judge by the brightness of her friend's smile the income and suitability of any male guests that made their bows.

And she wished that it mattered. She truly did. Miranda was trying so hard, and Esme knew her prospects, and the urgency of the situation, if she wished to avoid the marriage that her father would choose for her. But she had always hoped, when she'd dreamed of the balls she was missing and suitors that she could never have, that her feelings would be engaged when it was time to choose a husband.

Perhaps that was the problem. She'd imagined herself doing the choosing, not waiting patiently to be chosen. Without Miranda's help, she might never have had any say in the matter at all. But in the end, it would be up to a gentleman to choose her. And now, having met the best that the neighborhood had to offer, she found herself wishing ardently that none would step forward.

'St John,' Miranda called out sharply, 'come here this instant and properly greet our guest. Because you are family, you may think you can slink past us and avoid the line. But the least you can do is make Esme welcome and thank your host before drinking our wine.'

St John rolled his eyes before saying with exaggerated courtesy, 'I am so sorry, your Grace, that living here most of my life led me to make myself at home.'

Esme could feel the duke stiffen and ready a response, and Miranda tensing at his side, ready to avert the conflict that she had created by calling St John to them.

And then she felt the tension dissipate, as St John's shoulders slumped in submission and he muttered, 'What am I about?' and began again. 'Of course, Miranda. You are right. I was being provoking and have no wish to spoil your evening with my behaviour. He turned to his brother, and said awkwardly, 'It really is quite splendid, to see the old house this way. For a moment, I was taken back to when we were boys and Mother held such parties here.' He scanned the room. 'Although I think your wife may have outdone her. Perhaps it is only that I am finally tall enough to see over the tables.' He leaned closer to Miranda. 'Did your husband tell you of all the times he led me here from the nursery, to steal cakes and lemonade? I was not always the scapegrace of the family. Marcus got up to his share of trouble and I was but a sweet and innocent child, following my brother's lead.'

The duke looked shocked, before admitting, 'He is right. I had forgotten it until now. But he is right in this. I always found the cakes we took from balls to be sweeter than the ones brought to the nursery to keep us out of the way. And as I remember it, it took very little effort to lead you astray.' He looked even more shocked and smiled as he said, 'It took no effort to lead you any-where, for back then you followed me like a puppy on a leash.'

St John turned from the dazed duke. 'And, Miss Can-ville, is a formal greeting necessary? For I feel I know you quite well all ready.' He bowed low over her hand and then rose and looked into her eyes for a moment too long, until she could feel her cheeks beginning to colour. 'You are looking most splendid this evening.'

Of course he must say that to all the young ladies and so it meant little. But she had seen herself in the mir-ror, and tonight it was true. The rose silk of her gown suited her to perfection. Her hair was dressed with care and accented with real pearls borrowed from the duch-ess. And, best of all, the skin of her arms and throat was unmarked. She was as pure and beautiful as any of the ladies present.

It was good that she had failed in her original plan, for what would he have thought had she disrobed be-fore him that first night, when the bruises were still fresh? No one chose fruit when the flesh was dis-coloured. They cast such aside. When choosing a woman it was probably no different.

She put those thoughts from her head and said, 'Thank you, sir.' And as she smiled back at him she felt the low fluttering in her stomach that seemed always present when St John was near. Or was likely to be near, or even mentioned in passing conversation.

It occurred to her that its absence accounted for the strange dead feeling when meeting the other gentlemen of the neighborhood. They might be very nice, but they all suffered from the disadvantage of not being St John Radwell.

He was looking at her as if he saw nothing unusual in her behaviour. Perhaps her feelings did not show on her face.

'Yes,' he said, nodding in approval at her appearance. 'If you insist on looking so well when turned out for a ball, and looking at them with such fine eyes and that hopeful smile of yours, I imagine the eligible men in the room will be quite helpless to escape. I must thank the Lord that I am immune to your charms or I might find myself in a great deal of trouble.' And, after another half-bow, he turned and went in search of the wine.

Immune?

'I must say, St John is on his best behaviour this evening.' Miranda was smiling up at her husband.

As though she were some kind of pestilence. A disease.

'Yes,' the duke replied, 'that is rather a surprise. This is the first time in years that I've not had the desire to strangle him where he stood.'

Perhaps it was a transferable desire, for Esme quite felt the urge to strangle him herself.

'Of course,' Marcus remarked, 'the night is still young. He will most certainly have done something by midnight that causes the old rage to return. But he is right about my mother's parties. And the cakes. Why, when my father was alive…'

Esme's mind wandered from the discussion, as her eyes followed St John's retreating back through the room. How dare he? She was trouble, was she, now? And he felt himself lucky to be able to resist. Then he must hope that his luck would hold for she knew, with a sudden wave of resolve, that the only head she wanted to turn was on the impressively broad shoulders of Captain Radwell.

She set off into the whirl of the ball, intent on having the best time possible. She enjoyed herself with an almost spiteful enthusiasm. She positively glittered with the joy of being there. The dancing was divine, the company superb, and when she was lead into dinner on the arm of a frightened young man, she found the food to be beyond all imagining.

And was honest in her praise. It was the most delightful evening she'd ever spent, though perhaps the wine was ever so slightly bitter, and the pheasant flavourless, and the trifle less than moist, when she caught the occasional glimpse of St John entertaining his dinner companion at another table. The girl next to him looked flattered at the attention, and Esme thought she could hear the girl's silvery laughter as St John relayed some amusing story, and saw her faint blush in the candlelight as he leaned closer to her. Then, suddenly, the girl turned her face to Esme and stared at her with unexpected venom.

Esme pushed her own plate away with dessert unfinished. What could she have done to anger the girl, and deserve such a look? It chilled her to think that she had somehow made an enemy on her first public appearance. She shook off the feeling and attempted to focus on the conversation of the gentleman next to her.

She was trying, God knew, but why must it be so difficult? Mr Webberly was pleasant, honest and interested in her. He was not so much older than she, and, according to Miranda, he stood to inherit many acres of excellent farmland. Although his face was not as devilishly attractive as some people's in the room, it was open and honest and he would probably make someone an excellent husband.

And she hoped it was not to be her.

After dinner, he stood up with her, leading her slowly in a figure of the dance and handing her down the set. She tried to imagine him standing up to her father, or breaking with tradition to borrow a coach and spirit her off to Scotland. The picture would not form. She glanced back up the row, and saw Mr Webberley turning a local girl in the same steps, and looked again in shock. It was the pale girl who had been sitting with St John and who'd looked at her with such spite. And the man holding her hand could easily have been a total stranger to the one Esme had just danced with. His spine was straighter and his gaze more direct when he looked at the new girl.

She sighed in relief. It would be wrong to want him for herself. Not when someone else wanted and needed him more, and he wanted her in return. Esme had but to see that they spent the evening in each other's company, and she need never worry about his attentions again.

She shook her head. It was foolish to think of his attentions as unwanted. What she wanted was unimportant, it what she needed that mattered. An escape from the marriage set before her. One solution should be as good as another, and it would be much smarter to put her own wants and needs ahead of those of a complete stranger.

And then she looked down at the end of the set, to see St John lounging insolently against the wall, scorn for the young couple dancing together at the head. As her new partner took her hand and turned her, St John caught her eye, and she saw his mirth at her discomposure. He glanced from her to Webberley dancing at the head of the set and raised his glass in a mocking toast, as if to wish her well on the nuptials.

So many emotions rushed through her at once that it was hard to feel them all. There was shame at being caught husband-hunting, and embarrassment that he'd read her mind so easily from across the room. There was a moment's pride at the way his eyes had run over her before raising the glass. He'd looked at her as a woman, not as a girl, and something about the set of his shoulders had said that he could show her what she wanted to know better than the callow youth she was dancing with.

And there was a rush of all the things she did not feel when she looked at Webberley. It was not love, precisely. It was something stronger than love, but not so long lasting, a bone-deep desire to ignore what was good for her, to forget the future and revel in the present, spending every moment she could in the arms of St John Radwell.

The crush was intolerable. Even though she knew the room well, she could not help but feel that she was in a strange new world, now that the guests were here. When the next dance ended she crept to the ladies' retiring room to catch her breath.

Conversation stopped when she entered the room, and she wondered if there was some rule of conduct that she should be following of which she was not aware. But the ladies in the room crowded protectively around one of their own, and Esme immediately felt like the outsider.

It was the girl who had been dancing with Webberley. On close inspection, she was a little older than Esme, and she held herself awkwardly, as though she was no more at home in her surroundings than Esme was herself. There were obvious traces of tears on her cheeks that a friend was trying to conceal with powder.

Esme stepped forward without thinking and said, 'Is there something I can do to help? Should I get the duchess?'

The friend of the pale girl said coldly, 'I think you've done quite enough all ready.'

'Ann, please don't make it any more difficult.' The girl released a watery sigh, and Esme feared that the tears so recently stopped were likely to start again. 'Do not trouble her.'

Ann's eyes narrowed. 'No, why should I do anything to help you, if you will not help yourself?'

'I do not understand,' Esme said quietly. 'What is it that I am supposed to have done to your friend, when until scant hours ago I'd never laid eyes on her?'

'It is nothing.' The pale girl laid a hand on the arm of her friend, in an effort to silence her.

But Ann would not be quieted. 'Nothing but that there is a limited number of eligible men in the area. And the number of marriageable females has just increased by one.' Ann gave her a pointed look. 'We are from the country and you are from London. You are fashionable, pretty—worst of all, you are different. The gentlemen of the area have known us our whole lives. We cannot give them novelty. One of them is likely to offer for you. And this means one of us is to be disappointed. At the moment, it appears it may be Elizabeth. And, of course, this upsets her. But if you have plans in another direction, you might do us the courtesy of telling us so and setting her mind at rest. I have enough powder for all.'

Several sets of eyes stared at her in accusation, and she froze, searching her mind for the correct response. It had never occurred to her that there might be other schemes afoot at a gathering of this type. 'I have no designs on the gentlemen present,' she faltered.

'Oh, really? You have danced three dances with Mr Webberley, which is more than enough to incite comment.'

Had it been three? If so, they had made no impact upon her.

'I am sorry. I had not realised.' She attempted an encouraging smile that was not returned by the gathering in front of her. 'But now that I understand how things are, I will be more careful of the impression I give to the gentlemen of the area. If you will excuse me?' She backed hurriedly out of the room and returned to the ballroom.

She found Mr Webberley standing near the refreshments. He seemed to be looking for a face in the crowd; although he smiled in greeting to her, Esme could not help but think that it was not she he had been searching for.

She took the lemonade he offered with thanks and asked, 'Who is the tall girl you were dancing with earlier? The one in the unsuitable red dress?'

'Unsuitable? I find it most becoming.' There was a hint of censure in his voice. 'Her name is Miss Elizabeth Warrant.'

She smiled to herself at how quick the gentleman was to rush to the girl's defence. 'Well, red is hardly the thing so late in the summer. And it does not suit her. She would do better to choose something brighter.'

'Her family is not able to spend so extravagantly as some, with a new gown for every occasion. But I think she is turned out well, indeed.' His eyes were still scanning the dance floor.

Aha. She was definitely striking a nerve. 'I only wondered because she seemed so upset in the retiring room just now, as though she were hiding herself away. This is sometimes the case, when a woman does not think she looks her best. Or perhaps she is ill.' She said it lightly, as though it were not worth noting, but she noticed the man next to her pale.

'Elizabeth is ill? I am a neighbour to her family. If she is not well, perhaps retiring early would be best. But it would be a shame to spoil the evening for her sisters—'

'So you would offer to take her home yourself?' She finished his sentence and left him with no choice in the matter. 'Oh, would you? You are too kind, sir, to take such good care of a friend. Shall I see if she needs assistance, while you ready your carriage?'

'That would be best, I think.' She watched as Mr Webberley went in search of carriage and groom. He was secure in the knowledge that he had come up with the idea himself. It was too perfect.

Esme returned to the retiring room, shutting the door with a definitive snap behind her. 'Ann?'

The sour girl looked up at her with reproach and said nothing.

'Leave off helping your friend, for it would not do to have her looking too well. She is deathly ill and must return home at once.'

'I beg your pardon?' Elizabeth said, showing some spine for a change. 'I have no intention of leaving you to—'

'But you must. For I told Mr Webberley you are taken suddenly ill. He seemed most concerned. And please stop flushing. It is making you look far too healthy. Ann, do you have powder in a paler shade, perhaps? We need to kill the roses in those cheeks immediately.'

Ann recognised what was happening and smiled in satisfaction.

But Elizabeth said, 'I feel fine.'

'No, you do not,' Ann replied. 'You need to be taken home this instant.' She was furiously applying powder, and Elizabeth suddenly looked quite faint.

And yet the foolish girl insisted, 'I cannot go home. I do not wish to. My sisters would be so disappointed.'

'Which is why you must leave them here, to ride home with your parents. There will be other balls for you, but no night with a moon as fine as this one.'

There was still no light of comprehension in the eyes of the unfortunate Elizabeth.

Esme explained, 'If I do not miss my guess, Mr Webberley has found your parents and is even now explaining his intention to take you home in his carriage. Borrow a maid from Miranda if need be, preferably one who is a bit hard of hearing and a trifle blind. Or perhaps the rules of propriety can be bent, because of your weakened condition and Mr Webberley's position as a trusted family friend. Judging by the speed he rushed to your defence when I questioned him, and the look in his eyes when he thought you were ill, you need have no fear for your reputation as concerns Mr Webberly. He will guard it against all comers once he has proposed to you.'

'Oh, dear. I feel quite faint,' said Elizabeth.

'I hoped for nothing less. Use it to your advantage,' said Esme and turned to go. As the door shut behind her, she could hear Ann exhorting her friend to not be such a goose as to walk unsupported, but to take the man's arm and 'hold on 'til the last trump, if that was what it took'.

She smiled as she left the room and moved through the crowd at the door to the ballroom, satisfied with a job well done. But when she glanced down the stairs she thought she saw a familiar coat disappearing into the hall below.

St John. She tried to keep her heart from beating a little faster at the thought of him, though he seemed to be making every effort to avoid her for the evening. He had not danced a single dance with her, although she'd seen him stand up for several sets with others, including that wet hen, Elizabeth. And while she could swear that more than once she'd caught him watching her from across the room, he'd made no effort to speak to her.

Perhaps he meant to take a turn about the gardens, as many guests were doing. Suddenly, Esme longed for fresh air. She hurried down the steps and out the door.

Miranda had done a charming job of arranging the gardens for the ball. The paths were lit by tiny lanterns, and benches had been set for guests to enjoy the smell of the roses and the light of the full moon as it played on the surface of the ornamental pond. It was a beautiful night for a walk, although somewhat chilly. Esme rubbed the skin of her arms, wishing she'd thought to get a wrap before venturing from the house.

She passed several couples strolling arm in arm, and groups or people talking and laughing quietly, their clothes and hair silvery with moonlight. But there was no sign of St John, and she was getting quite far from the house. The path was no longer lit, and she suspected that this was a signal from Miranda that guests need go no further.

But she was not technically a guest, was she? She was a resident of the house, at least for now. And there was nothing to fear on the duke's estate. The full moon lit her way well enough. Perhaps just a little further…

'Looking for me?' St John's voice came out of the gloom behind her and she caught her breath.

'No. I mean, yes. Yes, I am. I wanted to…' The words froze in her throat.

'I'm sure you did, darling. Alone, in a dark garden, and so far away from the other guests. But I already told you, no. Did you think, once I saw you dressed in satin with stars in your eyes, that I might change my mind?' He strolled towards her. His movements were deliberate, with an almost animal grace, and his steps on the gravel of the path made no noise.

Was he different, or was it moonlight and champagne that made him seem so much more dangerous than he did during the day? She glared back at him, hoping that he would read her expression and ignore the shudder that travelled through her body as he taunted her. 'You really are the most odious man.'

He shrugged. 'As I've been trying to tell you, love.'

She tossed her head. 'It would serve you right if I found someone else.'

'Serve me?' He laughed. 'Alas, you'd not be the first missed opportunity, Esme. I will be wounded, but I shall survive. And it would be cutting off your nose to spite your face, when there are men in there who would have you honourably, to seek dishonour out of pique at me.'

It was her turn to laugh. 'They'll have me, will they? When they learn that there is no fortune that paid for these pretty clothes?'

'I'm sure many—'

'Then I fear, for all your debauchery, that you are much more naïve than I, St John. Without my father's consent, I have nothing. Of course, I can wait until I am of age, and I can do as I please if my father will allow me from the house. But how will I survive? I have no money, and no way to support myself. Again, I will have nothing. I do not fool myself so far as to believe I am such a great beauty that men will lose their hearts and all good sense. And it seems that many of the young ladies in the neighbourhood have plans for those same gentlemen that Miranda would choose for me. While they might find my company diverting, they will return to the familiar when it is time to offer marriage.'

She smiled back towards the house. 'I've already had to send Miranda's first candidate for my hand to assist a young lady who became most indisposed when she saw me monopolising him. If the gentleman has a lick of sense, he's making use of a trip in a closed carriage to convince the girl that she need fear nothing from me in regards to the disposition of his affection.'

'And if he has no sense?' St John asked in amusement.

'Then I believe the girl was being instructed, as I left her, in how to fake a swoon. If he cannot be moved to action when the moon is full and the woman he loves is near senseless in his arms, then I want no part of him either.'

There was a bark of laughter from St John. 'You set a trap for him so that he would marry someone else? Esme, darling, you do not understand husband-hunting at all.'

'It was for his own good, I assure you. Miranda meant well, but Mr Webberley was not intended for me. I could not very well have taken him away from the girl who loved him, and rejoiced in my success. It would have been wrong.' She turned away from him, looking out over the lawn, and wrapped her arms around her body, feeling the chill in the air. 'I should not have agreed to come here. It is folly to think that I will fit any better here than I might at home. Miranda should not be burdened with my problems.'

And the air warmed again as he stepped close behind her. 'While you continue to be a trial to me, Esme, you are no burden to my family. Miranda is overjoyed at having you. Now set your mind to rest and trust her to make you a match.'

'But I do not want them.' She hadn't meant to be so candid, but it was too late to call the words back.

'Not still dangling after me, are you? Little fool. I thought I'd made it plain enough. I can give you only one thing.'

She turned to face him, standing in the circle of his arms. 'Only the one thing I want. And yet you will not give it to me.'

She felt him tense, but he did not pull away. 'Offer to ruin you.' He stepped closer, then, and his arms slipped around her waist, pulling her close. 'To be here with me now is already your undoing, should someone find us.' He bent over her, and his lips brushed her hair. 'You should know better than to let a man take liberties with you, love, especially not a man such as myself. You are lucky that I have new-found self-restraint.' He put her from him and made to walk away.

'Self-restraint? You?' She remembered him, scolding his mistress loud enough for the whole street to hear. She could not help herself. She laughed. Then she stepped close to him again, tipping her head up to look into his face. 'Perhaps it is true. For all the stories I've heard told about you, St John, you cannot be as bad as people say.' Her voice fell to a whisper. 'Because you have me, alone in the dark. You can do as you will with me. And all you do is talk.'

He seized her and pulled her to him again. And then his fingers touched her chin, guiding her lips to meet his. He brushed lightly over her mouth, murmuring, 'And now I am done talking. Open your mouth, that I may kiss you better.'

She parted her lips in surprise, ready to ask him what he meant to do, when his mouth came down on hers and he showed her. His breath was in her mouth and then his tongue, filling her. He was stroking her with it, and his hand held her head so that there could be no escape.

Not that she could ever want to get away. She relaxed and let him take her mouth. Her body longed to be closer to his so she pressed against him, slipping her bare arms inside his coat and letting the warmth of his body take the chill away.

And it occurred to her in a haze of heat that what he was doing to her she could as easily do to him. And she slipped her tongue into his mouth, stroking in return.

He pushed her roughly away from him and dropped his hands to his sides. 'Just as I thought. Totally inexperienced.'

'H-have I done something wrong?' She reached to touch his sleeve and he brushed her hand away. 'Because I could learn…'

He snorted. 'If I wished to be a teacher, I imagine

you could. But I would much prefer a woman who knows what she's about. To have to endure the fumblings of a green girl, to be gentle and careful of her pride and her delicacies? To initiate? When I want a virgin to bore me in bed, then I'll propose to one. But for now, Esme darling, my tastes require something that you cannot possibly offer me. Marry one of the young bucks in that ballroom. Take your pick of the crop. In a couple of years, when you are thoroughly tired of each other, then return to me with some experience and we shall do well together. But for now, will you just leave me in peace?'

She had been trembling from cold, but now it was shame that chilled her, and she turned and ran, back into the house, far, far away from the man behind her.

St John waited for the tide of animal lust that was rising in him to subside. She had clung to him, grinding her little body against him, and moaning softly into his mouth. And the feeling of her tongue as it had slipped past his teeth… It would have been so easy. He closed his eyes and spoke to the darkness. 'I trust you saw it all.'

He heard his brother step out from behind a nearby tree and on to the path beside him. 'Of course I did. You knew I was here. We walked out of the house together.'

'But you could have left us alone. Instead you stood in the dark and watched me kiss her. Are you a chaperon or a voyeur?'

He waited for an explosion from Marcus, but it did

not come. 'I trusted you to do the thing we asked you to do and nothing more.'

St John glared at his brother, whose face was unreadable in the shadows of the garden. 'You trusted me…but not so much as to leave her alone with me. Thank you, brother, I know how much your trust is worth.'

There was tiredness in Marcus's voice when he spoke. 'Considering our past, did you expect me to trust easily?'

St John sighed. 'I suppose I should not have expected you to trust at all. But I have done what Miranda asked, I think. I have broken her heart to the extent requested. Am I to be sent away?'

There was a long pause as he waited for Marcus to answer, and he steeled himself for the dismissal. It would not do to care too much in his brother's presence.

And then Marcus shrugged. 'As long as you don't bother the girl further, you may stay or go, as you please.'

St John stood very still, while considering the words. His brother did not care if he remained? Apathy was a far cry from the open animosity that he was accustomed to, or the rejection he expected. And before the girl had interrupted, they had been chatting in a way that was almost civil. Perhaps there was hope. 'Believe me, I have no intention of bothering the girl. And I sincerely hope that the girl is done bothering me.'

But somehow, he doubted that that was the case. She was likely to bother him very much, if he remained.

'You know my rules, and appear to be abiding by them,' Marcus said. 'Then do as you will.'

St John's mouth quirked into an ironic smile. 'By which you mean, I am to do as you will.'

'Is there some problem with that?'

'None that I know of. You had suggested nothing I didn't intend before arriving. I merely resented being told.' He forestalled his brother's retort. 'But not so much as to kick over the traces to annoy you. I am not five, Marcus. Nor even five and twenty. If you do not treat me as a spoiled child, I will promise not to behave as one.'

His brother's laugh came in a sharp bark, startling in the silence. 'Very well, then. Stay.' And the duke turned and walked towards the house, leaving St John alone in the darkness.

Chapter Seven

As always, breakfast at Haughleigh was superlative, and Esme reminded herself to count her blessings before partaking. While last night's ball had not been a triumph, it had been more enjoyable than any other she had experienced. Miranda had seen to it that she'd looked her best, and she had received compliments from many of the gentlemen she'd danced with. The music had been wonderful, as had the champagne and the dinner. She was the toast of the evening.

Of course, she had not become betrothed, as Miranda might have hoped, but that was a rather unrealistic goal for her first entry into local society, so Esme did not count it as important. Instead, she had done a good deed for Miss Warrant and effected an uneasy truce with the other eligible young ladies of the community. Surely this must count as a positive.

And she had received her first kiss. Her pulse quickened at the memory of it. It had been more than delightful, at first. The feel of his lips and his tongue and the strength of his body against hers was everything she had hoped it would be. If she could manage to forget the last moments, when St John had laughed and dismissed her, it would have been the most perfect night of her life.

She glanced across the table. St John looked like death warmed over. If he had not the decency to leave her alone, or the willingness to follow through with what he started, or at the very least the kindness to cry off without insulting her—she smiled to herself—then the least he could do was to look the morning after as he did now. Clearly an excess of drink had left him out of sorts, for his eyes were red and his hand trembled, and it appeared that the clink of glasses and the chink of the silver on china was almost more than he could bear.

She rattled her fork against her plate and watched in satisfaction as he winced and closed his eyes.

The duke was sorting through the post and passed a letter down the table to her. 'Miss Canville, your father, most likely enquiring after your health.'

'Thank you, your Grace.' She took the envelope and noted with satisfaction that there was no tremor in her own hands as she broke the seal.

My Darling Daughter, I trust this finds you in good health.

She felt her mouth go dry at the sound of her father's voice in her head, the innocent words dripping with venom.

She paused and took a sip of water before continuing to read.

It was, no doubt, some girlish fancy that led you from the house in the night. Do you dream of escape from the responsibilities placed upon you? I think the sooner you accept the truth, put such foolishness aside, and return home, the better and easier it shall be for both of us. You know I do not like to be kept waiting.

In her mind, a picture flashed of the last time she'd defied him. He had invited his friends to supper, and she had cried off from playing hostess because of a megrim. The menu had been prepared, and the library was set for cards after the meal. There had been no need for her to attend, since the group of elderly gentlemen who were her father's favourites rarely noticed her presence during the meal or missed her when she retired after it. But he had insisted that she come down to dinner. She ignored his repeated demands that she appear at the table, curled up on her bed with the headache pounding in her ears. What good would it do her to sit downstairs, dazed with pain, embarrassing him in front of his friends? Surely he must understand that this was better.

And at last he had come upstairs to get her. His voice through her bedroom door was reason itself. He would not raise it, lest someone hear and he might embarrass himself. 'Do not make this difficult, Esme. You know my anger grows with my impatience.'

She'd whispered, 'I am sorry. I am so sorry', knowing what would come. And then loud enough so that he could hear through the door, 'I'm sorry, Father. I do not feel well enough to attend you.'

His voice became more insistent. 'You will not escape punishment by waiting. And he'd begun to count. Slowly and evenly. 'One, two, three…'

Would it help to apologise again? Would it be any worse if he had to open the door and drag her from her room? She'd left her bed and stood next to the door, hand on the knob.

'Four, five, six…' His cane tapped impatiently on the floor in the corridor, keeping time with his voice.

She sat frozen in the spot, knowing that it was folly to wait, but still afraid to open the door.

'Seven, eight…'

And finally she'd broken through the fear and turned the knob. 'I am sorry, Papa. So sorry.'

And without another word, he'd pushed her back into the room and closed the door. He spun her to face the wall and she'd listened to him count along with the blows of the cane on her back and shoulders. He'd stopped when he reached eight and watched impassively as she slumped to the floor at his feet.

'Next time, I trust you will learn to come when you are called. You know I do not like to be kept waiting. Now, pull yourself together and come down to dinner. The guests are waiting.'

'Esme!' The voice was real and in the room with her, and startled her back into the present. She opened her eyes and was staring into the worried gaze of St John.

'Is there something the matter?'

'No. No, I am fine.'

'The look on your face…'

'Was no worse than the look on yours, I'm sure. You of all people should understand the results of too much wine and not enough sleep, and sympathise, rather than shouting at me.' She rubbed at her temple, soothing an imaginary megrim.

'Too much wine?' His eyes narrowed. 'When you left me last night in the garden, you seemed none the worse for it.'

'I'd had more than enough, I assure you,' she snapped.

'Really? And I thought you wanted more.'

She raised her hand to strike him and struggled to turn the gesture into something innocent before he noticed how he'd hurt her. But before she could regain control, St John had snatched the letter from off the table where she had dropped it.

'St John,' Miranda warned. 'Do not torment the girl.'

Esme looked across the table, and flushed with shame. She had forgotten that they were not alone. Miranda and the duke were staring at her in concern.

St John unfolded the letter. 'I apologise for the impertinence.' He glanced down at the note. 'I was afraid that there was something here that might have been upsetting.' He scanned over the words. 'That does not appear to be the case. It seems innocent enough.'

Miranda turned with controlled fury to her brother-in-law and said, 'All the same, it does not give you the right to read another's mail. Give her the letter and apologise this instant.'

'It is all right,' Esme said as placidly as possible. She returned to her breakfast, trying to pretend an appetite for the food in front of her. 'There was no harm done.'

St John was still looking at her; she could feel his eyes burning on her until she looked up to meet them. 'I think perhaps there was. I am sorry, Esme. I humbly apologise for any wrong I have done you.' He said it so slowly and with such emphasis that she suspected the words had nothing to do with the letter in his hand.

'It was nothing, really,' she murmured, staring back down at her plate.

She heard him fold the letter, and he slid it along the table, until it was in front of her again. She snatched it up and tucked it into her sleeve. 'Esme.' His voice was quiet, but insistent. 'Esme, look at me.'

She looked up.

His face was solemn, but encouraging. 'I am sorry, truly, that I have made you unhappy. If I were not sure that Miranda and my brother could find a better solution—' He stopped. 'No, even if they could not do better for you, I am not sure there is any way I could help. But whatever I do now, no matter how cruel it may seem, I do it because I want what is best for you.' And he laid his hand on hers and gave it a gentle squeeze.

She ignored the way her heart leapt when he touched

her and said with her most obedient voice, 'Thank you, St John. I understand.'

She understood very well. She had found yet another man who was intent on doing what they thought 'best' for her, with little regard to what she might want for herself. But now that she had escaped from the tyranny of her father, it was only a matter of time before she set St John Radwell straight about what would be best for both of them.

She smiled down at her eggs and took another bite.

St John closed his eyes and watched the patterns of light and dark play on his eyelids as a breeze stirred the leaves above him. It was so pleasant to be sitting thus, under a tree in the garden, wondering whether a small nap might be possible and if it would help or hinder his appetite at lunch.

He should not get used to it. If he stayed too long at his brother's estate, Marcus would begin to wonder at his motives. It would not do to have to explain that his pockets were to let and he needed charity, yet again. The truth of the matter, that he could not afford to live elsewhere, would quite spoil the appearance he was trying to create that he was perfectly capable of surviving without help from the family.

The sunlight was warm on his upturned face. Good, English sunlight, he reminded himself. Not the cold and rain of Portugal in spring. No fears of battles past or still to come. And no sign of Esme Canville.

It was impossible to relax if he needed to maintain a constant defence against the girl. He had told her as politely as possible at breakfast that anything between them was an impossibility. And she had smiled her inscrutable smile and agreed with him so easily that he suspected she did not agree with him at all. If he was not careful, he would find himself in the awkward position of defending his honour from her unwanted advances.

The thought made him smile. Five years ago, when he had no honour to defend, life was simpler. He would have looked into those blue eyes of hers and fallen without a second thought. He imagined what it might have been like, and let himself drift away to thoughts of a sweet and willing Esme, and the sound of a single fly buzzing somewhere far above him.

But before he could lose himself in what had the makings of a very promising dream, he was roused to full consciousness by the sound of children's voices, distant, but growing nearer. A girl's hesitant quaver. The boy, firm and insistent.

He smiled. Ever Marcus's son, the next duke even in leading strings. He rose and walked toward the sound. It would not be a violation of Marcus's order, if he were to watch over them from a distance.

'We mustn't,' little Charlotte argued. 'Nurse doesn't know where we have gone. She will be cross.'

'Nurse will not miss us if we hurry, Lottie. What good is a trip to the country, if it only means more lessons in a different room? And you want to see the horses, don't you?' Young John was pulling her hand, but she refused to move.

There was a pause, as the girl considered. And then a hesitant, 'Yes.'

'Good. Then let us go to the stables.' John tugged again and they were in motion.

St John rolled his eyes. No nurse, and out for an adventure? Damn Marcus's rules. He'd be minus a nephew if he allowed the children to wander into trouble. He followed at a distance as the boy led the girl to the stables, jollying and then bullying her by turns to keep her moving.

St John breathed a sigh of relief when they neared the building, assuming that a groom would be along shortly to send them back to the house. But no adult arrived. He hesitated for a moment and then strode into the barn, after the children.

And his heart stuck in his throat to see them, standing beneath the head of a stallion, within an easy kick of the great, sharp hooves. The horse was eyeing them with suspicion, as the next duke explained to his sister that this would be his horse, once he had talked to Father.

St John stepped forward with care, in order not to startle the beast, and laid a hand on its neck, stepping between it and the children. 'It will not ever be your horse, lad, if your father catches you here without permission. Horses can be dangerous with people they do not know. I'm sure Marcus meant you to see them when he could show them to you properly.'

'He doesn't have time.' The boy pouted and St John gave him a stern look.

'Not today, perhaps, but he soon will, I'm sure.'

'He said that he and you would run away and have all sorts of adventures when you were little.'

So Marcus did remember their youth with fondness. He must be getting soft in his dotage, or children had clouded his view of the past. 'And did he tell you how much trouble we got into when we did? Proper punishment from your grandfather for stunts like this. We were boys, of course, and deserved what we got. But you would not want your little sister to pay for your wilfulness, would you?'

The boy looked doubtful.

'Or to see her stepped on by those great hooves, there, for standing too close?'

The boy looked very worried indeed now.

'I thought not. There'll be time enough for horses, and adventures, too, for this is to be your house and you'll be in it all summer and for many summers to come. Patience, my boy. You must learn to wait, not rush headlong into trouble, or your mother and father will be grey before their time. But no harm done today, and if you hurry, you can sneak back into the nursery before you're missed. Go through the kitchen garden and up the back stairs, and no one will see you. It is the way your father and I used, often enough. Now, go.'

The children hurried off, and he breathed a sigh of relief as he watched them nearing the house and going through the door.

'St John Radwell advocating patience and obedience? I never thought I'd see the likes of that.'

St John tensed at the sound of his brother's voice growing nearer. 'They are your children. You could have done it as easily as I.'

Marcus stepped into the stable and closed the door behind him. 'And missed that fine speech? Not for the world. I came in search of my missing children. You know boys and horses.'

St John nodded.

'But I never expected to find you here with them.' There was a trace of tension in Marcus's voice. 'I thought I told you to stay away from my family.'

'To avoid setting a bad example. I thought if I were to set a good one that the warning did not apply. And look at this animal.' He gave the stallion a gentle pat and it tossed its head and displayed a row of sharp teeth. 'I could not very well let them wander into danger, and then claim that I was following the letter of the law, could I?'

Marcus said softly, 'At one time, perhaps you could have. He is the heir, you know. He stands in your way.'

'To this land? Any desire I had for it is gone, along with many other youthful fancies. I'd only have made a mess of things had I found a way to them. This is better. The people are prosperous, the house well cared for.

I've heard no more than the usual amount of nonsense out of the House of Lords, since you took a seat on the bench. The land and the title are yours, brother, and they appear to suit you. Enjoy them in good health.'

'You've truly changed, then?'

St John shook his head and soothed the horse. 'I never attempted fratricide, no matter how I threatened. I don't think, even then, I could have harmed a child, had there been one. I was never the threat that you thought I was, and never so dangerous as I wanted to be. If I have changed, it is because I'm wise enough to admit it.'

St John could almost feel the surprise emanating from his brother. 'And the other day, at luncheon?'

He sighed. 'I was taking a nap. In my room. Much as I was trying to do under a tree in the garden, when your whelps disturbed me on their way to see the horses.'

Marcus continued to quiz him. 'Is there a reason you do not sleep in your own bed at night, but must doze during the day? A guilty conscience, perhaps.'

'Would it surprise you to be right? I admit it. I cannot sleep, because I am afraid to close my eyes. Since Portugal, my dreams are rather more vivid than I might like.'

Marcus nodded his head in involuntary sympathy.

St John continued, 'I manage as best I can, with drugs at night and what rest I can steal during the day. I am sorry to be such a grave disappointment to you, but most days, my bothering the maids will mean nothing more than shouting at them for waking me.'

'You sound like an old man.'

He laughed softly. 'Perhaps. The war aged me, right enough. But I thought many nights as I lay there, knowing I would face death in the morning, what better place to come, should I survive, than back to my brother's home. For no matter how old and feeble I may become, you will always be older still. It makes me feel so much better.'

Marcus laughed and said, 'That is much more the sort of comment I expect from you, St John.'

He nodded. 'I am glad that I am finally living up to your expectations. And as requested, I will avoid your family, unless the situation is pressing, as it was today.'

'About that. Well.' Marcus cleared his throat. 'Perhaps it is not necessary to keep so strictly to the rules. If you wish to see the children, I see no reason why you cannot.'

'Your son is very like you, in looks and in manner.' He could tell he'd spoken right, for his brother seemed to swell with pride.

Marcus looked back toward the house. 'He will be difficult, I think, when he comes of age. Stubborn. Like his father.'

'Perhaps. But you will have a beautiful daughter to take your mind from your troubles. Very like her mother.'

At the mention of Miranda, Marcus said nothing, but the silence was cold air between them.

St John spoke again. 'Once, I was quite jealous of you on that count, Marcus. You cannot deny that you have a beautiful and charming wife. But time has softened me. Now, I merely envy you, and some day hope to be as fortunate. But I no longer begrudge you your happiness.'

He reached into the pocket of his coat and removed the box with the necklace. 'Here. Before you look inside, remember that pride runs as strong as stubbornness in our family. Take these back and do not refuse me. Give them to your daughter, when she is of age. May they be as fortunate a gift to her as they were to me.'

And, before his brother could respond, he turned and walked away.

Chapter Eight

He was trapped at another of Miranda's damn come-out balls for Esme, and St John gritted his teeth and counted the hours he had yet to remain social. There had been dinners and dances enough for a full London Season, whether at Haughleigh or some neighbour or other returning the invitation. Music and dancing kept him up most nights, and the constant teas and garden parties, with guests tramping through the house at all hours, left him unable to rest in daylight.

Without the laudanum, he could not seem to get through an untroubled night. And the lack of rest had left him out of sorts. He wanted nothing better than to sit by the fire to pass an evening, pretending to enjoy a book. Instead, he must remain dressed and upright, and out of the clutches of the Canville girl and any other neighbourhood chit with designs on him.

He had quite frightened away the other girls with a

cool demeanour and a dark look. But Esme continued to be a thorn in his side. She had weathered rebuffs that should have sent her to her room in a flood of tears. Sharp words held no terror for her, coldness was ignored, and he rejected lechery as far too risky, since it was more likely to be met by eager curiosity than hysterics.

She continued to respond to everything with a patient smile and the occasional knowing glance that told him she trusted in his heart that he did not mean to hurt her.

And, damn it all, he did not mean it. It was all the more galling to know that she knew. He never should have apologised for the kiss in the garden. But she had sat beside him the next morning at breakfast, looking so unhappy and alone that he could not bear the sight. How was a man to enjoy his kippers with those sad blue eyes staring in his direction spoiling his appetite?

It had undone a good night's work in his efforts to dissuade Esme Canville. He had tried again and again since that night to turn her affections. Kissing in the garden had been a risk, even with Marcus standing guard over the girl. He'd come too close to losing control of himself. Better to keep a respectful distance and fill the void around him with enough sarcasm to repel every female in a five-mile radius.

An inexperienced girl should have been crushed, as all the others were. And an experienced one would have had the decency to pretend that his barbs had struck home, and perhaps to respond in kind.

But Esme remained a curious mixture of naïveté and world-weariness, which both annoyed and intrigued him. It almost made him wish…

He shook himself firmly. He wished nothing, other than to be back in his rooms in London, away from damned balls, damned musicians and annoying young women. After a few days' peace and quiet and a good night's rest, he could find some other way to strengthen the fragile truce with his brother that did not involve forced courtesy, formal dress and dancing. If they communicated by mail, he could be back at the family table by Christmas.

He lounged against the wall, cultivating a pose of well-bred indolence, and watched the dancers spin by as his head pounded out a rhythm to match the musicians. There was Esme, floating past him in a whisper of satin and a flash of white teeth. Her pale hair was piled high on her head, smooth in front but with an elegant arrangement of braids in a crown set with tin rosebuds to contain the curls that cascaded down the back. The gold satin of her gown gave a warm glow to her skin and he saw hints of the delicate flesh through the tissue of her sleeves. The man who partnered her whispered something to her as they waited at the bottom of the set, and the diamond drops trembled from her ears as she laughed.

And St John waited for her glance to flash in his direction, searching for signs of jealousy or interest on his face as he watched her flirt with the man. She'd been watching him like a hawk at these events, looking for any sign of interest or weakness. The strain of watching her watch him, and maintaining his look of schooled uninterest took considerably more energy than the legitimate boredom he was accustomed to feeling.

But her glance did not come.

He felt naked, missing the feel of her eyes always on him. She was truly looking at her partner, and she smiled again.

She had spent too much time with the blighter she was now dancing with, for he'd seen them together for most of the evening. St John struggled to remember the man's name. Something effete. Possibly with a hyphen. No rank, no title, no family. Expensive clothes and no way to account for them. Good looking, of course, in the way that foolish women liked, but clearly pockets to let and up to no good. How many dances had they shared? He was not sure, but certainly it had been more that enough to cause gossip.

On the next turn, her partner's hand slipped to touch her body, momentarily caressing the curve of her waist.

Her eyes widened in surprise, but not in insult, and she did not pull away as the man pretended not to notice the liberty he had taken, so that it might appear accidental.

St John felt a dull pain in his hand and looked down to see his nails digging into the palm of his closed fist. He relaxed purposefully, and glared back at the dancers.

The music ended, and the man was leading Esme away from the crowd, past the refreshments and down the steps to the garden. St John felt the hairs on the back of his neck stand up. It was a dangerous situation. He scanned the room for his brother, who was playing host at the far end, oblivious to the danger Esme had placed herself in. What was Miranda after, letting Esme walk out with that man? The stranger was angling after an heiress, and she was too new to put him off.

And so it fell to St John to watch the girl's reputation for her. The irony was exquisite.

He followed them at a distance. The man had tucked her arm through the crook of his own, and she leaned into him, standing closer than St John felt was appropriate for two who had just met, one of whom was a green girl.

He watched the pair conversing.

The man's smile was ready enough, as he gazed down at Esme, but, from where he watched, St John thought he detected a certain predatory glint in the eyes, perhaps a hardness around the mouth, hidden behind the cynical smile. The man was no doubt assessing Esme's wealth, trying to draw her out about her father, and any possible settlement or allowance. And he must like what he heard, or he'd have moved on by now.

And Esme was gazing back at him, smile bright, head tipped up to catch his words, displaying her fine white throat to perfection. She was standing too close, in St John's opinion. Far too close. She might think it necessary to hear the conversation, but knowing her acquaintance as he thought he did, the man was speaking more softly, to draw her near.

Conniving bastard. His fist balled in his pocket, and he again forced it to relax. Then he signalled to his brother, gesturing him to his side.

Marcus pointed to himself in exaggerated surprise at the command and then strolled down the room to him. 'You summoned me? Are you not enjoying the evening?'

'It is a dead bore,' St John snapped. 'But then, these things always are.'

'Then your agitation is a sign of ennui.' Marcus had a self-satisfied smile on his face that was most irritating.

St John gestured in the direction of the interloper. 'I was just looking at the man there, chatting with Esme.'

'Smythe?' Marcus shrugged. 'He is new to the neighborhood and quite popular with the ladies. Miranda singled him out as a possibility.'

St John frowned. 'Well, you'd best nip that in the bud, if you wish to play at guardian.'

'And why do you think that?'

'Just look at him,' St John said, making no effort to hide his disgust.

Marcus was unimpressed. 'He seems an admirable match.'

'A fortune hunter, I'd wager.'

'Well, of course you'd wager. But you would lose. As far as I can ascertain, his reputation is impeccable.'

St John shook his head. 'Then you cannot be in possession of all the facts.'

Marcus chuckled. 'I have at least met the man. You are in possession of no facts at all.'

'But I can see what is before my eyes. The man is false coin.'

'And what business is it of yours?' Marcus was examining St John far more closely than he observed his guests.

'None, I suppose, other than that I want what is best for the girl.'

'You sound more like a jealous lover than a concerned friend,' Marcus said.

St John snorted. 'Don't be ridiculous. I feel responsible, that is all. To set my mind at rest, I need to know that the girl is going to a better place, should she choose not to go home.'

'Then you must trust the girl to know her own mind.'

'As far as I can tell, she has no mind at all. Pretty she may be, but the little hen-wit should not be allowed out without a keeper, Marcus.'

He smiled. 'She seems to like you well enough.'

'And if that isn't evidence, I know not what is.'

'As you will. But the girl is perfectly safe amongst my guests. If you wish her to dance with someone else, that is a matter between you and Esme.' And Marcus walked away, ignoring his protestations.

St John stayed to keep watch over the pair. Marcus was blind if he thought Esme safe with Smythe.

The man was all flash. Just the sort to turn the head of a girl as naïve and unworldly as Esme. His coat was well cut, no doubt with the tailor's bill still in the pocket, along with numerous gambling debts and perhaps a *billet doux* from a mistress or some other man's wife.

St John knew the type well enough, having seen him in the mirror for years.

And there was Esme, smiling and nodding, gazing up into his face, leaning even closer.

Smythe leaned in as well, touching her hair again as he spoke into her ear. And then he clasped her hand warmly and brought it to his lips.

St John viewed the tender scene through a red haze, and watched as Esme turned and went back into the ballroom alone.

St John glared in Esme's direction and she caught his gaze as she passed him. Her chin came up a fraction of an inch, and her smile brightened. Her eyes were full of the devil.

St John waited until Esme lost herself in the crowd of the ballroom.

But Smythe remained in the garden, moving further away from the house.

St John followed at such a distance as to remain unnoticed. When they were clear of the other guests, and a good distance from the house, he caught up with the man and laid a hand on his shoulder. 'Smythe, is it?'

'I don't believe we've been formally introduced.'

The man swung around easily to meet him, and favoured him with a cool stare.

'I think we can waive the formalities in this instance. You may now give to me what you took from the young lady just now, and I'll see it safely returned to her.'

'I have no idea…'

St John smiled. 'Don't you? Why not look in your left breast pocket. You'll find a single diamond eardrop.'

'Oh. That.' The man waved his hand dismissively. 'I picked it up from the floor. I was going to restore it to my host.'

'You picked it from the ear of the lady in question when you were in intimate conversation, earlier. And now, I suppose, you are about to tell me that you were looking for my brother, the duke, in the garden? It really is far more likely, sir, that you meant to exit quietly with the diamond in your pocket. And that you took one, not two, because one missing earring is an accident, while two are a theft.'

The man shrugged. 'I took one because it was all I needed.' He reached into his pocket and tossed the earring back to St John. 'Your brother the duke? Then you must be St John Radwell. I'd understood that you were banned from the house because of your bad character.'

St John sneered. 'As is evidenced by your own presence here, my brother is none too particular about the company he keeps. When he sent me away he was not inviting common thieves to his parties.'

Smythe leaned against the tree behind him. 'That is quite unfair. I am a most uncommon thief. Until now, I was never caught. But, as they say, set a thief to catch a thief.'

St John relaxed slightly. 'I have been called many things, drunkard, gambler, scoundrel, but never thief.'

'Perhaps not to your face. If we were to ask the husbands of some of the ladies you've entertained, they might use the term.'

St John shrugged. '*Touché*. Point to you, I think. If you are trying to goad me into a duel, you will not succeed.'

The man laughed. 'A duel? What a quaint notion. But I thought perhaps you meant to challenge me. For the honour of the girl, or perhaps your brother's house?'

'I let my brother protect his own house, although I'll thank you not to steal while under this roof.'

Smythe shrugged. 'I doubt I'd have much luck a second time, having been caught here once. You have but to put a word in the ear of your brother, and I'll be banned from the premises just as you were.'

St John sighed. 'How shall I put this so it is best understood? A duel would be troublesome, and messy. You would be dead on the grass in a matter of minutes, and I would be left to explain to all and sundry the reason for the quarrel. The whole thing would most likely spring back upon me and show me in a poor light.'

Smythe nodded.

St John continued, 'Your reputation must be exemplary, or my brother would not allow you in his home. You will turn out to have an aged mother, or a weeping sister, and I will be the duke's unloved, younger brother who has been nothing but trouble for years. People will have no problem believing that I pushed you into it. So we shall not duel over this. The diamonds were borrowed, by the way, from the duchess. And my brother can afford many more to replace them, but I would not see Miss Canville distressed at the loss.'

Smythe snapped his fingers. 'So it is my interest in the girl that troubles you?'

'The girl.' St John sighed again. 'Let us say that I consider myself responsible for her welfare. And if I find that you have borrowed anything else that did not belong to you, or found any more of her lost items, if I see you hanging about her, making calf's eyes at her person, her non-existent dowry, or her borrowed jewellery, it will go hard for you. While I wish to avoid scandal, and would hesitate to call you out, I would have no trouble waylaying you on a dark street and slitting your throat from ear to ear. I could sleep with a clear conscience, knowing that the world is a slightly better place for my actions.'

Smythe smirked back at him. 'You do present a most persuasive argument.'

St John nodded. 'I thought you would find it so. Do you agree to my terms?'

'And if I do? It ends here?'

'I don't plan to go to the Runners, if that's what you mean. Or tattle to my brother. It matters not to me what method you use to seek damnation, or whether you do it from boredom or need. As long as you leave my brother and his guests alone. And the girl, of course. There is nothing there to interest you, in any case. She is quite poor and, from what I understand, already affianced to an earl.'

'The girl alone was quite interesting enough. The earrings were merely a distraction.' He saw the warning look in St John's eye and corrected himself. 'But alas, it would be unfair of me to trifle with such a charming young lady.'

'I am glad that we have reached this understanding. And you are leaving for the night.'

'Well, I had thought…perhaps one more dance.' Smythe gazed back toward the house.

'Let me clarify. That was a statement, not a question. I will give your apologies to your host, and to Miss Canville. Good evening.'

St John watched the man shrug and continue into the darkness in the general direction of the drive. Then he turned back towards the house.

When he entered the ballroom again, he saw Esme look toward the garden with interest. It annoyed him to see her eyes slide past him and search for another.

Be damned to all that. Now she was pretending she did not see him? He'd give her reason to take notice, if that was the game she wished to play. He strode forward purposefully and took her by the elbow, steering her in the direction of the stairs.

'St John? What is the meaning of this?'

'We must talk.'

'We can do that as well here as—'

'The devil we can,' he snapped.

'There is no need to resort to such language—'

'Since when have you cared?'

'Or physical violence.' She yanked her arm out of his grasp.

'Violence?' He hadn't gripped her arm too tightly, had he? 'I did not hurt you, did I? I assure you, there was no intention…' He touched her arm again to reassure himself, and then remembered himself and dropped his hands to his sides.

'Well, not violence,' she admitted. 'But you do not need to tow me like a barge. Merely ask me, and I will accompany you outside.'

'As you do any man who asks?' He could not keep the asperity out of his voice.

'What…? Oh, Mr Smythe.' She smiled, remembering him. 'We were gone for but a moment, surely. No one noticed.'

'I noticed. And I followed.'

She stared at him in amazement. 'You spied on us?'

'Us? Well, there will be no "us" with that particular man. I've seen to it.'

'You are seeing to my honour again, are you?' She was laughing at him again. He could see it in her eyes.

'Someone must.'

'And a fine one you would be to guard it. A fox in the henhouse, some might say.'

'Better me than Smythe. He was taking liberties.'

'He was a perfect gentleman and then kissed my hand, whereas, when you had me in the same spot, you kissed my lips and then insulted me.'

'A gentleman? Ha!' He could not resist a contemptuous laugh as he reached into his pocket for the earring.

'Yes. A gentleman. He was just explaining to me that, however much some parties might like to see us make a match, it would be quite impossible, as his heart was otherwise engaged. And when I told him I understood, he was so grateful he kissed my hand.'

'What utter nonsense.'

She was not laughing any more. Her temper broke over him. 'No, you are the one speaking nonsense. First you kiss me, then you send me away. You say you want me to find a match, but when a gentleman that I could fancy shows the slightest interest, you drag me away from the party and fill my head with lies. Perhaps you are like my father, and will only be satisfied when you see me unhappily married. What reason could Mr Smythe have had to tell me such? What could he hope to gain? And why is it so hard for you to believe, St John, that a man might be willing to resist temptation for even a moment, if he loved someone else. Perhaps your heart is as cold as you claim, for you always need see the worst in others.'

The words stung him, and his hand closed around the earring, before letting it drop back into his pocket. 'All right. I will concede that others might have motives that are honourable, and that I should not treat all so harshly. And if what you say is true…'

He could see the storm gathering behind her eyes again and rephrased, 'Of course what you say is true. I would have no reason to doubt it. You tell me that there is nothing between you, and so I will not worry further on the subject. But please, in the future, take care whom you are alone with. It would not do to be caught in the moonlight with too many young men.'

Esme rolled her eyes. 'Says the man who took me alone into the moonlight not once, but twice. Yes, St John, I will take care not to follow you, the next time you insist on speaking to me alone. And now, if I may go back to the ball?'

He could feel the heat rising in his face and ignored it. 'Very well. I think I have made the point well enough. Oh, and, Esme…'

She turned back to him. He reached into his pocket and produced the earring. 'You must have dropped this. I found it on the grass in the garden.'

Her hand flew to her ears and felt the lobe that was bare. 'Oh, dear.' She put a hand to her heaving bosom. 'Thank you, St John. I could not have lived had I needed to explain to Miranda that it was missing.'

And then she smiled, and the weight of her gratitude struck him like a physical force. For a moment her look held no mischief and her smile no calculation or hidden meaning. There was only relief, and thankfulness, and admiration. He was her hero for returning the diamond, even if the circumstances of its recovery were wrapped in pretty lies.

'Well, then, you needn't have worried. But I am glad that I could be of service to you. Most glad indeed.' He was fumbling to get the words out, staring down into those luminous blue eyes.

She took the drop from him, reaching to her ear. 'This is difficult to do without a mirror, perhaps I should—'

'Here, let me.' Why had he said it? She must have intended to go to the ladies' retiring room. It would have been the most proper course of action for them both. Instead, he took the thing back from her, and she stepped closer to him. A hint of her scent reached him as he bent over her, and he took a breath and held it, hoping she didn't feel the slight tremor in his hands as he touched her ear with one hand and replaced the jewel with the other.

And then it seemed only natural to leave the hand at the back of her head, as he leaned back to admire his work.

'St John?' Her head tilted in his hand, and her lips were ever so slightly closer to his, smiling expectantly.

It was maddening. How many women had he known? And how many had he known more intimately than this? His mind had never gone blank when they looked at him. His mouth had never gone dry when he'd spoken to them. His hands had never trembled to touch them.

He broke free of the spell, and jerked his hand away. 'I was just making sure that they are even. And secure. Everything is fine, now. Just fine.'

'Then you had best take me back to the ballroom, before someone notices our behaviour.'

'Yes. That would be best.'

Although he couldn't help feeling that the one person he least wanted to notice his behaviour was Esme Canville.

Chapter Nine

'St John, I wish to speak to you.' The duke's voice carried through the open door of his study and into the hall.

Damn. Six years ago, when he had been up to every kind of devilment, the study door had been shut tight and Marcus had left him with the run of the house. But now, when he wanted nothing more shocking than a nap in the garden and some peace and quiet, he could not get past the doorway unnoticed. The duke found any excuse to call him in.

He gritted his teeth and turned back to play obedient younger brother. 'What have I done now, your Grace? Come, tell me. I can tell by the set of your shoulders that I'm about to catch some type of hell. And, for once, I can't think of anything I might have done to deserve it.'

'You have done nothing objectionable, much as it surprises me to admit it. But I wish to ask your opinion of something.'

'My opinion?' St John said, in shock.

'Yes, you idiot. Despite what you may think, I value the views of others. And I cannot take this matter to Miranda, as you will soon see.' Marcus threw a stack of letters down on the desk and said, 'Read.'

St John sat in the chair before the desk and picked up a paper.

Your Grace,

As you are well aware, it's been weeks since my daughter has come to your home and I would think that by now there would have been an end to her little problem. It does not do to coddle the girl when she is in these moods, or to encourage her to disobedience…

St John looked up doubtfully. 'Well, I suppose there is some truth that you are encouraging her to be disobedient.'

'Only because you presented me with the problem. If you had not dropped her on my doorstep, she could have been as disobedient as she chose and it would never have come to my notice. Read this one.'

St John's eyebrows arched as he read. 'This seems to imply that you are holding her against her will. He's gone as far as he can, without being actually insulting, hasn't he?'

'Too far. The implication is definitely there.' Marcus's tone darkened and St John was pleased to see the duke's anger directed at someone other than himself.

'This is private correspondence. Canville is a nobody. Toss the letters in the fire and think no more about it.'

'But there is this one, where he's threatening to go to *The Times* and raise a scandal if we don't return his daughter.' Marcus slapped another letter down on the desk. 'The man is obviously mad, but I don't see what's to be done to keep him quiet. I have corresponded in return and think it will buy a little more time. But I've also spoken to my solicitors. If Canville chooses to press the issue, there is nothing for it but to return the girl to him. He is in the right. She is not of age and we cannot keep her here without his permission. I have no wish to disappoint my wife or see harm come to the girl, but we are running out of time in this matter.'

St John sighed. 'I am sorry that I brought this upon you. I wanted what was best for Esme, but was at a loss as to what that might be.'

Marcus shook his head. 'As am I. It might help if we knew more of her relations with her father. What was in the letter you took from her at breakfast?'

'It would be impolite of me to repeat it,' St John said.

'It was equally impolite of you to take it from her. Now be of some use and tell me the contents of the letter.'

'Nothing as inflammatory as his letters to you. He told her he was impatient for her return. She seemed upset, but I expect it had as much to do with my behaviour to her as with her father's. You watched me bring her near to tears at the ball.' He could not keep a hint of accusation out of his voice.

'Well, the girl will have to return home if we cannot find her a suitable match.' Marcus was looking at him with undue interest. 'I don't suppose you would have anything to say on that score.'

'I would say that it is an excellent idea and that you should proceed with it, post haste.'

'You know that is not what I mean.' Marcus paused. 'I watched you last night, and I wondered if you might be taking a more personal interest in her situation.'

St John looked at him in amazement. 'You allowed me here for the express purpose of being a bad example. I am sorry if I am not living down to your expectations. If I find it less than pleasant to toy with an innocent girl, without the reward of an actual seduction, or if I care when she walks out with an unprincipled rogue, it does not mean that I am considering matrimony.'

'But I have seen the way you look at Miss Canville. You hold her in regard, do you not?'

'As I do many other young ladies of the *ton*. I do not wish to marry them, either.'

As usual, Marcus ignored him and issued a command. 'You are three and thirty. It is time you marry someone.'

St John laughed. 'And since you have a female that needs marrying, you are ready to offer me up to fix the situation? I have news, your Grace. You are the one who needed to get an heir, not I. I am the younger son, and have not money, inclination, or any pressing desire to get myself leg-shackled, especially not to one as poor as myself. If you were offering an heiress, someone with twenty thousand a year and a house in town, then perhaps we could make a deal.'

Marcus reached into the desk drawer and produced the jewellery box that St John had so recently given him. He opened it and turned the emerald necklace out onto the blotter where it glowed green in the afternoon sunlight. 'There is more than enough here to make a fresh start.'

'As well I know,' St John said with exasperation. 'Have you forgotten that I used it for that purpose once before?'

'And yet you returned it to me, when you could have used the price of it to establish yourself.' Marcus's voice was low, but insistent. 'What you did was not necessary.'

'For you, perhaps,' St John said.

'If you have no prospects, then it was foolish to waste money on baubles, when you could set up a household and have more than enough to spare. Or do you plan to return to the service? If you do not wish to stay in England and marry, than there is nothing dishonourable in a military career. Unless you received some wound that would prevent you—'

'Marcus!' St John cut his brother off in mid-tirade. He took a deep breath before continuing. 'First of all, the necklace is not a bauble. When I took it from this house, it was a treasured family heirloom. Since you have the title and the rest of the entail, it might not seem significant to you. But it was important to me that it should be returned.

'I have no plans to return to the army. I am not wounded in any way. Do not concern yourself on that account. It is just that...' He should not have to share all the sordid details of his recent history with his brother. He was a grown man and did not need to justify his decisions. 'I will just say that it was time for me to leave the service. I left honourably and will not be going back.

'And lastly, as you point out, I am three and thirty. I am not the overgrown boy who left here five years ago. I am my own man, not one of your tenants, or a servant to be ordered about. I am sorry if my apparent lack of direction concerns you, but you must trust that I know my own mind and may have plans in place that cannot be discussed at this time. While I appreciate your concern for my future, I will not allow you to plan it for me, especially in such a way as to include Esme Canville.

'And now, if you will excuse me, I believe this interview is at an end. If you wish to turn me out of your house for my less-than-respectful attitude, so be it. But in the future, I would prefer that you refrain from meddling in my life, just as I have promised to stop interfering with yours. Good day, your Grace.'

And for the first time that he could remember, St John left his brother open mouthed and incapable of further argument.

Chapter Ten

St John stared into the fire in his room, trying to calm his restless spirit. He could no longer tell which he found more disturbing, the situation or the girl. Being back in the house and trying to navigate around his brother's whims took more than enough energy. But to add Esme into the equation? It was more than a sane man could bear.

At the ball the night before, she had *agreed* with him. And since, then she had been polite and co-operative. And once again he was left with the feeling that she meant to smile and nod at him and then do just as she pleased. Miranda's plan had seemed easy enough when he was to toy with her and walk away.

But when he walked away from a woman, she was supposed to collapse in despair, not turn and follow. He had never expected to find himself running ahead of her, as she pursued.

And she'd managed to catch him often enough since she'd arrived at Haughleigh, only to smile her innocent smile and set him free. He'd have easily overmatched her, he assured himself, if he'd been able to rest. But the sleepless nights were catching up to him and the cat-naps during the day were of no help. He needed rest.

He'd promised himself, once he came to Haughleigh, no more laudanum. And it had been easy enough when the family was still in London and could not see his odd hours and strange behaviours. He could sleep the day away without inciting comment.

But now there were expectations. Despite it all he must rest at some point or he'd find himself quite unable to manage the girl or his own family. If they did not find a match for Esme soon, the pressure from Marcus would increase. And then Miranda would join in as well. Some day he might wake from a nap to find himself walking from the altar, tenant for life with Esme before he knew what he'd done. And then he'd be responsible for her for a lifetime instead of a few weeks.

Certainly a small dose of the drug in his brandy would not hurt. It would mean an easy night and, come morning, a head that was sharp, if not exactly clear. He poured a glass of spirits and reached into his pocket for the phial. Toby had hidden the first one, for he did not approve of the habit and seemed happier thinking that the supply was cut. But Toby had not checked the pockets of St John's dressing gown.

He carefully measured a few drops into the glass,

swirling the brandy to mix it. And as he raised the glass to his lips…he thought of Esme. How quickly the drug had taken her. And how pale she'd looked, lying on the sofa, lost to the world and to herself. He had done that to her, however inadvertently.

She'd not questioned him on it, not heaped him with the reproach he must truly deserve. Except for that moment when she'd mocked his lack of self-control.

She was right, of course, he had no self-control, but it did not matter. He needed sleep and for that he needed the drug. He raised the glass to his lips.

And in his mind, he saw the flash in Esme's eyes and the slight, contemptuous curl of her lip. She had looked inside him and seen his bravery for what it was, a sham.

She was a thousand times braver than he, willing to hazard anything when she'd come to him, if it meant escape from her father and marriage. Any man would be proud to have her, once he'd seen that blazing spirit. He half-raised the glass again, in toast to the girl, but the look of contempt hung before him and he could not bring the brandy to his lips.

He did not deserve her affection. He did not even desire to be worthy of it. But nor could he drink, knowing what her response must be should she find that the drug was his master and not merely his crutch.

He sighed and raised the glass again. 'To absent friends.' Then he splashed the brandy on to the fire, watching it flare and catching a faint whiff of the liquor before it sizzled and was gone.

He untied the belt to his gown, slipped it off and climbed between the cold and clammy sheets of his bed. Demons of the past be damned, he would rest tonight. He closed his eyes with no small amount of trepidation—and thought of Esme. Dear, sweet girl. As he imagined her now, she was smiling at him. Full of approval, but also full of mischief.

It was hard to imagine her face without the playful undercurrent of one who knew more than she was telling. It really was a shame that she was a young lady of virtue and not the demi-rep she wished him to make her. He could easily imagine the same smile, close beside him some night, her head on the pillow, her blonde hair tousled, her cheeks flushed with passion.

The Esme of his imagination was wicked in her abandon and more than willing to take his mind off the laudanum, should he but ask her to. If he reached for the drug, she would twine her fine white arms around him, drawing him back on to the bed to kiss him until he forgot everything but her.

She would do nothing of the kind, he reminded himself. A decent young lady, such as herself, would be shocked at the suggestion, and horrified that he was making her the subject of his bedroom fancies.

But what harm could it do to think of her thus as long as he did not act upon his baser desires? He had told her often enough that he was not interested in a physical relationship. As long as he kept his thoughts and hands to himself, she need never know otherwise.

And he needed to find something that would help him to an untroubled rest. If he could not have the drug, then for a few sweet moments, before sleep took him, he would have his imaginary Esme, to do with as he pleased.

The voices came to him from a distance, as though through water. There was Esme's shocked cry of 'St John,' and a man's stifled curse.

And then the blow hit the side of his head and he staggered and fell.

It was strange. Instead of darkness as he lost consciousness, the opposite was true. There was light. A growing number of candles as the room brightened and swam into focus. It was a bedroom, he realised, but not his own. And for the first time he felt the chill air on his bare skin.

'Damn you, I said get up.' Marcus's voice was terse, and St John felt, rather than saw, the bedsheet thrown at his bare feet.

'So that you may knock me down again?' He lurched to his feet, shaking his head to clear it.

'Cover yourself.'

He was naked, and shivering. He scooped up the sheet and wrapped it hastily around his waist, and glanced across the room and into Esme's shocked face. She was huddled in the bed, knees drawn up and the coverlet pulled to her chin.

And then Marcus stepped between them and slapped him full in the face.

If any remnant of unconsciousness had remained, the slap cleared the fog. 'I can explain…' he began, then realised that, of course, he couldn't. Not in any way likely to be believed by his brother.

'You have abused my hospitality for the last time, St John.' His brother's voice was colder than he'd ever heard it, and there was murder in it. 'We will settle this at dawn, if you can find someone to second you.'

'I cannot fight you.' It was true. A duel would be a disaster for both of them. And Marcus could solve this so easily by banning him from the house yet again. 'This was an accident, I swear. It is not as it appears. If you will but listen—'

'I will not listen to you any more, as you twist the truth out of all proportion to gain my sympathy.' Marcus seized him by the shoulder and yanked him from the girl's room and into the corridor, letting him stumble over the sheet that hindered his legs to fall at the base of the opposite wall.

Marcus stared down at him, his lip curled in disgust. 'No, St John. I have listened too many times in the past. And this time, like a fool, I believed you. I thought you had changed. I trusted you.' Marcus shook his head in amazement. 'I trusted you not to dishonour the girl, and thought it was true that you wanted what was best for her. And then you attempted something even more despicable than I could have imagined of you.'

'You can't honestly believe that I meant to…' St John struggled to his feet.

'I will not let you use my home as a brothel, you contemptible wretch. This ends tomorrow, St John. At dawn. And do not think of leaving the house before that time, or I will chase you down and shoot you like a dog in the road.' And Marcus refused to speak another word, pulling a chair into the hall to sit as guard at Esme's door, leaving St John no recourse but to return to his room and await the morning.

There was a faint glow of the sun in the eastern sky, and the grass was still slick with dew. Footing would be less than ideal. But there was little breeze to affect the aim of a pistol shot, and the temperature was excellent for fencing. All in all, it was a better day for battle than many he'd had in Portugal. That he would need to face his brother on such a fine morning sickened him.

'This is a mistake,' St John tried again.

'Entirely yours. It is too late to apologise, St John, you must know that.' The anger was still there, but he could see the tiredness on Marcus's face. His brother looked old.

And Marcus did not understand what was about to happen. How could he? St John walked to the trembling footman who had been bullied into serving as his second when Toby had flatly refused to stand with him. Toby had looked him gravely in the eye and said, 'If you mean to kill a man, then at least do it for better reason than a woman's honour. I'd rather help you do murder than to listen to you talk about honour and then go and kill the duke, who never deserved it.'

Even his valet was ashamed to be seen with him. It was not as if the duel was by his choice. He'd tried apologies, both written and verbal, sending urgent notes to the duke via the servants. But Marcus would not budge.

St John had seriously considered running away. At least it would spare Marcus what would happen if they duelled. But it would mean running from Esme, and letting her think that he'd meant her harm. And there was the fact that, somewhere at the back of his mind, he would rather die here and now than to turn tail and avoid the fight. If he could not reconcile with his brother, then maybe it was best to admit the fact and end the quarrel in blood as Marcus had often threatened to do.

St John examined the weapons. As the challenged, he had the choice. He'd rejected pistols as too quick and inelegant to settle the age-old argument. There was no chance to change your mind, once you pulled the trigger.

But Marcus had brought the duelling swords that had hung over the mantel in the study since their grandfather's time. 'Do you remember these, Marcus? We used to play with them as boys.' He lifted his sword and gave an experimental swipe at the air. He felt the edge. The weapons had not been cared for. His sword was not as sharp as he would have liked, had he actually wanted to fight. It would not cut. But the point was true, God help him. He'd need to be careful.

'And Father gave us a whipping because they were not toys.' Marcus voice was distant, though they stood side by side.

'They still are not.' St John paced off the distance and watched as his brother picked up the other sword. He made one last attempt, before they began. 'I never meant harm to the girl, although you do not believe it.'

And now Marcus cut the air with his blade. 'You were naked and in her room. It does not matter if she invited you there.'

'Damn you, Marcus,' he snapped, finally angry enough to draw blood. 'If you care so much for the girl and her reputation, you will mind your tongue and take back what you just said. I was not there at her invitation. She had no fault in it. It was mischance. It was an embarrassing mistake, but if someone must pay for it, it will be me.'

'And if you care for the girl, there are other ways to salvage her reputation.' It was Marcus who saluted first and took his stance, which was stiff and unpractised.

'Planning to march me down the aisle of the chapel at sword point?' St John laughed. 'The Reverend Winslow would like that, I'm sure. When it comes to the sacrament of marriage, the Radwells can be counted on to entertain, if nothing else.'

'The thought had occurred to me. But her father might not consent. It would have to be Gretna Green for the pair of you. She would be willing, I'm sure. She has been mooning over you since before we came down from London. There is a carriage at the ready and a suitable head start could be arranged. Say the word and we can end this.'

'If I was willing. As I've told you before, I am not. Not to save the girl's honour or my own. If you mean to kill me, Marcus, then get it over with. I am beyond tired of your empty threats.' He saluted in return and prepared for the attack. 'But is this fight for Esme, or Miranda, or Bethany?'

It was a low blow, but it had the desired effect. Marcus charged forward, unprepared, and St John was ready to parry the first cut and respond with a feint.

Marcus had regained his temper and knocked the blade out of the way with his own sword. 'Shall we say that it is for a lifetime of wrongs, committed by you against our family?'

'Fair enough. Will this settle it, then? When one of us lies dead?' St John reached with a lazy attack, and let Marcus parry and riposte watching the timing of his brother's action. The speed was almost such that he had to work to avoid it.

Almost, but not quite.

Marcus's breathing was ever so slightly laboured, when he said, 'I suspect that death will be the only thing likely to stop you from dishonouring yourself further.'

'How will *your* death stop me from doing anything?' St John engaged his brother's blade and pushed him back with a series of actions that were parried with difficulty.

'For that is how this will end, Marcus, if you insist on continuing. I do not fight to lose. I never have. And after several years on the Peninsula, you will find that I have no trouble stomaching what I am likely to do today if you continue to threaten me.' He took control of the blade again and forced Marcus back, as he parried three swift attacks, one after the other.

Marcus was tiring and his foot slipped in the grass. St John ignored the advantage and paused, letting his brother regain his balance. When Marcus found his feet, he lunged forward and St John was deliberately slow to parry. He waited for the impact of the blade and the pain when it pierced his shoulder, but none came. At the last minute the point of Marcus's sword swerved to the side, slicing St John's shirt and leaving a scratch on his arm.

He glanced down with indifference at the blood on his own sleeve, and then up to his brother, who looked as white as if the cut were in his own flesh. 'Clearly, only one of us has the stomach to fight, if a little blood frightens you so. But then, you aren't much better at this than any other country farmer. I left a wide enough opening, dear brother—why couldn't you have taken it and run me through?'

'Don't think you can win my clemency by reminding me of our parentage.'

St John laughed. 'Your clemency? I have not needed that in a very long time. Now, fight if you mean to. I grow weary of waiting.' He let the duke attack again, and responded with an ineffectual parry, waiting for the point to pierce his flesh. Again, Marcus changed direction at the last second and St John felt the sting of the blade as it opened a shallow cut on his other arm.

He looked at it in disgust. 'There. I am wounded again, and have had better scratches from the kitchen cat. Are you ready to call a halt, or must we continue?'

Marcus stepped back and took his guard again. 'Call a halt? As always, St John, you are trying to walk away in the middle of the fight, leaving me to deal with the consequences. If you cannot leave her alone, you must marry the girl. I am sick of your cowardice.'

St John felt the blood creeping into his face, and forced the rage into his gut to save for the fight. 'Now, Marcus, you are the one who has gone too far. You sit on your precious land with your lovely wife, and think that because you have money and power, and had the good luck to be born first, you have the right to decide my future. Then, when you lack the guts to run me through, you call me coward.' He attacked, then, again and again, forcing his brother to give ground. 'And now, I must finish this, since you cannot. If you do not kill me, you will not see another day. My apologies to your wife, and your children.'

He paused, and smiled at Marcus, giving him one last opportunity. 'But do not worry about them. When you are gone, I will love them as if they were my own.'

Marcus lunged again, wild and off balance, too angry to focus his attack, which went wide. And St John caught the blade with his own, and held it, driving the guards up and back into a blunt blow to the face. Marcus's nose streamed blood and he was dazed as St John knocked the weapon easily from his hand and brought his own point down and to the side so that he could close the distance between them. He struck Marcus across the throat with his forearm, and followed him to the ground.

His brother lay beneath him, struggling for air, St John's knee in his stomach and an elbow at his throat. And he saw the look of final recognition in Marcus's eyes, as he'd seen it in many other men on the battlefield, when he understood that he had lost and this was how it all would end. Then St John drew his sword arm to the right and let the dulled blade slide harmlessly across his brother's windpipe before tossing his weapon aside.

He rolled off his brother and collapsed on the grass beside him, closed his eyes and listened to Marcus retch and gasp for breath. The grass was cool and wet. The sun was not truly risen. How long had they been fighting? Scant minutes. But then, it did not take long to kill a man. He'd learned that well enough.

It would be good, to lie here and to not ever have to rise. Peaceful. He heard the first birds, waking in the trees. He could feel a slight chill as the shadow of his brother crossed his face. 'Can you finish it now, Marcus?'

The voice above him was hoarse. 'I cannot kill an unarmed man.'

St John laughed, and felt a tear on his own cheek. 'I

can. At last, something I know I can do better than you. But I doubt I can kill you, even for calling me coward. And perhaps I am a coward, for I've been unable to summon the strength to kill myself. I'm sorry, big brother, but that is one more job you must do for me.' He leaned his face into the grass, smelling the greenness of it and the coolness against his fevered brow. 'It is so peaceful here. Let it end for me, now. Do what you meant to do. Please.'

Marcus's tone became more ragged still. 'Get up and fight, damn you.'

St John could feel himself beginning to tremble. 'I don't need you to damn me, Marcus. I've done that for myself. Bad when I left you, and worse when I returned. There was dishonour on my name, but now there is blood on my hands. So much blood. They made me a hero for it.' He laughed until his body shook 'And I can still hear the screaming. Without the laudanum, I cannot pass a still night. You've seen what happens without the drug. When I am in that state I do not know what I am doing. But I know what I'm capable of. And I must never inflict that on another. I am so tired. Of the drugs, and of life. Dear God, let it end.'

There was a noise that sounded almost like a sob, and he felt his brother drop to the grass beside him. And then Marcus lifted St John's head and slipped his rolled up coat beneath for a pillow.

'Rest. I will watch for you. You have nothing to fear.'

And for a moment he almost believed it.

* * *

He startled awake, some time later. The sun was higher in the sky and Marcus was leaning against a tree, a few feet away. He rolled on to one elbow, and asked, 'How long?'

'An hour. Maybe a little more.'

He stood up, and shook the wrinkles out of his brother's coat, handing it back to him. 'Thank you. That is more sleep than I've had for weeks.'

His brother shook his head. 'Finally, the duel I knew must come, that would settle things between us, once and for all. And in the middle of it, you fell asleep. My pride may never recover.'

'You were a formidable opponent.'

Marcus's smile was sad. 'You are not nearly so accomplished a liar as you used to be. You were more honest before, as we fought. I am a farmer, and you are a soldier. I was foolish to challenge you and am lucky to be alive.'

'I lied to goad you when I said you had aught to be afraid of from me. Whether you are living or dead, your house and your wife shall have nothing but my respect. I know I can never repair the wrongs I've done you, but I can at least leave you in peace and try not to make the present situation worse.'

'Leave? The devil you will. You've finally come home.' Marcus removed a flask from his pocket, and drank deeply. 'There is enough here for two, if you are interested.'

St John grinned at his brother. 'Thank you. I think I am.'

They waved the coach away and walked back towards the house, and St John felt lighter than he'd felt in ages. He searched his mind. That was not accurate. He could never remember feeling this way. He glanced over at his brother, walking wordlessly beside him. Without looking up, Marcus again offered him the flask. He was not alone. He took another drink. The brandy felt good, even on his empty stomach. The duke opened the door to the house and let him pass in first.

St John smiled as he saw Miranda before him.

His smile faded as she threw herself at him, striking at his face and chest, moaning tonelessly through her tears. And over her shoulder, he could see Esme, huddled on the stairs, also crying, but weak with relief.

Then Marcus stepped into the room after him. 'Lady wife, contain yourself, and unhand my brother.'

Miranda looked up from her tears at the sound of his voice, and rushed to him. 'We heard nothing, and when I saw St John, I thought you dead. Blood!' She sniffed. 'And brandy.' She shot an accusing look at St John, from the shelter of her husband's arms. 'What did you do to him?'

Marcus chuckled and mopped at his face with a linen handkerchief. 'Broke my nose and ruined my shirt, I think. But you will notice that he has two very nice cuts on his arms from me.'

'He could easily have killed me,' supplied St John,

trying without success to be helpful. 'But he chose not to.'

From the stairs, Esme gasped.

'Overgrown boys. Playing with sharp sticks.' Miranda slapped at her husband in frustration, and then held him close, clinging around his neck. Which must hurt like the devil, St John reminded himself. He'd made no effort to be gentle with his brother when he'd choked him. There would be bruises tomorrow. He shot an apologetic look to Marcus, who rolled his eyes in response and jerked his head in the direction of the girl weeping on the stairs.

Esme was still trembling, and wet-cheeked as he strode up the stairs to her. He stopped short, a few steps below her and knelt at her feet. 'Miss Canville. I humbly apologise for invading your room last night. I can but beg your pardon, although it was an unforgivable offence.'

'I thought you were dead,' she whispered, unheeding. 'Or had murdered your brother. And that it was my fault.'

He looked up at her earnestly. 'This was but the culmination of an old quarrel. And we've never needed much excuse to fight.' He paused and corrected himself. 'Not that I consider my disrespect of you a small thing. On the contrary. I…I deserved…'

She shook her head. 'It is all right. If your brother had not discovered you, there would not have been a problem.'

'No problem?' He lowered his voice so as not to alert the couple in the foyer below them. 'Of course there was a problem. You had a naked man in your room.'

'But you were that naked man, St John. And I have nothing to fear from you. Besides…' she smiled '…I'd never seen a naked man before. It was very educational.'

After years in brothels and gaming hells, and five years in the army, St John was at a loss for the last time he'd blushed. But that was before he'd met Esme Canville. 'You should not have looked, and, even if you did, you should not mention the fact.'

'Really, St John. It's not as if I'm likely to comment upon it at dinner. And in truth you are very handsome, even more so without your clothes. You cannot pretend to be surprised that I should look at you if you came to me naked in the night.'

'I didn't come to you, you silly girl. Not intentionally, at least—I was not in possession of my senses.' He hung his head in embarrassment. 'Sometimes, in my sleep, I wander.'

She smiled. 'So, you mean to say, once you were relieved of the unnecessary restraints you place on yourself, you came to me?'

'I am sure it was not that way at all,' he sputtered, hoping she did not realise how close to the truth she'd come.

'And removed your clothing?'

'There was no clothing to remove. I never find it necessary, on warm nights.'

She leaned closer and whispered, 'Really? I had no idea. Is that common amongst men?'

He pulled away from her and ran a nervous hand through his hair. 'I pray to God you never find out what is common amongst men. You should be familiar with only one man: your husband.'

She shook her head in disbelief. 'And if I elect to have none, I am to remain in chaste ignorance for my entire life?'

'Well—' he threw his hands into the air '—yes. You should.'

She smiled. 'Then I fear, thanks to you, it is too late for me already.'

'Thanks to me? Thanks to you, and your feather-brained attempts to destroy your honour, I could have died today, or killed my brother.'

She leaned close to him again, her eyes sparkling and intense. 'And that was my great regret. But masculine pride must take some blame for that situation. You admitted that to me before.

'And, as is typical of the male gender, you didn't spare a moment's thought to anyone else, when you found a reason to fight. Miranda and I sat for hours, afraid to speak, each knowing that the one's happiness at the outcome would mean the other's despair. When you walked into the door, I was shamed to find that I did not care that the duke might lay dead somewhere and that my only friend's heart was broken beyond repair. I was only glad that I could see you again and know that you lived.'

Before he could stop himself, he'd reached out and taken her hand. It was small and warm, and his breath caught in his throat as she twined her fingers with his. 'I am alive, and so is my brother. I promise, things are better between us than they have been for many years. I have you to thank for that. And I am grateful. But I do not wish to spoil the truce when it is so new, by abusing his hospitality. Please do not ask me to. I cannot give you what you want. No decent man would help you achieve dishonour with another. And I am certainly in no position to offer you better, as you would deserve.'

Her eyes shone with fresh tears, but he hardened his heart against them.

'I beg you, Esme, let Miranda find you a husband, or go home to the one your father has chosen for you. Once you are wed, you will be safe from your father and free of many of the restrictions you face now. Marry, Esme. Do it soon. And marry anyone but me.' And he pulled his hand away from hers and walked back down the stairs to his brother.

Chapter Eleven

Esme tossed in her bed, unable to sleep. The clock on the mantel was ticking more loudly than before. The sound of time passing was deafening her with its finality.

She punched her pillow and rolled to find a cooler spot. Her plan had lost all sense, at some point. She had hoped to find freedom by casting off her virtue, selling herself until she could find another way on. And then it had seemed possible that Miranda might find her a husband and she might never return home to her father's choice.

But that was not enough any more. She'd known, as she waited for the men to return from the duel, that she'd been foolish enough to fall in love. And with St John Radwell, of all people. If she'd woken one morning and made a plan to break her own heart, she could not have chosen better.

It was more than friendship between them. He wanted her, as a man wanted a woman, no matter how much he might protest otherwise. He could not offer for her, as he kept insisting, and yet he wanted her all the same, or he would not have come to her room when sleep deprived him of inhibition.

She groaned and rolled again, pulling the pillow over her head. The man took the strangest time to find his honour, just when she needed him to be a cad. She doubted, should he take liberties with her, that he could manage to free himself from the obligation of marriage. It might have been true of the infamous rake that she'd heard so much about, but certainly not the man that she'd come to know.

St John held her at arm's length, meaning to protect her, no matter what that protection might cost to her chance at physical happiness. But if he would not have her, than some other man must, or she must return home. She could choose a loveless marriage, or life as a spinster in her father's house, doing penance for her mother's deceit.

She threw back the covers and planted her feet on the floor. There would be no sleep tonight. Not with the memory of St John, standing naked over her bed the night before. His skin had seemed golden in the moonlight, and she'd taken her fill of the sight of him before calling out to waken him from his trance.

Which, she supposed, proved her father right all along. A decent girl would have shrunk in horror, or perhaps screamed for help. At least she should have shielded her eyes from the sight. But she'd longed to touch, and to explore. And she'd hoped that he'd take just a few more steps and come into her bed to cover her body with his own.

It had been most disappointing when the duke had come to rescue her and spoiled everything.

And now, her thoughts of what might have been left her warm and restless in the cosiness of the room, and she longed to throw her nightdress aside and lie bare on the cool sheets, as he must do.

She stood up and moved away from the bed and the wild ideas rising in her mind. It was far too late to ring for a cup of tea, but perhaps a book from the library… The walk would cool her blood and a nice volume of sermons would cool her fevered brain. Sermons made her long for sleep in the chapel on Sundays. They would be just the trick now.

She crept down the hall to the stairs, the cold marble under her bare feet making her shiver. This was much better, listening to the night noises of the big house and feeling deliciously alone and at peace. She opened the door to the library and paused on the threshold, sensing the presence in the room before she saw him. Candles were lit and there was a crystal decanter of brandy on the small table beside the couch and a snifter already poured, although it gave no sign of having been touched. Above the back of the sofa, she saw the outline of St John's head with the firelight behind it, the warm glow giving a halo to his golden hair.

Without turning, he said, 'You might as well come in, Esme. The open door is making a draught.'

'How did you know…?'

'That it would be you?' He laughed softly. 'Who else would it be, cutting up my peace, keeping me awake nights?'

She stiffened. 'If I disturb you so, then I had best be going.'

'Don't be a goose. I smelled your perfume.' He glanced back at her, over his shoulder. 'And I can see my attempt at wit has failed. Never mind it. What brings you here, at this hour?'

'I should think that would be obvious. What would bring me to the library at this time of night?'

'You could not sleep and wished something to read.'

'But of course,' she said with more bitterness than necessary. 'And you have come for a brandy before bed.'

'This hour vary rarely finds me curled up with a good book, if that's what you're hinting at.'

She walked into the room and dropped into the chair next to the couch. 'While I am not allowed to curl up with anything else.'

He nodded. 'As it should be. You will not find me curling up with you, tonight, whatever I might have tried last night.'

'No,' she snapped. 'Never with me. Although you might at least pretend that the idea is not so repellent.'

His smile was sad, and there was a haunted look in his eyes that gave her pause. 'Do not think that, dear Esme. You are not in the least repellent. If you only knew…' He paused, as if lost in thought for a moment, then went on, the softness disappearing from his tone. 'As a matter of fact, I could quite enjoy you, my sweet, given half a chance. So young, so tender, so naïve. But I have given my word to my brother not to trouble the guests while I remain under his roof. So I must admire you from afar, and brood into the fire on what might have been.' He sighed, and it was mockery. 'I must exercise self-denial. It is a perversion that I've not yet experienced, to stare at you thus, with bare feet sticking out from under your nightdress, and use only my imagination.'

'Self-denial,' she scoffed. 'And that is why you've sneaked off to the library for a glass of drugged spirits.'

His head snapped up and the look in his eyes was sharp with pain and shame. And he grabbed the snifter in with an impulsive shudder and pitched it and its contents into the fire. The brandy made the flames flare blue, before they settled again, the light glinting off the shards of crystal on the hearthstone. His voice was harsh. 'There. Are you satisfied? There will be no drug tonight. Or sleep either, since if I doze I am likely to walk as I did last night, shaming myself and my family more than this filthy habit already does.'

She went to him, and reached out, but when her fingers touched his arm he drew back as though burned. 'Do not touch me, if you value your virtue.' He stalked back to the couch and collapsed into a seat, glaring past her, into the fire.

She walked to him and dropped to her knees on the rug in front of him, blocking his view so he had no choice but to look at her.

'Well, then.' His tone was gruff. 'Are you still here? I thought I made it clear that your company was unwelcome.'

'No,' she whispered. 'You said that my touch was unwelcome. And so I will not touch you. But neither will I leave you alone while you need me.'

'Need you?' He sneered.

'You need someone, for I do not trust you to be alone. And I am the only one here. Would you prefer that I got the duke?'

'No.' His hand shot out and seized her gently by the wrist. He sighed and closed his eyes. 'Please. I would not wish him to see me this way. For the first time in our lives, he has begun to treat me as an equal, and not a constant source of disappointment. For him to find me now, unable to marshal my base needs for the laudanum, would undo much.'

'Then let me help you.'

His eyes were open, and he was staring into hers with that sad smile again. 'I would if there were aught for you to do.'

'But there is.' She smiled. 'If you cannot sleep without the drug, then I will stay awake with you, until you are tired enough to go to bed. I can distract you.'

His mouth quirked and there was a long pause as his eyes travelled over her body. 'I have no doubt that you could be most diverting, but I believe I've made my position on that quite clear.'

She was blushing. She could not help it, and she turned her face away from his so that he might not see it. She rose from the carpet and walked to the table near the window. 'No, silly. I am sure I saw some cards here, in the drawer of this table. Perhaps a few hands of something might pass the evening in an agreeable way. Whist?'

He rolled his eyes. 'Whist requires four persons. Be honest, now, Esme. What do you know of cards?'

'Very little. It is one of the many things that my father found too wicked for me to partake in.' She pulled the little card table close to where he was sitting and passed the deck to him. 'And so, you must teach me. I am afraid that I'm likely to be a rather slow pupil. It is lucky that you have all night.'

He smiled at her and shook his head. 'I am alone in the dark with a beautiful woman, she is barely dressed, and we have the whole night to spend together. And this vision kneels at my feet, offering to relieve my suffering. And then we play cards. Esme Canville, you must swear that no mention of this night will ever escape your lips. Never mind your precious virtue—my reputation as a danger to womankind will be utterly destroyed.'

He shuffled the deck and said, 'Very well. Cards it is. We will not bet, because it would hardly be fair of me with so inexperienced an opponent. Let us begin with a simple game of *Vingt-et-un*.'

When he sent her to bed, the clock was striking four, and she had begun to nod over her hand.

'Go back to your room, Esme. If you miss your beauty sleep, I do not wish to be held responsible for it.'

'And what of you?' He was very tired, but she could see the lines of strain in his face were not as pronounced as they had been.

'What of me?' His smile was wan. 'I will stay up for a time yet. The dawn is peaceful. I have reason to know. I have seen it often enough. When the first birds are singing, I find it easiest to rest.' He walked her to the door of the library, then stopped and impulsively seized her hand and brought her fingers to his lips. 'And thank you. You are right. It helped.'

She felt her heart soaring in her chest like the first singing bird. 'I will come again, tomorrow night.'

He shook his head. 'I should say no. I have a care for your reputation, girl, even if you do not. But I am so tired.'

She smiled. 'You should say no. But you won't. I cannot make you any less tired, but I can stay with you until this time passes. You have done much for me, bringing me here and giving me a taste of freedom and the friendship of your family. But I have done nothing for you but cause you grief. Let me do this one thing.'

'Very well.'

And he closed the door softly behind her as she found her way back to her room.

The next night found him pacing the library, restless as a caged animal. He would make several circuits of the room, then return to the couch, fearing that she would find him thus and interpret his nerves for weakness. But eventually the restlessness in his legs became too much and he was on his feet again.

It should not matter to him what she thought, for he should not be allowing her to sit with him. It was improper. Innocent enough as yet, but it would be far too tempting in his current condition to substitute one vice for another.

But it had felt so good to have her at his side the previous night that he had not noticed the hours slipping by. And she had been so eager to help him. He hadn't the strength or the desire to refuse.

The clock on the mantel struck twelve and he drummed his fingers on the table before him. It was later than last night. Perhaps she had seen sense and would not come. Or maybe she was so tired from the previous night that she had retired early and forgotten her promise to sit with him.

He had seen her, dozing in the family pew at chapel, and smiled as Miranda nudged the poor girl awake during the sermon, again and again. She needed her rest and it was wrong of him to wish otherwise.

But he found the prospect of an evening without her almost unbearable. After she'd left him at dawn, he'd remained in the library, and dozed fitfully as the sun had come up. Marcus had found him there, and kicked his boot to waken him, asking what he was about.

He'd begun to explain the insomnia, but had caught Marcus staring at the card table in front of the sofa. St John had hastily laid a game of Patience and had avowed that it calmed his nerves, when he was restless at night.

Only to see Marcus glance to the second chair. His brother had given him a pointed look and remarked slowly and with emphasis, that cards were a harmless enough way to pass the wee hours, as long as one was careful what games one played. And then he'd said no more about it.

St John had been left with the impression that his brother guessed much more of the truth than he cared to admit. But if that was the case, then he'd been given tacit permission to meet with the girl unchaperoned.

Obviously, married life had softened his brother's heart, or his head.

He heard the door click and rushed back to the sofa to arrange himself in illusory comfort as the door opened and Esme entered. 'Here to spend the late hours with me, after all?'

'As I said I would be.' She took the seat across the table from him as he shuffled the cards.

'I thought perhaps you would not come.'

'Miranda came to my room to speak to me about my feelings on the gentlemen at our last ball. And to remind me of my duties to my honour. I think she is concerned that I am still too fond of you. I could hardly send her away because we had an assignation, could I?'

He felt a moment's alarm. 'This is not an assignation.'

She cocked her head to the side. 'Well, what would you prefer to call it? I am open to suggestions.'

'I would prefer not to call it anything at all. It is merely two people meeting, with a card table between them. The word assignation makes it sound…'

'Clandestine? Well, it is.'

'No. Intimate.'

'It is that as well, St John. Not physical intimacy, perhaps…'

'Not physical intimacy, at all.' He hurriedly dealt out a hand of piquet.

'I meant emotional intimacy. I dare say in a few short weeks you've got to know me better than any human being ever will.'

'Surely your husband—'

She fanned the cards he dealt her and tapped them on the table in annoyance. 'If and when I find one. The man my father has chosen was not intrigued enough to meet me before the betrothal. Am I to suspect this sudden interest in conversation will magically blossom on our wedding night?'

St John glanced down at her body and swallowed the lump in his throat. The lawn of her nightdress was not sheer, and the wrapper hid most of her body. Bet he was suddenly aware that there was very little between her smooth, pale skin and the night air, and that what garments she wore were loose and easily removed. He forced his eyes back to her face. 'No, I doubt that your husband, when you find him, will be in the mood for conversation once he has you alone.'

'And yet you have no trouble engaging me in discourse. Possibly because you made it abundantly clear, after the kiss in the garden, that I hold no interest for you.' She smiled back at him a little too brightly. 'And thus you are willing to speak to me as an equal and have come to know me better than any other human.'

'About that kiss—' His mouth snapped shut. The last thing he need do would be to tell her how pleasant it had been, or there would be no managing her.

'And what of it? I would rather not think overly long on it. I had been quite enjoying it, until you spoilt it. It was my first kiss, but of course you noticed that, as you pointed out my inexperience. I suppose one must start somewhere. I will no doubt do better, when I have opportunity to kiss again.' She rapped the deck on the table with her knuckles. 'Now look to your cards.'

She remembered the rules of the game well enough to beat him repeatedly. It might have helped if he'd been able to concentrate on the cards in his hand instead of the lips of his opponent, and the idea that she might have an opportunity to kiss again—nay, must kiss, if they meant to get her properly betrothed before sending her home—and when she did, the kiss would be with someone other than him. And if that had been her first kiss, she'd shown natural aptitude and a willingness to adapt to the needs of her partner.

Miranda must find her a suitable husband, and quickly. For Esme was right in one thing: it would be a waste to give such kisses to an old man, even for a fine fortune, an early widowhood and a chance to escape from her father.

She would lose her innocence in more ways than one on the first night, once she saw what it was she'd been yoked to. Her playful nature would change to cynicism. In no time, she would be as jaded as any of the ladies of the *ton*.

And she'd come dangling after him some night when her husband was away, just as he'd told her to. There would be no teasing conversations, no time for games at all. Just a hurried and vigorous joining before she returned to her home.

Until the next time the hunger grew in her and she came to him. And he would not turn her away. He sighed.

'Is there something the matter?' She looked up in puzzlement.

'No. Nothing. Really.'

She returned to her cards.

After she was married, her visits would be so different from this. And when they saw each other in day-light, she would be unwilling to meet his gaze. She would have no wish to talk or laugh with him. She would studiously avoid him so as not to cause gossip.

Of course, she was ignoring him now as well, all her focus on the cards, biting her lip in concentration. When she let it go, it had a bee-stung quality that begged attention, and she rubbed at it with the tip of her tongue...

And without warning, he threw the cards aside, and leaned across the small table, gripping her firmly by the shoulders and bringing his mouth down upon hers.

'Oh, St John. We mustn't.' She struggled but for a moment, before dropping the cards and clinging to the lapels of his coat.

He slipped his tongue into her mouth and tasted her between the words of protest. He could feel her body relax in his hands, surrendering to him as the kiss grew deeper.

When he moved his lips to her ear, she took in a breath and let out a great sigh. 'Well, we probably shouldn't. I think. Oh, dear.'

And then she ceased talking entirely and turned her mouth to his to let him kiss her again. With some hesitation, she began to kiss him back, slipping her tongue between his lips in tentative exploration. She paused, and he could feel her waiting for a repeat of the rebuke he had given her in the garden. And when it did not come she became more bold, nipping at his lip, and losing all fear as she took his mouth with her tongue.

He was at once happy with and frustrated by the table between them. It kept temptation in check to feel the wood pressing against his legs. But she was leaning over it, her robe brushing the discarded cards to the floor as she tried to get closer to him. She balanced a hip on its top, pivoting and reaching for him to wrap an arm around his neck.

It was dizzying to feel her so close, rubbing against his body, begging for more than he dared give. He released her shoulders, placed his palms flat on the table, and pressed down until his wrists hurt, denying the urge to stroke her hair and face, or to touch the breasts pressing against his chest.

There was a crack of splintering wood as a table leg gave way and tipped her off on to the floor and sent him stumbling after to lie in a heap beside her and the broken table on the Aubusson rug.

There was a horrible moment when she lay face down on the carpet making no sound at all, and he feared that she might be more broken than the poor table. And then she rolled on to her back, shaking with silent laughter.

And he rolled to her side, leaning on his elbow and watching her laugh. It was strange, he thought. She smiled often enough, but very rarely did he see her so overcome by mirth. The healthy flush in her cheeks and the twinkle in her eyes as she squeezed out tears of laughter was quite the most attractive thing he'd ever seen.

Finally, she managed to control herself sufficiently to speak. 'All right, St John. I must agree with you. You are a truly wicked man. For now I've broken my host's furniture while dallying in the library with you. What am I to tell Miranda?' She rolled to face him, plucking at his coat with her fingers.

'That is simple. You are to tell her absolutely nothing.' He rolled away from her and stood, brushing an imaginary fleck of dust off his trousers, and examined the table. 'See? The pins that held the leg have snapped, but it fits into the top like so.' He forced it back into a rough approximation of what it had been and smacked it sharply with the heel of his hand. Then he carried the temporarily intact table back to its place by the window, setting it down carefully so as not to disturb it. 'There. Almost as good as new.'

She looked doubtful of his repair. 'But the first time someone makes use of it…'

'Perhaps. Perhaps not. It will break, should they try to make love on it. I believe we have proved that right enough. But it should last a hand of cards, as long as the players are not too strenuous in their betting. And now, little one, I recommend that we steal away to bed, so that we may be as far away as possible from the scene of the crime, should it collapse before morning.' He offered her a hand off the floor and she rose gracefully, standing too close to him for common decency.

He took a cautious step back and led her to the door to the hall. 'Sly, my dear, but not sly enough. You will not tempt me into a repeat of that incident, no matter how appealing the idea might be.'

And then she smiled in triumph and he realised she was not going to deny it. 'At least now I know you were shamming in the garden the other day. You do not wish to be my teacher? Then, my darling St John, I will have to be the one who teaches you.'

And she turned without another word and walked away from him, down the darkened hall.

Chapter Twelve

'And you are sure the first two will not suit?' They were taking their breakfast tea in the morning room. Miranda was chewing on the end of her pen, but seemed strangely unconcerned by her lack of success as a matchmaker.

Esme nodded. 'Both are otherwise engaged, although I will admit to the smallest amount of regret when it comes to Mr Smythe.'

Miranda smiled. 'He is most appealing, I agree. Handsome, well dressed, and with gallant manners, although a bit of a rakehell. Rather like St John, don't you think?'

Esme choked on a crumb from the scone she'd been eating, and took a careful sip of tea. 'Really, I hadn't noticed. Unless you mean in the sense that they have both told me that an association with me would be impossible. But Mr Smythe, at least, had the grace to appear disappointed.'

'Hmm. Most unfortunate. About Mr Smythe, I mean. I would hate for you to pin your hopes on wringing an offer out of St John. He really can be the most contemptible villain.' But she was smiling as she said it, which seemed out of context. She continued, 'Although I suspect he would be a devoted husband. He is a hopeless romantic and thus is afraid of confessing affection lest his heart be broken.'

Or any more furniture.

Esme looked down to hide her laughter and toyed with her spoon, trailing it aimlessly around the cup of cooling tea. 'I suppose… He will be a fine match for someone, should he be so inclined.'

'Well, know that your father would never approve. I am sure he would find Lord Baxter much more suitable. Mature. Stable.'

Which made Lord Baxter sound quite boring, really. Miranda was clueless when it came to matchmaking. Esme said, 'I do not wish to choose a husband based on the wishes of my father. If I could find someone who wanted me, who I wanted as well, then I doubt my father's wishes would signify greatly to me. Truth be told, if the man cannot withstand my father's displeasure, then it matters not whether I want him, for my father's displeasure is the only factor in this plan that can be assured.'

She thought of the new letter she had received at breakfast. The words were not threatening, merely curt. Another insistence that she get over her megrims post haste and return home to meet her betrothed. But she could imagine the look on her father's face as he wrote them, and the tone he would use if he were speaking. The one that told her, without saying the words out loud, the painful consequences of inaction.

'Well, we shall see if my last candidate can fulfil your requirements.' Miranda smiled again. 'I was thinking something less formal this time. A card party, perhaps. Enough couples to make a few tables of four, some cheese and fruit. Simplicity itself.'

'Cards?' Esme thought of the game she'd just played so successfully with St John and felt a blush rising in her cheeks.

'You do play whist, do you not?'

'Badly.'

'Do not worry.' Miranda waved off her objections. 'We will practise before the event. A few rubbers in the library. You can partner with St John…'

'That would be…most interesting.' She tried to keep her tone neutral.

That evening, they sat around the same table that she and St John had used the previous evening. He was seated across from her and the duke and Miranda were on either side. The game went well enough and she played as best she was able, although it might have been easier to concentrate if she'd partnered with someone who had been less prone to inappropriate laughter.

After taking another trick, Miranda commented, 'Esme, you and St John play admirably together.'

'But not so well as to win the rubber,' Esme responded.

'Winning is not the most important thing,' Miranda insisted. 'What matters is pleasure in the game and an evening spent in good company. Your partner does not seem to mind losing, do you, St John?'

'Miranda, look to your cards,' the duke cautioned his wife.

'We are losing?' St John asked. 'I barely noticed. I was too busy admiring this table.' He tapped the top with his finger. 'Is it new?'

Esme tried to kick St John under the table, and was most embarrassed to see the duke flinch in response.

Marcus ignored the misplaced kick and answered his brother. 'This table and its mate have been in the library since we were children, as you should well remember. Stop talking nonsense and deal.'

'It is still sturdy, despite its age.' St John shook the table, which showed no sign of collapse.

Marcus snatched his wine glass from the table, before it spilled. 'St John, if you must destroy the furniture, please wait until I've finished my port.'

'Hear that, Esme? My brother has given me permission to destroy the furniture.' St John grinned at her and raised an eyebrow.

'No more port for you,' Marcus responded and combined the contents of St John's glass with his own.

'This table has a mate?' Esme glared across the table at St John.

'Didn't you notice? It is under the window in the library. At one time, there were three of them, but they are rather easily broken. Weak legs.' He rattled the table again.

'I think the third table is upstairs in the portrait gallery. St John, have you shown Esme the family portraits?' Miranda suggested.

'Or they could play cards,' suggested the duke and the group fell into comfortable silence, punctuated by the occasional snort of mirth from St John.

She stood before him later, when they were alone in the library, hands on hips. 'That was horrible of you, St John. Letting me continue for half the evening in fear that the game was likely to collapse out from under us, when all the while you knew it was a different table.'

'They are easy to tell apart, if you know them. There is a chip in the veneer of the one we broke.' He pointed to the table that he had set for their nightly game. 'This one is unmarked and perfectly safe.' He walked to the other side of the table and sat down.

She glanced across at him. The tiredness on his face was even more evident than the night before. At some point, he must give in and sleep, or die from fatigue. And the way he had moved when he saw her, it almost seemed that he was keeping the table between them, which was ridiculous. A man who had faced Napoleon should have nothing to fear from her.

'Shall we try to improve your game for tomorrow? We cannot play a real game with only two, but perhaps with practice you might learn to bet.' He reached for a glass and decanter on another small table near the couch, and poured himself a glass.

She stared at it in suspicion.

He smiled. 'Not drugged, I promise you. Only the port of which my brother was so protective. And with reason. It is excellent. Portuguese, as it should be. It would have been criminal of me to spill it. If you do not trust me, you may taste from my glass.' And he offered her his wine and poured another for himself.

The port was rich, and it warmed her blood, but she detected no trace of the drug that she had taken in London. She sat the glass down on the table. 'You are right. It is very good. But I should not finish it. So late in the evening, it will likely go to my head.'

He nodded. 'That is wise of you.'

She stared across the table at him, remembering his kiss and the feel of his arms around her, and did not want to be wise at all. She picked up her glass and took another sip of wine, letting the warmth build inside her. 'I suspect that, should a young lady alone in circumstances such as this have too much wine, certain men might be prone to take liberties.'

'Perhaps.' He set his own glass down.

'Of course, with me you will do nothing. Much as

you are doing now.' She sighed and watched him as he watched the rise and fall of her bosom. Fire danced in his eyes when he looked at her, but he made no move to act. 'I am disappointed in you. You have a reputation as a dangerous man.'

'Well deserved. But that is in the past, I assure you. You are safe with me.'

'In the past? Tell me, then—what did you do in this illustrious past of yours?'

'I never plied a woman with port and made her fight for her virtue, if that is what you suspect.' He smiled, remembering. 'I did not favour the sort that would put up a struggle over something of that nature. The virtue of the ladies I favoured was long fled by the time I got them alone.'

'Oh, really? Were the ladies terribly wicked? And were you?' She tried not to sound eager for the story, but could not hide the curiosity in her voice.

He reached for his wine glass and filled it slowly. 'Not wicked. But they were not adverse to passing a pleasant afternoon picnicking alone with me in a certain secluded spot I know on my brother's property.'

'Is it pretty?' she asked.

'Very.'

'Then you must show me tomorrow.'

He glared at her. 'I most certainly will not. I would not take an innocent out into the woods without a chaperon. My brother would have my head for suggesting it. Any woman who shared a basket and a bottle with me

on such an outing was already quite sure of what she
wanted. And it wasn't jugged pheasant and fresh air.'

She looked disappointed. 'So you are not really a
practised seducer because seduction was unnecessary?'

'I am a practised seducer because I enjoy it, love.
When a man persuades a woman to spend a time in mutual pleasure, he should do it with grace and style, even
if the conclusion is foregone.' He took a deep sip of the
port, savouring it before swallowing.

'And what was your method?' She drummed her fingers on the table top. 'You are smiling again, and in the
strangest way.' She waited for him to speak, and he did
not. So she stared back at him, and felt the seconds grow
long and the air grow heavy, and the oddest thoughts
took shape in her head.

'First, I make sure I have the lady's full attention.'
His voice was soft, and she felt herself leaning closer
to him.

She drew back and broke the connection of their
gaze, taking another sip of her own wine. 'And what
happens after you have got their attention?'

'It depends on what they wish to happen.' He reached
over and took the wine glass from her hand, and sipped
from the spot where her lips had been.

A shudder went through her as she imagined the
touch of his mouth on hers.

He smiled at the response.

She watched in silence as he held and warmed the
wine in her glass in his cupped hand, his fingers caress-

ing the bowl. At last he pinched the stem between his fingers.

She felt her nipples tighten in response. 'Oh, dear.'

He looked down at the outline of her breasts against the lawn of her nightrail and the subtle peaks forming. As she felt his eyes upon her, the effect was becoming more pronounced.

When he spoke, his voice was mild and his face was all innocence. 'I really have no idea where I get such a reputation as a rake. It seems I need to say or do very little, and yet the ladies I am with have the most outlandish ideas. One minute I am enjoying a quiet lunch with a charming young widow, and the next, she is imploring me to drink champagne from her navel. I do not understand how it happens.'

'You do not have to oblige them,' she said, feeling the heat grow in her belly.

'But it would be churlish to deny such pleasant and accommodating ladies. And I quite enjoy champagne.' He was looking at her again over the rim of his wine glass with that curious intensity.

Her heart was pounding madly and the room was becoming warm. Her gown had seemed light before, but suddenly it was heavy and constricting and curiosity burned in her like the port. She took a gulp of her wine and reached for the ties of her gown. 'Would port work?'

'Would port work for what?' And then he saw the look in her eyes. 'Dear Lord, Esme. I meant that hypothetically. Or historically, perhaps. Not in the present tense. I was an idiot to mention it. It was only fatigue and one too many glasses of wine that persuaded me to mention it at all.'

She undid the bow at her throat and let the bodice gap. 'Oh, really? I think you discussed your method because you wanted me to hear it. You were willing to satisfy my curiosity, because you knew what I would do.' She reached for the next tie.

'Stop that, this instant, Esme.'

'I am not worried. We have been uninterrupted for two nights now. Tonight will be no different.'

'I will go to my room and leave you here alone,' he threatened.

'I seriously doubt that. You will not seduce me, for you wish me to seduce you to avoid the blame of it. Let us see if I am right, shall we?' She pulled slowly on the ribbon to let the bow unravel.

'Tie up your gown again and go to bed. I have had quite enough port for the evening, and you have had far too much.' He reached to take the glass from her, but she pulled away. It tipped and the wine spilled on to her, soaking the thin cotton of the gown. She could feel it clinging to her skin.

'Damn.' His gaze was frozen, staring at her breasts.

She looked down. The wine had rendered the fabric almost transparent. She could see the outline of her nipples clearly, as could he. 'Is there something the matter with them?'

'Perfect,' he muttered softly to himself. 'Absolutely perfect.'

'Really?' She relaxed. 'Well, that is good to know. But I certainly seem to have made a muddle of things. Perhaps I should go to my room and change.'

'Like hell you should.' He shoved the table out of the way and fell on his knees before her, pulling her forward so he could take her in his mouth, sucking her breasts through the wine-soaked fabric.

Her breath caught in her throat and she leaned her head forward to rest her cheek against his hair as he buried his face against her, his mouth searching for the opening of the gown to lick at her bare skin. The wine was chill on her, but his lips were warm, as were his hands as he parted the cloth and slipped the bodice to her waist. Then he pulled her out of her chair and laid her down on her back in the middle of the rug.

He stepped away from her, then, and she wondered what he meant to do. Then he reached for his port and lay down on the rug beside her. Slowly, he dipped his finger into the glass to catch a few drops and let them drip upon her breasts. Then he stroked her with his fingertips, massaging the wine into her nipples and drawing tiny circles on her body until her breasts ached for his lips. At last, his head dipped close and his mouth touched her and his tongue licked away the wine.

His teeth had caught a nipple and he was pulling gently on it, and she arched her back, hands clawing at the carpet. She reached to touch his hair, cradling his head as he moved to the other breast. She stared up at the ceiling above her and felt the world turning beneath her, spinning out of control. St John's hands travelled to her waist and held her fast as he sucked and bit and stroked until she was writhing beneath him, straining to be closer to him.

And then he stopped. He reached for his glass again and she held her breath as he poured it on to her belly. He set the glass aside and lay upon her, covering her breasts with his hands and tracing a lazy pattern with his tongue on the flesh of her abdomen, before drinking the wine he had poured. Then he raised his head to look into her eyes.

And he froze. There was a sound at the door. He held out a hand, warning her without words to stay where she was, on the floor and out of sight. Then he jumped to his feet and resumed his seat on the sofa, snuffing a candle, and dimming the room as the door opened.

'Master St John?'

'What is it, Wilkins?'

'I did not realise that you were still awake. Will you be needing anything?'

'Nothing, thank you. I am fine here in the evenings and do not require your service.' St John paused. 'But wait.' He reached for the port decanter and a single glass and walked to the door to hand them to the butler. 'You can dispose of this for me before I drink it all. It does not do to be alone with one's thoughts and a full bottle.'

'Yes, sir.'

Esme heard the door close and remained on the floor, waiting for her heart to stop pounding in her chest. St John loomed over her, half-lost in shadows, half-lit by the dying fire. He offered her his hand, and helped her to her feet. He pulled her close and whispered, 'And now that *my* curiosity is satisfied, we must stop.'

'No,' she gasped.

'Yes,' he said. 'The butler is on his way to the servants' quarters with half a bottle and my blessing. You have more than enough time to return to your room undiscovered. But it was a near miss, all the same.' He pulled her nightrail back up on to her shoulders and began to do up the bows. 'I have taken grave liberties with you, but done you no permanent harm. We will stop before that is no longer true.

'Do not think you can tease me, Esme, and make me dance to your tune. Another man would not be half so patient with you as I have been and would have greedily taken more than what you were offering tonight.'

He tied the last of the ribbons and led her towards the door. 'But I want better for you than that. You deserve more than a few moments' happiness. You deserve a lifetime. And when you find the man that can give you that, it would kill me to think that I have ruined your chances by stealing from you what rightly belongs to him.'

He opened the door and looked out into the hall. There was a moment's hesitation before he sighed and said, 'And now you must go to bed before someone finds you here.' He pulled her close and gave her an innocent kiss on the lips. 'And to answer your question, yes. Port works quite as well as champagne.' Then he pushed her out into the hall and shut the door behind her.

Chapter Thirteen

The next afternoon was as Miranda had described. A modest gathering of tables for four, and Esme was to be partnered with the last gentleman on Miranda's list. She hid a yawn behind her hand. She was still only passable at whist, and, try as she might, she could not raise the enthusiasm to become better.

Of course, once one had played cards with St John, one was unlikely to be satisfied with tricks and trumps and playing for pennies. She could not help feeling that the game became much more interesting once one had put down the pasteboards and pushed the table out of the way.

Miranda had suggested a simple, sprigged muslin gown for her, and the pink rosebuds that covered it went well with the flush in her cheeks as she thought of the previous evening. She would be playing cards on the very spot where they had lain the night before. And they might be playing on the very table where he had taught her how to kiss.

And she must not think of any of this again. Miranda had finished greeting her guests and hurried to her side, taking her hand in an encouraging squeeze. 'You look lovely today, Esme,' she said. 'Like a breath of spring. You are in fine colour as well. Are you excited at the prospect of meeting his lordship?'

'Yes. Of course, that is it.' Esme hoped her smile wasn't too dazed to be convincing. But in a moment's lapse, she had forgotten the reason she was there. This was to be her last chance at marriage. If Lord Baxter was the best that Devon had to offer, than she should do her best to appear suitable to him. Spinning fancies about St John when she should be concentrating on the man in front of her would be no help at all.

Miranda said, 'It is good to see you are looking forward to this. Men take notice when a girl is interested, and are flattered by it.' Miranda took her hand and led her across the room to meet her card partner.

'Miss Esme Canville, may I present Lord Baxter.' Miranda introduced them, and the gentleman bowed low over her hand. He was certainly gallant enough. The bow was deep and well formed. He was not as young as Webberly, or Smythe, but nowhere near as old as her father's choice for her. Baxter's hair was steel grey, and his face was lined, but not unhandsome. His eyes were not kind, but neither were they cruel.

He was not perfect, but he seemed the sort of man

she could grow fond of, given time and opportunity. She smiled back at him, polite and encouraging. 'I am honoured to meet you, sir. I understand we are to be partnered at cards this afternoon. I hope you will be patient with me, for I am new to the game of whist.'

'New to the game?' He dropped her hand. 'Then perhaps you would do well to partner someone as inexperienced as yourself. He looked at Miranda. 'Is there no other I could play with?'

Esme's heart sank.

Miranda was obviously nonplussed at having her seating arrangement questioned by a guest. It took a moment before her smile dropped back into place and she said, 'Why, no, Lord Baxter. I believe the tables are already set. Perhaps another time. But today I am most eager to have my friend in experienced hands as regards the game. And I was certain that you would be the best teacher for her.'

'Well, we can hardly expect to win, if we are unevenly matched.'

Miranda ignored his objection. 'Winning is hardly a consideration on such a pleasant afternoon as this. We are playing for amusement, and not high stakes, after all.'

'Winning not important? How like a woman to say such a thing.' Lord Baxter harrumphed. Esme had heard the noise from her father's friends, when there was mention of liberal government and difficulties with the lower classes, but had never expected to hear it from the lips of a potential suitor. She schooled her face into a neutral expression.

Miranda smiled and nodded, although there was a flash of irritation in her eyes. 'Yes, I suppose it is. But then, with children to raise and a household to run, we have little time for things as important as cards. You will be playing against the duke and myself. My husband has much the same problems with me as you will have with Esme. He finds it most trying. But it means we will be evenly matched.'

Esme thought Miranda must be as accomplished a liar as she was a card player to make the last statement sound convincing. She and the duke played as though they had a single mind between them. And now that Baxter had made her angry, Esme doubted that she would show the man mercy and lose to protect his ego.

Miranda led them to their table. Esme examined it. It seemed to be the one from the library, but it was hard to tell. Perhaps it was the mate. Several of the tables in the room looked alike, and the cloth covered the chip in the veneer. She must hope for the best. At an afternoon party there would be no reason for boisterous play. Things would be fine.

The game started well enough, but it seemed that she could not play with sufficient skill or speed to please her partner.

'Dammit, gel, you've lost the rubber for us again. If you cannot take the trick, then do not lead with such horrible cards.' He pounded the table for emphasis.

Esme cringed. And behind her, at a neighbouring table, she heard St John chuckle. 'I am sorry,' she said quietly to her partner. 'It was a terrible hand. It could not be helped.'

'A more experienced player can compensate for a bad hand,' he grumbled. 'For the next, see to your cards and waste no more time gossiping.'

Since she had not spoken a word during the last hand, the charge was most unfair. She was preparing to tell him so when he gave several firm taps on the table with his finger.

Esme could swear that she felt a slight wobble, which subsided when the tapping ceased. Was that normal? Perhaps she was being over-dramatic.

Miranda shot her occasional worried glances, and whispered when they had a moment alone, 'I am so sorry. I had not remembered him in this way at all. Perhaps it is competition that brings out the worst in him. When I met him, he seemed a most retiring and polite gentleman. Please forget my suggestion that you might make a couple and let us do our best to get through the afternoon. Do not think that this is your last hope. We will find a different way.'

Esme breathed a sigh of relief. 'Do not trouble yourself about it.'

'But you looked so worried. If he distresses you so, you can move to another table.'

It was Lord Baxter that ought to move, given the fragility of the furniture. But how to offer that suggestion?

Best not at all, Esme thought. 'No, I am fine.' She smiled with more confidence than she felt. 'Let us go back to the game.'

But St John was unable to let the matter rest. After a light refreshment, he convinced Marcus to trade tables and seated himself opposite Miranda, nodding to the two ladies. 'I have convinced my brother to give over your company for the afternoon, dear Miranda.' His eyes twinkled as he said it.

'And Marcus approved?' she asked with a trace of suspicion.

'We discussed it, and thought it was best that there be a change.' His weight shifted ever so slightly in Esme's direction. 'It is better not to let tables become too unmatched. I am too weak for the play over there. Marcus has far more skill at cards then I. He suggested that you partner me, although I must admit that I have not the patience for whist.'

Esme waited to see if lightning would strike, or the ground would open and swallow them, for all the outrageous comments passed as fact in an effort to gull Baxter into enjoying the foursome. She was tempted to point out that St John was an excellent card player. She had seen it herself. And he had professed a great love for this particular game. But then she remembered that they'd had no such discussion during their one evening of family play. It had been one of their nights together when he'd shared the information, so she could not possibly know it.

Lord Baxter was looking in frustration at the table of experienced players where he felt he belonged. Then he glared at St John. 'A man who cannot handle his cards is not much of a man, in my opinion.'

Esme noticed a steely glint in St John's eye at the insult, and watched it fade to innocuous good humour, when his lordship slapped the table top with his hand.

'Unlucky at cards, lucky at love,' countered St John. 'May fortune favour you in the next hand.'

'I fear we shall need it,' muttered Esme, trying not to smile.

'Ehhh?'

'Nothing, sir. I was merely seconding Captain Radwell's wish.'

St John dealt a hand and proceeded to play so ineptly that even Esme could best him. And when she won he congratulated her with excessive courtesy. She wondered if it would still be considered ungentlemanly to cheat at cards, when one were deliberately losing?

But apparently the Earl did not care from what source his win came. He stomped his feet and pounded the table in glee as he took the winning trick.

The table gave a decided lurch to the left and Esme braced it with her knee, amazed that no one else seemed to notice, although she suspected St John's smile as he lost had nothing to do with the game. And his eyes danced with mirth as he suggested another rubber.

Lord Baxter grinned like a predator. 'You don't know when to let well enough alone, do you, boy? Best leave the field, if you cannot handle the play.' He paused as if changing the subject. 'I understand you are just back from the Peninsula. Has the war ended, then?'

St John was silent for a moment, and Esme stifled her own desire to comment. But to have a woman answer for him as Baxter taunted him as a coward would only make things worse. She held her breath, waiting for the response.

St John blinked, and said with innocence, 'No. The war is most decidedly not over, at least not for those of us who have actually seen battle. But I have faith that the gentlemen still serving there can settle Boney without my help.' And then he said quietly, but in a tone that could not be disobeyed, 'Deal the cards, sir.'

Baxter stiffened and he dealt quickly, turning his attention to his hand.

Play began in earnest. St John raised his eyes from his cards and looked to Miranda and she smiled back. They were in communion as they took trick after trick. Esme felt a surge of jealousy, for it was clear that speech was unnecessary for them to be in harmony. She found herself wondering what had happened in the past that made them so sure of each other now, since Miranda played almost as well with St John as she did her husband.

Esme glanced to her own partner. He played as if he did not know she was there, and yet berated her each time they lost a point, slapping his palm upon the table for emphasis. He was boorish and horrible and all the things she wished not to see at breakfast every morning for the rest of her life. And she slid her leg away from its bracing position against the leg of the table and resigned herself to the inevitable.

It was clear that they would lose, and St John grew more courteous and pleasant, even as Lord Baxter grew more irate.

And, as Miranda reached to take the final trick to win the rubber, Baxter's hand came down upon the table and it collapsed, spilling cards in all directions and landing the contents of Baxter's wineglass into his own lap.

'I…I…I…' Baxter looked in horror at the ravages of the game.

Miranda raised her hand and servants appeared and spirited away the mess on the floor. She looked up at Baxter and said, with a brittle smile, 'That was most edifying.'

'Best two out of three?' St John asked.

And Esme kicked him smartly in the shin, not caring that there was no table to cover the action.

That night she came down to the library as she had for the previous three, to find St John in his usual chair in front of the fire, a book lying neglected on the floor beside him.

He rolled his eyes at her and picked up the book, trying to make it appear to her that she was an interruption. 'I had hoped, after last night, you would have sense enough not to come. It is too great a risk for you to meet with me.'

She sat down on a chair near the couch. 'Perhaps I am not here for you at all, and only came to the library to look for a book. That is a harmless enough impulse, is it not? And I am successful in my quest, for there are many books here, including the one you have chosen. What is it, please?'

He rubbed a hand over his face. 'I have no idea. I picked it at random and have read no further than the first page.'

'Well, then, I shall certainly not choose that one.' She stared at him in appraisal. He looked even more tired than he had the previous evening.

He sighed and said, 'My eyes can barely focus on the words, and yet when I close them, I do not sleep. This must end soon, or I shall.'

'Then do not waste breath trying to send me away. You cannot lose me so easily, St John. While I know you still suffer, I will not leave you. Do you wish me to read to you?'

He closed his eyes and shook his head.

'Well, is there some other way you might like to pass the time?'

He opened his eyes again, staring at her in disbelief, but said nothing.

'I would suggest cards,' said Esme, 'but I think I have had quite enough of them for one day. I have never been so mortified in my life. What you did to Lord Baxter was most unfair.'

St John drew himself up to sit straighter on the

couch. 'On the contrary, what he was doing to you was most unfair. I observed you from across the room. You appeared to be most uncomfortable, and there was that great oaf, hounding you over missing tricks.'

'It was nothing,' she insisted.

'To you, perhaps. But I cannot abide those men that treat cards as though they were life and death, but talk of battle as though it were a card game. And bullying a woman over a game? He was beyond insulting. At one time, I'd have called a man out over less than that. If I thought that I could puncture him with a sword and let out some of his ill humour today, I'd have seriously considered it.'

He smiled at her. 'But the method I chose was better. If the man insisted on making an ass of himself with his boorish behaviour, he needed the barest nudge from me to do so in a way that everyone could enjoy.'

'You made it quite impossible for him to court me in the future,' she said. 'He would never dare show his face here, after the scene this afternoon.'

St John snorted. 'As if you would wish him to. Do not tell me you harboured a deep-seated affection for the man, based on the way he criticised your card play.'

She frowned. 'What I might wish for is not the point, St John. He might be the last hope for me, here in Devon. In my current situation, I cannot afford to be too selective.'

'Well, be more selective than that. I do not care if he is the last man in Devon, or the last man on earth, Esme.

You should not tie yourself to him. Better to go back to the old man your father has selected. He will at least have the decency to die soon, and leave you a widow. But Baxter was most robust as he pounded on the furniture. I think we could count on him being a healthy boor for several more decades. He was not for you.'

She stalked to the window and stared out over the darkened garden. 'You don't understand at all, St John. It should have been my right to make that decision, not yours. I could have managed with Baxter, given the chance.'

'And been miserable for the rest of his life, or yours.' St John had come up behind her and laid a brotherly hand upon her arm. 'He was not a good match for you, Esme. You did not suit. You are a treasure, a gift to be cherished. And when you give yourself, it should be to a man who is worthy, not a lout like Baxter.'

She shook off his touch and stared intently into the darkness, willing away the tears of frustration that she felt forming in her eyes. 'For all your experience with them, St John Radwell, you know nothing of what it means to be a woman. You talk as if I may have my choice of any available man, and then you think you can decide for me whom I will choose. You call me treasure, but then suggest I must go home to let my father auction away my gifts without my consent.

'You refuse to see the truth. I am no more special than a hundred other girls. And I am running out of options. If I wish to marry, and live honourably, as you insist I must, then when a man offers for me, any man at all, my answer must be yes, because there may be no second chance. Whether I get any pleasure from my choice is immaterial.'

His voice was sad when he spoke again. 'Very well. Perhaps I do not understand. But if you mean to marry without passion or love, then you should know that there are pleasures still within your control.'

He stepped behind her and wrapped his arms around her body; after a moment's hesitation, she let herself relax into him and be held. She'd have thought it a comforting gesture, if not for the rising heat inside her that proved her reaction to him was not one of solace.

He let his hands rise to her shoulders and trail down her arms to take her hands in his, meshing their fingers together. And then slowly, he led her hands upward to wrap around herself and touch her own shoulders. She could feel the warmth of his body behind her, and his breath against her hair, and the smoothness of her own skin where she was touching herself above the neckline of her nightrail. And then, he was leading her again. Lower, smoothing her hands over her body to cup her own breasts.

She gasped in shock, unsure of what he expected of her, and felt the thrill of the weight in her hands, gasping again as his hands contracted and made her squeeze, gently. Then he was leading her fingertips to her nipples, guiding her until she was massaging in gentle circles.

Her breath quickened as the feelings rippled through her, and she heard his breath quicken as well, and felt the occasional phantom touch of his fingers, still locked between her own.

And then he took one hand and led it down over her belly, pulling her body tight to his. Their fingers were flexing and twisting together and she felt the cool breeze against her skin when the hem of her gown began to rise as he worked with her to bunch the cloth in her hands.

And suddenly, her hand was beneath her gown, and he was stroking with her along the smooth expanse of thigh, up and up, until she reached the place between her own legs.

She tried to pull her hand away, sure for a moment that there must be something very wrong of her to want this, but he was squeezing with her other hand at her breast, and she was absently rolling the nipple between her own fingers. As the warmth spread through her blood, it was hard to care what caused it, or to worry about the right or wrong of it. She only knew that she wanted more of what she was feeling and that St John would show her how to get it. So she relaxed again and let him guide her.

He bore down with the lower hand, and she very quickly discovered things about her own body that she'd either never known, or had done her best to ignore. The slick wetness of it, the secret folds, the way it became more and more sensitive as she stroked.

He was rocking gently with her, and she could hear his breath coming fast behind her, and felt his teeth grazing her neck, then her shoulders. His body was hard against her, and it seemed that she was not the only one enjoying the touches of her own body, that somehow he could feel her pleasure as well as she.

Their hands were pushing harder and deeper against her, swirling and rubbing and stroking, and letting the fingertips delve…

Inside? Yes, inside, oh, yes, definitely there. She was kneading eagerly at her own nipple and she heard his breath in her ear, matching her gasps and felt his lips against her throat.

The feelings rolled through her like building surf and broke suddenly and the newness of it and the shock of pleasure took her and she sagged against him, spent, her legs no longer able to support her.

His arms were around her, keeping her safe. And then he stooped to catch her behind the knees and lifted her in his arms to carry her to the divan. It had been so wonderful that she could hardly speak. But there was more, she was sure, and she wanted it all, and wanted it from St John more than any other man.

He sat beside her where she lay, looking into her eyes and his expression was an amazed sadness. When his lips came down to touch hers, he covered her mouth and she opened it, letting her tongue stroke his. She bit at his lower lip, and was surprised to hear him moan. His hands were rough against her, now pulling her close and stroking her back and her legs, catching her hips and holding them tight. And she followed his example and touched him, feeling the broad shoulders through the linen of his shirt, and the hard muscles of his chest and his back, and the tight, smooth wool of his breeches.

He jerked as if shocked, and pulled away from her, and she reached for him again. But he was murmuring, 'No. No. No.' It was almost a laugh, and almost a groan of pain. She could not tell which. 'No, dearest. Not tonight. Not ever.'

He tried to pull away from her and she clung to him, trying to draw him back.

'No. I cannot, I must not, and I will not.' He was backing towards the door now, shaking his finger and smiling at her. 'You are like absinthe, my dear, like the laudanum. Small and sweet, and intoxicating. I could lose my soul in you. And lose my mind in pleasure and wild fancies without you. Do not tempt me to it, just now when I am trying to be good.'

She rolled to face him, and watched him watch her as her nightdress shifted to reveal her bare breasts in the moonlight. And for a moment, she thought he would come back to her, as he took a step, against his will, to be closer to her.

But then he turned again and grabbed the door handle with conviction, yanking it open and stepping decisively into the hall.

She sighed. 'Well, tell me, at least, that I am helping you to sleep.'

He laughed, bitterly. 'If you only understood. Sleep is the last thing on my mind. And now, Esme, this must end between us. I will play no more games in the night with you. I am too fatigued. I can no longer trust myself in your presence, or fool myself, as I did after last night, that it will be cards and conversation if we meet again unchaperoned. Come to the library tomorrow, if you wish, but you will be here alone.' And he blew her a kiss and closed the door.

Chapter Fourteen

She came down to breakfast the next morning, trying to ignore the thoughts forming in her head, the overwhelming fear that she was out of options, out of ideas, and out of time.

And there was another letter, sitting beside her plate.

She broke the seal with trepidation and read the words quickly, before St John came down to the table and took it from her.

Daughter,
   The time for foolish games and procrastination has ended. We both know that you are not ill, unless one wishes to count sick to death of respecting one's parent. Or perhaps too pained by a decent life to continue in it.
·   *You have spent quite enough time with your fancy new friends to cure a host of imaginary ills.*

*You have four and twenty hours to find your
health, or I will come to Devon and find it for you.*

*I have enclosed passage for you on the mail
coach and will be there to meet it tomorrow evening.*

*If I do not find you there, rest assured that I will
find you wherever you may be. I will drag you
home by the hair if I must, if that is what it takes
to prevent you following in the footsteps of your
mother.*
Your loving Father

She folded the paper quickly and stuck it into the
sleeve of her dress as St John came to sit beside her. He
smiled warmly at her as he helped himself to eggs and
toast. 'Good morning, Esme, and a fine morning it is.'

She stared at him as though he were mad. Fine morning, when she would have to go home? He couldn't
know, of course. But she couldn't very well show him
the letter. It would only make him angry with her father.
And there was a limit to what anyone could do about
her father. 'I suppose it is,' she replied.

He tapped the table next to his plate. 'Seems sturdy
enough.' He picked up his fork.

'St John,' Miranda said in a warning tone.

'I am just being cautious. I have seen evidence that
the nearness of Miss Canville might lead an otherwise
calm man to destroy the furniture. Sitting as close as I
am now, I am merely assuring myself that, should I be

overcome by passion during breakfast, the table can withstand me.'

'Oh, for pity's sake,' Esme snapped. 'Do not quiz me again about yesterday. I have never been so embarrassed in my life.'

He smiled at her. 'And why would you feel any responsibility for what happened to Lord Baxter?'

'Why, you know full well that—' She stopped just short of announcing the truth in front of the family with their morning tea. 'Lord Baxter was there to meet me. This would never have happened if not for my visit.'

'I'm sure he would have done some such thing at another gathering. The only difference would be that you would not have been present to witness it.' He forked up more eggs before saying, 'Where did you find the old goat, Miranda, and whatever made you think he was fit for our Esme?'

'*Our* Esme, is it now?' Miranda cocked her head. 'Very well, then. I chose Lord Baxter as suitable for *our* Esme because of his exemplary behaviour on Sundays at chapel. He seemed most solicitous, if a trifle dull. How was I to know it was the exception and not the rule?'

'Well, good riddance to him. I am glad he revealed his true nature before wasting any more of our time. But I believe Esme has quite run through her first supply of eligible men, Miranda. She is the most spendthrift in courting them. You must find her another.'

'Must I, now?' Miranda pushed away from her own

plate and folded her arms across her chest. 'Let me apprise you of the situation. There are none left to choose from. Any name I can think of is either unsuitable or already on the way to the altar.'

St John gave his full attention to buttering his toast and said, 'Look in London, then. I am sure you will find someone, if you try.'

Miranda spoke with unnecessary clarity, 'If we take her to London, then we will have to return her to her father's house, for there is no way the ruse of her illness will hold. I cannot very well parade her in Vauxhall, while telling her father she is too ill to leave her bed.'

'You will think of something, dear sister, for you are prodigiously clever. I have the greatest confidence in you.'

Miranda's eyes narrowed. 'If all it takes is cleverness, then perhaps you could apply yourself to the task. Surely you know of someone suitable. Perhaps someone who has already met her and who seems to greatly enjoy her company. Someone who at three and thirty needs to settle down, and find a wife.'

St John stared at his plate, refusing to look at her, and said slowly, 'I know of no one suitable. Would that I did. But I do not. I say this because I hold Miss Canville in the highest esteem. I wish that it were otherwise, that there was some way I could help in this. But it is quite impossible.'

'Would you both please stop talking around me as though I am not present?' Esme snapped. 'I know what you are trying to do, Miranda, and I thank you for it, however misguided it may be. Just as I could see from the beginning that it was hopeless. You knew before we started that those gentlemen would not suit, did you not? And you hoped that, eventually, St John would come round. But we are out of time. And he does not want me. How many times must he say it? I swear I am as tired of hearing it as he is of repeating himself.' The envelope scratched at her arm and she twisted one hand against her sleeve, wringing the fabric nervously. 'Now, if you will excuse me, I think I have had quite enough help from the both of you.' And she turned and exited the room with what dignity she had left.

'Esme.'

She hurried down the corridor toward the back door to the kitchen garden, almost running in an effort to escape the voice behind her.

But his strides were longer than hers, and he was gaining ground. 'Esme. Stop this instant. I wish to speak to you.'

She wiped at the tears in her eyes with her sleeve and heard the paper rustling beneath, a continual reminder of what she must do now that there were no choices left to her.

'And I do not wish to speak to you, St John. Now please leave me in peace.'

'Then you do not need to speak to me, but you need to listen. I will not have you running from the table to cry in the garden over the likes of me. You will at least let me explain. I doubt it will hurt any less, but you must understand my reasons for not offering for you.'

'They are clear enough, for you have told me repeatedly. I am green, I am naïve, I am far too boring for a man as worldly as yourself.'

He laid a finger across her lips. 'Do not put words in my mouth. There is nothing wrong with you, my dear. If, by some miracle, I could be a different man, I would marry you in an instant, and I would want you to be just as you are, strong and clever and more than a match for me.'

'Then you do love me,' she whispered. 'I know you do. And you cannot help but know how I feel about you, for I've taken no pains to hide it.'

He turned away so she could not see his face. 'What I may or may not feel for you or any other woman, and what you think you feel for me, is immaterial to this discussion.'

'That is always the way of things, is it not? What I want, what I need, what I feel, is immaterial. I am a possession to be handed from place to place. Your needs and my father's are of the utmost importance, and when you hurt me, you will salve your conscience with the fact that it was for my own good.'

He wheeled on her. 'When I hurt you, which I most assuredly will, it will not be for want of trying to avoid the fact. I am attempting to make this as painless as possible, for both of us.'

'Then you are failing, St John,' she snapped. 'For I ache at the thought of leaving you.'

'But you are not leaving me, Esme. We will think on it, and in a day or two we will find an answer. You may be heartsick now, but you are alive to feel it, unlike the other women I have loved. And heartache is not a physical malady. You will survive. But you will not trap me into marriage with melodrama.'

'Of course not. When I behave thus, it is giving in to girlish hysterics. You are the only one permitted to wallow in melodrama, while I put on a brave face and go home to my husband.'

'That is the most ridiculous—'

'Show me the scars, St John. The physical wounds that pain you so that you must hide in your room with your laudanum.'

'I am not hiding.'

'Of course you are. The brave war hero, and his unsteady nerves, who allows me to humiliate myself before him, but will not take my love or my body. He would much prefer my pity.'

'You came to me. I did not ask for your pity, or your love.'

'But you are lucky to have it. You need me, St John, whether you admit it or not. To prove to you that you are not the base seducer that you wish people to believe you, or so low and villainous as to be undeserving of a woman's love.'

'Do not think, Miss Canville, that I am some empty vessel, waiting to be filled with your foolish romantic notions. I do not need you, or any other. I am fine as I am.'

'Liar.'

'You do not know me.'

'I do.'

He flinched as the words stung him and said, 'Because you cannot see a mark on my body, that does not mean that I am not marked within.' He strode away from her down the garden path and muttered, 'You cannot know what it was like.'

'Then tell me.'

He sighed and turned back to her, dropping on to a nearby bench. 'You will give me no peace, until you have had it all, will you? Very well. Perhaps the truth will be the best way to shake you off. It goes back to long before the war. Do you understand why I had to go away?'

'There was a falling out between you and the duke.' She looked away delicately.

'I told you more than that, did I not? He sent me away because I would not leave his wife alone. But it goes back even further then that. I was young and foolish and I loved. I can hardly be faulted for it, can I? And I was reckless, as you wish me to be now. I did not want to wait, and talked the girl into a haystack and out of her clothes. Maybe it was too easy. Perhaps she loved me and I was the first. Perhaps she was merely bored and I was one of many.

'But when she found she was with child, she could not find me, and I lost her to a better man.'

'With child?' murmured Esme.

'With child.' His smile was cold. 'My feelings were less than sympathetic to my brother after his first wife died, and he less than sympathetic towards me for being fooled into marrying her when she carried my child. When he married Miranda, I tried and failed to take her from him. I went away and time passed, and I found another love while in Portugal.'

He sighed. 'She was a beauty, that was certain. And innocent in a way that my first love was not. And I was not about to make the same mistake again. I courted her properly and her father respected my suit. In Portugal...' he held his head higher at the thought '...I was the gentleman I never was in England. And I had the love of a great lady. Maria was not just my equal, but my superior in birth. She'd have been a countess, had she been English. She loved me, and thought me heroic, and I tried to live up to her ideals. I worshipped her, and I vowed not to make the mistakes of my youth. I never touched her, I swear. I barely dared to kiss her hand.'

The pain in his eyes was unbearable, and Esme sat beside him and took his hand in hers.

He shook off her touch. 'When we met, there was a proper chaperon, a duenna, present at all times. But to be allowed to spend time in her presence was enough for me. And I swore that after the war was settled, and her country free, I would return for her, and make an honourable offer.

'Her father favoured my suit, even knowing that I was the poor younger brother. He respected me. He trusted me.' St John laughed bitterly. 'It was hard to choose the bigger fool between us. If I'd been the man she thought I was, I'd have insisted that she come away with me. I'd have written to Marcus and begged him to take her and keep her safe until I could come home. But I was too proud to ask for help and too eager to please her father, and I did nothing.

'The war parted us, but I thought her safe, inside the walls of the city. But when the time came to take Badajoz…' His eyes were blank at the memory of it, and his face was a mask of pain and exhaustion.

Esme sat in silence beside him. She ached to do something, anything that would help him, but dared not stop him.

'I tried to get word to her before the siege began, but the French were holding the gates and the letters did not get through. Her family had a place in the country, and she needed to get away before the war came to her. But her father thought it safer to be behind the walls, with the protection of the French, than to be in the country alone and at the mercy of any soldier, English or French, who might happen by.

'It took so long, and so many men died. The walls were almost impenetrable, but finally we broke through.'

This time, when she offered her hand he took it, and held it in a painful grip as he continued the story.

'The men wanted their revenge. There was no controlling what happened, once it started. It was like a madness running through them. They wanted to punish the town for not opening the gates. But it was not the French they punished. It was old men and women and children. It went on for two days, before we officers were able to take control again. And I looked for her all that time. Her house was empty. Burned to the ground. I found her father, wandering mad in the street, but he could tell me nothing.'

St John sat, shaking in the morning air. 'And at last I found her. At the base of the wall. Her servants were weeping over the body. The soldiers had come. Our soldiers. And they'd beaten her father, and burned the house. And taken her.'

There were tears in his eyes.

'And her damned honour would not permit her to live with the shame of it. She thought I could not love her. That I could not forgive things that were no fault of hers. And she'd thrown herself off the wall.

'She was right in one thing. I could not forgive what happened. Not my men, who I could not control. Not myself, for letting it happen. My love of her had been the end of her, just as it had Bethany.'

'It was not your love that killed her,' Esme argued.

'Nor could it save her. In the end, it mattered not whether I was reckless or cautious, respectful or a rogue. They are dead and I am still here. My brother hated me, Maria's father cursed me for an English dog.'

He looked to her, stricken. 'Don't you understand? What can I offer you? What do I have left to give? I have no money. No home. My protection is worthless. I know not what fresh disaster I can bring down upon you, if you continue to pursue me. But I want no part in it. I cannot promise that your future will be happy, or free of pain. But at least I will know that I was not the cause of it, should some harm befall you.'

He looked away on the next words. 'I…I…care about you too much for that.'

'Liar,' she whispered. 'If you truly cared, you would not talk such nonsense. Let me tell you the truth of things, St John. Twice you loved, and twice you lost them. And once they were gone you punished yourself and everyone around you. You behaved so scandalously that your own brother drove you away. You found a new life and a career, only to walk away from it to hide in your rooms, drugged to insensibility.

'And now you are afraid that if you admit you love me, it will all happen again, but that this time you will not survive it. Do not tell me that what you are doing is in my best interests. It is nothing more than an effort on your part to protect your own heart. You think you would rather feel nothing at all than to be hurt again.'

He sat on the bench, shoulders slumped and head hung, refusing to meet her gaze. So she dropped to the ground and knelt at his feet, taking his hands in hers. 'I cannot promise that I will live for ever. No one does. But I seriously doubt that when I die it will be from love of you. I do not care that you have little to offer in the way of security. All I need is your arms about me, and I will be safe enough.'

And yet he said nothing. She waited for the words she longed to hear. Any sign that his resolve was weakening. But she received only silence in return.

She stood up and brushed a fallen leaf from the hem of her gown. 'Very well, then. If you insist on feeling nothing, than I must feel for both of us. Perhaps, when I am gone, you will see things differently. You will have gained little and lost much. And I hope that the next woman you love is more fortunate than I have been.'

He would not look up, but at last he spoke. 'There will be no next woman.'

'Do not be a fool. You had a mistress, and when there is money enough, you will have another. And some day you will decide you want an heir, and for that you will need a wife.' She was too angry at the thought even to cry.

His voice was without emotion. 'Perhaps what you say is true. But you do not understand men any better than I do women. I never said that I would live without the company of women. But I will not have to love them to get what I need from them.'

'Then I am happy that I failed to win you, St John,' she said. 'You are every bit as bad as I have heard. You could give a woman more happiness than I am ever likely to see. But your plan is to use them and give nothing of your heart in return.

'At last I agree with you. Marriage to you would be worse than the union my father has chosen for me. At least if I marry a stranger who wishes only to use my body for his pleasure, I'll have no foolish notion that I am doing it for love.'

As the tears started to fall, she turned and went back to the house.

This time, he did not follow.

Chapter Fifteen

Esme lay in her bed, hopeless of sleep. She had spent too many late nights in the company of St John, followed by sweet dreams of him and long luxurious mornings in bed. And now he expected her to give him up without protest and go back to her old life as though nothing had happened. Her mind might see his reasoning, but her body refused to be denied.

The clock struck eleven and she listened as another minute ticked away, counting out the seconds until tomorrow when she would do what she must and return home. It had been too long already and she could no longer impose upon the hospitality at Haughleigh, or face St John over breakfast, knowing that there was no future in it.

Perhaps Miranda could find another possibility for her in Devon. Perhaps not. But she dare not wait longer and have her father come to fetch her. Suppose he followed through on his threats and dragged her away by force in full view of her friends?

The horror of it overwhelmed her. If he succeeded, it would be bad enough, but if they tried to stop him there would be scandal. To the world, her father would manage to appear the wronged party, an elderly man who was only concerned with the welfare of his daughter. The Radwells' intentions in helping her at all would be suspect. And, as usual, no one would be interested in her version of events or allow her to choose her own future.

So she must accept the fact that her attempt to control her destiny had been an utter failure. She could not, try as she had, bring St John up to scratch to offer marriage or lower him sufficiently to take her as a mistress. He was content to let things stay as they were.

Of course it was all to his advantage, that their relationship was no closer. He professed to enjoy her company, but he wanted to pretend that what was happening between them did not matter, and what she saw when she looked into his eyes meant nothing, which made it all the more unbearable.

Surely he did not look thus at every woman he had dallied with. When they were in the garden, he had opened his heart before her. He had even wept. And he had almost confessed the depth of his feelings, but in the end he would not even allow her the consolation of hearing the words.

Very well. She would leave him, if that was what he

wanted. But she would not go before taking from him all that he could give. St John owed her that at least, if he expected her to go home and marry Halverston. If there was to be no love in the marital act? She swallowed her fear. Then she must learn to use others as they wished to use her.

He had said he would not be in the library. Then he would be staying in a place he did not think she would dare to come. A decent young woman should not even know the location of a gentleman's bedroom because she would have no reason to visit it.

Esme had been filled with trepidation when she'd asked directions from the maid who cared for her room. Suppose the girl gossiped?

What did it matter? Tomorrow she must leave for London and would never see the house or its staff again. She had given the girl one sovereign for the information and another one to hold her tongue. And then she had crawled under the covers to wait until the house was asleep.

She swung her feet out of the bed and stood, afraid now that the moment had come. And then she untied the bodice of her nightrail and let it fall to the floor. She picked up her dressing gown and wrapped it tight around her. As the silk touched her naked skin it woke her body, and she felt the heat rising within her. The fear subsided, replaced by desire.

She took no light when she left her room, and walked silently down the corridor toward the wing on the other side of the house where she knew that there was one member of the family still awake. When she arrived at St John's room, she rested her ear against the door, listening for sounds within. All was quiet, but she could see a sliver of light under the door that showed candles were still lit.

She took a deep breath to renew her courage, grabbed hold of the door handle, turned, entered, and shut it quickly behind her.

At the sound of the opening door, St John had risen from his chair, tipping over the table next to him that held brandy and a book. He was in his own dressing gown, ready for bed, although she doubted he expected to sleep. His posture as he turned to face her was of a man ready to repel attack. But then he recognised her. She saw the joy on his face erased by pain and sadness and bone-deep fatigue. Without realizing it, he'd taken a step to be nearer to her, but then he got control of himself and stopped before coming closer.

'Go back to your room, Esme.'

'No. I will not let you send me away again. I know what I want, St John.' She held his gaze and reached behind her, turning the key in the lock of his door. 'Do not deny me.'

'But I must. You are mad to want it. And you must stop before it is too late. If you go now, no one need ever hear of this. But if I do as you ask, someone will find out, and there will be hell to pay for both of us. Go away, Esme, with your honour still intact.'

She reached for the knot of her dressing gown and undid it, letting the robe fall open and drop from her shoulders and to the floor.

'No.' But his voice shook as he said it, and he was looking at her, all of her, standing bare in front of him. There was hunger in his eyes.

She could feel the beating of her own heart, as she waited for him to respond. It seemed forever before he moved, although she could hear his breathing, deep and unsteady as if he had run a great distance to stand before her and look at her body.

Then he closed the gap between them, snatched her dressing gown from the floor, seized her shoulder and turned her roughly towards the door to push her from the room.

She heard the gown slip from his fingers and the gasp as he saw her back.

Esme turned and reached for the robe, picking it up and wrapping it about her to cover the scars. 'There. You have seen. I'd hoped to hide them in darkness, or that it would not matter. It is not as if they show when I am clothed. They are low enough on my shoulders that no one need see, even in a ball gown. Miranda has assured me it is so. But if you can do nothing else, tell me truthfully, will it change things when my first lover sees my back?'

St John reached for her, and smoothed the robe down off her shoulders again, and she could feel his breath on her bare skin, as his hands followed the tracery of scars on her back and shoulders. His voice was ice. 'Who did this to you?'

'My father. It was the day my mother ran away. He came back from riding, and the crop was still in his hand when he discovered the note. He was so very angry, angrier than I'd ever seen him, and I asked him what the matter was.

'And he told me that my mother was a dirty whore, and that I would be no better, if I did not learn.' She closed her eyes, and could still hear the sound of the crop, cutting the air, and the lines of pain lancing across her back as it made contact with the flesh. 'When he was done, I ran to the attic and hid. It took several hours for the servants to find me. My governess was afraid of him, and did nothing. But she held my hands as the maids cleaned the wounds. They told me that the scarring might have been less if they'd tended to me sooner, but the blood had dried and my dress was stuck to the wounds. The cleaning and dressing hurt almost as much as the whipping.' She smiled sourly to herself. 'He learned, after that, to do things that did not leave a mark. An open hand may leave a bruise, but it heals quickly enough. A blow from a cane hurts, but it does not break the skin. And a fist does not need to strike hard to make the intent clear.'

'I will kill him.'

She shook her head. 'You will not. Because I do not see what good it would do either of us, at this late date, to have him dead and you in prison for it.'

He pulled her close to him, and wrapped his arms around her, cradling her against him, and she could feel the places where his own robe gaped and his skin touched hers. 'But I am afraid,' she said softly, 'that any man who sees the scars might think…' she swallowed hard and forced the words out '…that I must have done something to deserve the beating. I've heard it said, when a woman lies with a man the first time, that it is difficult. There will be pain, I know that. It cannot be helped. But perhaps, if there was a chance, if the man believed I was innocent…

'But if he has bought and paid for something without flaw, only to find it marked and spoiled…' She finished helplessly, 'There is nothing I can do.'

'There will be no pain.' His voice was a raw whisper in her ear. 'It is the breaking of the maidenhead you fear, and that happens but once. I will do that for you, but nothing else. Do not fool yourself into thinking that what we are about to do means more than that. I cannot marry you, Esme. And I will not offer you less than that. When the time comes, give yourself pleasure before your husband comes to you, so that you are relaxed and ready for him. Then let him do what he wants and trick him with a drop of blood on the sheets and a maidenly protestation of discomfort and fear. We men are easily gulled when we are aroused.' He reached to untie his own robe, and it dropped to the floor with hers, and she could feel the cold air on her skin, and warmth where he touched her, and his sex thick and hard, pressing against her from behind.

He turned her to him, and his lips found hers, his hands tangling in her hair. Her lips parted eagerly, and she sucked his tongue into her mouth, letting him thrust gently with it, before his mouth slid lower.

'You have nothing to fear, Esme. You are innocent. Soft and beautiful and perfect.' He took a nipple into his mouth, running his hands over her breasts and her belly, tracing the curves of her, and stroking over the scars on her back as if wiping away the memory of them.

Her breasts seemed to swell and grow hard, even as the rest of her felt soft and liquid and he was walking slowly forwards, taking her with him, backing her up until her knees hit the bed behind her. He pushed her gently down and she collapsed backward. Then he spread her legs and knelt on the floor between them, sliding his hands underneath her and pulling her body close to meet his mouth.

She bit her lip against the pleasure, trying to remember to brace for the pain that would soon come. But there was nothing but the moment, and the feel of his tongue exploring her, and the growing tension in her body as it slipped into her, before retreating to find her centre.

And then he'd replaced it with his fingers, thrusting slowly while his mouth worked magic. She clutched the sheet in her hands and hung on as though expecting the world to shake her loose, and his fingers stroked faster, until she thought she could stand no more. Then she lost herself in him, trembling and helpless as he pulled her up to lie on the bed and covered his body with her own.

And he whispered softly, 'One thrust, I swear. That is all you need and all I dare take. And the pain will be over and I will pleasure you again.' And she felt him, hard against her, pausing at the entrance to her body, before pushing inside of her. There was tightness, and a shock as he pushed home. He stopped and let her body adjust to the size of him and the magical feeling of being part of another person.

And then he was pulling away from her. She felt the friction of their bodies, and knew that one thrust was not enough for him to feel what she had felt from him. As he pulled away, she arched up to follow him, raking her nails along his back and pulling his hips back to hers.

He pulled away again, and again she followed, twining her legs around his and locking their bodies together, rocking herself against him until she felt him groan, and knew he was helpless to deny her or himself. She revelled in her ability to control him, even though he was bigger and stronger than she. And then he pushed her hips back down on the bed, and she let him come again and again into her, as her body learned to accommodate him, and she arched against him again, tightened her muscles as if she could keep him with her always instead of just one night. He shuddered and thrust harder, and then one last time, before collapsing into her and against her. And then he rolled off her body and lay beside her. Exhausted.

'Esme.' It was all he said, but he said it with such

wonder, that the one word was enough. He was gazing at her through half-closed eyes, and as she watched he smiled and sighed, and then his eyes drifted shut and she felt his body relax into sleep beside her.

She lay for a moment, watching him sleep, and then looked up into the canopy of the bed, feeling the aches in her body and the strange newness of it.

He would have to marry her now. Despite all his claims of wickedness, his sense of honour ran deep and true. He would not cast her off, now that they had lain together.

The thought gave her no pleasure. To be married to him should make her happier than anything in the world. But to know that he had done it because she had been foolish and selfish, and despite all his protestations that he'd no wish to marry, to know that now he would throw his own life aside and wed her to hide her dishonour?

He was trying so hard to change his reputation, but if he married in haste, there would be talk. Everyone would guess the reason for the wedding and would count the months before the first child was born, sure that it had been conceived on the wrong side of the blanket.

It was unbearable. She was no better for him than the other women he'd loved. His memory of them was clouded with guilt and regret. But they, at least, had had the good sense to die, and would not have to see the look in his eyes that she would see as he spent his life in atonement to her.

She laid her hand upon his shoulder, feeling the hard, smooth muscle of it. It was a good strong arm, and he'd protected her with it for as long as he'd been able.

But now it was her turn to protect him. From himself, if need be.

And she climbed out of her lover's bed and returned to her room to do what was best for both of them.

Chapter Sixteen

Through the linen of the sheet, St John could hear the clock chiming on the mantelpiece of his room. It seemed to go on and on, which was strange.

Ten, eleven, twelve.

That couldn't be. He could see, from the light filtering through the cloth, that it couldn't be midnight. Which would make it…

Noon?

He threw back the covers and stared at the clock. And the reality of the night before came swimming into view.

Esme.

He turned back to check the bed, and realised how ridiculous that must be. He'd known he was alone when he'd awakened, but was at a loss as to how or when it had happened. Had he really taken her last night, despite all his good intentions, common sense, and his oath to his brother?

There was a telltale spot of blood on the sheet next to him.

He ran a hand through his hair and swung his feet out of the bed. He was an idiot. Careless. Foolish. He had only himself to blame for the ruin of the poor girl.

He'd been tired, of course. Pushed beyond reason, and overcome by the girl's willingness and the sight of those scars on her back. And then the feel of her skin against his and the tightness of her body around him, and the way she'd clung to him like a vine. It had been madness to think that he could have taken just a taste of her and been able to stop before satisfying himself. It must have been the exhaustion that let him believe he could control what happened once she lying naked under him.

Which was no excuse this morning. He'd fallen asleep immediately after like some kind of lout, not even making sure that she'd found her way safely back to her room without discovery. Suppose she'd fallen asleep with him? The consequences…

Of course, it had not happened. The fact that he was still breathing was proof enough of that. Marcus would have shot him dead on the spot, not waiting for anything so formal as a challenge.

So the girl had gone back to her bed without his help. And he'd had the first good night's sleep in over a year. Twelve hours, free of drugs, and he was awake and clear headed, with an appetite for lunch. Strangely optimistic, for all the stupidity of the last few hours. And with an obvious plan before him and hope of a bright future.

He would dress and find Esme. He would pull her aside and offer for her, and if it didn't make her happy, then be damned to her feelings. They would be on their way to Scotland and married before lunch tomorrow, and there would be no more of this talk of the *demimonde*, or other appropriate young men, or even her father's objections. If there was a problem later, he would appeal to Marcus to go to Canville and force the issue, in the way only a peer could. The man couldn't be such a fool as to refuse a connection with the Radwell family.

He sighed. It would not be as he'd intended, with a house and a fortune to offer her. There would be none of the safety and stability that she deserved. And the violation of her father's wishes, the breach of promise and sudden elopement, might stretch the patience of the regent beyond the breaking point.

There might be men more deserving of her. There surely were. Men who would never hurt her. Men who could be trusted to care for her better than he could.

But none of that mattered any more. He loved her. He had tried not to, he'd done everything in his power to avoid the fact, but still, he loved her with body and with mind. And so she would have to settle for him. A lifetime with Esme would give him more than enough chance to make it up to her. His heart was pounding with happiness at the thought of it.

He called for his valet and dressed hurriedly, trying not to smile back at the rumpled sheets. If Toby guessed the truth and had anything to say in the matter, he was wise enough to hold his tongue. Then St John raced down the steps to the dining room, in time to catch the footman who was clearing his unused plate.

'A little late this morning, St John? Or should I say afternoon?' Marcus tossed his napkin aside and pushed his own empty plate away.

'I was asleep.' St John said.

'I gathered. And you did not resort to…' He paused significantly.

'No. No, I didn't. The worst is over, I think. And I did not stir, once.'

Miranda was pretending not to know the meaning of the conversation, but he could see the obvious relief in the set of her back. 'We had hoped as much. Your valet was unable to rouse you, and Esme said that we should not trouble you. But she has left you a letter.'

'Letter? Whatever for?' He glanced around the table, suddenly aware that there was no sign of recent clearing away at Esme's usual place. The linen was free of crumbs, without so much as a wrinkle to show use. 'What she has to say to me couldn't wait until afternoon?'

'You don't know?' Miranda looked disgusted.

'Apparently not. Or I would not be inclined to say, "Know what?" Where is Esme and why is she writing me notes for lunch?'

Miranda looked puzzled. 'She said it was all settled between you. And that this was for the best. That you

would agree, which I thought was rather harsh of you.'
Miranda shot him another disapproving glance. 'Even
if it is true. While I am happy for your recovery from
your difficulties, it would have been nice of you to at
least say goodbye, knowing as you did her tender feelings for you.'

'Say goodbye? Why would I have to say goodbye?'

Miranda was staring at him as if he'd gone mad, and
even Marcus was looking at him as though he was some
kind of idiot. His voice rose, despite his efforts to maintain his new-found calm. 'Dammit, woman, where is my
Esme?'

'Your Esme, as you've decided to think of her now
that she is gone, has returned to her father's house, as
you have been encouraging her to do for weeks.' Miranda slapped an envelope down on the table in front
of him. 'She left you this. And now, if you will excuse
me, I'll leave you with a cold luncheon and what I hope
are regrets.' Miranda swept out of the room on an icy
cloud.

St John felt the growing dread as he looked at the letter in front of him, and his hands trembled as he seized
the fish knife beside his plate and slit the seal.

Dearest St John,

*For that is always how I will think of you. You
are dearer to me than anyone and always will be,
whether you would or no. And despite what you
may claim, you have been my truest friend, and*

my love, and the only man in my life who has meant me no harm and has always tried to put my needs ahead of his own.

Despite your protestations, and your own lack of faith in yourself, you are the strongest, and bravest man I've ever met, and you've taught me to be strong and brave as well.

And now, I must make hard decisions, and do what I hope will ultimately be best for both of us.

When I came to you on that night that seems so long ago, I thought I had no options, and no chance for happiness. I've come, with your help, to believe that this is not true.

I know I can't marry any of the men that I've met while here, no matter how honest they may be or how appropriate you may think them. And it is not because of what happened last night. Do not trouble yourself on that account.

The plain truth is: I do not love them. If they are honest and good, then they do not deserve a wife who cannot come to them with her virtue intact and her heart empty of love for another.

I love you, St John. Even if you do not want to read the words, you know that they are true. And now you are telling yourself that you took advantage of that last night.

Do not be such a ninny. It is most unattractive in you, and I will not hear it. If a woman waits until your mind is addled with fatigue and comes naked to your bedroom, refuses to leave, and clings to you, even as you try to pull away, than it is vanity on your part to claim any credit for the seduction.

You told me again last night that I was not to expect marriage, or come crying to you for my lost virtue, after I'd carelessly thrown it away. And I do not and will not, for I have no regrets for what happened between us. This morning, I feel stronger than I have ever felt before, and at last see a way forward that might lead in time to happiness.

I am going home, St John, to my father and the marriage that he has arranged for me. My new husband may be everything I suspect. But as you have often pointed out, a married woman enjoys freedoms that a girl does not. Even at the worst, it will be better than remaining unmarried and in my father's house.

And as you have also pointed out to me, he is old. And rich as well. It looks quite horrible, as I write this, but marriage to the earl will not be a life sentence on my part.

I had thought, when I came to you, that a few years was the same as for ever. But now I believe that, if you are happy, as you have made me, one night can be for ever, and years of hardship will pale to scant moments when compared to it.

I can't, in good conscience, take a lover after

I've given my hand to the earl. The secret of last night will be difficult enough to keep, although the lies will be a light burden when weighed against the moments that I will treasure in my heart for as long as I live, no matter what may come.

And I will probably be a rich widow in a few short years. I will now ask something so audacious that it will make all my previous behaviour look conventional. But could you wait for me, St John? It is not my place as a woman to ask it, but if there is anything in your heart for me, could you keep it safe until I am free to come to you?

I know it must pain you to let the world think you are marrying for money, and I cannot expect you to think of me if your heart is drawn to another, or to remain faithful to me, in any case. You have wants and needs of your own. But please, St John, please, wait for me, and, if you want me, come to me when I am free.

Whatever the future may bring, and whatever my body may do, I will never give my heart to another man and will always remain,

Your Esme

He stared at the words on the paper, as though he could will them to change.

'Not what you expected?' His brother's voice startled him from his reverie.

'How could I expect this? How could I know?'

'That the girl would leave?' His brother could not contain his sarcasm. 'You idiot. How could you expect anything else? It is what you wanted all along, what you yourself encouraged her to do.'

'No.' He cleared his throat nervously. 'I knew she should go. I just did not expect that it would be so hard to let her leave. If she had given me one more day, I would have offered…'

Marcus sighed. 'If she had given you one more day, then you would have wasted it as you have wasted all the others. Sunset would have come and you would have had some excuse to put it off until tomorrow, and tomorrow after that.'

'No.' His own voice was sharp. Too loud in his own ears. 'Today would have been different. Everything is different, now.'

'Don't be a fool. Of course it isn't.'

He looked up, and his brother met his gaze.

Marcus sucked in his breath. 'Dear God. Tell me you didn't do what I suspect you did. Under my roof, while the girl was in my care. Tell me you did not break your promise to me.'

St John looked at the plate before him and the food held no appeal. 'I can tell you whatever you wish, but I had hoped to try the truth for a change. Last night— it is as bad as you suspect. Perhaps worse. I have nothing to say in my own defence except that I tried to avoid it. And when it happened, it was for love and not mere conquest. And then I fell asleep. If the girl were standing before us now, I would offer for her in a heartbeat.'

'But she is not. She has gone back to London, to the man her father has chosen for her.'

St John felt his throat tighten. Wealth and position. It was not the first time that a woman had chosen them rather than him.

He could offer her love, of course, but she must have realised what it would mean to be the wife of a pensioned soldier. And now, of all times, after weeks of wheeling and conniving and trying to break his will on the matter of marriage, she was being practical and taking him at his word. Now that she'd won, and got what she wanted from him, she'd decided she wanted the money as well. And she was offering to keep him, once she was rid of her troublesome husband.

His fist closed on the letter, and he crushed the sweet words in his hand. 'Very well, then. She is probably right in any case. I cannot ask her to live on love, and I certainly cannot compete with the match her father has arranged.'

Marcus snorted in disgust. 'Coward. You could go to her now, and she would come away with you. So all your talk of love and offers was nonsense.'

He sneered back at Marcus. 'And I suppose you would allow me to live off you, with a wife and children in the bargain?'

'I could afford it, you know.' Marcus considered.

St John shook his head. 'But I could not. Allow me

some pride, at least, to want to be able to support a wife before taking one.'

'Well, you are right in that. It is easier to manage with an income. Old Halverston can certainly afford the keeping of her, but surely—'

There was a subtle clearing of throat as the butler entered. Marcus looked up, as the man stooped to murmur something. He shot St John a confused look. 'Were you expecting news from London?'

'No. Not really. I—'

'There is a footman, in Prinny's livery, at my door. And looking for you. Before we go out in the hall, do I want to know what you've done and how much it's likely to cost me, or were you going to leave it as a surprise?'

St John shook his head and rose, as if still sleepwalking, to go to greet the servant. And the probable truth of it seeped through to him, leaving him numb with the shock.

The footman was there, bowing stiffly and offering the letter, signed with the royal seal, St John took it, and thanked him, and assured him that there was no reply, but that he would be leaving for London shortly and would wait upon the regent at his convenience.

His hands trembled as he cracked the seal and read the contents of the letter.

'Well, what the devil is going on? Do you mean to keep us all in the dark?' Marcus was shouting at him, and he heard it through the fog in his head. It sounded very much like the Marcus of old, which was pleasantly familiar. He passed the letter to his brother, and sank on to the nearest bench.

'What nonsense is this? Miranda, read these words and tell me that I am going mad. The Earl of Stanton is dead without heir and my little brother has been named successor to the title. For meritorious service to the crown and uncommon bravery in the face of the enemy.'

Miranda snatched the letter from his hand and there was a squeal of delight.

'Am I to call him Stanton, now? Captain was bad enough. But his lordship? There'll be no end to it, I'm sure.' There was a fierce joy in Marcus's words and St John felt a cuff to the head before his brother's arm wrapped around his neck. 'Wake up, Johnny. Do not stand there like an idiot. Your problems are solved. There is pen and paper in the study. Write to Esme and tell her to cry off. Write to her father with a better offer. You are Halverston's equal now in title and land. His superior, if I remember the Stanton entail. If you are serious in your feelings for her, let us take the news to London.'

St John reached into his pocket and withdrew the letter from Esme, smoothing the crumpled paper. He refolded it carefully and tucked it into the pocket over his heart. Title, wealth, reputation, and security. He could lay them all at her feet, along with his heart, and she need never worry again.

'Toby!' he bellowed in a voice that carried through the house. 'Pack my bags. I'm going to London to get a wife.'

Chapter Seventeen

St John stared out over the crowd in the rented rooms that Esme's father had chosen for her betrothal party, searching for any sign of his beloved. Surely even her father would not leave the girl locked in her room for the celebration.

In the week they'd been apart, St John had written her daily, informing her of his intentions. If Esme received his letters at all, she either chose not to answer or was not allowed to. He assumed it was the latter. He had to, or lose his sanity. Surely, after the heartfelt letter she had written him, she could not chose Halverston.

Letters to her from Miranda went unanswered as well. Marcus's correspondence to the father could not be ignored, but it was answered with brevity. The girl was well and most grateful for their help, but she would be needing it no longer.

At last, St John received a similar missive from Canville, denying his suit and informing him that Miss Esme Canville was otherwise betrothed and viewed his attention as harassment. Any further letters from him would be returned unopened and he must cease all attempts at communication, for they were unwelcome.

It pained him to read the words, and they left the continual, nagging fear that they were based in truth, and not merely the ruse of her irate father.

St John's worst fear was that an attempt to visit Esme might only lead to her punishment. He vowed to stay well out of sight of Canville, and had vacated his rooms across the street from the home. Instead, he had taken discreet residence in the Stanton town house, awaiting the formal announcement of his title. It was more luxurious than he'd anticipated, almost as fine as the Haughleigh residence. But despite a full staff it felt empty to St John because it lacked the chance to stare out the window and catch a glimpse of the woman he loved.

Canville had wasted no time, once he had Esme back under his control. Marcus had seen the official announcement in *The Times*, shortly after their arrival in London. The banns had been read once, already. There were but two weeks left before St John lost her to Halverston.

Not lost, he reminded himself. She would be his, in any case. honour be damned, he would haul her from the church on her wedding day if need be and take her away to the continent. Never mind the scandal.

But Marcus had assured him that it would not be necessary. They would gain entrance to the betrothal party, where it would be difficult to put them off without public embarrassment. The duke would intercede with Canville, and St John could explain things to Esme. All would be settled.

St John had his doubts that things could be handled so easily, but admitted it was the best course of action. Canville might slam the door of his home in their face, but it had always amazed him how many other doors opened without question for the Duke of Haughleigh.

St John watched his brother explaining their situation to the hired footman at the door of the hall. The Radwells were friends of the family. Clearly, their invitation had been lost in the post. Such a burden to have to deal with the mistakes of others. But what could one do?

St John tried not to grin and spoil the effect. Marcus was making it up out of whole cloth, and following it all with a look of noble disdain, turning to irritation as the servants hesitated. When he suggested that they get Mr Canville and explain the reason for denying entrance to a peer, the footmen wilted before him. Marcus waved aside their offer to announce him.

They proceeded down the stairs toward the receiving line and St John made to rush forward, only to have Marcus lay a steadying hand on his arm. 'No need to hurry, Johnny. Remember, we are trying not to call attention. The father is at the base of the stairs. Leave him to me. I think it wise that you keep to the far side and avoid the line entirely. Stay out of sight if you can. Your objective is on the dance floor, with her betrothed.' Marcus sniffed. 'The poor girl.'

They stared down at the couple dancing below them. The floor was nearly empty. The guests that showed any interest in the music looked on in disapproval as the guests of honour waltzed before them. Had they no blood left in their veins? Who could find it so terrible that a couple soon to be married might wish to dance in each other's arms?

St John erased the man from the couple below and thought only of the girl. Some day soon, he would have Esme, and then every dance would be a waltz.

The couple turned so that St John could see her face. Dear God, when he was hers he hoped that she did not look thus. She was staring into the eyes of her husband-to-be, and seemed to all the world like a bird trapped by a snake.

St John glanced at the man with her. Every bit as old as she had said. And strangely familiar. The name Halverston was not known to him. But had he met the man? When and where? If it had been during those last months before he'd gone to Portugal, it was quite possible that they were acquainted. He recalled little more about most of that time than the drink and the blue-devils that followed it.

St John searched the man's face, and found it stern, but not unkind. What had he said, to make her so frightened? And why, when he looked at the man, did he feel a chill?

The music had ended, and the earl linked his arm in Esme's, taking her toward the balcony at the end of the room.

St John went down the stairs and pushed his way through the crush, following a distance behind. Esme had been right to be concerned about her future. There was not a face under fifty in the crowd, and most were much older than that. Had she no friends her own age, no confidants to explain her situation? He had hoped all along that it was some girlish exaggeration that had brought her to him. Merely a spirit burning too bright that her father had sought to break with violence.

But it was worse than that. She had known what she must return to, and had thrown herself at him with all her might, seeking all the pleasure she could in their brief time together. To leave Haughleigh must have been like returning to the tomb.

But she needn't worry any more. He would take her from this place tonight and all would be well. He had but to wait until she was alone and spirit her away. If he could catch her eye, signal her in some way…

But her gaze was only for the man beside her. As it should be, only two weeks from the altar. And yet, all wrong. He knew from experience what Esme should look like, if she were in love. If she were happy. The woman before him was blank and empty.

Drugged? Could it be? Or merely frightened? When he talked to her, he would know.

Halverston had taken her on to the balcony and into the moonlight, and other couples gave them a wide berth, allowing the earl to steal a few moments alone with his supposed beloved. The last of the guests came back into the ballroom, and pulled the door shut behind him with a sly smile, leaving Halverston alone with Esme.

There was no way he could step out on the balcony and interrupt, without inciting comment. It would be best to wait. St John stood only a few feet from them, hand pressed against the glass in the door, watching. He had an excellent view of the couple, but was obscured from them by the potted palms that decorated the balcony. He would have ample warning, when they came back toward the door, and could step to the side and accost Esme as they passed.

If he could bear to watch as the earl stood with the woman he loved in the moonlight. It would only be a few more moments he reminded himself. And what was to fear from Halverston, really? The man was old and frail and wanted an heir. He was choosing youth and vigour, and hoping for the best. He was of very little threat to a woman with as much life and strength as Esme. He would be fortunate to lose her, for she would lead him a merry chase should he win her, the poor old fool. St John watched them.

The earl spoke to her, and at first she did not seem

to hear. She stared out over the balcony at the pavement below, seeming lost to the man next to her.

Her lack of attention seemed to annoy him, for he caught her by the shoulders and turned her gently to face him, speaking directly to her.

She was attending, and her eyes went wide with fright, before fading to blankness again.

And the old man pulled her close to him in an embrace. They were caught in profile in the moonlight, youth and age together. The earl spoke urgently into the girl's ear and there was the flare of fear in her eyes again, before she shut them tight, as though if she could not see she would also be unable to hear.

And St John watched as the earl's hand dropped from her shoulder to her hip, first smoothing the fabric of her skirt, then caressing, then urgently kneading the curved flesh, holding her tight against him, so that she could feel him and know what he meant to do with her.

Esme shuddered in revulsion.

And suddenly, he remembered where he'd seen Halverston. It was no common brothel, but the kind of house where a man need not use his right name. Where if he had enough gold to offer, he could indulge his darkest whims without fear of retribution.

And the girls there had been afraid of him.

Blood was pounding in his ears as St John seized the door handle, ready to charge on to the balcony and pitch the man over it, should it prove necessary.

And then strong hands fell upon his shoulders and yanked him back into the room.

'What is the meaning of this?' He made as if to shake them off, but the servants that held him were not to be dissuaded.

'Let me go this instant.' People in the crowd were beginning to notice. And the two burly footmen that held him were hurrying him out a side door.

'Let me go, you bas—'

A fist connected with his gut, and the man still holding him pushed him down the stairs and into the street.

He knelt on the cobbles, struggling to get his wind back, and heard the voice of his brother above him.

'That did not go as well as one might have hoped. But at least I was allowed to walk out on my own two legs, so I shouldn't complain.'

'Rank hath its privileges,' St John gasped.

'Apparently.'

He glared up at his brother, who was staring back at him in bemusement. 'Help me up, your Grace. We need to be going.'

'You have another plan?'

St John nodded. 'Esme will be mine before the week ends. But first, we must go to a brothel.'

St John stared intently at the opposite wall, devoting his full attention to a watercolour of an undraped and attractive female rather than the more shocking scene in front of him. The sight of his brother the duke, relaxing on a red velvet divan and chatting with the madam in a notorious house of ill fame, was disconcerting. Marcus must recognise the sort of place they'd come to, and yet he acted as though this visit was no different than lunch with the vicar.

St John checked himself. The man was two score, and had no doubt visited a brothel at some point in his life. But somehow, he'd never believed that his proper, older brother had tasted of life's vices, preferring to imagine him celibate.

And yet Marcus seemed quite at home, but it was the ladies who were discomfited. There was no small amount of giggling in corners, and pointing, and whispers behind hands about the rank of their new visitor. But when the duke's eyes met theirs, they shrank from him in awe.

He must learn the trick of it, the effortless dominion that Marcus achieved over his surroundings wherever he might be.

He looked back at the girls in the room, who had greeted him with all the warmth and eagerness that he wished to feel from Esme.

The madam gazed from him to his brother with knowing eyes, and refilled their wine glasses. 'If not entertainment, then what have you come for, Johnny? Or am I to call you Captain Radwell, now?'

He cleared his throat, embarrassed at the familiarity of her greeting. 'You will soon be calling me Lord Stanton, although the news is not yet public.'

He was surprised to notice her reaction, as her posture improved and her gaze became less forward.

'But that is neither here nor there for one of such old acquaintance, Annie. I am here seeking information only.'

'You ought to know that nothing in this house is free, your lordship.' She'd dropped easily into using the new title and there was a hint of subservience in her voice.

'If you wish money, name your price. But I think you'll have payment enough when I tell you what I want, and what I mean to do with what you give me. I offer you a chance to settle an old score. Your clients sometimes talk in moments of intimacy, do they not? Lord knows, I often said things I wouldn't care repeated.'

She seemed indignant at the suggestion. 'But we do not share this information. You know us as whores, sir. But that does not mean we are spies or blackmailers.'

He smiled back at her. 'Nor have you been able to use what you've learned to your advantage, I suspect. Whereas, if someone like myself, or perhaps my brother, were to find facts damaging to say, perhaps, the Earl of Halverston—you call him Eddie, when he is here, I believe—we would be able to take the information to the proper authorities.'

'And why the sudden interest in Halverston?' But her eyes were glittering with something other than avarice.

'On my last visit to your establishment, I had the

misfortune to meet him. I heard the cries of the girl he had been with and saw the marks upon her body.'

'It has been five years,' the madam reminded him.

'But I have not forgotten. The change in my status puts me on equal footing with the old lecher. And the reconciliation with my brother puts me slightly ahead. The fact that Halverston is betrothed to a young lady who I hold in esteem—well, that outweighs the first two reasons, for I will gladly tear the black heart from his body before I let him have her. But if there is a way to administer justice quickly, quietly, and legally? All the better. You will lose his custom, of course, but I wager you'll be glad to see it gone.'

She relaxed into the cushions beside the duke and signalled a girl to bring them another bottle of wine. 'You are right in your suspicions. He is like—you will forgive me, your lordship—the French pox. Impossible to get rid of, and growing steadily worse.' She glanced up at the girl holding the wine. 'Please ask Emily to join us.'

They sipped their drinks in silence; and shortly after, a girl entered and sat with head bowed at the end of the couch. She was pale and blonde and St John's stomach rolled as he noticed her marked resemblance to Esme.

Annie announced, 'Gentlemen, this is a favourite of Lord Halverston. Emily, these gentlemen would like your help.'

'Friends of Halverston?' Her eyes darted up to meet theirs, and she looked from one to the other in suspicion and growing anxiety. Her voice was steady as she said, 'Certainly, anything you gentlemen may wish.' But her expression said otherwise.

'You have nothing to fear, my dear. We will not be going upstairs. What we need can be settled in this room, and you will be paid handsomely for your time, if you are truthful.'

She nodded.

'You are intimately acquainted with Halverston?'

Her laugh was bitter. 'There is no one else who is more so, because no one else will have him. I have been assured that I need do nothing else, if I can keep him happy and away from the rest of the girls, and there is a bonus in it for me. When the old bastard dies, and I hope and pray daily that he does so before finishing me, I'll have enough money to start a house of my own, or retire to a more respectable trade.'

St John struggled to control a shudder of revulsion, and he could feel his brother leaning forward in concern for the girl. 'We will take you from here today, if you wish, and give you all the money you need to start anew.'

She looked at them appraisingly. 'That would leave him with no distraction. And who would he turn to then? I might save myself, only to see his tyranny inflicted upon some other poor girl. Gentlemen, do not have a care for me. If you are so great and good, if you have any feelings for the welfare of those such as myself, then kill the monster.'

St John reached a comforting hand to the girl, then, fearing it would be misconstrued, let it fall back into his lap. 'We were hoping you could help us in some way. Has he ever spoken of anything, any wrong done outside this house, that we might use against him?'

She nodded. 'Because no one cares for the wrongs done inside these walls.'

St John flinched at the words, but shook his head. 'If there is nothing else, then I assure you, he will die for this. I will kill him myself. He is too old to call out, and the world will see it as assassination, and not justice. But if there is something that we could make into a public scandal…'

'Then you can be rid of him and remain free of his murder. And I will be rid of him as well.' The smile spread slowly across her face. 'Go to his house, your lordships. There is a drawer in his desk, the contents of which will be most interesting to you. He trades with the French. Many things. Brandy, silks, currency.'

Marcus shook his head. 'Many nobles engage in black-market trade. This is hardly news. Their patriotism wears thin, it seems, when they realise that a protracted war will separate them from French brandy.'

'But there are other secrets that will interest you, your Grace. Years of debauchery have left his estates depleted and it is more expensive to appear rich than to quietly husband what wealth you have. And to feed his appetites here is no small thing. Much of what he wishes to do, when alone and above stairs…' A cloud passed over the girl's face, and she shook her head as if to clear the memories. Then she smiled a cold, brittle smile. 'As with any service, when things are difficult or dangerous, they often cost more. He has squandered his wealth, and now he must find ways to refill the coffers. He is none too particular about how he does it.

'Halverston has friends in the War Office. He is in a position to overhear many things, the names of spies, troop movements. Information that can be slipped to his French contacts, in exchange for money and comforts. And when he finds a man in power who is prone to sins of the flesh, he encourages the perversions and then turns them against the sinner, who must buy his silence with money or secrets.'

St John's lip curled in revulsion. 'A spy for the French. And a blackmailer.'

'Yes,' Emily said. 'And he brags about it to me, knowing that there is no one I can tell. Is it not bad enough that I must give myself to the old lecher, and be used to debase his friends? To know that I am paid for with French gold is even worse. There is a safe in his study, where he keeps papers that he wishes to copy, and the names of his contacts in England and in France. If you have those, you have him.'

'Then we must find a way into his household, to get them. A safe, you say? This will be devilishly difficult.' Marcus was puzzling over the situation, when St John began to smile.

'Difficult for us, perhaps. But I think I know of a solution.' He touched the girl lightly on the arm. 'Emily, we will need to know that the earl is to be away from home, so that we are free to operate. I hesitate to ask…'

She smiled the same hard smile as she had before, and tossed her head. 'If you swear to me that it will mean an end to him. Then you shall hear from me when he is to visit, and I will do whatever is necessary to hold him here.'

He leaned forward and kissed the girl lightly on the head. 'You have my eternal gratitude, Emily.' Even as he said it, he realised how little that was worth. 'And what protection I can offer.'

He could see the calculation in her eye, and the knowing look that passed amongst the girls.

St John cleared his throat. 'I do not know how best to phrase this offer, since I've never done such before…'

There was another flurry of silent communication in the room, and several giggles expressing doubts that he was inexperienced in offering a *carte-blanche*.

'But I wish to take you from this place and offer you a residence. I would be willing to meet all expenses. And in exchange…'

Emily's lips quirked in a knowing smile.

'You would be required to look out of the window.'

The smile slipped from her face and was replaced with confusion.

'And tell me what you see, of course. By letter. It's probably best that I stay as far away as possible. But if you could report on the girl in the room across the street. If you saw her. To know that she's all right. It would mean so much.'

There was a stunned silence from the girls in the room. And Emily repeated, 'You are offering to keep me, your lordship?'

He mumbled, 'Well, not as such…'

'And all you wish is that I look out of a window.'

'And let me know about the girl across the street. You can go today, if you like, to inspect the apartments. They are yours as long as you need them.'

And she laughed. It was the first sincere sound he'd heard in the house since arriving there.

'Would you like more tea, Miss Esme?'

'No. Thank you, Meg. Really. I am fine.'

'Something else, then? A bit more bread, perhaps? Consommé? For dessert, there are some cakes that cook says used to be your favourite.'

Esme pushed the food around on her plate and tried to look satisfied. 'No. I've had enough, really.'

The maid looked worried and whispered. 'You've got to eat more, miss. You're not taking enough to keep a sparrow alive.'

Esme looked up at her helplessly. 'I know. Tomorrow, perhaps. Today, I am not feeling well.'

Meg nodded in sympathy. 'I know just the thing. Herb tea. Some camomile to help you sleep and black haw to ease the discomfort. You'll feel right enough in a day or two. I'll bring it right back.'

Esme watched the girl as she walked to the door of the bedroom and through. She heard the decided click of the lock once Meg was in the hall. There had been a hesitation before the bolt had shot home. She was sure of it. It was Meg's duty to lock the door, 'to keep Esme from any more foolish wandering' as her father had put it. There was some small comfort in knowing that Meg did not enjoy her job.

She stared out the window to the apartment across the street. Empty, or so it appeared. What good it would do her to see him, she did not know. One more glimpse and she wouldn't be able to carry through with what needed doing, if she was ever to get out of this bedroom. She must walk down the aisle free of tears and hesitation, and to go to her new husband willingly.

She must force herself to think of Halverston thus. Husband. Even fortified with several glasses of wine, she could hardly bear his touch on the dance floor. And then he had taken her out on to the balcony and confirmed her worst fears. He had whispered poison into her ears as his hands had strayed over her body, with the party guests only a few feet away.

Halverston would die soon, she assured herself. And she would be free of him, and her father.

But it would be better if she did not see St John until after the deed was done, and she had become used to her new life.

She looked across the street at the empty rooms. If he was not in the room across the street, he must be staying in the apartments of his mistress. The thought sickened her.

And she scolded herself for her missish sensibilities. He would have other women. She was sure of it. She should take comfort in the fact that he cared enough for her feelings not to flaunt the other women under her very balcony. If he could wait the few weeks until she was married and out of this house, before staging any more public scenes, that would have to be enough.

It was foolish of her to hope that he would return to his rooms alone, pining to be near her. Foolish to be thinking of him at all. He had promised her nothing, other than to help her avoid pain. And she had given herself to him, so the chase was over. His interest was probably waning with each passing day. It had been idiotic to write him the letter, and she had no doubt proven herself to be the green girl he had accused her of being. He had never claimed to be anything other than a rogue. And such a man as that did not spare feelings for the girls he'd dishonoured. They did as they pleased and be damned to everyone else.

She had hoped that she might be increasing, which would solve some problems, but create others. She could merely have announced it to her betrothed before the wedding, and marriage would have been impossible. But there was a chance that her father would have beaten her, if he found out, and it would not have been good for the baby. Still, she would have had a bit of St John with her, and that would be something.

And then she could have gone to him, with an heir in her belly and he would have had to…

No. She squeezed her eyes tight against the fantasy. That dream was just as likely to end with a look of disgust on his face at being saddled with the expense of a bastard. He could not afford a wife. What would he want with a child? And suppose he married her and their union was marked with coldness and bitterness because she had trapped him into it?

But that point had been moot. She was not now or ever likely to carry St John's child, and the aching misery inside her could not be cured with black haw tea.

A light flickered in the window across the street and, unable to help herself, she snuffed the candles in her room, plunging it into darkness, and stepped out on to her balcony in the chill night air and crouched behind the balustrade, hoping to catch a glimpse of the man she loved.

A footman was lighting tapers in the room she knew from her single visit to be the sitting room. He was pulling back Holland covers and hurriedly laying a fire. She looked closer.

It was the man that St John had called Toby. If his servants were there, then the rooms were still his. The wind brushed lightly against the hair on her bare arms and she felt a shiver of excitement.

The door to the room opened and she held her breath.

A girl entered. Not much older than herself. And alone. Her dress was satin and had been fine once, if a trifle gaudy. It had the appearance of long use and it fit her ill.

She looked hesitantly around the room, unsure of her new surroundings. She stroked the crystal decanter that rested on the tray next to the table and poured herself a glass of what appeared to be sherry. Then she settled down on the couch, drawing her legs up under her. She sipped the wine and smiled.

It was a look of total and almost sexual satisfaction. The look of someone who had seen harsher times, but was content with her present circumstances.

Esme felt the panic rising in her, and hurried back into her room.

Her worst fears were manifest. St John had found another.

Chapter Eighteen

Anthony de Portnay Smythe lounged in the back of a rather unsavory pub in an even more unsavoury inn of London, enjoying a mediocre whisky. Its flavour was rendered much more subtle by the knowledge that he had purchased it with ill-gotten gains.

His fence was examining the sack of jewels collected from the latest week's work. A gold signet from a rather repellent young marquis. A diamond necklace and matching earbobs from a dowager with a penchant for gossip and gin, and a set of emerald studs from a barrister in Kent who had been more successful at the gaming tables than in court. The last had been devilishly tricky to get, since the only open window to the house was on the third floor.

'Fifty quid.' Edgar the fence was being difficult again, but Tony was having none of it.

'They're worth a hundred.'

'And I'm giving you fifty. The signet's got to be

melted down. It's worth nothing as a ring with that crest on it. Any fool will know where it came from.'

'But the gold is good. And it's heavy.' Tony stroked the necklace beside it. 'And look at those stones. They're worth ninety, all by themselves.'

'If I could sell them.' Edgar pointed to the emeralds. 'One of the studs is missing. Sixty.'

'I was in a hurry. I fell out of the damn window getting back. No time to count them. Seventy-five.'

'Done.' Edgar scooped the jewels off the table and into his pocket, and dropped the money on the table without counting it.

Tony sorted through the coins. The money had been counted out before they'd started to argue. That old bastard. Edgar had known they'd end at seventy five, but he'd haggled anyway.

It was embarrassing to be so predictable.

Edgar moved away, and they studiously ignored each other as though the meeting had never taken place. There were similar people performing similar transactions at nearby tables, and Tony ignored them as well, preparing to drink the rest of his whisky in peace.

Tony enjoyed his visits to the Blade and Scabbard. It was the only place in London he knew where a man was guaranteed absolute privacy, no matter the size of the crowd. Since no one wished to be seen there, one did one's fellow patrons the courtesy of not seeing them. Despite the busy tables around him, Tony might as well have been drinking alone in his rooms.

A shadow fell across the table. And there was a scrape of chairs as two men drew seats on either side of him and the illusion was shattered.

'Good day, Smythe.' St John Radwell on one side and his brother the duke on the other. Tony allowed himself to feel alarm, but took care not to let it register on his face. The jig was most decidedly up.

'Good day? I suppose. I hadn't really noticed. Not much for the daylight hours, myself. Well, gentlemen, it's been charming. Now, if you'll excuse me.' He gave them a cheerful smile and rose to go.

There was a hand on each shoulder, pressing him firmly back into his chair. His body met the wood with more force than was necessary. St John Radwell smiled back at him. 'Not just yet, I think. First we must have a little chat.'

'Well, we seem to have covered the weather. And that leaves me…' Tony considered '…nothing to say for myself. Not a thing.'

The duke's voice was a gruff rumble, with no trace of his brother's false warmth. 'If that was meant to excuse your stealing my wife's earrings, it was sorely inadequate.'

'No. An excuse would be something more like, "I did not know that they belonged to your wife when I took them", or "it was one earring, and not a pair", or "your brother stopped me, so really it was nothing at all."' Tony continued to smile and spread his empty hands to prove that he was no threat. If they meant to do him harm, then they must live with the fact that he was an unarmed man, and the devil take them for their brutality.

'I fail to see where attempted robbery in my house can be construed as nothing at all.' His attempt at levity was wasted on the duke, who gave no indication of possessing a sense of humour.

'Frankly, robbery is a bit out of my line as well. Burglary,' Tony corrected. 'That's the ticket, gentlemen. Burglary. I prefer that the owners of the swag not be present when I collect from them. Most times, the people I take from can spare the loss and deserve the theft. Miss Canville had done nothing to me, but I was sorely in need that night and meant to make do with the one jewel. If it's any consolation, it would have troubled my conscience had I succeeded and caused her distress. And I would have found a way to pay her back, when I was able.'

'Well, that makes it all better, then.' It was St John, speaking again, and his voice dripped sarcasm. Of course, Radwell had wanted to plant him a facer just for dancing with the girl. Stealing the earring had given him a better reason.

Tony took a moment to regret the whole evening at Haughleigh as a mistake, and then said, 'Well, is it off to the Runners, then? Or into the alley to teach me a lesson? Since I never took anything from you, an apology is all I can offer in reparation.'

'Not quite.' St John was now grinning at him in a

most unpleasant way, and Tony remembered his threat. Perhaps a simple beating was not what they had in mind. To end the evening bleeding his last in a ditch somewhere was definitely not part of his plans.

He looked pointedly at Radwell, hoping to jog his memory. 'You said that we were quits if I left Haugh-leigh and the girl. And I have. I've stayed far away from both. On my…' he paused '…too late to swear on my honour. Upon my soul. I still have one, not that it's worth much to you.'

Radwell smiled. 'That is true. You have followed my instructions to the letter. But it appears that you have not reformed your character. My brother and I cannot very well look the other way, after seeing you trading in stolen goods tonight.'

'Of course you can,' Tony retorted. 'It is no business of yours. And frankly, gentlemen…' He looked around the room at the ragged band of cut-purses and criminals seated at the other tables '…it is in the best interest of your health to leave this place quickly and forget you saw me here.'

Radwell glanced around the room and snorted. 'If I be-lieved that the men assembled in this room were capable of fighting as a unit, I might, just might, be concerned. But you know as well as I that they will scatter when the first body hits the floor. Their concern will be for their own necks, not yours. There is not a thing I can do to you, in plain sight of your fellows, that will incite comment or notice. And if I leave money on the table for the barmen, I won't even have to clean up the mess afterward.'

Tony let the words sink in. The body on the floor would be his and no one would care. He was alone and there were two of them.

It had always been so peaceful at the Blade and Scabbard. He had but to mind his own business and he could enjoy a quiet drink. And now Radwell and his brother had spoilt the ambiance.

He sighed. 'Very well, gentlemen. Do what you will. But if possible, leave me the strength to get home and enough money for a cab.' He closed his eyes and waited for the first blow.

'We are not here to administer punishment.' The duke was almost formal in his pronouncement and the new tone was less menacing than that of his brother. It was most pleasant to hear the voice of someone who did not particularly want to kill him because he'd flirted with Esme Canville. 'Get on with your suggestion, St John.'

Tony opened his eyes. Radwell was looking at him with cool speculation. 'I've seen your skills at pickpocketing and sleight of hand. You took that earring, and Esme never felt it. Those talents will probably not be needed, although stealing the thing in the middle of a crowded ball bespeaks impressively steady nerves. And I've heard you, just now, talking about climbing in windows, so you must not be afraid of heights. Also useful.

'But how are you at opening safes?'

Dear God. To even admit such was folly. It had to be some sort of trap. If not, what were these men planning? Tony proceeded with caution. 'It depends upon the lock. There are picks that will open most locks, if the user has skill with them. But if it is a Bramah lock, then nothing will work. They are said to be unpickable.'

'Then for your sake, I hope you have both the picks and the talent to use them. And that we are not dealing with this Bramah lock. Or that rumours are not true.'

They wanted him to open a safe. He stalled. 'Well, some time spent in observation of the premises will establish—'

The duke said, 'We have done all the observation that is necessary.'

Tony sighed. 'I meant observation by me.'

Radwell went on as if nothing had been said. 'A young lady of his acquaintance assures us the owner will be gone tonight until well after midnight. The safe is on the wall behind the desk. The servants do not appear to care overly about their master's well being, so detection is unlikely. They were stealing his brandy in clear sight of the windows, when we left.' Radwell grinned at him. 'As they say, there is no time like the present.'

'This is easy for you to say, since you will not be the one taking the risks.'

Radwell sneered. 'Nor are you, since we will be there to haul your miserable carcass out of danger, should a problem arise. The young woman distracting the earl is the only one hazarding her life this evening, and she assures us that she is up to the task, as long as we can finish the job tonight and arrange for her safe departure from her current place of employment.'

Which was all cryptic enough, so Tony ignored it. 'And what assurance do I have that you will be there waiting for me, should something go wrong?'

'You have our words,' the duke proclaimed, as though this should be enough.

'And if I do not help you?'

'Then you know what I will do to you.' Radwell looked almost gleeful at the prospect.

'Which shows me what your word is worth, since you promised once before to do nothing.'

Radwell shrugged. 'My word is not worth so much as my brother's. And desperate times breed desperate measures. Let us sweeten the pot. If you do not help us, you will have more trouble than you can ever imagine. But if you do, you have your freedom, our gratitude and the contents of my purse.'

Tony rolled his eyes. 'And I'll wager your purse is empty. I am not so green as all that. Try again.'

'The contents of my purse, then.' And the duke tossed a bag out on the table where it landed with a resounding clunk.

Tony undid the string and poured out the money inside. He would not have to work for a very long time. And the temptation of house-breaking and lock-picking with permission from the nobs was really too much to resist.

But suppose it was a Bramah?

Then he would pick it and have the great pleasure of bragging about the adventure later. He would be infamous. He returned the coins to their bag and slipped the lot into his pocket. 'Gentleman, we are in agreement. Tell me what I am to get, and point me to it.'

'Do you seriously think we can trust him?' Marcus looked doubtful, which St John found strangely annoying.

They sat in a carriage, across the street from the earl's town house, staring out the windows and up to the darkened rooms above.

'Not far, I should suspect. But that is not the same as not at all. We can trust him to do this one night's work. I saw the look in his eyes at the end. He is hooked fast as any fish by the sight of the money and the lure of the theft. He will open the safe, steal the papers and come back to show us he's done it. If the incident with Esme was any indication, he is very good at what he does, but does not dare to brag about it. I doubt he can resist the chance to let someone else see him at work, without fear of repercussion.'

'But what of blackmail?'

'To him, or to us? If this goes according to plan, there is nothing we need fear revealing. If it does not? All the risks are his, and we have but to deny the whole thing.'

Marcus arched a disapproving eyebrow.

'Or we can acknowledge him and our motivations. If the papers exist, as I'm sure they do, there is no one who will fault us for our rash actions. I doubt there is any behaviour that could touch the Duke of Haughleigh and his spotless reputation. While I?' He thought of the Regent and wondered if the ink had dried on the letters patent that assured his title. And he realised it did not matter. If he could have Esme, then he would kiss his own aspirations goodbye and not think twice. 'Well, if we are discovered, I doubt that scandal can do much to mar my record.'

As they watched, the window of the study opened, and a figure stepped out on to the narrow ledge, edged to the side and carefully shut the window behind him. Two stories above the pavement, Smythe walked to the corner of the building as easily as if he was on a city street in daylight, and hooked a leg around a bit of ornamental stonework, before starting his climb to the ground. He made the descent easily, dropped into the landscaping, and reappeared in a moment, straightening his clothing, and brushing the dust off his jacket. Then he strolled toward the carriage as though he had not a care in the world. He opened the door, took a seat across from them and pulled a packet of papers from a pocket of his coat. 'I believe this is what you were looking for, gentlemen. I stopped to read them to make sure. You had but to tell me the reason for this endeavour and I would have been a willing participant. I do not deny that I am a thief, but I am no traitor and would see those that are get the punishment they deserve.'

'And I suppose this means that you will be returning the money my brother gave you, since this was done for King and country.'

Smythe's expression was unreadable. 'I am a patriot, sir. Not a saint.'

St John had expected as much. 'And while you were in the safe, you did not help yourself to its other contents?'

Smythe grinned. 'It would have been a shame to waste the trip. There was very little there, truth to tell. Only the papers and this.' He pulled a small box from his pocket. 'I believe it is intended to be a wedding ring.' He revealed a heavy gold band, small enough to fit a lady's finger.

'Keep it, with my compliments on a job well done,' St John responded with satisfaction. 'He will not be needing it, in any case.'

Marcus was examining the papers, and looked up, giving a solemn nod. 'As bad as we'd hoped, and worse. These need to go to the Foreign Office, immediately.'

St John smiled. 'And I will wait for the earl to come home. We will have a discussion. It will be edifying for him, and most satisfactory for me.'

'And what of me?'

St John looked up at Smythe, and realised he'd all but forgotten the man was there.

'You, sir, are a paragon, and I will fight any man who says otherwise. I will be staying here to await the earl, but my brother will give you a ride to wherever you choose to go.'

Smythe looked doubtful. 'And that is all? No threats, no warnings to mend my ways?'

He grinned and clapped the man on the shoulder. 'I should think not. If I had anything else I needed taken, I should certainly keep you in mind. But if you are hoping to use me as a reference? Then I think that is an unlikely event. Let my brother drive you to your lodgings and I would hope that you forget this evening, just as I plan to forget your part in it.'

Smythe smiled and his body relaxed into the squabs, tucking the box of rings back into his coat. 'Very well, then. It has been a pleasure doing business with you, gentlemen.'

St John allowed himself to be presented and entered the study of the Earl of Halverston. Although he had never before been in the room, a week's covert observation of it left him with a sense of déjà vu.

'Good evening to you, sir, and to what might I owe the pleasure of this visit?' Halverston was a gracious host with a pleasant smile, and had not St John known better, he would have observed nothing more than the distinguished elder statesman and pillar of the community that others saw when they met the earl.

St John ignored the old earl's proffered hand and Halverston returned his appraising gaze. Halverston was more formidable than he'd remembered, although

St John's memory of the man as he'd behaved in the brothel removed some of the gloss from the image of gentility before him now. This man might be old, but his fine clothes masked the frailty of his legs. His eyes were not clouded by drink, but cold and shrewd, no matter how warm the greeting he offered.

St John glanced back at the butler, lingering near the door. 'What I have to say is for your ears alone, my lord.'

The earl arched an eyebrow at the impertinence of it, but gestured the servant away, reaching for the decanter to pour a whisky for his guest, which St John left untouched on the desk.

'Very well. We are alone. And now, sir, speak your mind. Have you come here to reminiscence about old times together?' He smiled in a way that hinted at the knowledge of shared perversions, and St John felt his stomach churn at the thought that he might have been looking into his own eyes twenty years hence, had not he changed the direction of his life.

'No, I have not. Although I suppose I should thank you for the brief glimpse into hell that our meeting afforded me. It was sufficient to tell me that it would be better to let the French put a bullet in my brain, than to grow into a poxy old lecher. But that is tangential to the matter at hand. Certain papers have come into my possession. Things which the Foreign Office will be very interested in. Until tonight, they resided in the safe on the wall behind your desk.'

The Earl was doing his best to appear uninterested,

but his voice was tense. 'And how might you know the contents and location of my safe?'

'You are indiscreet in so many ways, your lordship. Not the least of which was telling a poor abused girl of your schemes with the French.' He pointed to the tapestry on the wall where the safe was concealed. 'You might wish to check the contents, to verify what I am saying, and then we will continue our conversation.'

The Earl rose, and his movements were smooth and sure as he walked to the safe to open it. But the return trip to the desk seemed to have aged him by a score of years. 'What do you want from me?' The question was hoarse and feeble, and St John wondered if he was supposed to feel pity for the pitiless traitor before him.

'Alas, what I want cannot be. I would wring the life from your scrawny body for your treachery and your perversion, and because you stand for so much that is wrong in the world. But that would be murder, would it not? And pleasant though it might be, and capable though I am, it would not help me achieve my ends. So I am willing to settle for second best.'

He stared hard into Halverston's eyes and felt the other shrink in submission. 'Firstly, there will be no more trading secrets with the French. The papers are on their way to the necessary authorities, and they will decide what it is they wish to do with you. That is not my problem. But I doubt that any of it will appear in *The Times*, as that would be of no use to anyone. You will be much more useful to your country, if the discovery of your treason is not made public.'

There was a glitter of hope in the old man's eyes.

'That is, unless you do not abide by my other conditions. Second: there will be no more visits to a certain house of ill fame, to Emily or any other girl. If you have any misguided plans for vengeance, know that the girl is safely away, and under my protection. Any attempts at retribution, or a return to your old habit in some new location, will result in public revelation of the scandal. Is that understood?'

The earl nodded, but there was a flush to his cheeks that made St John suspect he was biting back his true feelings on the matter.

'And last, you are to cry off immediately from your engagement to a young lady of my acquaintance. Do not think that you can continue in the way you have been going, with a young wife to get an heir on. No girl of gentle birth should be forced to remain in your poisonous company, and certainly not Esme Canville. Do I make myself clear?'

'So I am to give up everything, my livelihood, my diversions, and my betrothed, or you will spread lies about me in the papers?'

'If you mean your treason, your perversion, and the poor girl who is being forced against her will to yoke herself to you? Then, yes, you must walk away from them all, or I shall tell the truth, your lordship, the total, unvarnished truth to anyone else who will listen. You have no choice in the matter.'

The earl laughed. 'Of course I have a choice. There is always another way, young man. Now get you gone from my study. For whatever I decide to do, I do not have to put up with your insufferably priggish presence for a moment longer.'

'Very well, then. I will be watching for the announcement of the end of your engagement. You have twenty-four hours. If you have not gone to *The Times*, I certainly shall.' He nodded and left the room.

St John walked towards the front door, signalling the footman for his hat and stick. He had not reached the exit before a single shot rang out from the direction of the study.

Chapter Nineteen

Esme felt her heart quicken in fear at the sound of the curses rising up the chimney from the room below. Her father was louder than he'd ever been, and she struggled to think if there was something she'd done to provoke it. She spoke only when spoken to, she never questioned his orders, no matter how outlandish they might be, and she responded promptly to all summons.

Except for the beating she had endured on homecoming, the last two weeks had been most uneventful. She had taken all meals in her rooms and had heard no objections from her father. At times it almost seemed he had forgotten her presence, although she was aware of him, moving about in his study beneath her. But now, it appeared that things were about to change.

She was on her hands and knees on the hearth in an instant, her ear up close to the flue of the cold fireplace, listening to the shouting in the study. It was impossible to tell what had upset her father so. There had been no visitors that she'd noticed from her prison window. Perhaps there was something in the post, or the papers. But he was now incoherent with rage and she doubted even if she had been in the same room with him she would have been able to ascertain the reason for it.

She heard the crashing of glass against the fireplace, which must have been the crystal decanters that stood on the corner of the desk. There were a series of loud thuds, which could only be the heavy, leather-bound books that lined the walls, striking the floor as he pulled them from their places.

There was a hesitant suggestion from the butler. An offer of port, or a whisky to calm the nerves, though it was still early in the day.

There came a shouted negative from her father and the slam of the door below her.

Which would mean one of two things. He was going out, or he was coming up. She stood, smoothing her dress and carefully wiping her face with a handkerchief. To appear untidy in his presence would only make the inevitable worse.

The door to her room sprang open, and she could see her maid, hesitating in the hallway behind her father.

'You.' The word was full of venom, and her father pointed at her with one hand, while gesturing wildly with the newspaper in his other hand.

She nodded politely. 'Yes, sir. I am still here.' She tried to keep the reproach from her voice.

'This is your doing, I don't doubt.'

'If it is anything to be found in today's paper, I do not see how I could be held responsible for it. I have not left this room in a fortnight.'

'Then you smuggled a message out with your maid,' he shouted. 'I am sure of it. And you've done something to upset him and this is the result.'

'Upset whom, sir? There have been no smuggled messages. I have no idea what you are speaking of.'

And he slapped her hard in the face with the paper, then held it before her eyes, pointing to an article on the front page.

'The Earl of Halverston is dead. By his own hand. What could have driven him to this, girl? I wonder.'

'I swear to you, sir, that I have no idea.' Her mind was racing. She would not have to marry him, then? But then she would remain with her father and there might be no chance of another offer or of escape.

He rattled the paper again and she flinched at the threat of a blow. Then he opened it so she could see the headline. 'In his study. A single gunshot. He was alone when it happened. But he had just received a visit from the brother of your former host.'

'St John?' The name had slipped out before she could stop it.

'And thus you betray yourself. Not Captain Radwell, like a decent girl would have called him. From you it is St John.' He was rolling the newspaper in his hands, and she watched with fascination as he formed it into a weapon. 'St John Radwell, who has been trying to gain entrance to this house since the day after your arrival here. What did you say to him? What did you let him do to you? And what does he have to do with this situation?'

'I have no idea. I swear.' She was backing away, and avoided part of the first blow, as it bounced harmlessly off her arm.

St John had been here.

'Don't lie to me, girl.' He stepped in and swung again, hitting her on the check. It was as hard as any slap, and her eye teared as her face began to swell.

'I am not lying. I don't know what happened. I swear it.' And she prayed it sounded convincing as the next blow struck her in the abdomen, doubling her over and leaving her gasping on the floor.

He stepped away then, and she felt Meg rush to her, supporting her as she regained her breath.

'And you.' Her father was turning to the maid now. She pulled herself upright and shook off Meg's protecting hands.

'She had nothing to do with it, sir. Whatever it is that you assume happened, it was my doing. All mine.'

'Very well. Then you can have her punishment as well as your own.' And he struck her again on the other cheek, with the back of his hand. He turned to Meg again, who was cringing behind her.

'Get your things and get out of this house. I do not permit disloyalty from my servants, and I will not let them come between me and the proper discipline of my daughter.' He strode from the room, leaving the quaking maid in his wake.

'Oh, miss,' she murmured. 'Oh, Miss Esme.'

Esme sighed. 'It's all right, Meg. Do not worry yourself. Here is what you are to do. When you leave here, go to the house across the street, to the rooms on the second floor. Tell the lady there that you are cast off without references, but that you would have mine if I could give it, and that I wish St John Radwell to find you a position with his brother or in his own household.'

'Oh, miss,' she said again. 'What of you?'

'I've managed before, Meg. I am not so soft as I appear. Now go, before my father sees you.'

The girl started towards the doorway. And then turned back to her. 'He'd have had to fire me for carelessness anyway, miss. For I'm always losing things. Keys, for instance. I have no idea what happened to the key to your room.' And she pressed the heavy brass key into Esme's palm and hugged her once before running from the room.

Esme went to the door and carefully locked it behind the retreating girl. It would do no good for her father to find her door open. She did not need an extra punishment. She needed to find the best way to use the resources at hand. She had the key. Which meant she could come and go as she pleased.

She would not be escaping the house through marriage, then. But, should she think of somewhere to go, she could at least get out of her room. With no money, she was little better than trapped. It had been foolish of her not to send a message with Meg. She could have begged for assistance from St John. Perhaps his visits meant nothing, but at least he had not forgotten her.

She knew of only one place that might take her in, should she leave the house in the dead of night, but it might have been easier, if the woman across the street had at least anticipated her coming.

Perhaps a signal of some kind. She walked to the window and looked out and into the rooms across the street, to see the lovely blonde woman rising nervously and turning to the door to greet someone. Surely Meg had not arrived so soon.

The girl was holding her own copy of *The Times* and seemed most agitated by something she saw there.

And then St John stepped into the room and went to the girl.

She dropped the newspaper to the floor and threw herself into his arms, hanging from his neck with her feet barely touching the floor, and she showered his face with kisses, as he smiled down at her.

The key slipped from Esme's fingers and dropped to the floor, forgotten. She would have no need of it now. The thought was vague and unfocused in her mind. She might be able to escape the house, but there was nowhere on earth she could go. Because the only alternative was far more painful than the thought of remaining where she was.

And, at last, the pain of her father's blows reached her, and she collapsed on the floor of her room in a ball of misery, and wept.

Chapter Twenty

St John chafed at the discomfort of his collar, which had been starched to a wooden level of stiffness, and the cravat, which was immaculate and knotted simply, although perhaps a trifle too tight. His coat was black superfine, his breeches the same, his hose silk, and his boots polished to mirror brightness.

He looked and felt like a well-dressed vicar.

He knocked on the door and waited patiently for the servant to admit him, dropping his new card on the silver salver presented to him. An earl. Would that be sufficient to impress Mr Canville? It was every bit as good as the title her father had secured for her. Better, actually, for his title was older, more respectable. The land was more productive. He'd been over it a hundred times in his mind, pointing out the advantages to himself.

Now all he had to do was prove himself to Esme's father.

The butler opened the door to him, and he could see the look of panic on the man's face, before his mask of imperturbability dropped again and he could inform milord that Mr Canville was not in.

'Then I shall wait.'

The butler cleared his throat. 'He does not wish to see you, my lord.'

'Stuff and nonsense.' St John waved the dismissal aside, while wedging his foot in the door as a pre-emptive measure. 'He was not in for Captain Radwell. But this is the first time the Earl of Stanton has visited. The title should at least get me over the threshold. Show me to the study, and call for Mr Canville. If he means to turn me off, he must do it to my face.'

The butler shrank before him like a retreating tide.

Hell and damnation, Marcus had taught him well. St John had assumed at first that having a title would be rather like being an officer. In the army, he had given orders and his men had followed. He could do so again as an earl. But his brother had explained that situations often demanded more diplomacy, as would the problem of Mr Canville. Then one simply had to pretend that the rules did not apply to one. Ignore. Dismiss. Proceed in good humour to do exactly what one wished, secure in the knowledge that the world revolved around one.

It had been most annoying, when his brother had used the technique upon him, and St John was happy to practice it fully on any who might oppose him now.

Mr Canville entered the drawing room, leaning

slightly on his stick, and greeted St John with a perfunctory nod.

St John watched the stick, with its twisted length and silver handle, and remembered the marks on Esme's back. His blood chilled, and then heated to a boil as he imagined grabbing the stick and using it on its owner.

He fought down the response and smiled placidly back at her father.

'And to what do I owe the pleasure of this visit, Lord Stanton?' Canville forced the title out through a tight smile, as if he had trouble crediting its validity.

The cheek of the man. Again St John's temper flared and he forced it down. It would not do to antagonise him. 'It is concerning your daughter, Miss Esme, sir. I became acquainted with her while visiting my brother's home this summer.'

Canville stared at him, unblinking.

St John continued. 'I was told that she had been betrothed, and that there was no hope for me. But the union will now be impossible, due to the unfortunate death of the earl. And I had hopes...'

'To court her, when the body of Lord Halverston is barely cold?'

'Not so soon, of course,' St John corrected. 'After a respectful time, if the lady is willing.'

'I could not think to give my daughter to one such as you, for the name St John Radwell is quite infamous.'

No more infamous than the old lecher you tied her

to before, you snake. 'No longer, sir, I assure you.' St John replied meekly. 'My brother the duke and I have reconciled. My time in the army had quite a transformative effect. I was awarded a peerage for my service to the crown.' *Which ought to be good enough for you, you tight old screw.* 'The title is old, and the land is fruitful.'

'There will be no settlement, if that's what you're after.'

'I did not expect one. It will hardly be necessary, for my income is ample and will be more than sufficient for both of us.'

'But there are others who would seek her hand.'

Already? 'I am sure that, given the chance to choose, she would receive my suit favourably.'

'Given the choice?' Canville's voice rose beyond the level of courtesy.

St John had put his foot in it and it was too late to back out.

Esme had been dozing and started awake as the book slipped from her lap and struck the floor. The dream had been most vivid this time and it was a shame that she had to wake and end it. It was a favourite of hers: the dream where St John came to the house and persuaded her father to let him take her away.

'I do not see what her choice has to do with anything. It is I who will dispose of her as I see fit.'

'Then I must assure you that my suit is superior to the others.'

The voices floated up through the chimney flue, faint but clear.

It could not be. What she thought she heard was the result of an overheated imagination combined with the last echoes of the dream. Wishful thinking and nothing more.

She hurried to the fireplace and fell to her knees on the hearth, brushing the remains of the previous night's fire to the side and pressing her check to the bricks along the back wall.

'I think you lack the necessary seasoning to make a good husband.' That was clearly the voice of her father. And he was talking marriage with someone.

She held her breath, waiting for the other man's response.

'But seasoning is something I can gain, with time.'

St John. She stuffed her fist into her mouth to keep from screaming the name aloud. He was in the house and he had come for her, just as he had in her dreams.

'Why should she wait when there are men already old enough?'

'I am three and thirty, titled and landed. I do not need to wait upon a better position, nor do I expect to mature, significantly.' She could hear the steel in St John's voice as he challenged her father. 'If you are waiting, perhaps, until I've lost some teeth, or my spine is not as straight? Then I shall wait as well, sir. We shall see who lasts the longest, myself, or the octogenarian you will no doubt choose as a fitting match to your daughter.'

'And wait you shall, for you will find, sir, that you can never meet my specifications for a fit husband for my only child. No amount of time, no money, no land can wipe away the stain of your past.'

'Much as nothing could stop Halverston from putting a bullet in his brain, when the truth would out.' She smiled as she heard St John's temper rising to equal her father's. 'You will find, sir, that I am of stronger stuff than Halverston. There is nothing I have done that I cannot bear to live with. My past is stained, but I have survived it and mean to make a better future.'

'And you may make your future alone, for you shall not have my daughter.'

That was that, then. Her father had refused him. There was a pause. Her heart sank as she waited to hear St John take his leave.

And then his voice came to her, cold with fury. 'You old fool, I've had your daughter right enough. For all I know my bastard is growing inside her now. Give her to another man, and I'll tell him so. You'll find it damned difficult to give her away after that.'

'Then I will give the foolish slut to no man at all. She can stay in her room and repent for the disgrace she's brought on this house.' Her father was shouting. She shivered, knowing what would happen once St John left her alone.

But his response was a battlefield shout that was so loud he could have been standing in the room with her. 'The devil she will. You've hit her, sir. I know you have, for I have spies watching the house. It is only my respect for Esme that keeps me from giving you the beating you deserve. I've tried the honourable course. I have been far more polite to you than you deserve. And yet you deny my offer?

'Very well. Perhaps I've finally found a man with less honour than myself. We will play the game by your rules, sir. I love her. She's mine. I will take her and to hell with you.'

Esme heard the door to the study slam open and footsteps striding into the hall. And then St John shouted, 'Esme! Where are you? Come down here this instant.'

She rattled ineffectually at the door, and then remembered the key and pulled it from its hiding place, fumbling it into the lock.

'Esme! Damn it, woman! Come out of your room so that I may profess my feelings for you.' St John's command was easily loud enough to be heard in the street.

The key hit home, the lock turned and she fell into the hall as the door gave way in front of her.

And strong arms caught her before her body could hit the floor. He pulled her to her feet and his lips were at her ear, murmuring, 'You didn't think it would be so easy to get rid of me, I hope.'

'I was afraid to dream it.'

'And you have nothing to fear now.' He was pulling her down the hall with him.

She cringed against his shoulder as they approached her father.

'Stop it. Stop it this instant, Esme, and go back to your room. And you, Radwell, get out of this house.'

St John's grip on her waist tightened. 'My lord. I believe that is the correct form of address for an earl, *Mr* Canville.' He spoke the 'Mr' with a crisp emphasis that left no doubt as to who was the better man. 'And now, if you will excuse us.'

'I will not allow you to kidnap my daughter, Radwell.'

'And how do you mean to stop me?' St John laughed. 'Better men than you have tried and failed to kill me. Perhaps you intend to call the Runners. I'm sure they will settle this quietly enough, once they see my livery. Halverston proved to me right enough that the law is different for the landed. And now, it seems, I must prove it to you. Your daughter is nearly of age, sir. Soon there will be nothing you can do to hold her. Most men would think you a fool to try. But I mean to take her from this house today. By the time you can summon aid, we will be well beyond your reach. Face it, you have lost.'

He turned back to her, pulling her close. 'And as to you, minx. You wanted a say in your future. You are coming with me this minute, or not at all. No questions, no regrets and no time to pack a bag. Are you ready? Yes or no?'

And in full view of her father, she raised her head to St John's and kissed him full on his open lips. When he pulled away, the look in his eyes was dazed.

'Oh, aye. You are more than ready. But am I ready

for you is the question?' He swept her down the stairs and out the front door. Her father's railing faded in the distance as she looked into her lover's eyes.

They ran for the waiting coach, which was black and with a strange crest on the side. She glanced at it in puzzlement. 'What is that mark on the door?'

'Your new coat of arms, my lady, once we reach Scotland. I've heard Gretna Green is lovely this time of year. And it seems…' he looked up at the sky as though trying to remember '—it seems I have a hunting lodge not too far from there. I wonder what it looks like. We'll soon find out. I mean to honeymoon there.' He pulled her into the carriage behind him and shut the door.

He took her hand and linked it with his own. 'And I have other land as well. A nice piece of Cornwall, ceded to me for service to the crown. And there are jewels as well, fit for a countess, for that is what I will make of you.'

Her heart skipped once in her chest before she spoke. 'Jewels are unnecessary. I am only interested in the man, not the title.' She bit her lip, and spoke with artificial cheerfulness. 'But I really must insist, if you mean to marry me, that you not flaunt your mistress in my face. To install her across the street from me might be convenient for you, but it was most painful—'

He leaned forward and kissed her with a passion that made argument impossible. 'Halverston's ladybird, not mine. I set her there to watch over you. When she heard of his demise, she offered to show me the depth of her gratitude, but I told her that my soul had no mistress but you.' He stroked her face. 'She saw your father strike you. When she told me, it was as if I felt the blows.'

'They were nothing.' She planted a kiss in his palm. 'It is over and I need never see him again.' She smiled. 'I doubt he will relent and approve my marrying you.'

'Then perhaps I shall not bother with marriage. I could keep you, senseless with pleasure, until you are totally ruined and have no choice in the matter but to take me as husband. It's me or nothing for you, Esme.'

She shivered with pleasure. 'And what of your newly found reputation?'

He laughed. 'I had need of it when I wanted to be a gentleman. But I am a noble, now, in case you haven't heard. As an earl, I can be as dissolute as I please and there is very little that can be done about it.'

The carriage set off at a dizzying pace and she allowed herself to lunge forward and collapse against him. 'So I am to be kidnapped by a heartless libertine and forced to submit?'

He looked at her fondly. 'Not heartless, for I dare say I found my heart when I found you, Esme, my sweet. But the rest is accurate enough.'

'Oh, my.' She fanned herself theatrically. 'The thought leaves me quite faint.' And she reached slowly for the hooks at the back of her bodice. 'Perhaps if I loosen my garments, it will be possible to catch my breath.'

'Esme, do not dare. For you know what will happen

to you, if you tempt me.' The warning was a low growl, but he smiled as he said it.

'Oh, dear.' She unhooked another hook. 'In broad daylight?' Her bodice was slipping down her arms and he lunged to pull the shades at the carriage windows.

'In a moving carriage? Repeatedly?'

'Repeatedly?' His wolfish smile had changed to a look of shock.

She steadied herself against the carriage seat and shifted to let the dress fall to the floor. 'Well, I am to be married, so if you mean to ruin me so totally, you'd best hurry. You are supposed to be terribly wicked, are you not?'

He paused to admire the scene, and then smiled and said, 'Wicked. Oh, yes. Terribly.' He was loosening his cravat.

'It is such a long, long way to Scotland.' She lay back on the squabs, one leg dangling and the other on the seat next to him and looped her hands through the leather strap above her head. 'And I am utterly helpless.'

'If you are the helpless one, then how is it that, since the first, you have been able to make me do whatever you wanted?' He tossed his jacket on to the floor beside her dress and reached to undo his shirt.

'Not true.' She smiled as she watched him struggling to remove his boots as the carriage rocked around them. 'I never got you to say that you loved me.'

He threw the second boot on the pile with the rest of

his clothing. 'Then you shall have your last wish. I love you, Esme. Allow me to demonstrate.'

And he did.

REGENCY
Collection

*Let these sparklingly seductive delights whirl
you away to the ballrooms—and
bedrooms—of Polite Society!*

Volume 1 – 4th February 2011
Regency Pleasures by Louise Allen

Volume 2 – 4th March 2011
Regency Secrets by Julia Justiss

Volume 3 – 1st April 2011
Regency Rumours by Juliet Landon

Volume 4 – 6th May 2011
Regency Redemption by Christine Merrill

Volume 5 – 3rd June 2011
Regency Debutantes by Margaret McPhee

Volume 6 – 1st July 2011
Regency Improprieties by Diane Gaston

12 volumes in all to collect!

MILLS
BOON

www.millsandboon.co.uk

REGENCY

Collection

*Let these sparklingly seductive delights whirl
you away to the ballrooms—and
bedrooms—of Polite Society!*

Volume 7 – 5th August 2011
Regency Mistresses by Mary Brendan

Volume 8 – 2nd September 2011
Regency Rebels by Deb Marlowe

Volume 9 – 7th October 2011
Regency Scandals by Sophia James

Volume 10 – 4th November 2011
Regency Marriages by Elizabeth Rolls

Volume 11 – 2nd December 2011
Regency Innocents by Annie Burrows

Volume 12 – 6th January 2012
Regency Sins by Bronwyn Scott

12 volumes in all to collect!

MILLS
BOON

www.millsandboon.co.uk

"To say that I met Nicholas Brisbane over my husband's dead body is not entirely accurate. Edward, it should be noted, was still twitching upon the floor..."

London, 1886

For Lady Julia Grey, her husband's sudden death at a dinner party is extremely inconvenient. However, things worsen when inscrutable private investigator Nicholas Brisbane reveals that the death was not due to natural causes.

Drawn away from her comfortable, conventional life, Julia is exposed to threatening notes, secret societies and gypsy curses, not to mention Nicholas's charismatic unpredictability.

www.mirabooks.co.uk

MIRA

HISTORICAL

Regency
MORE THAN A MISTRESS
by Ann Lethbridge

Merry doesn't need a man—no matter how handsome he is! Sadly society takes a different view and she is to wed Charles Mountford. The Marquis is more than happy to make her socially acceptable, but only if she acts publicly as his betrothed and privately as his mistress!

Regency
THE RETURN OF LORD CONISTONE
by Lucy Ashford

Miss Verena Sheldon is more than a little surprised when Lord Conistone—notorious womaniser and the man who broke her heart—returns from London. Even more surprising is the effect he still has on her. But Lucas has returned with a secret that will surely drive Verena from his arms for ever...

SIR ASHLEY'S METTLESOME MATCH
by Mary Nichols

Determined to overthrow a notorious smuggling operation, gentleman thief-taker Sir Ashley Saunders will let nothing stand in his way! Until he runs up against spirited Pippa Kingslake, who's just as determined to protect her own interests...

On sale from 6th May 2011
Don't miss out!

Available at WHSmith, Tesco, ASDA, Eason and all good bookshops

www.millsandboon.co.uk

0411/04a

HISTORICAL

THE CONQUEROR'S LADY
by Terri Brisbin

To save her people and lands, the lady Fayth is forced to marry the commanding Breton knight, Giles Fitzhenry. The marriage is as unwelcome as the deep desire which stirs each time she looks at her husband's powerful, battle-honed body...

SURRENDER TO AN IRISH WARRIOR
by Michelle Willingham

Tortured soul Trahern MacEgan is a born warrior, forever scarred by a lost love and untameable by any woman. Yet can Morren Ó Reilly, who is no stranger to suffering and still shrinks from a man's touch, be the one to bring light to his dark world?

MAIL-ORDER GROOM
by Lisa Plumley

Fleeing scandal, stage sensation Savannah Reed swaps sparkles and satin for calico and wool to be Morrow Creek's telegraph operator. Through the wires she finds her new leading man, but when he arrives shot and left for dead on her doorstep Savannah suspects she's jumped out of the limelight and into the fire...

On sale from 6th May 2011
Don't miss out!

England's Forgotten Queen

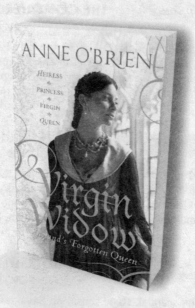

Anne Neville is the heiress and daughter of the greatest powerbroker in the land, Warwick the Kingmaker. She is a pawn, trapped in an uncertain political game.

When the Earl of Warwick commits treason, his family is forced into exile. Humiliated and powerless in a foreign land, Anne must find the courage and the wit to survive in a man's world.

www.mirabooks.co.uk

"The arrogance! To think that they can come here with their town bronze and sweep some heiress or other to the altar."

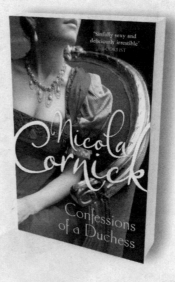

When a feudal law requires all unmarried ladies to wed or surrender half their wealth, the quiet village of Fortune's Folly becomes England's greatest Marriage Market.

Laura, the dowager duchess, is determined to resist the flattery of fortune hunters. Young, handsome and scandalously tempting Dexter Anstruther suspects Laura has a hidden motive for resisting his charms…and he intends to discover it.

www.mirabooks.co.uk

"Blackmail is such an ugly word, Miss Lister. It is essential that I marry you. So let us call it a bargain."

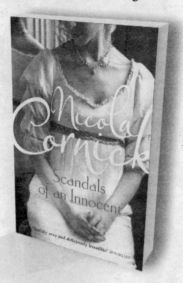

When a law requires all unmarried ladies to wed or surrender half their wealth, maid-turned-heiress Miss Alice Lister is a prize to be won!

Now the insufferably attractive Lord Miles Vickery is certain he can gain her fortune by blackmailing her into marriage. Of course, he doesn't yet know he's falling hopelessly in love with this formidable innocent...

www.mirabooks.co.uk

"I promise that I will release you tomorrow – when the hour of the wedding is past."

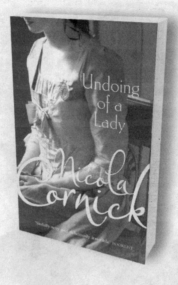

Nat Waterhouse must marry an heiress.
Lady Elizabeth Scarlet vows there is just one way
to save her childhood friend from a loveless
marriage: kidnap him!

When her inexperienced attempt flares into intense
passion, Lizzie is ruined…and hopelessly in love!
Now the wild and wilful Lizzie must convince Nat
that they are a perfect match – in every way.

www.mirabooks.co.uk

Sparkling ballrooms and wealthy glamour in Regency London

Immerse yourself in the glitter of Regency times through the lives and romantic escapades of the Lester family

Now the news was out that the Lester family fortunes had been repaired, Harry Lester knew the society matrons would soon be in pursuit, so he promptly left London for Newmarket.

Fate, however, proved more far-sighted, having arranged for a distraction in the person of Mrs Lucinda Babbacombe. Lucinda is a beautiful, provocative but unwilling conquest – who to Harry's irritation cannot be ignored.

Immerse yourself in the glitter of Regency times through the lives and romantic escapades of the Lester family

Jack Lester had every reason to hide the news of his recently acquired fortune: he wanted an attractive, capable bride who would accept him for himself, not for his new-found riches.

But he had to make his choice before the society matrons discovered the Lester family were no longer as poor as church mice. He must convince Sophie, the woman of his dreams, to marry him as poor Jack Lester.